HIDDEN YELLOW STARS

also by

REBECCA CONNOLLY

A Brilliant Night of Stars and Ice

Under the Cover of Mercy

HIDDEN YELLOW STARS

REBECCA CONNOLLY

SHADOW
MOUNTAIN
PUBLISHING

Image Credits:
p. 276: Photograph of Andrée Geulen and Ida Sterno, courtesy of Andrée Geulen-Herscovici. Image found on www.yadvashem.org.
pp. 278–79: Photographs of Ida Sterno and Andrée Geulen © United States Holocaust Memorial Museum, courtesy of Andrée Geulen-Herscovici.
p. 282: Photograph provided by the author.

Visit us at shadowmountain.com

Portions of this book are historical fiction. Characters and events in this book are represented fictitiously.

Library of Congress Cataloging-in-Publication Data

Names: Connolly, Rebecca, author.
Title: Hidden yellow stars / Rebecca Connolly.
Description: [Salt Lake City] : Shadow Mountain, [2024] | In the title, the "a" in "stars" is represented by the star of David. | Includes bibliographical references. | Summary: "The story of Andrée Geulen and Ida Sterno, who worked with the Committee for the Defense of Jews to hide more than three thousand Jewish children in Belgium during World War II"— Provided by publisher.
Identifiers: LCCN 2023036169 (print) | LCCN 2023036170 (ebook) | ISBN 9781639932344 (hardback) | ISBN 9781649332509 (ebook)
Subjects: LCSH: Jews—Belgium—History—20th century—Fiction. | World War, 1939–1945—Jews—Rescue—Fiction. | Jewish children—Belgium—History—20th century—Fiction. | World War, 1939–1945—Jewish resistance—Belgium—Fiction. | Belgium—History—German occupation, 1940–1945—Fiction. | BISAC: FICTION / Historical / 20th Century / World War II | LCGFT: Novels. | Historical fiction.
Classification: LCC PS3603.O54728 H53 2024 (print) | LCC PS3603.O54728 (ebook) | DDC 813/.6—dc23/eng/20230807
LC record available at https://lccn.loc.gov/2023036169
LC ebook record available at https://lccn.loc.gov/2023036170

Printed in the United States of America
Lake Book Manufacturing, LLC, Melrose Park, IL

10 9 8 7 6 5 4 3 2 1

For my family members who perished in the concentration camps:
ZSIGMOND, SARAH, AVRAHAM, BENO, EDITH, LEAH, HEDI,
PINKHAS, ESTER, SANDOR, DAVID, LILI, MOSHE, GERSHON, HERSCHEL,
RAKHEL, FERENTZ, RIVKA, GOLDA, and TOVA.

Discovering you through the research for this book has
illuminated my family history in a way we had only dreamed of before,
and I am sorry I did not know you sooner.
And to the many other relatives of ours yet to be discovered
who may have suffered the same fate.
May peace be upon you all.

And to Galaxy Minstrels and Counters for helping
to keep the Dementors at bay while I wrote this book.

And so we must know these good people
who helped Jews during the Holocaust.
We must learn from them,
and in gratitude and hope,
we must remember them.

—ELIE WIESEL,

author, philosopher, and Holocaust survivor

HISTORICAL CHARACTERS

Members of the Comité de Défense des Juifs
(Committee for the Defense of Jews, or CDJ)

Andrée Geulen, aka Claude Fournier
Ida Sterno, aka Jeanne, aka Ida Hendrickx
Claire Murdoch, aka Catherine
Paule Renard, aka Solange
Suzanne Moens (Moons), aka Brigitte
Ghert and Yvonne Jospa
Maurice and Esta Heiber

Other historical figures

Odile and Remy Ovart
Dédée (Andrée) Ovart
Sister Marie-Aurélie
Hélène Gancarska, aka Miss Goris
Icek Glogowski, aka Fat Jacques
Madame Dumont
Dr. Hendrickx
Dr. Duchaine
Horse Head (*Pferdekopf*)
Dago
Jenny
Madame von Volden
Madame Martine
Regina
Charles
Madame Brat
Raoul
Victor Martin
Victor Hendrickx

All accounts of families and children come from true accounts, though most of the names have been changed or created for the purposes of this story.

CHAPTER 1

Whoever bears this mark is an enemy of our people.

—NAZI PROPAGANDA LEAFLET, 1942

Brussels, Belgium
September 1942

Yellow stars were emerging.

One here, another there, still another a bit further on. Making their presence known yet providing very little light. Scattered about her classroom like some cruel evening sky.

They were not the first she had seen, not by a long shot. Who could have failed to notice the bright symbols foisted upon people about Brussels? Normal people, average people, simply minding their own business and going about their lives.

Now they could not have normal, average, or simple lives. Now they were forced to stand out within the public, branded as though one's religion and heritage ought to be so shameful.

Jews.

She had heard it talked about in the streets; nobody had suspected this many Jews in their city, in their neighborhood, in their street. It wasn't always said with disgust, but sometimes . . .

Andrée Geulen had seen plenty of cruelty and evil in her scant twenty-one years of age. The Spanish Civil War and its mass of fleeing refugees into her country had seen to that. But she had never seen anything like this.

And that she had to see it in the children she taught was enough to make her angry.

Not just angry.

Livid.

What had these *children* ever done to know the shame of being sneered at? Of having things thrown at them? Of no longer being free to befriend those of their choosing?

Day after day, she had seen her sweet Jewish students come into class clutching their books to their chests in an attempt to hide their blaring stars. To cover the shame that they now had to carry. To try, little as they could, to blend in once more.

Those stars . . . To represent the Star of David, what the Jewish community treasured so, and yet have its emblem mean something so terribly unholy to anyone. Any Jew over the age of six was to wear it and thus become targeted by the murderers of the soul otherwise known as the Gestapo.

How were any of them supposed to bear a life like this? How were their neighbors and friends of other faiths supposed to stand by and watch?

Andrée's only consolation was that the burgomasters had unanimously refused to distribute the stars to the Jews of Brussels, but that only meant that the Judenrat had to do it instead. Jews having to brand their own because the Nazis were in charge and the Nazis said so.

Well, the Nazis were not in her classroom, and she was not going to allow the shaming of children to stand where she could make a difference.

"Children," she said with gentle firmness, "please fetch aprons from the hooks on the back wall. From now on, you will all wear them from the moment you arrive until the moment you leave. Is that understood?"

"Yes, Miss Geulen," they intoned as one, their small chairs scraping against the floor as they rose to do as she bid.

She might have imagined it, but she thought there may have been looks of relief on the faces of her Jewish children, if not flickers of hope. If she was correct, the aprons would cover the hideous stars completely, and all of her students would look the same.

Again.

The war of the outside world had no place in her classroom, nor did its cruelty.

She smiled at the line of little ones needing her help in fastening the aprons about them, and quickly tied the ribbons for them, one after another. They filed back to their seats like little orderly soldiers, most of them unaware of the significance of the moment. School was simply a way of life, and the addition of an accessory for the entire class need not make sense.

What a blessing children were! What resilient creatures! What innocent beings, so filled with goodness and light, seemingly unable to be touched by darkness or even negativity.

And yet . . .

Andrée glanced around the room now, stars gone, a sea of young faces looking up at her expectantly.

Someone was missing.

At least two someones, if not three.

She forced herself not to frown as she considered the list of students in her mind. "Where are Camille, Henri, and Lilly? Has anyone seen them?"

The sea of students created a somber wave with their shaking heads.

Three students missing, none of them siblings. There were any number of explanations for such a thing, but something cold settled in Andrée's stomach. Something sinister and clawing that made her pulse race and her throat tighten.

She was not prone to such bursts of sensation, but ever since the Nazis had occupied Belgium, she had been feeling them more and more. Not fear, exactly, nor anticipation. Not quite anxiety and nothing so easy as dread. Some combination of feelings that had found harbor within her from the very moment Belgium was no longer her own and sprang to attention at random intervals.

Such as missing children.

It could be nothing. It could mean an illness was yet again making the rounds of young and active students, as it often did. It could all be explained by any number of coincidences.

Yet Andrée did not believe in coincidences anymore.

A sudden burst of painful heat in her chest ignited a thought that made her turn toward the blackboard, away from the children who might notice the change in her countenance.

Every one of the three children missing from her classroom would be wearing the star.

Three *Jewish* children missing from her classroom.

The heat eked its way to the pit of her stomach, searing the previously cold sensation and creating an abominable ache she could not begin to soothe.

That could not be an accident of fate, and she would not delude herself into thoughts of optimism. Not at a time like this, not with the world enduring its present torment.

And not when it involved children.

Andrée cleared her throat and took up a piece of chalk, writing upon the blackboard with trembling fingers. "Today is Wednesday. Can anyone recollect the date?"

The rest of her instruction for the morning passed in a blur, the pattern of subjects and students eager to answer the same as any other day she had taught. She had joined the staff as a substitute teacher for the remainder of the term, and the joy of teaching was never lost on her. She had hopes of a permanent position becoming available soon, but as war was raging across Europe, she could not know what the future would entail for her.

Her own time as a student had been marred by conflict. From the moment her teacher had informed their class about the Spanish Civil War, Andrée, who was then only fifteen, had not known life as a standard student might have done. She had not been able to rest for thinking of the refugees fleeing their native country due to the dangers and had pledged to do something for them. She had gone so far as to demand that her parents do something to provide relief or aid, something to soothe the pains of humanity. After all, they had raised her to be a Christian and engrained in her the importance of those attributes they associated with such people and such a figure. Would they, then, give her exceptions for such demands?

To her relief, they had not.

Some of their neighbors had housed Spanish refugees in their own homes, but the Geulens had not been able to do so. Her father's physical handicap made their own state of living complicated at best, and bringing another person into their home might have provided less than comfortable refuge. But they had been active in their community in giving what they could and offering help and support to their neighbors and friends.

An important lesson, her father had told her once. The secret to life, with all its vast intellectual pursuits and wide opportunities of interests, was to help and serve one another.

He was a proud, intelligent, cultivated sort of man, and rather bourgeois, but the two of them shared a knack for strong argument that her mother could not understand.

It had upset them both when Andrée had abandoned the Roman Catholic faith, let alone a faith of any kind, but her staunch defense of her stance and of the indignity of the injustice of the world had brought about an unwieldy truce among the three of them. So long as she continued to live by that all-important lesson, her father had relented, he would say nothing more on the subject of religion.

And he never had.

Then the Nazis had come to Belgium. She had been finishing up her schooling in Andenne when bombs had begun to fall, waking them all up from sleep. The Meuse River was close by, and the bridges had been a prime target for German bombs. For the safety of the students and staff, the school had been evacuated. Teachers had escorted students home, and those who would have needed the now bombed-out bridges over the Meuse were reduced to rowing across the water in small boats in order to reach the train station.

Andrée had been forced to take her final secondary school exams in a school in Brussels rather than at her actual center of education.

Now she was a teacher, albeit in the same state of war that had taken her childhood from her during her time as a student.

What sort of a world was this for children of any age to be brought up in? What could they be taught that would truly make a difference through any of this?

Entering the staff lunchroom, Andrée moved to a table where three other young teachers sat, deep in conversation. They offered almost hesitant smiles as she reached them.

"Miss Geulen," greeted Monique, the most senior of the group, her blonde hair bearing the perfect waves of pin curls. "Nicole and Veronike were just saying they are missing some Jewish students from their classes this week. I have noticed one of mine gone as well. Have you any that are missing?"

Andrée nodded, swallowing against the renewed tension in her throat. "Yes. Three."

All of the women shook their heads. "What is happening here?" Veronike whispered, her green eyes wide with concern. "We have all seen those horrid stars, marking them like cattle, but now . . ."

"I have two students," Nicole murmured, dropping her voice lower, "who wear their jackets with the lining on the outside. Their mothers thought it would be better. I wish I could tell all of them to do the same. But then"—she shook her head somberly—"one of the other students announced to the entire class that the girl wore her jacket in such a way, and hung it in such a way, because she had a star on it."

Andrée gaped at the story, her appetite nearly vanishing entirely. "Who would do such a thing?"

Nicole's expression turned grave. "The headmistress's daughter."

There was nothing to do but lower her eyes. Shame filled her for being employed at a place where the children were subjected to such behavior. That their headmistress was, perhaps, not curbing the behavior of her child. That the children from non-Jewish homes were learning such behavior.

"I had to break up a fight yesterday on recess duty," Monique broke in, cracking the heavy silence with an equally heavy tone. "One of the boys had gone up to a Jewish classmate and asked him what he was doing to their country."

Veronike released a sound of distress, her hand going to her throat. "Children are not naturally vicious. They are learning this behavior, aren't they?"

"If not at home," Andrée agreed, "then from the world around them. Trying to make sense of the abuse and destruction. The targeting and the shaming." She paused, recollecting an experience over the summer that had opened her eyes to the reality of the situation for the Jews.

She had kept it in her heart in order to protect those involved, but with these sympathetic, sweet fellow teachers . . .

"Over the summer," she went on, "I was assisting with children in Andenne. Staying overnight and trying to make them comfortable away from home, that sort of thing. One night, a little boy hugged me especially tight and told me that his name was not what I thought. He was Jewish, and his real name was Charlie. And he told me it was a secret. I had never thought there would be Jewish children in hiding, but there he was, living and breathing among his fellow students with a false identity. So young and tender, yet he knew the importance of his secret. I can only hope he did not share it with others, but I cannot regret that he did so with me."

Nicole had tears in her eyes while Veronike's flowed freely down her cheeks. Monique was sitting back in her chair, her arms folded tightly across her, jaw set.

"We will have to do something to prevent this," Monique muttered in a tone too somber for her appearance. "These children disappearing and suffering so among us."

They nodded, individually and as a group, but no one said anything further in their agreement.

Andrée looked around at them, feeling just as lost within herself as her companions seemed by their expressions. "What will we do?"

Nicole met her eyes, apparently haunted by the question. "What *can* we do, Andrée? The Gestapo are everywhere, and Queen Elisabeth has already insisted that no Belgian Jews can be taken away."

"The problem with that," Veronike countered with a sigh, "is that so many of the Jews here are not Belgians originally. The Queen's proclamation protects very few people at all, for all the good Her Majesty was trying to do."

"At least she is trying," Andrée pointed out. "Surely we can try as well."

Monique managed a smile for her. "You are trying. The aprons are an excellent solution."

Nicole began to bite her lip in a show of uncertainty. "If we can do our best to keep our classrooms a safe and warm place for our students, they will know that here, at least, they have nothing to fear. Will that be enough for now?"

"It will have to be," Veronike replied. "We are powerless in all else."

Andrée bit back a response that most certainly would have been tart and argumentative, adding nothing to the conversation at hand. But she hated the word powerless. Despised it. She would not accept that she was completely powerless in anything, no matter what was at stake. She might not have a clear idea of the course of action she could take to help her students, let alone their families, but she would not concede to being powerless against the tyrants in their country. Not for a moment.

She silently began to eat her lunch, her mind spinning, her heart bright, not with warmth, but with indignation.

Something must be done, indeed. And somehow, in some way, she would find it.

CHAPTER 2

Only members of the nation may be citizens of the State. Only those of German blood, whatever their creed, may be members of the nation. Accordingly, no Jew may be a member of the nation.

—POINT 4, NAZI PARTY PLATFORM, FEBRUARY 1920

A weekend in Brussels would be just the thing.

Ida Sterno inhaled the aroma of the street along which she walked, capturing the fragrance of fresh bread from a bakery, the dampness of the cobblestone, the distant petrol of a truck, a slight waft of florals from the parfumerie . . . It was a strange combination, but it seemed to bring Brussels more to life than what her eyes alone could tell her.

She could have done without the petrol hovering among the rest, as it was evident that the truck it came from belonged to a Nazi contingent engaging in some pointless exercise or activity. It did not help that the star on her coat felt like a branding upon her skin, signaling to all that she was a target of particular disdain. Informing the soldiers up ahead that *she* was their enemy, rather than the Allied soldiers they might combat in war.

Reminding her that she was somehow less than human.

Her marriage to Victor helped, in some ways. All interfaith weddings between Jews and Christians seemed to, technically speaking. It did not get her out of wearing the vicious beacon that was the star, but it kept her from having her livelihood destroyed, as others had. It did not even matter that their marriage was purely logistical and that they did not, and likely never would, live together. She was, legally and lawfully, Ida Hendrickx.

Poor Victor. Married to a Jewess in a time when that was less than ideal. It was refreshing that he had not minded when the marriage had been arranged by her brothers, and he did not mind it now. At least, Ida did not think he minded. It had been some time since she'd last written to him, let alone asked his opinion.

Even if Ida was non-practicing, the Nazis did not care. Jewish by birth and heritage was enough. More than enough.

And she was done with it.

She'd left her job at the factory in Charleroi because of these stars. Not because she had been forced to wear one, but for the trouble that could arise for the factory *because* she had to wear one. She did not want to be employed anywhere that had to enforce that rule under German ordinance, and the gas and electric plant for all of the Hainaut region was one of those unfortunate compulsory locations.

What exactly she would do for work now was not clear, and what was available to her, thanks to the star, was even less so.

But she had come to Brussels this weekend to try to forget what lay before her, and to avoid considering her options for a short time, at least. If she could.

"Ida? Ida Sterno, is that you?"

Startled to be recognized, let alone called out, Ida glanced around quickly, almost panicked, given the present circumstances. Her fear evaporated when her eyes fell on the figure of Yvonne Jospa, whom she had known from their days in social services school.

Ida gaped momentarily, then started for the table at which Yvonne sat, nestled just outside of a café. "Yvonne! I had no idea you were in Brussels!"

"And I know for a fact that you are *not* living here," Yvonne laughed, rising to hug her tightly. "Charleroi, isn't it?"

Ida nodded, the relief of smiling for joy nearly as much as that of a warm hug. "For the present, yes."

Yvonne pulled back, giving her a stern look through narrowed eyes. "For the present? Do explain. Please, sit."

"Ghert isn't here?" Ida asked, not wanting to take his seat.

Yvonne shook her head and gestured for Ida to join her. "He is not. I am enjoying some brief time out on my own. Your company is just what I need to fulfill such enjoyment."

Never one to turn down a warm invitation, Ida sat as indicated, grinning at her friend. "How is Ghert?"

"Busy, of course." Yvonne chuckled at the mention of her husband, though there was a new strain around her eyes as she did so. "He is always so busy."

A repeat of the same statement, and no additional information.

Interesting.

"And Paul?" Ida asked, choosing, for the moment, to let the subject of Yvonne's husband pass. "How old is he now?"

Yvonne's smile became perfectly free of strain. "Nearly five. And impatient to be much older. But he is a sweet boy; I do adore him."

"Good."

"I heard that you married, Ida," Yvonne said almost at once. "Are you happy?"

Ida barely avoided a laugh. "Very. I'm forty now, and as independent as I please. Victor is perfectly content to live as he does and wishes me to live as I do."

"Then he isn't . . ."

"He isn't," Ida confirmed. "My brothers arranged it, and everyone is satisfied with the arrangement. He is a good man. And the hope is that I am now safe, so to speak." She shrugged, not willing to go into much more detail on the subject.

Yvonne didn't seem quite convinced.

Ida felt her throat tense. "It isn't that uncommon, you know. There's even a term for it now: a *mariage blanc*."

"What's wrong with the term mixed marriage?"

"It is that, too."

Now Yvonne looked completely confused, and it took Ida a moment before comprehending why.

Then she laughed. "It is a mixed marriage, certainly. But a *mariage blanc* is a different kind of marriage. No relations, if you will."

"None?"

"None. It was arranged specifically for protection. As I said, Victor is a good man. Very good."

Yvonne exhaled audibly through partially pursed lips. "Oh my . . . yes, he most certainly is. I had no idea that . . . and you say this is becoming common?"

Ida smirked. "I don't know about common, but it is not so uncommon now as it was. Belgium as a whole isn't as devoted to the ideals of our invaders as they might like, and some are taking it as a personal affront, though they are not the targets."

"I love those people," Yvonne admitted with real fondness. "There are some wonderful humans all around us, in spite of everything."

Ida was far less inclined to view general humanity in such a rosy light, and she scoffed, mostly to herself. "There is also a surprising number of ignorant humans everywhere, as it happens."

Yvonne looked a trifle bemused by that but said nothing against it. She would be a fool to deny the statement, and Yvonne had never been a fool. She was rational, she was reasonable, and she was wise. Never foolish.

Yet there she was, sitting openly in a café in Brussels, smiling in the flickering sunshine as it peeked out from clouds, as though it was 1920 and they would be shortly returning to their classes at school. Was the woman living in the same world in which Ida was living? She certainly did not seem to be, given her general air of serenity and good humor.

Ida looked her friend over, noting slight signs of the passing of time, but nothing to especially age her. No particularly haunting look, no signs of oppression or fear. She looked, as it happened, perfectly content somehow.

Then Ida noticed one very striking omission from Yvonne's ensemble.

The telltale star.

"You don't wear one," Ida said without emotion, hoping her friend would understand the reference.

Yvonne's brow creased and she tilted her head in confusion.

Ida placed a finger on the table surface and quickly traced the shape of a star.

"Oh. No, I don't." Yvonne's lips curved in a very small smile.

"How?"

"Simple. When we registered in Brussels after first moving here, we neglected to put down the key requirement for which that particular emblem is intended."

Ida's eyes widened as she stared at her friend, her heart doing some combination of skipping and jumping as it processed the possibility of such a thing. They were in public, though the neighboring tables were mostly vacant of people, and her words must be chosen with the greatest care, for Yvonne's safety as well as her own.

"How?" Ida asked again, lowering her voice.

"Certain documents," Yvonne hedged, still smiling. "Ghert is very active in his work, and he must be permitted to continue to do so. And the lack of the emblem proves most useful. And we are always looking for others willing to rid themselves of the emblem in order to serve a greater purpose for those who can't."

Yvonne was taking a great risk in saying as much as she was, even without the specific words. Ida might not know exactly what her friend was referring to, but she certainly knew enough to understand the danger involved in the discussion.

And she was dying to continue it.

"Well," Ida pretended to muse, absently tracing on the table surface once more, "there is nothing keeping me in Charleroi now. I have left my job at the factory. Might there be something here in Brussels that I could do relating to social services?"

Yvonne's smile spread slowly but surely. "Oh, indeed. I am doing some work in the field myself at the moment. It involves children, specifically. We could certainly use your expertise and skill. Given the times we live in, it can be challenging . . . carries a particular risk, you understand."

Ida nodded in faux understanding. "And Ghert would be able to secure the certain documents enabling me to work with greater ease here?"

"Naturally." Yvonne's eyes narrowed and her bottom lip tensed, probably from biting the inside. "He has two jobs, really. One more public than the other. And I assist in the less-public part, particularly as it relates to children. We are seeking alternate housing for them. Safer housing, given the turbulent times." She widened her eyes meaningfully. "And certain documents can go only so far with children."

Ida's jaw slowly seemed to loosen from its tightness, and she would have fully gaped had she allowed her lips to part. If she was understanding this coded conversation correctly, Yvonne was finding accommodations for Jewish children. Safe accommodations. Now that the Gestapo were beginning razzias—or raids—of Jewish homes and businesses, it was growing more common to see people loaded into large trucks, each bearing the stars branded upon them.

"And the parents?" she eventually managed to ask, keeping her tone businesslike, as if she were in a job interview.

"Our work enables them to act in their best interest," Yvonne said carefully. "Without having to consider the children as well. They trust us to do what is needed. And word is spreading, so you can imagine the opportunity for you, should you be interested in the position."

Children only. No parents. Which meant they were hiding children.

Hiding Jewish children from the Nazis.

There would be an incalculable risk to that task. Dangers upon dangers. Every Jew without access to the false documentation Yvonne had been referencing would be identified by the Association of Jews in Belgium, the AJB. Created by the Nazis to purportedly aid the Jews in Belgium, the AJB provided almost no real aid to its people but did keep detailed records of the names and locations of all Belgian Jews, which they of course were obligated to turn over to Nazi authorities upon request.

Belgium hadn't been turned into a prison for the Jews as yet, but there was no telling what the Nazis had planned for them. Ida knew full well that many Jewish families had fled when and where they could, and those who could not either dealt with the situation at hand or hid themselves somehow.

It had never occurred to her that there would be people actively working to assist the Jewish people in thwarting the Nazi mistreatment of them. Jews working around the system they were forced into and saving some of their own. But why would there not be? In a world filled with all sorts of minds, all sorts of personalities, why would there not be hearts like her own that cried out for justice and ached for action in the defense of it?

Ida stared at her friend, nearly breathless as her thoughts spun on the topic, on the possibilities, on the opportunity that was before her.

There was no fear in the prospect.

Only hope.

"Are you interested?"

"Yes," Ida heard herself say amid the excitement humming about her ears. "It sounds like a perfect opportunity for me."

Yvonne's smile matched the energy now racing through Ida's limbs. "I hoped you might say so. When can you start?"

Ida matched her grin. "When I have a place to stay in Brussels. Shall we start looking?"

"No need. Between Ghert and our other associates, we have several options." Yvonne nudged her head toward the street, and they rose from their table, starting in the direction she indicated and linking their arms.

Ida felt on edge immediately. "Are you certain you want to walk with me? I'm . . . marked."

"Which is nicely covered by my walking beside you for the present," Yvonne replied smoothly, apparently unconcerned. "And in a moment, we shall turn your coat inside out. As soon as we turn on the next road, away from those we wish to avoid."

Ida glanced up the road, noting the truck she had caught the scent of earlier. Ice raced through her veins, in spite of the bravery she had felt only moments before. Here and now, she was nothing more or less than a Jew, subject to their treatment and harassment, and to the humiliation that such behavior would bring.

She would love nothing more than to be rid of these feelings, and to help others be rid of them as well.

Yvonne kept her close, turning down the next small street, rubbing her arm. "Breathe. We are out of sight, so take your coat off and turn it."

Ida did so, wishing she still had feeling in her fingertips. "It will be a pleasure to be rid of the thing, but what will we do about my looks? I hardly look Aryan."

"There are any number of people that do not look Aryan," Yvonne reminded her. "You will soon get used to it. Now, would you like to hear about the first assignment I have in mind for you?"

Startled, Ida paused with her now reversed coat half on. "Already?"

Yvonne chuckled. "I hardly imagine you to start on it today, but I thought you might like to hear what it will be once you are here and ready. Something to look forward to, eh?"

Ida shook her head in disbelief and adjusted her coat, taking her friend's arm once more. "Yes, if you can speak about it openly."

"There is a school here in Brussels with a sympathetic headmistress. The Mother Superior at the Sisters of the Very Holy Savior convent in Anderlecht has told us about her and her husband, and the good work they do, and we think they might be open to hiding some children in their school. It would be an excellent opportunity, if we can find a way to bring it about."

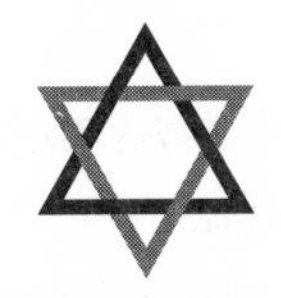

CHAPTER 3

It is questionable to even speak of a "Jewish people," since there is only a limited and widely varied sense of real consciousness of being a people.

—JOHANN VON LEERS, NAZI PARTY OFFICIAL, 1933

Gatti de Gamond school, Brussels
Spring 1943

"Miss Geulen, could you come speak with me in my office a moment?"

Andrée paused a step, looking at the headmistress, Madame Ovart, in surprise. "Of course. Is everything all right?"

Madame Ovart smiled warmly and waved for her to follow. "Yes, everything is fine. I only wish to have a quick word while many of our students are away for the holiday."

That was fair enough, Andrée supposed. The Pentecost holiday had taken the majority of their students away from the school, which allowed for a bit of breathing room for the staff to prepare forthcoming lessons and attend to the remaining students more personally.

And for Andrée, who lived in the boarding dorms of the school, it was a chance to enjoy more peace than she typically would in caring for the boarding students.

An interview with the headmistress was not exactly what Andrée had anticipated during this semblance of a break.

She ran through her recent activities in her mind, involuntarily looking for any moments that might have earned her a word of correction, but none stood out in such a way. Were there day students that were having difficulties at home? Or some family issues with the boarding students? The school was a non-confessional one, but, as far as she knew, the students were all Catholic, so the continuing abuse of the Jews in Belgium should not be a direct issue.

She was quick to silence any comments from her students that followed the barbaric trend to verbally abuse Jews, though there were none in their ranks. She had not been able to find a direct way to help her poor Jewish students in her last post as a substitute teacher, aside from doing her best to make them equal in her classroom and showing them respect and affection. Here at the Gatti de Gamond, there were none to help, but there were certainly plenty in the community that she could help, if there were a way.

The world was a dark place at present, and it was only going to get darker if something was not done.

They moved into the headmistress's office, where Andrée saw a woman with dark hair sitting in a chair facing the desk.

"Miss Sterno, this is Miss Andrée Geulen, our boarding teacher here," Madame Ovart greeted, rounding the desk and gesturing a hand back toward Andrée. "Andrée, Miss Ida Sterno."

Miss Sterno rose and turned to face Andrée, smiling a little. She was older than Andrée, but not quite to the age of Madame Ovart, whose only child was nearly an adult.

"Pleased to meet you," Andrée said with a quick nod. She gestured to the door behind her. "Should I close the door, madame?"

"Please," Madame Ovart answered, taking her seat. "Then come sit beside Miss Sterno here."

Andrée did so, then sat as directed, even more curious about the reason for this meeting, especially as there was someone else in the room with them.

It was all she could do to avoid looking at Miss Sterno to try to figure out what role she played in whatever this meeting was about.

Madame Ovart folded her hands together on the surface of her desk and gave Andrée a serious look. "What we are about to tell you, Miss Geulen, is not to leave this room."

The statement caused an instant tension to form in Andrée's throat, and she struggled to swallow against it. "I understand," she eventually managed to say.

"Good," Madame Ovart said with a clipped nod. She gestured to Miss Sterno and said nothing further.

Miss Sterno cleared her throat, taking some kind of cue from the gesture. "Miss Geulen, I am a member of an organization called the *Comité de Défense des Juifs,* or CDJ. It is a part of the Belgian resistance, and a very particular group within it. I work in the children's sector of the organization, and I have been working with Madame Ovart for some weeks now."

Andrée blinked and looked at her headmistress quickly, but only received a small, tight smile in return.

"Doing what, exactly?" Andrée asked, looking between the two women.

Miss Sterno's smile was less tight and held a significant note of confidence in it. "Hiding Jewish children, Miss Geulen. Protecting them from the razzias and deportations. Giving them the best chance of surviving all of this."

Hiding the children? There was nothing that could have surprised Andrée more, though she immediately saw the wisdom of it. The faces of her sweet Jewish children from the previous fall with horrifying stars on their coats flashed before her mind, and she wished she had thought of hiding them somehow. Taking them home with her and finding safe places. Her parents would have allowed it, she was certain, and then some of those sweet faces might not have disappeared from her class.

But where was Miss Sterno hiding them? And what did Madame Ovart have to do with it?

Andrée turned her attention back to the headmistress, a subtle realization dawning. "You're hiding some here."

There was no question in her words, and none in her mind. Madame Ovart was a good woman, a Christian in more than just faith, and a humanitarian above all else. She and her husband had insisted on their school being non-confessional, which was far from the normal arrangement of religious institutions in Belgium. They had wanted a school that would not pressure the students in the same way that confessional institutions had done for generations, and it would allow, in theory, for students of multiple faiths to attend without issue.

Including, also in theory, those of the Jewish faith.

There had been no new students recently, so she did not anticipate that Jewish students were currently in attendance, but that did not mean there were no Jewish children in the school.

Madame Ovart's smile spread, and she looked at Miss Sterno. "I told you she was quick."

"I never doubted you," Miss Sterno returned. "You're right; she'll be a perfect addition."

"Addition to what?" Andrée all but demanded.

Miss Sterno turned to face her more fully. "For the CDJ, Miss Geulen. We would like you to join."

Andrée felt her brow ripple into a frown. "I am not Jewish."

"Exactly," Miss Sterno returned, surprising her. "I need a non-Jewish partner to assist me, as I am suspicious just by the way I look, even without the star." She gestured to her own dark but graying hair, dark eyes, and general features. "You, on the other hand, are perfectly Aryan with your pale locks and bright blue eyes."

"Ergh," was all Andrée could say, finding the would-be compliment rather disgusting, given the host to whom the obsession with such looks belonged.

Miss Sterno laughed at the reaction. "It will prove very useful, Miss Geulen. I have filed false paperwork in Brussels to avoid being on records as a Jew and being forced to wear the star, but word can still get out. Having you as my partner will give us a safety net for our work with the children."

It sounded useful, it sounded commendable, and it sounded as though it could work, but to accept such an invitation, given her employment here at the school . . .

Andrée looked at Madame Ovart, unsure what to say.

The headmistress was smiling fully now. "I would not have brought you in here to meet Miss Sterno if I did not approve. I am unable to join, as my husband and daughter would be at risk, not to mention the students and school, but I will continue to do my part as I am able."

"What are you doing at present?"

Madame Ovart sat back in her chair, her hands resting in her lap. "We presently have several Jewish children among the day students, and twelve Jewish students and their headmistress actively hiding in the school. Among the boarding students and staff."

Andrée jerked in her seat, her fingers clutching the armrests tightly. "What? I haven't noticed any new students arrive, or new staff!"

"They have been here since before you started." She drummed her finger on the surface of the desk, almost seeming amused by the conversation. "They are all here during the holiday, for obvious reasons, and they all go by different names than what they were born with. And they all sleep in the attic bedrooms. We thought that was best so they might have the privacy to share with each other the things that might expose their truths to the other students."

"Miss Goris!" Andrée said at once, putting a hand to her throat as she recalled the boarding teacher who stayed in the attic bedrooms as supervisor.

Madame Ovart nodded. "Her true name is Hélène Gancarska, but yes. She is their headmistress. All of them have been hiding in plain sight here, and Miss Sterno has been facilitating both their delivery here and the means to care for them. And, as I understand, that would be similar to the duties they would ask you to fulfill, should you accept the position."

Andrée looked to Miss Sterno for confirmation, which was given with a brisk nod. "And the risks?" she asked, lowering her voice.

Miss Sterno gave her a tight half smile. "Well, we're in a war, even if the battlefield looks a little different than one might expect. I won't lie to you, Miss Geulen. We're risking everything. Not merely our own lives, but those we're trying to help, those we are working with, those we love . . ." She shook her head before shrugging. "Everything. Every single thing. If that is too much, I only ask that you maintain discretion about what you've heard here."

There was no doubt of that, regardless of whatever decision Andrée came to. Even if she could not take part in the operations of the CDJ, she would fully support them in any way possible. There was nothing she wanted more than to keep the abuse of Jews from continuing, and she was passionate about giving herself to such a cause, but with the risks being what they were . . .

"I want to do it," Andrée said slowly, knots in her stomach raveling and unraveling in an uncomfortable pattern, "but may I have twenty-four hours to be certain?"

Miss Sterno nodded, her smile staying in place. "Of course. In the meantime, Madame Ovart and I need to discuss further details for our present friends. Until you are certain, it would be safest if you know as little as possible. Would you mind?" She nudged her head toward the door.

"No, of course not." Andrée rose and brushed at her skirts, sparing a smile for the headmistress. "You have my discretion, madame. You can trust me."

"I know, Andrée. There has never been a question of that." Madame Ovart returned her smile with an encouraging one of her own that Andrée took for a dismissal.

She nodded at them both and walked out of the room, her mind full of scenarios and questions that she had never before imagined. Wondering if she was capable of the things she had heard about, the things she was now considering, the things she wished she had thought of before. Wondering if she could join these brave men and women in resisting the schemes of the Nazis and protecting those who were no longer able to defend themselves.

Hadn't she dreamed of doing great and brave things from the moment she had heard about the refugees in the Spanish Civil War? Hadn't she been desperate to do something, anything, to help the situation? Hadn't *action* been the thing she'd most craved at that time?

Hadn't she been longing to take any sort of action in the present situation? For her students, her neighbors, her countrymen, her fellow members of humanity?

And now, action was being offered to her. The chance to do more than sit around a table and bemoan the situation with fellow sympathizers. To actually change the situation for those they could reach. It would not be enough for everyone, but it would be everything to each someone they helped.

Would it be enough to make any difference?

Would that be enough for her?

She chewed the inside of her lip as she walked up the stairs toward her room, wondering if she ought to turn back now and tell Miss Sterno she accepted or if she ought to truly wait the twenty-four hours she had asked for.

Her family would need to be told something to protect them, but she wasn't staying with them, so housing her throughout the endeavors would not be a problem. She wouldn't have risked them by staying there anyway, had she not been boarding at the school. They were not particularly close in her adulthood, and she had no reason to change that now.

Or when she joined the CDJ.

If she did.

Which she planned on.

But she wouldn't interrupt the present meeting between Miss Sterno and Madame Ovart. They had built a relationship of trust over however many weeks and months they had worked together, and she would not interfere with that at the moment. There would be time enough to forge her own relationships and connections once she officially joined.

She did not need to rush this.

What she would need to do is avoid viewing the students she now knew to be hidden Jewish students with an excess of compassion and sympathy. She always viewed students with some of both, but now she knew the truth about some of the most vulnerable . . .

She could not risk anyone guessing their secret because she could not hide her feelings for them.

But Andrée would make a note to take part in the bedtime routine for those students tonight, which was not outside of her realm of duties and would raise no suspicions. It was the perfect excuse to show a little extra care without being blatant.

Hours later, doing just that, Andrée found herself smiling as she tucked in a girl of nine who seemed to be struggling with the concept of sleeping for more than an hour at a time. It was not so uncommon for this particular child, but it especially amused Andrée now that she knew more of the child's background.

Such innocence despite the danger and the abuse, such a simple display of childish normalcy at a time when children were fast becoming adults. It was encouraging, refreshing, and heartwarming. There was no telling what the child knew of her situation, let alone that of her fellow students and teacher, but she certainly knew enough, given she almost certainly had to use a different surname than the one given at birth or used at her previous school.

And yet she could still innocently struggle with consistently staying asleep.

Or was that a newfound affliction brought on by her new reality?

That was a far more humbling thought, if not more likely scenario.

Andrée tucked the sweet girl in a little more securely as she attempted to doze off once more. Was her name really Marie, or was that different, too? Had she been forced to train herself to respond to a different name for months? Forced to forget her family and home life? Forced to grow up in the space of weeks instead of years?

It was all Andrée could do not to scoop the sweet child into her arms and hug her tightly.

She allowed herself to tousle Marie's hair before pushing up from the small bed and moving out of the room of sleeping children.

A thundering on the stairs startled Andrée from her reverie and forced her sharply back into the present. Harsh German voices barked orders as the thundering neared her, backing her up instinctively toward the children's rooms.

There wasn't time to shout much of a warning, and there was nowhere for them to go this high into the boardinghouse. No way out, no escape, no options. They were coming for them, and nothing could be done.

Stern, angry faces appeared on the stairwell, nearly all bearing the telltale blue eyes and fair hair that the Nazis preferred, and all of whom had their eyes and guns fixed on their aim.

The bedroom.

One glanced at her and indicated with his gun that she should enter the room as well.

The scene she came upon could not have been more different from the one moments before. Children were dragged out of bed by their hair, tears and screams ignored, their treatment that of animals rather than young humans. Marie was among them, rubbing the sleep from her now streaming eyes, lined up beside her fellow classmates, nightdress askew.

Other teachers from the school were marched into the bedroom, including Miss Goris, as well as Madame Ovart and her husband. But, strangely enough, not their teenage daughter.

The Germans were in plain clothes, which told Andrée they were Gestapo rather than soldiers, but there was no consolation to be found in that revelation. A denunciation had taken place; it was the only reason why they should be here at this time of night. Someone had told the secret police where Jewish students were hiding.

Children. The Gestapo were hunting down children.

Andrée could have snarled where she stood.

The room was now filling with people, teachers roused from their beds, students from other rooms, even the kitchen staff, all standing together and waiting for the Gestapo razzia to commence.

A tall, chiseled German with a narrow mustache stepped forward, looking at the children. "All *Juden* come stand on this side. Everyone else, stand opposite," he ordered in accented French. "Now!"

The children did as they were bid, trembling with every step and every breath.

He surveyed them all, then produced a whip and slowly walked up the line of non-Jewish children. "Any child that lies to me will receive such a whipping from me that he will remember it for the rest of his life."

A small boy, no more than four, stared at him with wide, dark eyes, then darted across to the Jewish side and embraced a girl who looked so like him they could only be siblings. He buried his face in her nightgown, and she clung to him, keeping her eyes straight ahead while silent tears continued to stream down quivering cheeks.

Andrée also shook, though it was not from fear. She ground her teeth and glared at the man with the whip, ready to tackle him to the ground if he moved to use it on a single child.

The man then moved to the adults in the room, eyeing each of them with coldness. "Each of you will be interrogated, and the promise I made to the children will stand for you as well. You are all under arrest, though it is up to you what the result of said arrest is."

He paused in front of Andrée, looking her up and down without interest. He shook his head. "Aren't you ashamed, Miss Aryan woman, to be teaching these little Jewish fleas and looking after them?"

Searing heat screeched its way up Andrée's spine, settling in the base of her throat. "Aren't you ashamed, esteemed descendant of the glorious Goethe and Schiller, to be making war on innocent children?" she returned in crystal clear German.

His lip curled in a sneer. "When you do not wish to be eaten by adult bugs, you crush them under your boot when they are young."

He had also replied in German, which meant the children did not comprehend, but several of the teachers did, and their gasps were enough to make the children whimper.

Andrée continued to stare at him coldly, daring him to say anything else to her, to attempt to defend his words, but he said nothing to her. No shame, no remorse, no adjustment to his attitude or sentiments. He lived by this mentality; they all did.

The world was consumed by this evil, and they were only living in it.

If she hadn't been certain of her decision to join the CDJ, she was convinced of it now.

The man moved over to the Ovarts, grinning at them in a purely malevolent fashion. "If your teachers tell us the truth, madame, monsieur, your daughter just might be spared deportation to Germany. You will certainly be transported regardless. Do you understand?"

They made no response, staring straight ahead.

The teachers, however, stared at each other and at each of the Gestapo in the room. None of them were going to risk Dédée, the Ovarts' daughter, though they probably knew little enough to consider lying about the situation anyway. They would share their honest thoughts and feelings, and it would wind up coming down to the Ovarts and Miss Goris for those directly involved.

Even Andrée could only admit to knowing about this situation today, which was exactly what the other teachers could say.

Her advanced information was only a matter of hours compared to the rest of the staff, and she highly doubted the interrogation would get so specific, unless the denunciation had taken place that very afternoon.

The officer turned to his men and barked quick orders, resulting in the children being marched out of the room, and then, of all things, he moved to the line of teachers and specifically pulled out Miss Goris, forcing her ahead with the children.

They had known exactly who they were looking for.

The Ovarts were also seized and taken from the room, leaving the remaining teachers there with a few of the Gestapo, no doubt for the aforementioned interrogation.

It didn't matter, whatever happened. The children and Miss Goris were probably being taken to Malines for holding, unless they were going to be transported somewhere more sinister. Andrée could answer any questions they put upon her, though she would certainly do so with spite enough to warrant her own arrest, if they wished.

Then, whenever they finished with her, she would stand on the streets outside the school and ward off all day students, both Jew and non-Jew, and send them back home for safety. There was no way the Gestapo would know only about the hidden Jewish students, and she was not going to risk any other children getting caught in this witch hunt.

And after she was sure that the children were safe, she was going to find Ida Sterno and officially join the CDJ.

Effective immediately.

CHAPTER 4

The Jewish spirit undermines the healthy powers of the German people.

—NAZI PROPAGANDA SLIDE, CA. 1933–1939

She had to ignore the tears. Whatever she said, however she reacted, the tears could not affect her.

If Ida, too, became choked up, it would upset the children far too much, and they could not spare the time for so much compassion.

Ida wasn't even collecting the children today. Andrée, Paule, or Claire would do so tomorrow or the next day, depending on the situation. But this mother was already crying and tempting Ida to do the same just in discussing what was needed.

"Your husband has already been taken, Madame Liebman?" Ida said as gently as she could while the woman's tears streamed unchecked down her cheeks.

She nodded, her pale countenance seeming more ghoulish than sickly. "Three weeks ago. I know it is only a matter of time before they come for us as well. I cannot hide adequately like this. I can barely exist, given the circumstances."

The soft giggles of the children in the other room offered a strange dissonance to the reality presently expressed by their mother and the discussion in which she was engaged. But it served only to emphasize what Ida and the rest of the committee always attested to.

Children were remarkably resilient.

Ida continued to take notes, forcing herself to remain distant. "Do you have family outside of Brussels, madame? Friends who could help you once we remove the children?"

"Yes," Mrs. Liebman murmured without any hint of relief or satisfaction. "There are options." She rocked in her chair a little, then leaned forward. "Where will you take them?"

"I cannot tell you that, madame," Ida told her, meeting her eyes and smiling with some sympathy. "It is a condition of the committee's involvement. We cannot guarantee the safety of anyone if locations are known."

Mrs. Liebman winced and turned away, nodding ever so slightly. "I know. But my heart . . ." She swiped at her eyes. "My children are all I have, Mademoiselle Jeanne."

There was some comfort in the professional distance imposed by Ida's code name, which she had learned to answer to just as readily as her given name, but it still did not completely soothe the compassionate pain that always accompanied these meetings.

If Mrs. Liebman was this emotional in just the discussion of intervention, the scene upon pickup of the children would almost certainly be much worse. Ida would need to warn whoever was assigned to escort the children to their new home—a situation infinitely more difficult than what Ida's routine involved now.

There could be no tears or fretting on the escort's part during the pickups, or the parents and children would suffer. The children needed as much ignorance as was possible, masked by joviality and enthusiasm. The Gestapo had spies everywhere, both within their ranks and within members of the general public who they had persuaded to their side; and distressed children walking along the streets with young women would attract attention. Would raise questions. Would put them all at risk.

It was for the best that none of the escorts were mothers. How could they pry children away from their mothers if they, too, felt the pains of such separations on an intimate level? It was agonizing enough to be witness to it.

Ida cleared her throat and returned to her notes. "And the names and ages of the children, Madame Liebman?"

"Irene, age twelve," Mrs. Liebman answered softly. "David, age ten. Alice, age six."

Jotting that information down, Ida raised her eyes to the woman again. "Any particular health issues we ought to be aware of?"

Mrs. Liebman shook her head. "None, Mademoiselle Jeanne. They are beautiful, healthy, sweet children, each one. And they miss their father." Her face crumpled and she buried her face into her hands, her slender shoulders shaking.

Ida's throat tightened and she set down her notebook and pen, swallowing hard. How could she remain aloof in the face of such distress? She had a job to do, but in the course of doing such work, it was easy to forget the horrors that were taking place daily among her fellow Jews. It did not matter that Ida had not been a practicing Jew for years, did not matter that she almost never prayed the Shema, that she was more Jewish by tradition than faith, or that she couldn't remember the last time she had gone to synagogue.

These were Ida's people, and the Nazis were not concerned with the dedication one had to the Jewish faith. They hated each and every one equally, and universally despised all that they were.

But Mrs. Liebman could not know that Ida was part of her community; that she was also at risk of persecution, deportation, and death; that she was living under false papers to move more freely; or that she had burned the stars she had once had to wear on her coat.

Still, she could not ignore the tears this time.

Would not.

Against her usual regulations, Ida reached out and took Mrs. Liebman's hands, squeezing gently. "I cannot make this easier for you, Madame Liebman. I cannot change the world we live in or what is happening. But I can get your children to safety and protect them from the denunciations that abound. I can keep them from following their father to the camps. I can hide them, madame, which will allow you to also hide more easily."

Mrs. Liebman sniffed, bobbing her head in weak nods as she gripped

Ida's hands in return. "I don't know what to do for myself or how to go about hiding, but I would do anything to protect my children, even if it will break my own heart." She raised her head and met Ida's eyes. "Do what you must, Mademoiselle Jeanne, to make my children safe."

Ida offered her a firm smile and nodded. "I will. You can be sure of that." She sat back, letting her hands slide from their hold on Mrs. Liebman. "You can expect one of our associates to arrive for your children the day after tomorrow. Kindly have one bag packed per child. Do you have any questions for me before I go?"

It was as though the question was deliberately snubbed. No reaction from Mrs. Liebman, no attempt to start the process of bidding her farewells, no indication that she had questions, thoughts, or feelings. There was only a blankness that seemed to come from deep within the soul.

An emptiness that humbled and a hopelessness that frightened.

Was this what the world had come to, then? An existence that became an inconvenience and a life suddenly devoid of light?

All the more reason for Ida and the others at the CDJ to continue their work and to redouble their efforts. Those who were arrested and deported, taken to the dreaded camps one heard about, would need something to live for, and knowing their children were safe from such a fate could be the difference between strength and weakness.

Ida rose from her seat and kept her expression intact. "Then I will bid you good day, Madame Liebman. If you need anything before my associates arrive, contact the AJB, as you did before."

This Mrs. Liebman heard, as indicated by her nod, but made no move to rise herself. It was no matter to Ida, who let herself out of the house and made her way down the street toward the secret offices of the CDJ. She was duty bound to tell the woman to contact the AJB if she needed anything, as that was the avenue through which any Jewish request for aid must go. But the Association of Jews in Belgium, though staffed by Jews, was more of a shell organization for the SS. Created by the Nazis with the pretense of enabling support to Belgian Jews, the AJB worked mostly as a means of cataloging the names and addresses of Belgian Jews. The work the AJB did often alerted the SS to families and individuals who might try to flee. Almost as soon as a family's information was cataloged by the AJB, the SS might take that information and carry out a raid on the family.

Fortunately, those same AJB lists were also how Ida and the rest knew where to intervene before a possible raid.

Maurice Heiber was their connection at the AJB, and he kept his position there only to further the actual help that the CDJ provided. He had joined the AJB with hope and good intentions at the onset of its establishment only to discover its true purpose and complete worthlessness when it came to providing relief. He and his wife, Esta, had been crucial to helping Ghert and Yvonne Jospa found the CDJ and set up the various departments and connections needed to finance the work. It was an impressive network, all things considered, and there were enough secrets between the departments that the organization would not be compromised in its entirety even if discoveries were made.

Because the AJB was how Mrs. Liebman had found them originally, it was the means by which she would need to request anything else. Maurice would know what to do when she contacted them.

Still, it was hard to imagine she would need anything else, unless she changed her mind entirely. Which, given her distress, was entirely possible. She would not be the first to change her mind, nor would she be the last.

But the truth of the matter was that no one, as yet, who had changed their mind had avoided deportation through their own means.

Ida did her best to explain this to those she met with before they confirmed their interest, and yet some still chose to trust in their own efforts rather than do what was necessary with the CDJ. Those were the cases that haunted her dreams, not the ones where they had failed, or where mistakes had been made or betrayal had come. The ones where they had offered the requested help, had a plan set up, and then, before the rescue could occur, minds had changed. Fears had taken over, forcing resolve away and tying fate to tremulous foundations.

All of this was made worse by the fact that one of the primary denunciators for the Gestapo was, in fact, a Jew.

"Fat Jacques," they called him, for evident reasons. His family had been taken away to the camps last year, and rather than hate the Nazis for doing so, he had given up hope and light to join them and pursue darkness. He was the one who had discovered what the Ovarts were facilitating at the Gatti de Gamond school and had told the Gestapo of it. He was the one who helped those who hated his people to succeed.

It was he who did to others what was done to himself.

Not even the Nazis could say that about themselves.

Fat Jacques was worse than they.

And he was the bane of the CDJ at the present.

Ida shook her head as she moved toward the offices in Rue de la Brasserie, taking her usual route of indirectness to ensure confusion for any who should follow. She had never felt that she was being followed in the course of her work, but she knew full well that these seemingly unnecessary precautions were what was going to save her.

They were what saved everyone who could be saved.

With men like Fat Jacques betraying not only his people but humanity, one could never take too many precautions. If only these families could understand that. The CDJ was not tearing families apart because they enjoyed inflicting torment upon already weakened spirits. They were trying to save the most innocent among them: the children.

The very future of the Jewish people.

There was, of course, the convenience to the adults of not having to consider options for themselves that would involve hiding or fleeing with children, which would enable their own efforts to be more successful, in theory. But ultimately, the object was to keep as many children from danger as humanly possible.

Sometimes that kernel of truth became lost in the need of parents to keep their families together. Ida could not, and would not, judge them for feeling such bonds, but neither could she deny that indulging in those feelings was putting them all at an increased risk.

She had returned to far too many now-empty houses to believe anything else.

Finally, Ida arrived at the offices and turned in, going beyond the facade placed for appearances and the secretary whose job it was to look busy regardless of the time or day, passing through another series of doors, and then entering the main room where her colleagues and superiors occasionally made appearances.

None of them spent a consistent quantity of time there, given the risks, and none of them kept the entirety of their information in this location, but it did make for a convenient meeting place and center of operations when it was needed. The Adult section of the operations had their own couriers and operatives, just as Ida and the others in the Children's section had; and the third section, that of Housing and Sustenance, worked in an entirely different manner from the other two sections. Ida knew almost nothing about how they worked, only that they did so, and that several of the locations she had presently housing children relied on the success of another section.

But she couldn't think about that now, nor about what the adult section would do for Mrs. Liebman. She could only look into the options for her three children and arrange their pickup with her operatives.

"Jeanne," greeted Esta Heiber, glancing up from her desk with a smile. "All well?"

Esta was the figurative head of the children's section, and her insight was invaluable to the entire operation, even if Ida had practically taken over with the increase in requests and need for operatives.

"Yes," Ida confirmed tightly, moving to the safe nearby to pull out a notebook, then to the cupboard across the room to fetch another. "All well." She couldn't give more information than that, not until the children were safely away and safely established elsewhere.

She jotted down the names of the three children into the first notebook, notating a code number beside each name. She read those through three times, committing them to memory, as Irene, David, and Alice could not retain their names when they were moved, and the complex system of records the CDJ kept required focus and intensity by the operatives involved.

Next, she opened the second notebook, which indicated locations, their capacity, and their code numbers. She'd already thought up a few options in her mind but needed to check availability before she settled on one. Once she decided where the children should go, she could pass their names and code numbers to Paule, Claire, or Andrée, whichever one was doing the pickup, as well as the code for the children's new location.

None of the operatives who helped physically relocate children even knew where this office was, as it happened. They met Esta and Ida in other locations, and the information on available housing locations was filled in by Esta or Ida when Yvonne Jospa and her associates sent it to them. No one knew all the pieces, so no one could give up the entire operation.

Arrests happened far too often for them to trust so much to so many.

Ida returned the notebooks to their previous places, then walked over to Esta, pretending to look at the papers on her desk. "123, 124, and 125," she murmured in a low voice. "Going to 322."

"Claude," Esta told her, giving the code name for Andrée.

Nodding, Ida pushed off the desk and left the office, going out a side door and heading toward the market. Her apartment was four blocks from the market, and it was always a great way to adjust her course before returning to her lodgings, given the variety of stalls and the varying number of people there.

Once she was in her apartment, Ida would write out the instructions for Andrée and meet up with her later. Meanwhile, Esta would take the numbers Ida had given her and record them in the notebook kept under her desk in a secret safe.

Then Andrée would create the false name for the child, teach the child that name, and ensure it was recorded in the notebook she had access to once the child was delivered.

It was quite a process to record every detail, but Esta had set it up with the full understanding that it would keep the children safe, should any notebook fall into the wrong hands, and that those who knew how the system worked would be the only ones who could ensure that families could be reunited when the war was over.

If any of them survived.

No, Ida scolded harshly, nudging her way through the people standing around the scant produce stall. She would not consider the possibility that every one of them would be captured, deported, and dead before the end of all this. They could be captured or deported, certainly. But it was highly unlikely that all of them would be all three of those things before the end. Especially as they could recruit others to continue the work.

They hadn't brought anyone else on after Andrée joined them, but Esta and Yvonne were constantly looking for more social workers or teachers to work with them. If there was ever a need, Ida knew they would provide her with excellent options. The work would continue, of that she was certain.

It would be fine. Even with Fat Jacques, the Gestapo, and the soldiers, it would work out, somehow.

She refused to believe they would fail in this.

It was only a few turns more until she was back at her apartment building, and she began the process of climbing the stairs toward her quarters.

"Mademoiselle Hendrickx?"

Ida turned at the landing to face down the stairs she'd just ascended. "Yes?"

Her landlady appeared, resting her hands on the railing as she met Ida's eyes, face impassive. "I'm afraid I will not be able to renew your lease here. You will need to find alternative accommodations."

"Is there a problem?" Ida asked, drumming her fingers against her thigh, more in absentmindedness than anxiety.

The landlady dipped her chin in a quick nod. "I'm afraid it has been made known to me that you are of a particular racial and religious persuasion that renders housing you more difficult than I am willing to endure. Therefore, you must leave."

The utter formality of the exchange was almost as irritating as the reasoning behind her eviction. Ida had maintained a good relationship with her landlady during the months she had been living in Brussels and had never had a single issue with her rent payments, the cleanliness of her place, or the conditions of the building itself. She was using a false name, but that had been easy enough, given her little-publicized marriage, and her paperwork showing such a name would pass even the most studious tests.

How in the world had the fact that she was Jewish made its way to the landlady's ears?

It wasn't even a question from the lady. It was a statement. An accusation. Something so clear, it seemed, that no argument would be accepted.

Yet she was not being arrested or invaded by the Gestapo, so the knowledge was a quiet one. She supposed she ought to be grateful for that.

"When would you like me out, madame?" Ida asked in a low, respectful voice.

"Immediately, mademoiselle. Apologies, but I must insist." The landlady gave her another nod, averting her eyes, then moved out of sight into another part of the building.

Ida released a slow breath, her heart pounding more after the fact than it had during the exchange. Anger was racing through her veins, as was pity. Irritation was flooding in, followed by sadness. She had no doubt that her landlady was a good woman, and that her actions were born from fear rather than judgment.

But it still put her in the situation of needing to find a new place to live, even with her false papers.

That was inconvenient, given all else she had to do. But she had no choice.

It didn't take her much time to pack up her belongings, all of her worldly possessions fitting neatly into two valises. Moving to Brussels to do this work had rid her of a great many needless items, which had been oddly freeing. She hadn't planned on it being a plus to relocate again, but it was certainly worth acknowledging.

She would simply take her bags with her to meet her operatives, and then find Esta or Yvonne to seek out alternative housing. They had helped her to find this place, and they had connections with other sympathetic people in the city. No one would know she was a Jew unless they spoke with her former landlady, but she would appreciate discretion and respect in the person from whom she would be renting. Anyone who was a possibility for hiding some of their families from the Gestapo would be a secure place for Ida to live.

Especially as she was not exactly in hiding.

Smiling for the benefit of anyone who would pass her, Ida moved along the streets toward the office she had set up for herself and her operatives, a quiet little flat in Rue du Trône. It was an unimpressive property and as very few people went in and out, it was of little interest to anybody. According to any town registries, it was an office of social workers, which kept most from asking questions, and was close enough to the truth to be proven by the background of those working within.

The exact nature of their social work was, of course, entirely unrelated to the general idea.

Ida sat down at one of the desks, putting her head into her hands and taking a moment to feel the strain of needing to find herself new lodgings amidst everything else. She would almost never be there. It would be purely a place to sleep and dress, and yet it was also supposed to be a location where she felt safest.

Now that had been taken from her. Was this the sort of anchorless sensation the children they hid felt when they were plucked up and taken elsewhere?

Paule was probably doing a run at the moment, which meant either Claire or Andrée would arrive, if not both. Claire had just returned from a delivery to one of their convent locations, so she could appear only to report. Or, as had happened before, none of her operatives could appear, given the variety of tasks and assignments they were engaged in. Which simply meant that Ida would have to send a message to one of them about meeting up in another place and time.

It was more complicated to think about than it was to accomplish, she decided with a small laugh to herself.

"Good morning, Jeanne," greeted the mellow voice of Andrée as she entered the office and sat in a chair nearby.

Ida grinned at her newest operative. "Claude," she greeted, using her code name. "Are you ready for another?"

Andrée nodded, holding her hand out to accept the paper.

Ida slid the information to her. "Three this time. Twelve and under. Mother is already teary, so be on the alert."

"Always." Andrée gave her a tight smile, then glanced at her bags. "Are you leaving, Jeanne?"

"No, simply in need of a new residence." Ida sat back against her chair, shaking her head. "Apparently, my landlady discovered something presently distasteful in a renter. I'm not worried; our friends know several locations."

Andrée countered her posture by leaning toward her. "My apartment has two rooms, one of which is unoccupied. I've barely been there two weeks—why not move in with me?"

Ida's eyes widened, the possibilities and conveniences of such an arrangement spinning about in her mind. "Are you certain?"

"Positive," Andrée confirmed with a nod. "I could help more with your load, if you'd let me, and we each wouldn't have to bear so much alone."

That Andrée could so easily detect the burdens Ida bore, after scant weeks of her involvement in the CDJ, was both a credit to Andrée and a sign that Ida could use such a partner while this work continued. Why shouldn't they become roommates?

"Very well, then," Ida said, smiling at her fellow conspirator and burgeoning friend. "Shall we?"

CHAPTER 5

All proposals that include a permanent presence, a permanent regulation of the Jews in Germany, do not solve the Jewish Question, for they do not eliminate the Jews from Germany.

—ACHIM GERCKE, NAZI OFFICIAL IN THE MINISTRY OF THE INTERIOR, 1933

"Mademoiselle Claude, where are we going?"

Andrée barely heard the sweet whisper of the young companion to her right. Her mind was too active, her heart too aching. How was she going to explain to Ida and Esta that she did not have three children with her, but only two? How were they going to ensure that Mrs. Liebman and her little Alice, just six years of age, were safe in their home?

How could Mrs. Liebman send away only two of her children and keep one with her?

Irene and David, now Eileen and Dirk, had been unruffled by the change, which made Andrée wonder if their mother had explained the change to them the night before. Or perhaps just that morning. Had their mother ever planned on sending all three away? Was the separation too much to bear? Had she somehow convinced herself that she was better able to care for her youngest than strangers?

Alice was not an infant, but a robust and quick girl of six. Andrée had seen that in only five minutes of knowing the family. But it would appear that Mrs. Liebman saw Alice as the baby she had carried in her arms most recently, the toddling child she had taught to walk, the curious little girl who had not yet managed words.

Whichever it was, Andrée had not been able to convince her that Alice ought to join her siblings in hiding, and she had not had the time to argue for long. There was nothing more that could be done for Alice if the mother would not give her up.

She had a terrible, sinking feeling about the predicament, and escorting only a portion of the Liebman children to their new home was unsettling, to say the least.

"Mademoiselle Claude?"

Andrée blinked, and looked at Eileen, trying for a smile. "Yes, Eileen?"

Eileen's brow furrowed, no doubt from the shift in her identity. "Where are we going?"

"Your aunt and uncle in the country, of course," Andrée told her gently, taking her hand. "You won't remember them; you were very young. But they are very excited to have you both come to stay for a while. There are cows and chickens and sheep, fields of wildflowers, plenty of fresh air . . . your aunt is an artist, and told me she would love to teach you, if you're interested. And for you, Dirk, there are plenty of hills to race across, since I know you are very active."

She made it sound as beautiful and fun as possible, hoping her enthusiasm would be catching for them. Nothing she said was a lie, apart from the fact of their hosts being in any way related to them. The farm was a beautiful place and one of the safest places they had ever found for hiding children. It would be a freeing experience for these children, who had only known city life and, more recently, been as cooped up as they were.

Neither Eileen nor Dirk had cried upon leaving their mother, each bearing a stoic, carefully blank expression. Something certain and determined rested upon both sets of features, even as their mother had openly wept and clung to them.

Alice had cried as well, clearly not understanding why her siblings were leaving, why she was not, why her mother was crying.

Andrée had facilitated several family separations by now, but there was something about this one that was particularly stinging.

She could not get Alice Liebman's tearstained face out of her mind.

Not her mother, not her brave older siblings, but her.

Left behind. Left in danger. Left with only her mother for family.

Andrée had separated siblings from parents before, but they had all been in hiding together, so they had been unified in that. They could find solace in knowing that they were not alone in their experience.

Alice would not have that.

After she delivered the two older Liebman children to their destination, she was going to meet with Ida and Esta, if she could manage it, and see if one of them could try to convince Mrs. Liebman to change her mind, to give them Alice as well. To let them save her.

She could not let this go.

Andrée looked across from her at Dirk, only ten years old and yet so mature and serious. Had the natural impetuousness of boyhood vanished because of the invasion? Or had it been more recent, with the arrest of his father?

There was a restless energy in Dirk, she could tell that by the way his left ankle bounced while he sat. There was no pattern to it, no reason for it, no sign of outward anxiety or worry. It just bounced, rather like every other little boy Andrée had ever seen when they were bored.

Dirk was going to love living on the farm. Assuming he could allow himself to forget his life in Brussels for a while. Some children could, some children couldn't. Which category would Dirk fall into?

The train jolted a little as they pulled into a station. Eileen and Dirk looked out of the window in expectation, then up at Andrée in question.

She gently shook her head and held up two fingers to indicate the number of stops they had before their arrival.

The children exchanged looks, then sat back against their seats with the same rough motions and scowls. If nothing else indicated they were siblings, that did.

It was for the best that they went to the same location. They would need each other, particularly with their youngest sibling not being hidden beside them. They would wonder about their father, their mother, *and* their little sister.

Life was not presently fair for these children. Or for any of their people.

Or for any reasonably humane people.

A faint shift in the train told them all it was starting to move once more, and Andrée decided to attempt to engage her young companions by telling them a story, something she had often done with young children she had taught or boarded with. Just like those sweet children who had been rounded up by the Gestapo and sent to heaven knows where.

She had been able to prevent the school's day students from meeting the same fate, thankfully. Once the Gestapo had finished interviewing her and, reluctantly, decided she had nothing to do with hiding the Jews, they had let her go. Rather than go home, Andrée had gone out in the streets by the school and was able to warn day students of the danger and tell them to return home at once.

The Gestapo hadn't taken a single one of those students, not after the initial roundup.

It didn't soften the pain of the loss of those boarding students, but it prevented a second series of pains from occurring due to others being arrested.

She missed those quiet, innocent moments of telling stories to children before bed. There was a lovely simplicity to it, a reminder of the beauty in the world and the purity of children, an illustration of hope and a portrait of bliss. It seemed cruel to bring the harsh realities of the world upon such a moment, especially when the world was filled with such evil at the present.

Here she was, telling a story to children on a train heading to the country, and it could not be further from those rose-tinted memories.

These children were fleeing for their lives, separated from their parents and sister, and hated for existing.

Would her attempts at a story bring them any hope or light at all? Would a story even distract them from what they had already endured and the unknown that lay ahead?

Somehow, she managed to tell a relatively entertaining story for the children, even though neither of them was fixed on the words coming from her mouth. She sensed they knew what she was trying to do, and they were content to let her try. It was a poor substitution for the moments of childhood they should have been having, but it was better than silence.

They had to pass for a family or family friends, after all, or they risked discovery. That was less likely now that they were out of Brussels, but she had been on a train in the country with Gestapo members before, so it was not completely out of the question. Still, this had been a quiet trip since they'd left the surrounding Brussels area, and the children were not inclined to chat.

Andrée could only hope that they would find some semblance of the children they ought to have been with enough time in the country.

The train began to slow, and Andrée glanced out of the window before nodding at the children and rising, pulling their valises from the shelf above their heads. She glanced back to see Eileen straightening Dirk's collar and cap, much like she had probably seen their mother do dozens of times.

It was both sad and endearing to witness.

They disembarked, children hand in hand, while Andrée had Dirk by one hand and the valises in the other. Well, one valise in hand and the other under her arm. She thought it best to maintain a hold on at least one of the children as a mother would have done.

She owed it to Mrs. Liebman to treat them as such.

A friendly cab driver drove them from the station to the farm, the children equally silent on that drive as they had been for the majority of the train ride. She wasn't going to force them to talk, not in front of a cab driver they'd never see again, and not at the age they were.

Younger children were more easily distracted, but these two . . .

The sooner they got to the farm, the better for them all.

The cab pulled off the road and onto a dirt path, a quaint and tidy farmhouse up ahead of them. Andrée began calling the children's attention to various aspects of the farm and the land, anything she could think of that might attract and entertain them for even a minute. They would not have anything left to explore if she kept this going, but she was willing to risk that.

If it was possible for the children to grow more silent, they did so as the cab stopped in front of the house.

Andrée opened the door and climbed out, gesturing for them to follow. "Come on! Let's go greet your aunt and uncle. They'll be so excited you're finally here!" She forced as much glee into her voice as she could, hoping it would be contagious, and pretended to brush at Dirk's shoulders when he got out.

The door to the house opened with a loud creak, and Andrée turned as though to present the children officially to the middle-aged couple that appeared.

"Eileen and Dirk Lybaert, this is your aunt and uncle, Marie and Luc Dupont." Andrée gently pressed her hands against their backs and moved with them toward the porch. "Say hello."

The children waved, stepping up to the porch, and the Duponts put their arms around them, leading them inside, away from the waiting cab.

Once inside, pretenses were dropped, and Marie Dupont sank down to the kids' level. "You may both call me Aunt Marie, all right? This will be your home for as long as necessary, so I want you to feel comfortable here. Be as loud as you want and as wild as you want, so long as you don't break anything that can't be fixed."

Eileen nodded with the eager obedience that came with being an oldest child, while Dirk began to smile for what had to be the first time all day, if not longer.

It was the most encouraging sight Andrée had seen in some time.

"Now, would you like to come upstairs with me and pick your rooms?" Marie asked the children, using just the right amount of invitation and amusement in her voice.

"We get to pick?" Eileen's eyes were round at the thought, her expression losing the haunting appearance she had been wearing.

Marie nodded, smiling at her. "You do. Our children are old enough to live away from us, and there are four of them, so there are a few rooms to choose from."

Eileen and Dirk gave each other excited looks, then nodded at their new aunt.

Marie laughed and led them upstairs, leaving Luc in the entryway with Andrée.

Luc gave Andrée a concerned look. "Only two? What happened to the little one?"

Andrée exhaled roughly, gripping the back of her neck. "The mother changed her mind with that one. Said she couldn't give up her baby as well. Nothing I said could convince her otherwise." Her eyes began to tear up at the thought of Alice, now that her siblings were out of her sight.

Luc shook his head. "Poor woman. She must be at her wit's end to keep one behind. No matter, we are happy to help Eileen and Dirk."

"Thank you." Andrée reached into the pocket of her skirts and handed over the details of the ration stamps and money that would be sent to help support the children. "As discussed, it should be regular, if there are any concerns about that."

Luc tucked the paper into the pocket of his pants without looking at it. "I am not concerned about that, Mademoiselle Fournier. We have sufficient to provide for them without assistance, though I won't refuse the help, if it can be spared."

"It can," Andrée assured him. "Though I will let you know if anything changes. I'll be reporting back on occasion to check in on them, and you. Just to be sure all is well."

"Understood." Luc looked up at the ceiling, through which the sound of giggling and the squeaking of mattresses could be heard. "That's a good sound, isn't it?"

Andrée smiled at the sound. "Yes, it is."

Luc sighed, folding his arms. "Who makes war on children, Mademoiselle Fournier? Regardless of race or religion or perceived wrongs, children should always be safe from persecution."

Now she smiled at this dear man, who would be so good for these children. "I could not agree more, Monsieur Dupont. I could not agree more." She jerked her thumb toward the door. "I'll get their bags and be on my way back to Brussels."

"I'll see you out." He followed her back to the cab and took the bags from the trunk for her. "Do you want to say goodbye?" he inquired, gesturing to the house.

Andrée looked at the building and imagined the children jumping up and down on the mattresses, giggling like the children they deserved to be. Swallowing, she shook her head. "Not unless they need it. Based on the sounds we heard, I don't believe they do."

Luc smiled and nodded at the cab driver. "Thank you for waiting for her. You'll see her safely returned to the station?"

"Of course," came the cheery reply. He got back into his cab and turned the key.

Andrée held out a hand to Luc, shaking firmly. "Thank you, Monsieur Dupont. For everything."

"You should be the one thanked, Mademoiselle Fournier. By comparison, we risk very little." He shook her hand again, gripping firmly.

Throat tightening against another wash of emotion, Andrée nodded and moved to the cab, sliding into the back seat. Getting back to Brussels would be important now so she could close this delivery and start the next one. Several tasks would need to be done—finishing the reports, putting down the official information into notebooks, sending word that it was done, and, of course, relating that Alice Liebman, also known as number 125, did not become Anne Lybaert.

That would throw a wrinkle into a few things, but, ultimately, it altered nothing for their plans.

There were more children that needed to be hidden, and they needed to get to them quickly.

Unless Mrs. Liebman changed her mind, Alice wasn't going anywhere with the CDJ. "What happens to me happens to her," Mrs. Liebman had told Andrée.

Couldn't she see that was exactly what they were afraid of?

But ultimately, if Mrs. Liebman could live with that, Andrée would have to as well.

They all would.

The ride to the station and the train back to Brussels were uneventful, as she had expected. There was entirely too much time to think, and entirely too many silent tears shed as those thoughts swirled. But she would be well enough, as always.

The separations had not gotten easier since she had started, but she was doing better when it came to orchestrating those separations. She was learning better ways to speak with the parents when she came, kinder ways of expressing what she could, being more apologetic for what she could not say, and finding more creative means of gaining the children's trust quickly. She had been told too many horror stories from Paule, Ida, and Claire, all of which she had learned from, and while she would never claim to be perfect in her efforts, she could say that she had benefited a great deal in hearing of their mistakes.

All of them wanted to be better in this, and all of them were as determined as the next to continue in their improvement.

And then there were the Nazis.

The SS men and the Wehrmacht soldiers were almost always about in the streets, which was one reason why they went to pick up the luggage separately from the children. But it was not unusual to see a few of them on corners, their eyes clearly asking the question of how Andrée could possibly be old enough to have a child of eight at her side, or whatever age her present children happened to be. They never stopped her to ask, never suspected anything, given the blessed Aryan looks she possessed that they valued so highly.

She had learned to smile at them when their eyes met. Had learned that friendliness when combined with her appearance diffused any possible suspicions on their part. Had learned to swallow back the burning anger and volley of sharp words she longed to launch upon them.

For the sake of the children she was saving, she could act the part required of her, knowing their safety depended on her abilities.

It was exhausting, she would not deny that, but it was also the most important thing she had ever done, of that she was certain.

Once back in Brussels, Andrée made her way, taking a roundabout route, to the Rue du Trône office. She was drained but eager to share what she had experienced and how everything had gone with her delivery. She wasn't sure if any of the others had dealt with a parent changing their mind on the day of pickup, but it was certainly something she needed to pass along so they could all be prepared for the situation.

To her good fortune, Andrée found both Paule and Claire, code names Solange and Catherine, sitting at desks within, Ida in her usual place, and to her surprise, Esta Heiber, their superior from the central office, sitting in the midst of them.

All looked at Andrée as she entered, their smiles small but welcoming.

"Claude, welcome," Esta greeted, waving her over. "I've only come to give you all some updated information."

Andrée nodded and came to the desk she usually claimed as her own, turning the chair to face Esta, as the others had done.

Esta was an elegant woman, more suited to a life of stardom than oppression and hiding, and, despite her youth, had a certain motherly air about her that was comforting. One might believe that a hug from her would soothe all infirmities and sorrows that could exist, and yet she had a will of iron that even Hitler would find himself quivering at.

Now, however, Esta looked pale and drawn, devoid of elegance and lacking in vibrancy. Someone or something had dimmed the light that came so naturally to Esta, and that alone was terrifying.

Andrée folded her hands in her lap and looked at the woman in anticipation, dreading and hoping at the same time.

"Some of you will know," Esta began slowly, her faint Polish accent still evident in her words, "that an asset of the CDJ and FI, Victor Martin, went into Germany last year. He's an academic, and thus is able to move about rather freely, all things considered. His professional interests provided an excellent pretext to discovering the fate of deported Jews, whether they are taken into Germany or Poland, or wherever other camps are springing up." The FI, or Front de l'Indépendance, was the larger Belgian resistance movement, of which the CDJ was just a small part.

What an important yet horrific excursion that would be! If there was anything that Andrée had learned since the invasion of Belgium and the start of war, it was that the Nazis were taking an exceptional amount of care with the news going out into the world and painted a rather cheery and innocent picture of themselves compared to the truth of the matter. Then there was the matter of their extreme secrecy about those camps they sent so many Jews and prisoners to. There had been invitations for teenagers to come voluntarily to something called working camps, which supposedly would save their families from deportation, but those teenagers, once sent away, were never heard from again, and some families were still arrested.

There were lies in abundance, drowning them all in their excesses and their depths, suffocating the average citizen and putting blinders on those who ought to look more closely.

But what was the truth amidst all the lies? That was nearly impossible to find, and if Mr. Martin had discovered any grain of truth . . .

"He spoke with inmates at some of these camps," Esta went on, her lips trembling as much as her voice. "And he has just returned to Brussels this week. He reported to my husband and the Jospas this morning." She lowered her eyes and swallowed with some apparent difficulty. "He says that people are being burnt."

A long beat of silence stretched among the group, not even their breathing audible.

"Burnt?" Paule repeated, her brow creased. "As in punishment?"

Esta wet her lips and shook her head. "As in put to death. There are . . . ovens. And chimneys. It is no burning at the stake for a sign to others; it is . . . horrific mass destruction. Elimination. And there are no distinctions made for gender or age. Witnesses have seen victims of every age, including infants, sent toward those chimneys."

The word seemed to deflate Andrée's lungs, and she could only sit and blink as the words attempted to find purchase in her mind. She had presumed there would be brutality in the camps, but she would never have guessed that the depravity of man could sink so low. Her mind flashed to the Ovarts, who had given her so much during her time at Gatti de Gamond. They had been deported to a camp somewhere after their arrest. Were they still alive? Had they been sent to ovens? Had their fate been even worse?

What could be worse than that, she did not dare to imagine, but she had no doubt that someone within the Nazi realm had thought of worse and was even now implementing it. Because obviously the world needed to become even worse for the Jews and for those who considered them human beings.

Andrée closed her eyes, forcing her lungs to fill with much needed air and then to release it slowly. This information changed nothing for them. The children needed to be saved from arrest and deportation, just as before. The risks of children going to any sort of prisoner camp—working, death, or otherwise—would likely mean death for them anyway, given the brutality of those who hated them. Those who considered them bugs to be crushed. Those who thought them less than human.

Their parents needed to be given the chance to hide, and having someone else protecting the children allowed them that chance.

The work they did here was important, and it needed to continue, now more than ever.

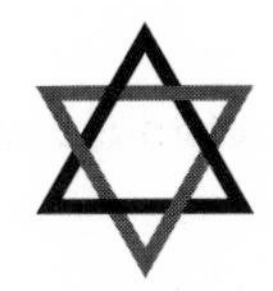

CHAPTER 6

Jewry is organized world criminality. The Jewish danger will be eliminated only when Jewry throughout the world has ceased to exist.

—ERNST HIEMER, *DER STÜRMER*, 1942

Her feet kept slipping on the damp pavement, but she would keep going at this rapid pace until she reached the clandestine offices in Rue de la Brasserie. She almost never received urgent summons, and it terrified her.

Not much terrified Ida Sterno anymore, but this did.

Esta needed her and needed her now. More than that, Ida did not know. In this day and age, more information could not be shared via note, but the possibilities for disaster were endless.

Was it only Esta that needed her? Was everyone all right? Had something happened to someone in the central office? Did she have an immediate need for some children that could not wait?

The thoughts came faster than her steps, and there wasn't a chance to let them fully form. There was not *time* for them to form.

It was almost curfew, and with her looks, she couldn't risk being out and about after that. Her coloring was dark enough to look suspicious to anyone looking for a reason to detain her. Only her Aryan operatives could dare so far, and even they could be questioned about it.

Ida dashed into the building with as little fuss as she could manage, wiping her shoes on the rug as she hurried in, shaking her uncovered head to do something about the rain clinging there. She made a beeline for the main offices then, afraid of what she might see.

There was only one person she could see within, and that was Esta herself.

She stared at nothing and was wrapped in a gray raincoat, the drabbest version of herself that Ida had ever seen. But if she was here, then she had not been arrested, so there was one fear dissipated.

Only five thousand more.

"Esta?"

The woman turned slightly, eyes focusing on Ida now. "Jeanne, hello."

She still used Ida's code name, even when they were alone? She must have been afraid of something, if not a few things.

Ida approached carefully. "Is everything well?"

Esta shook her head. "Do you remember a little boy with the surname Schilderding? We placed him in a crèche."

"Of course!" Ida smiled at the memory. "Such a healthy, happy boy. Moshe, wasn't it? Changed to Michel?"

The way Esta's throat moved made Ida's stomach clench.

The silence that followed tightened it further.

"The crèche had an outbreak of diphtheria," Esta murmured hoarsely. "He was stricken hard with it and taken to *Hôpital St. Pierre*. His mother has been struggling with his absence, you'll recall. Writing several letters to us about wanting to see him. Maurice has had to be very clear, almost stern with her. When he found out the boy was in hospital, he wanted to invite the mother to come and see him for reassurance." Esta paused, her voice breaking. "Only the boy is now dead. Dr. Hendrickx could not save him."

Ida sank onto the nearest surface, which was her desk, and groaned softly. "Poor boy. Poor mother. Has Maurice told her?"

"He wants to meet us there," Esta said, sliding her hands into her coat pockets. "We will tell the family and, hopefully, help them process the grief."

"How do *we* process the grief?" Ida whispered. She shook her head, feeling as though her chest was quivering from her heart and spreading outwards. "We're the ones who placed him in that crèche, who vouched for his safety, who promised that he would be taken care of, and now . . ." She buried her face into a hand, the tears welling and falling from her eyes in almost the same moment. "Did we do this to him, Esta?"

Esta moved to her quickly, taking her free hand. "We have no control over diphtheria, Jeanne. You know that. We had no way of knowing that would be a problem at the crèche. We cannot promise health, only safety. And he was safe. This was out of our hands."

Ida dropped the hand from her face and met her friend and mentor's eyes. "Will the parents see it that way?"

She could see the pain she felt reflected back at her and felt comforted by its revelation. She was not alone in this, and she would not be alone when they were with the parents. They could all grieve together, in their own ways.

That would have to be enough.

They moved out into the mild downpour, linking arms as they walked through the quiet streets. Curfew came and went unnoticed by both of them, the blocks of houses passing one after the other. No words were exchanged between them, and none were needed.

No words could properly accompany such a sense of foreboding.

A lone figure stood outside of the Schilderding house, drops of rain pelting the surface of his fedora and shoulders of his raincoat with visible sprays.

It wasn't often that Maurice Heiber met with the families that requested their assistance. Due to his work in the AJB, it was safer for everyone if his work with their smaller, more clandestine operation remained administrative and protected. But apparently, this particular situation warranted his direct attention.

Ida could hardly blame him for that.

He looked up as they reached him and smiled without joy. He

leaned in to kiss his wife on the cheek, then nodded at Ida. "You've been apprised of the situation?"

Ida returned his nod. "I have."

"Good." He exhaled and turned to step onto the porch, knocking firmly, then stepping back. "Which one of us are they going to recognize?"

"Me," Ida said, clearing her throat and doing her best to arrange her features in a composed manner.

The door opened, an older man with a beard answering, the star on his smoking jacket telling them what they already knew. "Yes?"

"Is this the Schilderding residence?" Ida asked in a small voice, wishing she sounded more like her age.

His eyes darted to all three faces. "Yes. My daughter and her family. Why? You Germans?"

"No, monsieur," Maurice broke in, shaking his head. "We are members of the CDJ, the *Comité de Défense des Juifs*. We . . . we were responsible for the hiding of your grandson."

His eyes widened. "Moshe?" He stepped back and waved them in.

The entire family came into the room, no one sitting on the available chairs and couch. The grandfather and grandmother stood beside each other, his hand on her shoulder. Mr. Schilderding leaned upon the chair, expression blank. The young Mrs. Schilderding had her arms folded tightly, her shoulders raised, her expression that of a woman tortured.

How would they cope with what they were about to learn?

"Monsieur and Madame Schilderding," Maurice greeted, focusing his attention on the parents themselves. "I believe you are aware that your son Moshe was taken to *Hôpital St. Pierre* for diphtheria after an outbreak occurred at the crèche where we placed him."

Both nodded, and Ida saw a new tension in Mrs. Schilderding. Her eyes widened and she looked at Ida suddenly, her head already shaking, her lips forming silent words.

"I am sorry to say," Maurice continued, his voice breaking, "that Moshe has passed away from the disease."

Mrs. Schilderding inhaled before the rest, the sound jagged and cruel to any ears.

Then she screamed.

Cry after cry as her heart was symbolically ripped from her chest again and again, her fingers clawing at her face and her arms. She turned toward the wall, slamming her palms against the surface as she wailed.

"I knew you had killed him," she roared through her tears, almost choking on the words. "I knew it! My baby, my poor baby, I knew it . . ."

Mr. Schilderding had lost feeling in his legs, it seemed, for he sank to the floor, burying his face into his hands, his shoulders trembling. His father-in-law, the stoic grandfather who had let them in, now turned to the nearest surface, a table, and began banging his head against it as he called the name of his poor, lost grandson.

Only Mrs. Schilderding's mother stood in absolute silence, still as a statue, barely blinking, but somehow upright. Slow tears trickled from her eyes and down her cheeks, unchecked and as somber as the mood around them. She had paled with the news, but her emotions, however raging, remained encased within her frame.

Which was the worst pain to experience? Or was it all one collective agony?

Ida found her own tears flowing amidst the mourning, wanting to say so much yet finding no words at her disposal.

Maurice was less paralyzed than Ida. He moved to Mr. Schilderding on the floor, crouching beside him and placing his hand upon the man's back. "I am so very sorry. We had not expected anything of this sort, could never have anticipated . . ." He looked toward Mrs. Schilderding, who was still lying against the wall, sobbing incoherently. "Moshe would almost certainly be well and whole if he had been safe enough to remain at home."

Mrs. Schilderding turned to face him, resting her back against the wall, her expression almost defiant.

Ida couldn't believe what she was hearing. What was Maurice saying? Was he going to put the blame on them for hiding Moshe? They had hidden hundreds of children already, and they could not guarantee anybody's health. Just last week, Ida had been working on relocating some children who had been discovered to have scabies and lice. They had medical professionals who worked with them to falsify medical records of children to keep them safe and in hospital if needed, but the majority of the time, the problems came from having too many children in close quarters.

How did one tell generous people who wanted to help that they needed higher standards of sanitation if they were going to take in children that were not their own? It was not a perfect process, but they were doing the best they could.

And if they were now expected to be health inspectors on top of everything else . . .

Maurice looked around at each member of the family in the room. "Moshe fell, despite his age, like a soldier, a victim in Hitler's war. That is how we must think of him. Were it not for this war, for the Nazis and their hatred, Moshe would be safe in your arms. And you are soldiers in this war. Sacrificing so much to try to save what matters most. This is not lost on us, my friends. We hide these precious little soldiers every day, and the loss of any one of them is cruel."

Mrs. Schilderding's father straightened from his place at the table, the redness of his forehead telling the tale of his reaction clearly. He sighed and came over to his wife, putting a hand about her waist. "You are right, monsieur. Moshe's death is not upon your head, but upon Hitler's. We must never forget that we hid our sweet boy to save him from Hitler."

"But he is still dead," Mrs. Schilderding whimpered. "My baby . . ."

Mr. Schilderding rose and went to her, taking her into his arms while his own tears continued. "Better he died cared for in hospital than at the hands of the Nazis."

His wife nodded against him, her face crumpling as more tears seeped from her eyes for her lost son.

Ida couldn't bear this, couldn't bear the rationalization, the separation of what had happened from what could have happened, the deflection of blame, however true it might have been. She felt responsible for the death of that baby, and no one was going to rid her of that burden. Logically, she knew Maurice was right. She knew there was nothing they could have done, no blame she could truly have taken on herself, but it was there all the same.

It was rooting itself within her heart.

To save a child from the Gestapo only to lose them to illness? Unacceptable.

But she would keep her pity for herself to herself. It did not belong in this setting and with this family.

They stayed only a few minutes more, answering questions as best as they could and advising them on how to carefully sit Shiva under the present circumstances. None of them were rabbis, of course, but as fellow Jews, they had some experience in religious rites.

Well, the Heibers did, being more devout than Ida.

Still, she was suddenly extremely interested in sitting Shiva and made it a point to look into other ways to honor Moshe according to their faith.

It was a quiet walk back to the office in Rue du la Brasserie, the Heibers holding hands while Ida felt the chill of the night without any reminder of warmth. The rain had stopped, but it did not improve the mood in the slightest. The night simply held an air of incompleteness without a downpour to mimic their tears.

The distant sound of shouting met Ida's ears, and she was suddenly on the alert, her eyes scanning every street and building for danger. Nothing could be seen, but she was carefully attuned to the noises.

"East," she breathed to the Heibers, who had stopped beside her. "Do we go around?"

Maurice shook his head. "The only shouting at this time of night is a roundup. Let me get closer and see if it is anyone we know."

"You're not going alone," Esta insisted, putting a hand to the arm she held.

Ida nodded her agreement to the statement. If there was something they could help with, they needed to do it quickly. It was entirely possible that only the father of the family was being arrested at this time, which would create a small but crucial opening for the CDJ to get the children moved out of the house. It had happened before, and it would certainly happen again.

And if the Gestapo or SS or Wehrmacht were occupied with an arrest or roundup, they would not be paying much attention to those breaking curfew.

So long as they remained out of sight, they would be perfectly safe.

Hopefully.

With just as much silence but much less emotion, the three of them moved down the streets of Brussels toward the sounds, doing their best to hurry without drawing attention to themselves. It took only two blocks before the sight met their eyes, and when it did, Ida covered her mouth to hide a gasp.

Mrs. Liebman, holding Alice in her arms, was standing on the street outside of their house while men in plain clothes went in and out of the house. A truck waited idly nearby, and it was clear that Mrs. Liebman was under guard. Ida could not get a look at her face, nor that of Alice's, but she had no doubt that both were distressed.

And that they were not going to remain at home.

One of the men came out of the house and tossed coats at Mrs. Liebman, barking orders in German and gesturing toward the truck.

"No!" Ida whispered, starting toward them.

The Heibers seized her arms and pulled her back, keeping her safely in the alley with them. "Ida, you can't!" Esta hissed into her ear, startling her almost as much by the use of her real name as by the strength of her grip.

"We can't do anything for them now!" Maurice told her with a gentle firmness. "Nothing!"

"She wouldn't let us take Alice," Ida told them, her voice choking on tears and the attempt to whisper. "She was going to, and then she . . . she . . ."

"We know, Ida," Esta assured her. She moved to stand in front of Ida, blocking her view. "We cannot do anything. We can follow her progress once they take her to Malines, but there is nothing we can do for her. Or for Alice."

Ida dropped her head to her friend's shoulder, openly weeping now. "It's not fair. It's just not fair—none of this is! Why is this happening? Why are they doing this? Why? Why?"

Neither of the Heibers had any answers for her, but she hadn't expected answers. She hadn't even known she still had these questions. The rise of the Nazis in Germany, the invasion into Belgium, the stars for the Jews. The questions had been there throughout each of those occasions and the outbreak of abuse against the Jews. But since she had started with the CDJ, the questions had faded as assignments and missions moved to the forefront of her mind. The rescue of children, the hiding of them, the locations suitable for them, the safety of her operatives . . .

There hadn't been time for the cries of her heart during all of that, let alone reminders that she had them.

But here, now, in this moment, those cries were the only ones she knew.

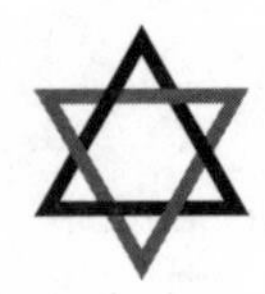

CHAPTER 7

"Jewish Murder Plan against Gentile Humanity Revealed"

—HEADLINE IN THE NAZI TABLOID, *DER STÜRMER*, MAY 1934

"Claude, we've got a change of plans."

Andrée looked up from her desk in surprise, covering her latest entry into the notebooks out of sheer habit. "What? Why?"

Ida gave her a slight smile. "The Mother Superior had a message relayed to us that we should not come today. Apparently, Jacques and the Gestapo are raiding there."

"What?" Andrée cried, echoed by Paule behind her. They exchanged looks and shot to their feet. "The convent is being raided? What about the girls?"

"I am told everything will be fine," Ida told them, her hands gesturing in a calming motion to them. "The sisters have a plan, and I will visit in a few days. We have worked with Sister Marie-Aurélie for some time now, and she is very capable, not to mention formidable. We must trust in her and her sisters to do what is best for the girls. Yes?"

It was all Andrée could do to avoid being moody in her response to the affirmative. Yes, the sisters were resourceful and capable, and yes, Sister Marie-Aurélie, the Mother Superior, was one of their strongest, most committed allies in this, but that did not mean that Andrée could just easily brush off a raid at the convent where at least fourteen girls were hidden.

Not that there was anything she could do about it.

Fat Jacques had been right behind the CDJ, it seemed. More denunciations, more arrests, more razzias, and he always seemed to be in the middle of it. She had yet to encounter him herself, but he was everywhere somehow. Betraying his people without shame.

Even the children.

If Andrée ever did come face to face with him, she would be hard-pressed not to kill him with her bare hands.

And she was against violence on principle.

Andrée sat in her chair again, looking up at Ida. "So, what will I be doing, then? Another pickup?"

Ida shook her head. "I need you to go to the café in Place Bara. There was a roundup there yesterday and a little girl was hidden by the landlady. She's about three or four years old. We need to get her out. Can you go?"

"Absolutely." Andrée looked at the notebook on her desk quickly, nodding to herself. "Looks like she'd be number 347. Do you know her name?"

"I do not, so you'll have to make the entry into Notebook 1 when you get her. Why don't you take her to 47? They should have room."

Andrée smiled at the suggestion. Forty-seven was the location of a quaint crèche run by the sweetest group of nuns, and the deliveries there were always some of her favorites. No child taken to that location would ever feel unloved or unsafe, nor would they feel like a lesser creature for being Jewish.

She could not say the same for all of the religious institutions that had taken in Jewish children. While their intentions had been good—or, at least, humane—they did not all view the children with the same generous lens that ought to have been used. One child Andrée had talked to on a recent check had told her that a nun had accused her of spitting on and hitting Jesus. Another convent apparently forced the hidden children to eat only dry bread for a day if they did not know the catechism.

Those places were not fit to hide these children and keep them safe. Others were more concerned about converting these children than anything else. Apparently, saving the children physically did not matter as much as saving them spiritually, in their eyes.

Thankfully, not all of the convents or monasteries had the same view. One of the priests had told Ida last week that a boy hidden in his boarding school wanted to be baptized to convert, which was not too unusual, as places of faith would have a strong influence on children living in fear, but the priest had suggested that the boy wait until after the war, to see if he felt the same.

Boarding schools, rectories, seminaries, convents. The children were hidden all over the place, and there were so many others placed outside of religious institutions. Family homes, crèches, farms, even hospitals, were housing children for them, and the numbers were fluctuating from day to day.

Neighbors were taking in children for their parents. Store owners hiding children from roundups. Villagers seeing the good that others were doing and wanting to follow suit.

There were so many good people doing so many good things in spite of the evil around them.

It was a reminder to Andrée that good still existed in the world. The Nazis hadn't eliminated that in their efforts to eliminate groups of people.

She finished the notations on her most recent assignment, then stashed their notebooks in their respective hiding places. Then she grabbed her coat and left the offices, intentionally walking at least three blocks in the wrong direction before readjusting to head toward Place Bara.

It was a beautiful day, so she kept her coat over her arm, strolling along as though she were merely on errands or enjoying the sun. No one bothered her when she looked pleased as punch to be alive, she'd found, so the smile on her face came naturally now. She could smile at the SS, a grumpy local, Fat Jacques, or possibly even Hitler himself, if she were on the way to pick up a child or was fresh off a delivery.

And because of how she looked, they would smile back.

It used to make her skin crawl, but now it was oddly satisfying. Especially when she carried the information of the child she was fetching in the very shoe she was walking in.

As she was now.

She kept her attention focused ahead and around her, as per usual when she was on her way to a pickup. Eyes sweeping the street, looking for anything even slightly suspicious or out of place, ready to alter her movements as needed to protect her identity and that of those she was going to save. Between the soldiers in uniform and the Gestapo in street clothes, she could never be certain from which direction the enemy would come.

As of yet, they had not come for her other than that night at the Gatti de Gamond school, but she would not consider herself out of danger until the war was over.

No one was out of danger until the war was over.

She soon reached Place Bara, and the café was easy enough to find, almost directly in the center on one side of the square. The square itself was remarkably empty for its location and the time of day, especially considering the fair weather. But, if what Ida said was correct, there had been a roundup the day before. That would thin out the usual patrons of any establishment, and the neighborhood would be quiet for some time.

It was the perfect time to collect a little girl who needed to be safe.

Entering the café, Andrée took the time to let her eyes adjust to the new lighting, then glanced around the room. Empty but for two elderly gentlemen eating silently at a booth in the corner. Local regulars, she'd guess, based on age and general physique.

Still, best not to make too much of a fuss about her arrival.

She moved to the door of the kitchen and knocked, feeling it best not to proceed into parts unknown without permission. That was what the Gestapo did, and she was not about to be compared with them.

A middle-aged woman came to the door and looked her over impassively. "Yes?"

"Claude Fournier," Andrée said, extending a hand out. "I am here for a pickup?"

The woman's eyes widened, and her lips parted ever so slightly. "Ah. You are? And how do I know . . . ?"

Andrée smiled at her. "Jeanne sent me. That is going to have to be enough."

She nodded and gestured for Andrée to follow her as they crossed the café to another door, one that could have passed as a door in any given house. Out in the corridor, a set of narrow stairs led upwards to a landing with doors on either side. They ascended the stairs and turned to the right at the top, only speaking when they had entered the room and safely shut the door.

"It was a large roundup," the landlady said in a low voice. "Chaotic. They knew we had people in the back room. Got them all. We only escaped arrest ourselves because there's a door to the outside, so they could not prove we knew they were there. I was able to sneak Nicole away during the procession out of there because she was so small and young."

Andrée nodded at the explanation, trying to picture the roundup in her mind. She hadn't witnessed one since the Gatti de Gamond, for which she was grateful. That had been a harrowing enough experience for an adult like Andrée. What would poor little Nicole be feeling and thinking after experiencing that?

"Does she have a bag?" Andrée asked, looking around the tidy apartment. "Or did the Gestapo take the bags as well?"

"All of the bags were left there, and she was able to point out hers afterwards." The landlady pointed to a small case partially obstructed by a table.

Andrée nodded and moved over to the case. "Perfect. I'll take this downstairs first and then come back up for Nicole, if you can have her ready."

"Of course." She gestured toward the door for Andrée while moving further into the flat, away from her.

Taking the case, Andrée moved out of the flat toward the stairs.

There wasn't much time if they wanted to get Nicole out of there before anyone else took an interest in yesterday's roundup. Occasionally the Gestapo would return to the site of the arrests to pick up any stragglers they might have missed in the arrest, or to discuss the situation.

She started down the stairs, pausing at the sound of German voices in the café, growing closer to her every second.

She cursed in her mind, glancing back toward the flat, then toward the café again.

There wasn't time to get warning to the landlady and Nicole upstairs. How in the world were they going to manage this?

Twisting her lips, Andrée continued down the stairs. It was better to engage them head-on than to let them march up into the flat and take Nicole. At least with talking to Andrée, there would be more time for Nicole to be taken elsewhere.

If they could manage it.

As she reached the bottom step, three men in plain clothes entered the corridor from the café, one of them with his arm in a sling. They looked at Andrée, looked at the case she carried, then all frowned with nearly identical furrows in their brows.

"Papers," the one in the sling barked.

"Of course," Andrée replied, reaching into the pocket of her coat and handing the papers over to him. She smiled as politely and warmly as she could and switched over to German. "Does there seem to be a problem?"

His eyes lifted to hers. "I'll know that after we look at your papers." He continued to read, then showed them to the man at his left. That man grunted and nudged his head toward the café.

"Come with us, mademoiselle," the slinged one ordered in French, gesturing for her to follow.

Andrée did so, careful not to show concern. They moved back into the café, the two older men still sitting at their table, and a young couple now sitting at another, both looking rather haggard and drawn.

They were not here for the food or coffee, that was clear enough.

One of the men pointed at an empty table while the other two moved to the couple. "Mademoiselle Fournier, please."

Andrée smiled at him but did not sit. "Might I make a phone call? I see a phone just outside in the square; you will be able to see me from the window."

He glanced over to his partners, occupied in their rather agitated conversation with the couple. "That should be fine."

"Who are they?" Andrée asked, following his eyes.

"Jews," he spat. "They were in the roundup here yesterday, but somehow escaped transport. We found them again today and brought them in. We'll be having them taken away and then interview you." He gave her a dark look. "Stay where I can see you."

Andrée nodded, still smiling at him. "Of course! Anything to help."

His look was unconvinced, and full of warning, but he moved over to his associates and the Jewish couple.

Andrée started toward the door of the café, her pace sedate and easy, coat still slung over her arm, case still in hand. She didn't need to hand over any evidence without their asking for it. She had no doubt they knew who lived here, and had some idea of what they would find, but she was an unlikely ally for the Jews, in their eyes.

She always was.

The Jewish couple rose from their table as she passed, the woman losing her grip on her purse, which fell to the floor and spilled its contents. Papers and coins and a compact were among the belongings, and Andrée instantly stooped to help pick the things up.

"I'm so sorry," the woman said in a panic. "So sorry, clumsy of me . . . I just . . . I'm so sorry, mademoiselle. Please, don't feel you have to . . ."

She met Andrée's eyes and mouthed something as she shoved one of the bits of paper into Andrée's palm, all the while cleaning things up together.

Andrée closed her hand instinctively around the scrap and handed the compact to her. "No harm done. We must all be a little more careful these days, yes?" She examined the woman's features quickly. Something about her seemed so familiar, and yet, in this moment, she could not recollect where or how she might know her.

The woman nodded, sniffled, and rose, stuffing the compact into her purse. "Yes. Thank you."

"Good luck, madame," Andrée told her, trying for a smile that was as polite as any Belgian neighbor might be. Then she continued out the door toward the phone, pointedly ignoring the paper in her hand for the benefit of the woman still in the café. If Andrée was being watched, they would be observing everything she did, including reading anything in her hands.

She picked up the phone and dialed Ida's number at the office, which only the members of the CDJ had.

"Hello?" Ida's voice crackled over the line.

"Hello, Mother," Andrée said in a cheery voice. "It's Claude."

"What's happening?" Ida asked at once, her tone firm. "Are you in trouble?"

Andrée laughed cheerily as the three men brought the couple out of the café. "I am perfectly well. I am going to be a little late for our outing today. Everything is perfectly fine; I simply have a delay. Some people wish to talk with me."

"Gestapo?"

"Oh, probably."

"The girl?"

"No, I haven't picked up your flowers yet either. That will have to be another time, all right?"

"Noted. Be careful."

Andrée eyed the men and the couple, occupied with the van nearby. She peeled open the paper in her hand and recited aloud as she read it herself, her heart dropping as she did so. "Seventeen Rue de Lessines, Deux-Acren. Yes, Mother, I know very well. I was just there eight days ago." In her mind, she replayed the exchange with the woman during the cleanup of the purse items, now placing her exactly with the visit she had made last week. They had a young boy that still needed to be placed, and they had hoped to keep him with neighbors or extended family. Andrée and the rest had only been waiting for confirmation from the family to officially remove him.

But what could the mother have been trying to say when she had handed the paper to Andrée? What word had she mouthed?

Then it occurred to her, and she looked at the van with interest. The one in the sling looked particularly malicious, and he glanced back at her on the phone.

Jacques. That must have been the word.

"Do you know, Mother," Andrée said slowly, "I think Jacques might be here. You remember him, don't you?"

"Claude, be careful. Are you compromised?"

"No, I don't think that's necessary, Mother." She laughed again and tossed her hair. "I will be there as soon as I can, hmm? We can always reschedule."

"Understood. Report in when you can."

"I love you, too, Mother." Andrée hung up the phone and turned back for the café. She had to trust that the landlady would do what was best for Nicole, and that there would be another chance to save her.

Meanwhile, the poor Jewish couple now in the van had silently asked for her help and relaying that information to Ida would ensure that the little boy now left alone at his home would shortly be relocated.

How awful to be caught up in the Gestapo's raid twice, with the thrill of escape between the two to give them hope! And now to be so particularly singled out . . .

The least Andrée could do was help their boy.

The landlady came into the café again, coming to Andrée. "Would you like anything while you wait, mademoiselle?"

"Coffee would be wonderful," she replied. Then she continued in a soft undertone. "Is she safe?"

"Next door," came the response. "Through the garden." She cleared her throat. "One coffee, yes, mademoiselle."

Andrée nodded and smiled up at her. "Thank you, madame."

She moved away just as the Gestapo and Jacques came into the café, Jacques coming to her table while the other two men moved to a booth nearby.

He was a beefy sort of man, more burly than fit, and wore a light-colored hat, which did nothing to minimize the size of his head. Tufts of dark hair were visible from beneath the hat, and his eyes, also dark, darted across various aspects of Andrée's appearance, as though he were doing much the same analysis on her.

Pity he wouldn't know nearly as much about her as she did him.

"Who are you?" Jacques asked her, adjusting the sling on his arm and settling further into his chair.

"Claude Fournier," Andrée recited with polite precision.

He raised a brow. "I can see that, mademoiselle. But who *are* you?"

"A social worker." She smiled and waited for the next question.

"Do you normally come to see Jews as part of your work?" he inquired without any of the politeness she was affording him.

Considering the man *was* a Jew, she wondered just what he had against so-called Gentiles helping Jews in life. But that was a conversation for another day and time.

Certainly not here and now.

"Religious persuasion is not on the paperwork we receive about prospective cases," Andrée replied with a light shrug of the shoulders. "I can only go where I am assigned, monsieur."

He made a slight grunt at her use of the word *monsieur*, though the emotion behind such a noise was impossible to identify.

"And the case you brought down?"

Andrée had thought of that and only smiled. "I saw it at the top of the stairs, and there was no name on the luggage, so I thought I would bring it down to help whoever it belongs to."

He was certainly not convinced by that, but without proof of anything otherwise, what could he say?

"You will give us any addresses for Jewish homes that you have,"

Jacques instructed with the brusqueness she had anticipated from the start.

"Monsieur," Andrée protested, sitting forward, "I have a remarkable case load at the moment. Given the uncertain times, families of all faiths and ethnicities are wanting help for their children or help to get their children into the country with relatives, or out of the country entirely. Only last week, I was tasked with helping the burgomaster see his older children safely installed in a boarding school in France. You can check that, if you'd like. I am sure the monsignor at the school would tell you."

"Your point?"

"My point is that there are so many addresses I have visited in the last week alone that I could not possibly recall all of them, let alone isolate which ones I thought might be Jewish." She shrugged again and tried to look as helpless as possible.

As it turned out, the burgomaster's children *had* been taken to a boarding school in France just last week, but the CDJ had nothing to do with it. They simply knew about it through various sources.

If Jacques or his associates decided to verify her story, they would find that it was true.

And if Jacques knew what a monsignor actually was, or what his role entailed, Andrée would eat the man's hat.

He continued to eye her for a long moment, then muttered something in Yiddish, which she only recognized by spending so much time around Jews of late. He pushed back from the table with his good arm, wincing and gripping the arm in a sling, before waving one of the others over.

Andrée sighed quietly as her interrogators swapped places, and smiled at the newcomer, prepared for more of the same questions. The slip of paper in her shoe seemed to be burning her sole, and she did her best to ignore the sensation.

"Where did I lose him, officer?" Andrée asked with a laugh. "And where would you like to begin?"

CHAPTER 8

By destroying the German people, the Jew wants to wipe out the core of Germandom, the source from the very beginning of time of the human strength that preserved it from being ruined by the Jews. The war the German people are fighting today is a holy war. It is a war against the devil. The German people must win this war if the devil is to die and humanity is to live.

—JULIUS STREICHER, *DER STÜRMER*, 1941

Once, it would have been unheard of for Ida to walk into a convent.

As a Jewish woman, what reason could she possibly have had to do so?

Now, it was just as common for her to go there as it was her own home.

If she had to be perfectly honest, Ida would have to say that the Little Sisters of the Poor on Avenue Clémenceau was her favorite convent. Sister Marie-Aurélie was the Mother Superior, and she was a kindred spirit for Ida if there ever was one. The nuns within her charge were as dedicated to helping children as she was, risked all they had to keep them safe and hidden, and showed them as much love as they claimed to live by.

It was a welcome insight into the lives of good people, regardless of specific faith.

Their usual visit to check on the girls hiding in this convent had been canceled, as the Mother Superior had received word that they were due to be raided. Until they heard from the Mother Superior again, none of them were to visit. It was their usual method and code, and today Ida had contact from the convent.

She was nervous to hear what had happened during the raid. She was excited by the prospect of a chat with her friend and fellow conspirator. She was eager to see the children, especially after enduring the raid. She was afraid that physical violence might have been used, if not damage to the building and its grounds.

She wasn't at all certain which feeling was the primary one that concerned her, but there was competition for the position.

As Ida entered the church, she looked around with observant eyes, desperate to find any changes that would inform her one way or the other. But the splendor of the place appeared the same, there were no new marks on visible surfaces, and there was someone playing the organ in the distance. There was no immediate indication that anything was amiss at all.

Keeping her composure, Ida moved down the nave as though she were a member of this congregation coming to pray. When she reached the aisles of pews, she turned right, walking away from the direct path toward the altar and down the cloisters toward the refectory and chapter house. It was her usual route, and, until she heard otherwise, she would continue on as normal.

A pair of nuns walked by, looking perfectly well and whole, and they smiled at her, bobbing their headdresses as they moved along. Ida had yet to master the names of the aspects of their headdresses, let alone what order they were placed in, but as she was not having to dress herself as a nun, she supposed it was not entirely relevant to her cause.

But if the nuns looked well and were moving freely, all could not be lost, could it?

She was nearly to the refectory when the familiar figure of Sister Marie-Aurélie appeared from the chapter house door, moving in her direction.

She, too, looked well and appeared perfectly serene.

One would never know there had been a raid there within the last week.

The Mother Superior saw Ida and grinned widely. "Jeanne! What a pleasant surprise, I was hoping it would be you that came. Not that I have anything against the delightful ladies that work with you, or with Mr. Heiber. But it feels more like speaking with a friend when it's you."

Ida returned her smile. "I feel the same, Sister. Is there a place we can talk? I'm eager to hear about your raid, if you can spare the time."

Sister Marie-Aurélie nodded and gestured for her to accompany her down the cloister, further away from the nave. Ida hadn't been this far into the building before, but it bore the same hallowed sense as the rest of the place did. It was not as ornate as the altar and various aspects of the nave were, which was why she enjoyed walking in these spaces. This space felt somehow more regal and statuesque than even the grand vaulting in the nave and the church proper.

This felt more like a place to worship, at least in Ida's eyes.

But she didn't worship anymore.

Didn't really care to.

Sister Marie-Aurélie surprised her by taking her into the atrium of the place, a beautiful grass opening in a square courtyard of sorts. There were well-manicured trees and flowers in portions, as well as a few benches, but it was the simple peace that the space created that caught Ida's attention. There was something in this atrium as sweet and innocent as the children she helped.

Ida could have sat in this place for hours. Easily and happily.

She might have to ask the Mother Superior if she would be permitted to come here when she needed time to breathe.

Provided she was able to find time for that.

Sister Marie-Aurélie gestured for them to sit on a nearby bench, and Ida did so, setting her purse on the ground beside her. There was something about the sister's countenance that made Ida more curious about this story she was about to hear. Something resembling pride—although the Mother Superior was far too humble for that—and playfulness, though well contained, and smugness, which was the most surprising thing Ida could have imagined seeing in a nun's expression.

And her eyes were positively dancing in the daylight, which made her smile almost irrelevant.

"Sister," Ida began, grinning herself, "why do I have the feeling that you are really going to enjoy telling me what happened?"

The sister laughed to herself, and, for a moment, Ida could have forgotten that she wore a habit at all. It might have been just two friends out in a park enjoying the Belgian sunshine.

But she was wearing the habit, which made her laughter all the more entertaining.

"Because I *am* going to enjoy what I tell you," Sister Marie-Aurélie assured her with a quick pat to her knee. "And you are very much going to enjoy hearing it."

The nun ought to have been an actress on the stage; she cleared her throat, tossed her headdress enough for the veil portion to float to the back of her shoulders, and smiled off into the distance.

"Fat Jacques and his Gestapo friends showed up at the convent," the Mother Superior began, somehow still smiling as she mentioned Fat Jacques and the Gestapo. "He showed me a letter denouncing us as housing fourteen Jewish girls there. The letter was anonymous, of course. No one wants to actually admit that they're turning in a religious institution to the Gestapo."

That was unfortunately true. Denunciations on Jews had come from neighbors, from business partners, and one even from a child living in the house who wanted additional money for her allowance, promised to her by a Gestapo officer. But when it came to churches, or anything related to them? There were rarely any names attached to the accusations then.

Which meant there was not a lot that could be done to prevent it again.

And the girls they had hidden at this particular convent had been happy and safe so far. To have them found by the Gestapo and Jacques was crueler than the usual denunciations.

"What happened?" Ida asked, feeling none of the enjoyment that she had been promised.

Sister Marie-Aurélie shook her head, still smiling. "They raided, of course. We were powerless to stop that and had to comply. They found all of the girls. Delighted to know there were fifteen instead of fourteen, though I cannot see how one additional Jewish girl helps them. At any rate, they did not have the means to transport so many."

"Wait," Ida interrupted sharply. "They knew they had around fourteen girls to pick up, and they didn't bring the means to transport all of them?"

The nun shrugged, which seemed a very un-nun-like thing to do. "We've never suspected Fat Jacques or the Gestapo were gifted with exceptional levels of intellect, regardless of their information or methods."

Ida snickered in surprise at that, which made the sister smile.

"So," she went on, "we were ordered to hold the children ready for them. I managed to convince them to let us keep them overnight, allowing them to get a good night of sleep, and assured them that they would be fully prepared with coats and belongings the next day."

"Seems reasonable," Ida agreed, tucking a stray lock of hair behind her ear and crossing her ankles. "But I am not the Gestapo, so I imagine they did not think so?"

Sister Marie-Aurélie hummed a sound of amusement. "Actually, they agreed to it." She looked at Ida fondly, still smiling, and plucked at the material of her habit. "Perhaps I wear the garb of someone inherently trustworthy."

Ida returned her smile. "Says the woman hiding children from the Nazis."

"Only our Lord is perfect." The sister lifted a shoulder in another shrug and tipped her face back to embrace the sunlight upon her cheeks. "But apparently, nuns do not lie. So, they left under the promise that the children would be ready in the morning."

There was something in the woman's tone that broke through the story playing in Ida's mind, and she narrowed her eyes at the woman beside her. "And were they? Ready in the morning?"

The sister cracked one eye open to look at her. "You are skipping ahead, my child. There was more that occurred that night."

Ida had not expected that, and she blinked in surprise. "There was?"

The eye closed again, and the smile spread. "Did you really think that I intended to do nothing to save the children after the Gestapo left?"

Chuckling more in anticipation than anything else, Ida gestured for the Mother Superior to go on, though she wouldn't see it.

No doubt sensing the invitation, Sister Marie-Aurélie continued. "I had our priest call the CDJ office and inform them of the situation. He came back and told me that they would quickly create a plan and intervene before dawn." She straightened and opened her eyes, turning more fully on the bench to face Ida. "A few hours later, several people arrived whom I had never met before. They told me Maurice Heiber had deemed it best that he not be included in the discussion of the plan, so as to keep himself free from suspicion when an investigation would happen."

Ida found herself nodding in agreement with that plan. If the Gestapo and Jacques already knew and accounted for the hidden children in this convent, any actions preventing their roundup would lead to a significant and harsh investigation. Maurice was in the AJB, where the information on Jewish families came from, so he was already someone that they would be aware of.

They needed to keep him safe from detection at all costs.

"What did they do?" Ida half-whispered, though no one could overhear their conversation.

Sister Marie-Aurélie smiled. "They decided it would be best to stage a kidnapping on our convent. Not only that, but an attack. They cut our phone lines, tied up our staff, ransacked some rooms . . . and then they tied all of us nuns up and put us in cells, gagged most of us, and locked us away."

Ida gaped at her in shock, trying to imagine the scene in her head and not being quite able to manage it. It seemed far too unlikely, and yet nuns did not lie . . .

Unless it was to the Gestapo.

"They covered their faces as they did this, of course," the Mother Superior went on, "so none of my fellow sisters would be able to identify those tying them up if they tried. I had to rely on my acting abilities, but it would suffice. Our would-be intruders then took the children away and left us like that until Jacques and the Gestapo arrived in the morning and discovered the distressing scene."

Ida began to laugh, more in disbelief than in humor, but the laughter soon shifted to hilarity. "Did they believe what they saw?"

Sister Marie-Aurélie laughed along with her. "Of course, they did! We were tied up in cells and gagged. We could not release ourselves from our bindings and our prisons. How would we *ever* have managed such a thing ourselves?" She grinned, quirking her brows before folding her hands across her stomach in a rather satisfied position. "They freed us, of course, and, though furious, had no option but to accept that terrorists had come and taken the children away."

"Oh, I imagine their faces were priceless to behold!" Ida chuckled, wiping away tears of mirth.

"It was the most delicious fury I have ever seen," the sister confessed, crossing herself and looking heavenward as though atoning for intentionally causing anger. "Your associates will, I have no doubt, inform you of the new location of the girls soon enough. And perhaps when enough time has passed, we may take more children in. But it would be prudent to wait. Given the, erm, trauma of our attack." She gave Ida a quick wink before sighing with satisfaction.

Ida shook her head. "That is a remarkable experience, Sister. And so brave of you and your sisters!"

The Mother Superior looked bemused by the praise. "The idea was not ours, my dear Jeanne. We simply agreed with it and endured a few hours of mild discomfort. Considering the alternative of our sweet children being arrested and deported, it was certainly worth the endeavor."

"And that is precisely what I wish everyone would think." Ida reached out and covered the sister's hands with her own. "There is a saying in the Jewish faith, Sister. He who saves one life saves all of humanity. I believe you and your sisters are saving humanity."

Sister Marie-Aurélie's smile turned warm and remarkably tender. "And we have a saying in the Christian faith, my friend. Greater love hath no man than this, that a man lay down his life for his friends. To us, this is scripture. And I could not face myself or my maker if I did not live up to this. As you do."

Tears began to burn in Ida's eyes, a tide of warmth rising within her as she let those kind words settle on her, as they filled the connection between her and this good, faith-filled woman beside her. Their lives could not have been more different, and they would never have had reason to associate with each other but for the evil they were united against. Yet here was true friendship, formed in the desire to do a greater good, to prove that no propaganda could turn them against their fellow man.

Regardless of faith, of race, of creed, or of any other perceived division, they would continue to devote themselves to saving as many families as they could. Would push themselves until they themselves were captured or stripped of their power to act. Would resist the devil that was the Nazi regime to the death.

And, it would seem, would embrace the faith of any among them, whether it be in God, in fate, or in man.

Faith of any sort was welcome in their ranks, so long as they were willing to act upon it.

The sound of clipped steps in the cloisters suddenly echoed in the atrium, drawing Ida's attention, and she looked about in all directions, as it was less than clear where exactly the sound was coming from.

Nothing surprised her more than seeing Maurice Heiber crossing over to them from the far side of the atrium. His expression was unreadable, as his eyes were lowered, but Ida found herself tensing as he approached, alert to any sudden change that must be made immediately.

She and Sister Marie-Aurélie rose when he reached them, the Mother Superior tucking her hands beneath the front fold of her habit. "Monsieur Heiber, welcome," she greeted. "I was not expecting you today."

Maurice swept off his hat and held it in front of him as he smiled almost sheepishly. "And I apologize for arriving unannounced, Sister. I was told you were out here with Jeanne and thought it wise to come and see you both at the same time."

"Is something wrong?" Ida asked at once.

"No, no," Maurice returned hastily. "No. I simply thought you'd like to hear what I came to tell the Mother Superior."

Sister Marie-Aurélie cocked her head. "You visited the family I told you about?"

He nodded. "I did." His eyes flicked to Ida. "There were concerns about a boy we placed. The family said he was stealing from them."

Ida blanched at the thought. Children were children, of course, but these children were certainly in precarious situations, and it was already a dangerous time to be a Jew. Any perceived sins could come down upon their heads tenfold simply because they were Jewish.

And what kindhearted family would want to house a thief when they could already be arrested for the child being there?

Maurice returned his attention to the sister. "I arrived at the house, and the parents told me what had happened. Their daughter, who is eight, received a Christmas gift last year of a manger scene of your nativity. After the holidays, she wished to keep this scene near her bed. Some days ago, the infant figurine and that of his mother disappeared, and only the boy we placed there could have taken it. He would not tell anyone if he had done so, why he had done so, or where the figurines were. And the family were not willing to risk their safety for a thieving child."

It was already a sad tale, this displaced child taking something that did not belong to him, for whatever reason, but to then refuse to accept responsibility for his actions . . .

But Maurice was not finished. "I went up to the room to see the boy," he went on. "He was more determined than defiant, which I found unusual for a lad of five. But, after lengthy questioning, he finally told me that he did not steal the figures. This I did not believe, so I asked,

'Did you take them?' And he shook his head with great emphasis. 'No,' he said. 'I did not take them. I hid them.'"

Ida shared a look with Sister Marie-Aurélie, then returned her attention to Maurice. "Hid them?" she repeated. "Why admit to that, but not the rest?"

"I thought the very same," Maurice admitted, turning the hat in his hands absently. "I waited for him to explain himself. He began to cry, and then said, 'Amelie told me that the Baby Jesus and the Virgin Mary were Jews, so I hid them. The Gestapo will not have them.' And then he cried harder. And, I must admit, so did I." He sniffed then and looked up at the sky, blinking quickly.

"Blessed child," Sister Marie-Aurélie whispered as she crossed herself before pressing her hands together in a praying motion.

Ida swallowed once, then again before she realized that tears were flowing freely down her cheeks. She swiped them away quickly. "Did the family hear?"

Maurice nodded, his eyes returning to her. "The parents had followed me up, so they heard it all. They were crying as well and embraced him. They are now happy to let him stay in their home. I thought you would wish to hear the tale, Sister."

The Mother Superior nodded, dabbing at her damp eyes. "Thank you, Monsieur Heiber. In times such as these, the stories of beauty help to get us through."

He glanced at Ida then, smiling in understanding. They had dealt with some truly distressing results with some of the families for whom they had hidden children, and there were no simple answers for those cases. There were still so many children to be saved, so many families to be assisted, and so many already hidden children to visit for wellness and safety checks. The circumstances changed all the time, sometimes daily, sometimes hourly, and they had to adjust to each and every one somehow.

But the sister was right: the stories of beauty, the stories of hope, helped to get them through.

CHAPTER 9

The end of the battle against the Bolshevist army in the East is German victory and therefore the victory of Gentile humanity over the most dangerous instrument of the Jewish world destroyers. The cause of the world's misfortune, however, will be forever eliminated only when Jewry in its entirety is destroyed.

—JULIUS STREICHER, *DER STÜRMER*, 1941

Something was wrong.

What, exactly, she couldn't say, but something was.

Andrée smiled at the mother who was currently standing with her in the hall. The woman was not much older than Andrée, and she seemed to shake where she stood. That was not so surprising; many of the mothers she saw trembled at the prospect of their children being taken away, even if it was for their safety. But this mother could not even look Andrée in the eyes.

It was not anger or hatred, not distrust or shame, not even sadness or grief.

It was fear.

How she could detect one emotion amidst the others was less explicable, but Andrée had learned much since beginning her time with the CDJ, and this was almost certainly fear.

There was no blaming her for that. The times were frightening, and hope was minimal.

But there was still something that made Andrée uncomfortable about this situation. More than usual.

She drummed her fingers along her folded arms, waiting for the father of the house to return from the child's room with the child himself. Andrée had already taken the child's bag away and stored it in a secure location.

Taking the child was proving a trifle more complicated.

"I'm sorry," the mother whispered, shaking her head. "He just wanted to say his goodbyes in private. He'll be along soon."

Andrée managed another smile, even knowing the woman wouldn't look to see it. "I understand. This is difficult for everyone, no matter the circumstances. But we really must be quick, for everyone's sake."

The mother did not seem to hear her and only cleared her throat. "John. It is time."

There was a faint shuffling from the bedroom beyond, but then the man appeared, the toddler awake but quiet in his arms. The remnants of tears were on the father's face, but Andrée could not allow herself to consider them.

She would have broken long before now if she had.

"Come now, darling," Andrée cooed, stepping forward and holding her hands out toward the baby. "Shall we go for a walk in the sunshine?"

The chubby little boy smiled at her, one finger finding its way into his mouth, making his appearance all the more adorable. Then he leaned toward her with eager arms.

Andrée could almost hear the hearts of his parents breaking as she took him, as his hands found her face, as he gurgled some innocent, toddler babble.

Their child would not return to their arms for what could be a very long time.

If ever.

His mother stepped to Andrée's side, brushing back her child's hair before pressing a kiss to his brow, her tears falling upon Andrée's arm.

"Right, then, young sir," Andrée announced in a playful voice, glancing around them. "There is your pram, so I think we are ready!"

She made a show of settling him into his pram and getting him situated, more to keep him entertained and distracted from the distraught countenances of his parents than anything else. If he noticed anything amiss with their behavior, he gave no indication, which must have been painful for them to see.

If Andrée had children, she would likely have found her task an impossible one each and every time.

"Will his name still be David?" his mother asked as Andrée and the baby moved to the door.

Andrée glanced back, intentionally not meeting the woman's eyes. "I cannot say, madame. Find us after, and we will reunite you. I promise you that."

Without giving either parent a chance to say anything further, Andrée opened the door and pushed the pram out into the street, chattering aimlessly with the baby as she did so.

A commotion up the street drew her attention, and she paused at the corner to look in the direction from which they'd just come.

Men jumped out of covered trucks, all in plain clothes, and stormed into the nearest building, barking orders in German. Moments later, people were shoved out of the same places, crying and calling out for each other.

The Gestapo was raiding in this street? Now?

Her throat threatened to close entirely, her heart leaping to the sky with a burst of panicked heat. She turned down the block and started away from the scene, pointing out nearby flowers to the baby.

Up ahead the street was being blocked off, and other Jews were being pulled from their houses. Roughly. Though the Gestapo were rarely ever respectful in their raids. Sounds of cries and screams, of anger and indignation, of hatred and fear . . . all somehow blended with birdsong and the wind blowing through the trees.

Those latter sounds should have stopped when the raids began. Should only occur when there was no evil around them.

When it was safe for everyone and anyone to notice.

The men setting up the roadblock saw her coming with the pram and smiled.

Smiled.

"Good day," one of them greeted, going so far as to tip his hat.

Andrée nodded at him, smiling in return. "It is, isn't it?"

He nodded and looked at the baby in the pram, smiling just as much at him. "Fine, strapping lad. It must be delightful to have him."

"Yes," Andrée agreed, her heart skipping amidst its panicked pace. "He is so happy; I cannot help but smile as well."

The man reached out and put his finger in the baby's palm, grinning as the tiny fingers curled around it, and laughed as the baby began to wave the finger he held.

"He reminds me of my own boy in Germany." He pulled his finger from the hold and ruffled the baby's hair.

What would have happened if he had known just where this particular baby had come from?

Andrée only smiled more fully at the thought.

She gestured to the blockade. "Am I able to go through?"

"Of course," the other man replied, gesturing that she do so. "We're only trying to stop Jews from escaping. This entire neighborhood is infested, and we're rooting them all out."

Which meant that, unless they were exceptionally lucky, this little boy's parents were about to be rounded up as well.

She could not have felt any closer to failure than at that moment.

Swallowing the sudden choking sensation, Andrée smiled at both Gestapo men and pushed the pram past the blockade. "Good day, then."

They bid her farewell and let her pass without any trouble, but Andrée did not look back toward them or toward any of the houses presently being emptied. She could not risk looking uncertain or suspicious, and the baby in the pram she pushed needed to get to safety now more than ever.

Eventually, the baby fell asleep, content in her care and completely ignorant as to the plight of his parents and his people. Andrée reached the offices in Rue du Trône and brought the pram inside the flat, but picked up her smaller companion and carried his sleeping form into the offices themselves. He nestled himself against her shoulder, his breathing gentle and audible with the slightest rasp.

What were his parents enduring at this very moment? The pain of losing him to parts unknown, followed by the loss of their neighbors, if not their own home? Had they been loaded up into the truck with those in their building? Were they on their way to Malines to await transportation to a camp?

Would they even care what happened to them if their son was gone?

Until Andrée could deliver the boy safely to his new residence, she would hold him like he was her own.

"Claude," Paule hissed when she saw her enter. "We are not supposed to bring children here!"

Andrée gestured to his sleeping form. "He is a baby and he will not remember. Besides, he is sleeping." She made a shushing motion and moved to her usual desk to check where she had planned on taking him.

She knew, of course, as she had memorized it, but the suddenness of the raids in the neighborhood had shaken her, and she needed to be certain the home she was taking him to would be safe, considering the day's actions.

"Any trouble?" Paule asked softly.

Andrée shook her head. "But there could have been. Raids happened all around me. Probably his parents, even." She shook her head, eyes stinging with tears. "The Gestapo smiled at me as I passed by their barricades. Smiled at *him*. They were pulling his parents, his people, out of their homes, and they ruffled his hair because he was in a pram pushed by me."

"Unfortunately, your fair looks are what make you a perfect person to do what we do." Paule shrugged and came over to them, holding her arms out. "May I?"

Andrée smiled and carefully handed him over, trying not to jostle him. "I may take him elsewhere, given the trouble."

Paule nodded, cradling him against her neck and rocking gently. "I would not blame you at all. There are a number of places open for a baby boy. Any of them will do." She smiled as she held him, her hand rubbing smoothly up and down his back. "He is a delightful love, isn't he?"

"You should see him when he's awake," Andrée murmured as she pulled out the location journal. "I have never met a happier child in my entire life. I only hope that he can keep that innate cheerfulness through all of this." She bit her lip, running her finger along the pages of locations, no place seeming safe enough for this sweet boy whose parents might, even now, be in danger.

She paused at the number of a location in the Ardennes and nodded to herself. It was far enough away to be safe and a pleasant village for a young child to be raised in. One family there had decided to take in some Jewish children, and then neighbors, inspired by the goodness of that family, had offered themselves as safe homes as well.

"There," Andrée said aloud, "267. That's where I'll go."

"Excellent choice," Paule praised. "A good location for a young boy learning to live."

"I thought so, too." She replaced the notebook in its cabinet and moved to pick up the suitcase she had stowed for him against one wall. "If I go now, I can be back here before nightfall."

Paule walked with her out to the foyer and settled the still sleeping boy into the pram. "Go. If they're still raiding the neighborhoods like you said, the train station should be easy."

"One can only hope." Andrée nodded at her and started out of the building toward the train station.

It was not a long walk, which was one of the benefits of their office being located where it was, but Andrée felt her heart pounding as though she had run miles. As though she herself were being pursued by the Gestapo. As though at this moment her life were at stake.

As though she *ought* to be running.

She boarded the train without incident, even receiving help from strangers to get the baby and pram settled easily. Once they were on their way, the baby woke and seemed mildly confused by his surroundings.

Andrée found herself immediately shifting into her role of teacher and caretaker. "Hello there, Dorian," she cooed, using the new name he had been assigned and standing him up to allow his legs room to stretch. "Have you had a good nap? You slept for quite a while. Yes, you did."

He grinned at her, reaching for her face playfully.

"I bet you're hungry, aren't you? Yes, you probably are. Shall we see what I've brought for you?"

A finely dressed woman walked down the aisle, pausing to smile at Andrée and the baby. "What a pleasant little fellow! He is simply adorable, and clearly loves you."

Andrée returned her smile, biting back any urge to correct the mistake. "Thank you, madame."

"How old is he?"

"Twenty months," Andrée recited, fidgeting with her bag to pull out some of the food she kept for her journeys. "And very active."

The woman laughed. "Ah, my boys were the very same at that age. The color of his hair I can see he gets from you. But those curls! Those must be from his father."

The mention of Dorian's father tightened Andrée's chest with pain, bringing to mind the image of the faces of both parents as they bid him farewell, possibly for the last time. Why hadn't she noticed anything as innocent and sweet as the child's curls and from which parent they had come? If he never saw his parents again, he ought to know who gave him such curls.

She blinked as she somehow maintained her smile. "I had curls as a child, but they grew out with age."

It was a true statement; it was simply not the reason Dorian had his curls.

Allowing inference was not dishonesty, was it?

"Ah," the woman said, still smiling. "Well, it's a pleasant sight to behold, a mother and son so happy and bright. Good day to you."

She moved on before Andrée could respond, which was well enough. There was no need to say much more.

Dorian busied himself with crackers on Andrée's lap and Andrée held him close to her, rocking gently as she allowed herself to gaze absently out of the window.

She remembered a song her father had sung to her during the sillier bedtime moments. She sang softly:

The orange chick
Who lays eggs in the barn
She will lay a little egg
For her little one
Who will go night-night,
Nighty, night night.

What songs had Dorian's father or mother sung to him to settle or soothe him? Or to play with him, or make him laugh? It was not as though she could sing him any Yiddish songs, even if she knew the language, but if they were any of the songs other children in Belgium knew, she could have sung those to him as well.

She didn't even know what number Dorian was for her. He was number 394, she knew that. But how many children had she hidden by now?

When would it become easier?

Would it become easier?

Andrée leaned her head against Dorian's curly one, continuing to sing.

The gray hen
Who lays eggs in the church
She will lay a little egg
For her little one
Who will go night-night,
Nighty, night night.

The brown hen
Who lays eggs on the moon
She will lay a little egg
For her little one
Who will go night-night,
Nighty, night night.

She sang song after song until they arrived in the Ardennes. Quickly and quietly, she made her way with Dorian, his pram, and his suitcase to the village. The house was easy enough to find, and the neighbors soon flocked with curiosity.

An older woman looked at Dorian in the arms of his new maternal figure, straightening her spectacles as she did so. "That is a Jewish child?" She looked at Andrée as though she had somehow tricked them all with the placement of Dorian.

"Yes," Andrée said slowly, confused by the reaction. "He is."

The woman looked at Dorian again, shaking her head. "Well, he looks like any other!"

Heat raced into Andrée's face, the pressures of the day and the strain of it all coming to the forefront of her mind, her fatigue unable to bear any more. "So, what did you think?" she snapped without reserve. "That he would have horns and a tail?"

The neighbor's mouth worked as though she meant to answer, but another put a hand on her arm, silencing her.

Andrée exhaled a shaking breath and turned to the mother of the home. She was scowling at her neighbor, but soon looked at Andrée with concern.

"It will be fine," Andrée assured her. "Dorian is a joy, and his parents have been rounded up by the Gestapo. He won't remember any of that. But he . . ." She swallowed hard, her voice breaking. "He seems to very much enjoy singing." She cleared her throat and lifted her chin, trying to return to business. "Someone will be checking in with you from time to time, just to see that everything is in order and that your needs, and his, are being met."

The mother nodded, rubbing Dorian's back and bouncing him a little. "Thank you, Mademoiselle Fournier."

Andrée nodded and turned to the others with a warning look. "I trust none of you will endanger him or this family. Enough has been endured by those who are *like any other*."

The neighbor in question did not meet her eyes, but the others nodded.

"Good night," Andrée murmured to them all, leaving the house without looking at Dorian again. Her eyes were already burning, but she couldn't cry in front of an audience.

She had talked with Paule and Claire and even with Ida and her associate Brigitte about their experiences so far, and she knew they had all had emotional occasions. But all of them had hidden their reactions from those involved. They had cried many times, but never in front of the parents or the children.

They saved their tears for the privacy of their homes or their walks back to their offices or homes.

Never to be seen by others.

Never.

As Andrée walked back to the train station to return to Brussels, she let her tears flow. Not sobbing. She wasn't going to allow herself that extreme or to feel the pain of the day that deeply. But she needed to cry, if for no other reason than to remind herself that she was still human among this work she did. It was its own kind of cruelty to the parents, but it was nothing compared to the harshness and evil that was possible through the alternative.

Sometimes, in the midst of the hard things she asked of others, she forgot that there were emotions for those engaging in the rescues as well as those experiencing them. She did not want to be without feeling or to be heartless in truth, no matter how stoic and calm she appeared to the parents. She was in pain most of the time with these sweet children, but she would never dare compare her feelings with those of the families she was disrupting and uprooting.

How could she tell anyone that she was feeling so much? How could she cry with the mothers and still take the children away? How could she indulge in emotion and accomplish the impossible? No, the emotions had to come later, as did the experience of her pain. The allowance of her pain.

Her permission to feel the pain.

She did not believe in God, but suddenly she wished she did. She wished she could find comfort in crying aloud and pleading for Dorian's parents to somehow be spared the death that awaited so many. She wished someone would intervene and take the whole sweet family away from all of this.

But she did not believe.

So, all she could do was cry and embrace the truth she knew deep in her heart: she was human.

Humans were flawed, but they were capable of great things. Horrible, evil, atrocious things, as well as daring, honorable, generous, and good things.

The latter just needed to be more powerful than the former.

And she would continue to cry in private over the work she did until the good overcame the bad, until the weak were the strong, until the oppressors were thwarted, until humanity prevailed.

Until the end, whatever end that happened to be.

It seemed an empty, silent train ride back to Brussels. Something devoid of life and light, and, while it was a chance to rest and recuperate from the stresses of the day, Andrée found herself wishing for the happy baby to be back in her arms. He would distract her from her own thoughts, force her to smile at his antics, and remind her of the beauty of such innocence in the world.

He was the reason she was doing this. He and the hundreds of other children just like him.

So that all of them would have a reason to smile in the future, even if it was harder to do so now.

Tired and drained, Andrée disembarked once the train reached Brussels and made her way back to the office to finalize her paperwork before she returned to the flat she now shared with Ida. The streets were quiet now, no sign of razzias, no sounds of distress or fear, only some distant crickets could be heard.

One would never know anything untoward had occurred that day.

Andrée yawned as she entered the offices and was startled to discover Paule, Claire, and Ida all within, their faces wreathed in distress.

Her eyes darted to each of them in turn. "What happened?"

Ida faced her, eyes puffy and red. "The Heibers have been arrested and taken to Malines."

CHAPTER 10

Deep and boundless hatred is an essential characteristic of Jewry. It is rooted in the Devil's blood of the Jews and can only be distantly understood by the other peoples of the earth.

—ERNST HIEMER, *DER STÜRMER*, 1943

Another day, another convent.

It wasn't the most helpful thought Ida had as she walked down the street toward her third convent of the week, but as the Catholic sisters were so eager to help with the saving of Jewish children, the CDJ wasn't exactly in a position to refuse them. It was a marvelous cover for them, as there were always children attending school there, most of whom no one paid any attention to.

It was the easiest place to hide children, all things considered.

But not all the convents had the same appeal as Little Sisters of the Poor did, and not all Mother Superiors were as warm as Sister Marie-Aurélie.

This particular convent was Ida's least favorite.

Ida entered the church and looked for any sign of a nun, wanting to get this over with as soon as possible. She had other locations to visit today for welfare checks, not to mention a few places she needed to go to for evaluation. And then there were the families that had requested help through their new system of the post box, which was proving a challenge to keep up with now that the Heibers had been arrested and taken away. Losing that position in the AJB had been painful for all of them, but at least Ghert Jospa still had his position with the *Front de l'Indépendance.*

The results weren't as accurate as the AJB had been, as far as locations were concerned, but setting up the post box for messages and requests for help had allowed people to put their addresses down with as much detail as they were comfortable with. And besides, Ida and her operatives had a fairly good idea of location based on generic information at this point. They had a solid cover story as being social workers that worked for any situation, Jewish or not, so if mistakes were made in location, no one should be any the wiser.

But she couldn't think about the stress of her position and the monumental number of tasks she had to complete, now that Esta and Maurice were imprisoned. At this moment, she had to be sympathetic and compassionate, listen to the concerns of the children, and ensure that all of them were not only safe but also comfortable.

One of the sisters she recognized walked by, sniffing in faint disgust at her. "Here to see them, are you?"

Them? Was that how they were referred to here?

Ida barely avoided spitting at the woman. "I am. Where should I go?"

"Rectory," she said with a dismissive hand. "I'll have them sent down."

She left before Ida could thank her, criticize her, or offer an opposing opinion.

Did she know that Ida was a Jew? Or did she simply not care enough to be polite to those who worked with rehousing Jewish children?

Had she placed children in a toxic situation that was physically safer than their homes but mentally and spiritually just as abusive as the Gestapo?

Ida pressed her tongue to her teeth, lifting her brows at nobody in particular, and turned to walk toward the rectory alone. She had never felt more unwelcome in her work, and she was racing against the Gestapo.

What sort of allies were these people anyway?

Biting her tongue with a semi-painful pressure, Ida entered the rectory and sat at the nearest table, waiting for the students to arrive. How they were going to keep the Jewish students from being outed to their classmates by this isolation she couldn't say, but she imagined the nuns had some process in place for the occasion.

Esta had taken care of several of these locations before now, and she would understand the details better. But until they figured out how they could get the Heibers out of Malines, if there was a way, she had to take on these tasks herself.

The younger children came in first, and they had little enough to say. They were impressionable, moldable to the nuns' wills and generally well behaved. She did note marks on the skin, though it was hard to tell if they were the result of average childhood antics or something worth more concern. She made a note of it all the same.

Dr. Hendrickx in Rue aux Laines had offered her services for welfare checks where health concerns existed, as had Dr. Duchaine at the Depage clinic, but the CDJ hadn't taken either up on that yet, more to protect them and their valuable positions than anything else, but Ida might call them in soon enough.

One of the older girls came into the rectory after the little ones, and Ida smiled at her. "Arlise, right?"

"Yes, mademoiselle," Arlise murmured in a soft voice, barely above a whisper. She kept her eyes downcast, and her hands carefully folded in front of her, submissive in the extreme and trying not to be noticed.

Ida didn't like that one bit. "Would you like to sit, Arlise?"

The girl shook her head faintly. "No, mademoiselle."

Arlise offered nothing further, and Ida watched her for a long moment, eyes darting from feature to feature of the girl's appearance. Clothing looked good enough, but she was covering the surface of her left hand with her right and seemed rather intent on keeping it so. Her skin was pale, which could simply be from a lack of being outdoors, but with all of that combined . . .

"Arlise," Ida prodded gently. "Do you remember me? I talked to your family before you were brought here. I'm not associated with the convent or the order. You can tell me anything and it won't get back to the Mother Superior or your instructors. It just goes into my notes, unless we need to intervene somehow."

The girl shifted her weight, her hands moving ever so slightly against each other.

It was the most movement Ida had seen from Arlise yet, and it encouraged her.

"Would you like me to close the door?" Ida offered, gesturing toward it. "Would that help?"

Arlise froze, which seemed to be answer enough.

Ida rose and closed the door firmly, then returned to the table and smiled. "There. Just us. Better?"

The girl's shoulders moved on a massive exhale, and she nodded. "Yes, mademoiselle." She sat in a chair now and laid her hands upon the table surface.

Her left hand was covered in welts and bruises, unable to lay as flat as her right.

Ida swallowed and met Arlise's eyes. "What happened?"

Arlise glanced at her hand as though it was barely a passing concern. "Several of the nuns use rulers on hands for wrong answers or talking out of turn. Not just on the Jews, but all of the students. But . . . a few seem to select the Jewish students more than the others."

"They know who you are?" Ida asked, eyes widening.

"It's never been a secret," Arlise told her. "All of the nuns know. The little ones seem to do well enough, but those of us who are older . . ." She made a face. "The Mother Superior cornered me yesterday, and she said, 'You are Jewish, but you do believe in Jesus Christ, don't you, now that you are thirteen years old?' And I didn't know what to say."

Ida held her breath, continuing to smile as gently as possible. "Why not?"

Arlise shrugged her narrow shoulders. "Because it's impossible, and unbelievable, for the Mother Superior to love a girl who is an unbeliever."

How the breaking of Ida's heart was not audible to them both, let alone everyone in the building, Ida couldn't say. But she felt it give way, almost directly down the middle of the organ, and could swear the pieces of her heart hit various ribs as they fell to the pit of her stomach.

The girl had been taken away from her home for her safety, taken from the arms of those who loved her, and placed here, where she now felt unable to be loved because she was a Jew.

Would the world ever be a safe and fair place for them and their people?

Arlise was thirteen. Such a pivotal age in a girl's life as she tried to figure out who she was as a person, what she wanted to believe for herself, how she viewed the world. And she was being hidden in a convent, safe but unloved, confused about what she should or should not believe because the world wouldn't allow her the freedom to decide for herself at the moment. She was old enough to take care of the younger Jewish children in this convent, and likely did so, but what hope or inspiration could she give them in this place? Their numbers were not great, compared with the other students, but there were enough of them to be able to band together for support if needed.

And what would happen if they did band together? Would they still be looked down on here for believing differently? Ida felt the need to go speak with one of their other religious allies, Father André, who ran a boarding school himself. He made a point to offer psalms to the Jewish students he housed, knowing they read them as much as his Catholic students, if not more, and that they might find comfort there. He never tried to convert any of them and refused to allow them to convert faiths, if they wished, until after the war was over and they were reunited with their families.

He was a man of faith, and a true man of God, she believed. That was the God she wanted to believe in. Not the one who divided them by harshness and cruelty.

"I am so sorry, Arlise," Ida murmured, covering her hand across the table. "That must be so difficult."

Arlise looked down, seeming to shrug again as though it was not such a terrible thing. "You get used to it. One of our teachers was talking about Jews and Judas the other day, and she said that she recognizes Jews right away. That they—we—are dark, have yellow skin, and large hooked noses. And she looked right at me as she said it. She went on with the lesson but made sure the entire class knew that the Jews killed Jesus and spit on him."

Ida closed her eyes, exhaling roughly. There was no way to hide her distress at this, nor to ignore the situation. The Jewish children were being mistreated here, subjected to the rampant antisemitism that the Nazis played upon for their own ends. The only thing that could be said about the nuns here was that they did not want the Jewish children imprisoned or dead.

But that, it seemed, was all they were willing to allow.

What could she do about this? Where else could she place these children? How could they intervene when there were already so many other children to place and greater risks of death and danger out there? Could they take them away? Could they talk to the Mother Superior and ask for more gentleness in treatment and more understanding in behavior? Did her authority extend that far? Did anyone's?

Sister Marie-Aurélie was of an entirely different order from the nuns in this convent, so she had no influence or authority on them. Ida could reach out to their friends at the *Oeuvre Nationale de l'Enfance*, Belgium's national child service—or ONE—who had made most of the religious connections for them, but would they be able to do anything either?

Was having the children here that much better than leaving the children at home and in danger with their families?

Ida had trouble swallowing, let alone trying to think, but she somehow managed to smile. "I'll try to make things better for you here, Arlise. Better for all of you."

Arlise raised her eyes to Ida, doubt and resignation filling their depths. "It's fine, mademoiselle. They're not the Nazis, are they?"

There was no good way to answer that question. Of course, they weren't. The Nazis were unmatched in their evil, and these nuns who had agreed to house Jewish children and keep them safe from such evil could not be grouped with them.

But that did not mean the children would be free from prejudice in these locations.

Ida had to keep smiling, though she did not have much else to say. "I will try to make things better," she said again, not knowing how she could.

She could not promise things would get better, but she could promise to try.

Which was all they were doing with these children anyway.

Trying.

There were only three more students to see after Arlise left, and their stories were relatively unremarkable, though they echoed the tone of Arlise's as far as the prejudice went. She had seen children in worse conditions, but there was something particularly heartbreaking here.

They had to do better in finding places to keep these children safe. That was the only way they could prevent the children from feeling the abuse that so polluted their homes and neighborhoods at this time. There had to be more homes and schools where the children would be well cared for, not just safe. Happy and safe. Healthy and safe.

Loved and safe.

Was that really too much to ask?

Ida decided to give up the rest of her morning schedule and go to the main offices. She needed to gather her thoughts and her strengths, needed to be reminded of the good things they were doing rather than the harsh things they were experiencing. She needed to hear from others that were engaged in the same work that it was, in fact, making a difference.

She was struggling to believe her own thoughts at the moment.

The screeching of tires brought Ida's head up, though she couldn't recall when she had begun looking down at her feet.

Fat Jacques was getting out of a car and moving to a nearby bench with another man in plain clothes, expressions determined. Other people moved out of their way, either moving deeper into the park behind the bench or avoiding the area entirely, as was common during Gestapo interventions. Ida hung back herself, tucking herself against a light pole, but did not leave the area. She needed to see this. Needed to know who was being arrested or interrogated. Needed to remind herself of the reality of life in Brussels at the moment.

She watched as Fat Jacques moved to one side and her eyes could fall upon the figures being questioned.

Her stomach plummeted and she gripped the light pole with tight fingers.

Ghert Jospa.

No. Anyone but him. They'd already lost Maurice to arrest; they could not afford to lose Ghert as well. And if they lost Ghert, would they also lose Yvonne?

Ida didn't recognize the woman on the bench with Ghert, but he had several contacts from the various organizations helping the Jews in some way or another. She certainly could have been Jewish, based on her looks alone, but despite what the Nazis and Gestapo thought, not all Jews looked the same.

Her throat threatened to close entirely as she watched both Ghert and the woman hand over their IDs to Jacques and his associate. The false IDs had been used time and time again by all of the CDJ and had not yet come into question, as far as she knew. That alone spoke to their quality, though it would not have done them very much good to have poor false IDs that could be easily spotted.

All of their false documents of any kind could stand up to scrutiny. They'd made certain of it.

Which meant Ghert ought to be just fine, and this ought to end well.

But Ida knew better than to blindly hope.

Jacques seemed particularly fascinated by whichever ID he held, and then looked at the woman on the bench for a long moment.

"False card!" he shouted suddenly, pointing at her.

Two men sprang forth from some corner of the park and immediately took the woman to the car and shoved her inside.

Ida's breath began to hitch against her lungs and throat, her fingers and toes going numb.

Please, she hissed in her mind. *Please, no . . .*

Fat Jacques pointed at Ghert's briefcase, his words unintelligible to Ida from this distance. But Ghert seemed to be confused by the request and asked several questions.

Ghert was rarely confused by anything, so Ida could only assume that he was acting in this.

She prayed he was acting in this.

But Fat Jacques was insistent, and Ghert picked up his briefcase, opening it and turning the case for the other man to see.

Time seemed to stop, as did sound, as Ida saw Jacques moving things around in the briefcase. Then he picked up a paperless package bound with string, and even from this distance, Ida could see what they were.

ID cards.

She closed her eyes in horror just as Jacques shouted again, only opening them when she heard a car door close.

Ghert had been shoved in beside his companion, and Fat Jacques was climbing into the passenger seat of the car, the Gestapo officer moving around to the driver's side.

Ida made no motion to get Ghert's attention. Doing so would have only drawn the Gestapo's attention to her, and they seemed to be in a rather short-tempered mood. Not only that, but the CDJ could not afford to lose anyone else.

There would be no defending the stack of IDs in Ghert's possession. He would be officially arrested and interrogated, and Yvonne . . .

Yvonne.

Ida turned on her heel and began to walk briskly, taking several shortcuts to get to the Jospa home. She wouldn't have known it as an operative, but Yvonne and Ghert had welcomed her to Brussels with a family dinner last year. She had since become far more acquainted with the city and orienting herself within it, so she needed no redirection to get there.

Yvonne might be at the office, but the Gestapo wouldn't know where that was. The Jospa home, on the other hand, would be on their registration with the city. If Yvonne and Paul were there, Ida needed to get them out.

Now.

There were no cars parked in front of the house, Ida could see quickly, and she nodded in satisfaction at not being too late. She knocked on the door repeatedly, her heart thundering in her ears, but no one answered.

She could not have been too late; they would need to verify Ghert's identity first, so Yvonne and Paul must not have been at home.

There was still time.

"Come to visit the Jospas, mademoiselle?" a neighbor asked with some concern, a washing basket on her hip. "They won't be home until evening."

Ida smiled at her, though her face seemed to object to such a motion under the circumstances. "I simply wanted Yvonne to know that Ghert has been arrested. I don't know what for, but I would hate for her to find out from someone else."

The neighbor's eyes went wide, and she stepped closer. "They're Jews, you know. I don't know the details, but they do so much for so many. If I see Yvonne, I'll warn her. If they've taken him, they'll come for her."

Ida did not trust easily, but something about the woman's expression spoke truth, and Ida put a hand on hers. "Please do. I'll try to find her and warn her, but they might come for her before I can."

"Paul stays with his aunt," the neighbor told her, looking up and down the street. "He'll be safe for now. But your people need to find a solution for both him and Yvonne. Something safer. We won't let them take her as well. I'll keep an eye out." She nodded at Ida, seeming as determined as any member of the CDJ that Ida had ever seen, and then turned back for her house.

There was nothing to do now but go to the offices, as she had planned, and hope that she might find Yvonne there, working on something or other. If she was not there, Ida would have to trust in the care of Yvonne's neighbor.

In a world where friend turned to foe, she could not say that she felt perfectly at ease with the safety of her friend, but she had little alternative.

The Nazi vice was tightening around Brussels and the CDJ, and Ida had to keep going. Had to help others to keep going.

Had so many more children to save.

She could do no less.

CHAPTER 11

Each Jew individually, and Jewry as a whole, is without a home. Jewry undermines every people and every state that it infiltrates. It feeds as a parasite and a culture-killing worm in the host people. It grows and grows like weeds in the state, the community, and the family and infests the blood of humanity everywhere.

—HERMANN ESSER, NAZI PROPAGANDIST, 1939

"Claude. Claude, wake up."

Andrée groaned and sat up, gripping the back of her neck. "What? Where are we?"

Claire snorted softly and handed her a bit of muffin. "Gare du Midi, where we fell asleep. Solange should be here soon. Are you ready for your pair?"

Blinking away the very little sleep she'd managed to get between train journeys, Andrée nodded. "Yes. Is it time for me to fetch them?"

"Mm-hmm," came the answer around a mouthful of food. "Go ahead. I'll wait for Solange, and one of us will be here waiting for you, just to be safe."

Andrée rubbed her eyes and took another bit of proffered muffin before pushing up off the bench she'd slept on. There wasn't much she could do about her skirts and the wrinkled nature of them, but she brushed at them anyway as she walked away from the train station.

Everything was more careful about their operations now. They checked in on each other more regularly, and, occasionally, spent the night with each other in train stations for safety. With the Heibers still in Malines and Ghert Jospa arrested, there was little room for error or carelessness. They could not afford to lose others, and they were doing everything they could to avoid that.

Poor Ida was almost never at the flat she shared with Andrée anymore, given the amount of work she had taken on. Yvonne Jospa was still involved, but from a safer distance and a secure location. Ida had mentioned that the neighbors had warned Yvonne away from her house when the Gestapo had been waiting outside for her, which had allowed her to make herself scarce and, eventually, safe.

Andrée struggled to sleep well these days with such significant arrests and troubles constantly on her mind. On days where she worked herself into exhaustion, of course, that was not a problem, but her dreams made her restless. She had cut off all contact with her family, for their safety more than her own, and she was feeling the lack of connection in peculiar ways.

She was not even that close with her parents and siblings. She had always felt different from them, and now she was acting with such daring and defiance of military authority . . . Her family hated the Nazis, she knew, but none of them were going to the extremes she was.

Still, separating families had made her more keenly aware of her own.

She had begun to look at these children she was saving as her own children, though she clearly had no idea of the depth and breadth of a mother's love and attachment. But from the moment she took them from their homes until they were safely deposited in their new locations, she adopted them. Each and every one. She became their mother, their protector, their friend, their guide.

She would have lain down her life for them without even thinking about it twice.

The two children she was fetching at the moment were old enough to ask questions but young enough to be resilient. They would likely understand what had been happening around them, to some degree, and would understand the necessity of their leaving. They might cry more because of that understanding, but that understanding, in turn, might also bring more comfort to their parents.

She prayed only that these siblings would not have to be parted from each other after they were placed. She'd already had to separate several sets of siblings, including a little boy who had already lost two other siblings throughout the course of this war.

The pain of such separations was, in some ways, worse than being separated from the parents.

But both were brutal.

Andrée reached the building she needed and entered as quietly as possible, moving up the stairs to the flat and knocking softly.

The door opened almost immediately, and the drawn mother stood there, clearly not having slept a wink the entire night.

Andrée would not blame her for that.

"Good morning," Andrée greeted. "Are they ready?"

The mother seemed to flinch at the words, and Andrée had to bite her tongue to keep from apologizing. She had to be all business in this, or the situation would become so much worse.

"Yes, Mademoiselle Claude," came the rough murmur. "Ruth, Aaron, it is time."

The children appeared, knapsacks over their shoulders, and hugged their mother tightly. There were no tears, no words. Only tight embraces and fervent kisses. Then their mother held them at arm's length, looking at both thoroughly.

She eventually nodded, and gently urged them toward Andrée.

For the children, Andrée smiled. "Good morning, children. Are we ready to catch the train?"

The girl, who was ten years of age, only nodded. Her brother, age seven, smiled just a little.

Andrée lifted her gaze to the mother, whose eyes were rapidly filling with tears. "Thank you," the mother whispered.

There was nothing Andrée could do but nod. Words would have been useless.

She turned and took each child by a hand, walking with them down the stairs, saying nothing while they were within the building.

Once they were in the streets, however, Andrée did her best to turn cheery. "Ruth, you are now going to call yourself Renée. You're not going to use any other name or call yourself something else, all right?"

Ruth—now Renée—nodded, again silently.

"And Aaron," Andrée continued, turning to the boy. "You are going to be Andre. Do you know what Andre means?"

The boy shook his head, looking up at her with all the innocence in the world.

"It means manly and well-built," she told him, smiling. "Do you think you can be manly and well-built?"

Andre immediately puffed out his chest and squared his shoulders, making her laugh.

"Yes, just like that!" Andrée squeezed his hand. "You must think of yourself as Andre now, my boy. There must be no other name that you respond to. Understand?"

He nodded obediently, glancing over at his sister.

Andrée looked at her as well, but the girl's focus was straight ahead, her fingers cold and unmoving within Andrée's hand. The light from a porch they were passing illuminated her face briefly, just enough for Andrée to catch sight of one tear slowly trekking its way down the surface of her cheek.

Was anything more heartbreaking than that sight?

It would do no good to ask what was wrong, though the question was on the tip of Andrée's tongue. What was wrong was that this girl had just been taken from her mother's arms, not knowing when she would see her again. Or *if* she would see her again. What was wrong was that she was leaving her home and being taken away to parts unknown for the foreseeable future.

What was wrong was that she was a Jew.

And that was a shameful statement to have to be made.

As though Renée had heard Andrée's thoughts, she asked, "Mademoiselle, why is it wrong to be a Jew?"

Andrée squeezed her hand gently. "It's not, darling. It's not at all. When we are on the train to the countryside, we can talk about it more."

Renée nodded, though it was clear she did not believe that the conversation would happen. Or was it that she did not believe Andrée's brief answer to the question?

How could she possibly explain to these children that it was perfectly right for them to be Jewish when they were leaving their mother for that very reason? When the world they lived in revolved around hating and abusing them? When they had been branded by those horrid yellow stars so that walking down the streets of their home had become an experience in being gawked at?

When their childhood as they had known it was ending and their identities lost?

Children were resilient, it was true, but children were also observant and curious. They did not believe as many lies as adults wanted them to, but they were content to allow the lies if they sensed the truth would be too arduous to get into. Children were adaptable, but they internalized so much more than could possibly be understood.

These children, who might not know precisely what it meant to be Jewish or grasp the attributes of their faith that made them so unique, were suffering for the simple fact of their identity, which they had not chosen for themselves. Their heritage as well as their faith. Their breeding as well as their heritage.

They were viewed as some sort of inferior and alien race that must be sponged out.

People are being burnt.

The words from weeks ago, on the report out of the Nazi camps, came back to mind, a haunting echo of the base reality of the world. These children could very well have been made to walk to their own burning death simply for certain aspects of their identities. With no debating over their youth or innocence, for their identities were no innocent thing, according to the powers that were. With no consideration toward allowing them to grow and develop into adulthood, where their faith could be more fully embraced, their virtues established, their own sense of humanity forged.

No, they were simply the spawn of insects and had thus earned an equal death.

"When you do not wish to be eaten by adult bugs, you crush them under your boot when they are young."

She shook her head at the memory of the words that night at Gatti de Gamond, still feeling the sting of them.

It was enough to make a sentient creature ill, when the details were accumulated.

She would dare any soldier of the Nazi ranks to personally walk a child alone to such a fate, had she not believed to her core that they had all been poisoned to view them without humanity.

What cankers on their souls must be growing from such views.

May they fester and bleed each one of them to a painful, poisoning death.

The train station was soon before them, the faint light of dawn beginning to creep into the sky and the surrounding areas.

Claire sat there still, a wicker basket at her feet that had not been there before. She turned toward the sound of their approach and smiled when she saw their silent trio.

"What a delightful group of travelers!" she greeted with a wave to both children. "I am Mademoiselle Catherine. Are you hungry? My friend Solange brought some breakfast, if you would like to eat before you get on the train with Mademoiselle Claude."

The boy nodded eagerly, while Renée remained impassive.

Still, Claire was undeterred and began handing out items from the wicker basket. The siblings sat on the bench and began to eat while Andrée moved to stand on Claire's other side.

"Solange checked in?" she asked softly.

"Mm-hmm," Claire answered, handing her a surprisingly warm pastry. "All is well. She went home to get some rest."

"Good." Andrée exhaled slowly and took a bite of her breakfast, letting the warmth of it seep into her chilled frame. "I'll go purchase our tickets, and once that is done, you do the same. We'll be fine here."

Claire nodded and turned to the basket again. "Let me see. I do believe there are some croissants in here. Is it too early for croissants, or—"

Small hands reached out at once, cutting her off, and Claire laughed at the gestures. Even Renée was eager for one, which made Andrée smile.

Perhaps the girl would find some light in this day after all.

Andrée moved to the ticket office, smiling slightly at the man in the booth. "Three tickets for Crupet, please."

"Ah, visit to the countryside, mademoiselle?" he replied as he rang up the expense. "Lovely this time of year."

"Indeed," Andrée agreed, "which is why we are going. The poor children are unwell and in need of country air."

He tsked sympathetically. "Poor lambs. The countryside will be the best thing for them. And with all those blasted Gestapo trucks clogging up our city air, among other evils, the sooner they are away from that, the better." He handed the tickets to her, his smile sympathetic. "Safe travels, mademoiselle. And may God bless those children to be well again soon."

"Thank you, monsieur." Andrée gestured a quick wave with the tickets before moving back to Claire and the children.

It was always refreshing to find people in and around the area who did not hold with the Nazi's ideals, though they did not necessarily know the children in question were Jewish. So long as they saw the children as children, it was enough.

She hoped he believed that his God could make the children well. Faith was a great motivator for those who had it. Unless it became the reason behind their evil actions. But that was not truly faith. It was some twisted, misguided rationale for deeds that they claimed were done out of faith.

Her Catholic upbringing had taught her that much, at least.

"We may board the train now, if we like," Andrée told the children.

"Mademoiselle Catherine, may we take some additional treats from your basket for the journey?"

Claire nodded, hoisting the basket up. "Take the whole thing, please! Otherwise, I will find myself eating it all myself and becoming quite sick!" She made a playfully pained face that had young Andre giggling and Renée smiling.

At long last.

Andrée grinned and took the basket from Claire. "Can you say thank you to Mademoiselle Catherine, children?"

"Thank you," they chimed together, their sweet voices blending in the sort of harmony that only siblings could create.

"My pleasure, dears." Claire rose and gave them each an almost maternal smile. "Safe travels. Perhaps I might come and visit you. Would that be all right?"

They nodded and hopped down from the bench, coming to Andrée's side and taking her hands. She turned them to walk toward the waiting train, helping both on board and moving to the first set of open seats. Once they were all situated, and Andrée had checked their surroundings, she turned to Renée.

"Now, Renée," she began in a low voice. "You asked me a question earlier. Do you remember it?"

Renée's eyes widened, but she nodded. "Why is it wrong to be a Jew?"

Andrée gave her a slight smile. "Yes. And while there is no one about, I will answer this for you. It is not wrong at all. It is even very good to be a Jew. There have been extraordinary people in the Jewish community. There are Mademoiselle Oppenheim and Monsieur Gierymski, both extraordinary artists. Bizet the composer. Einstein and Bohr, both physicists. Disraeli, a prime minister of Great Britain, was born Jewish. There are simply marvelous individuals of Jewish descent."

"Then why . . . ?" Renée frowned, her lips twisting in thought as her brow creased. "Why do people hate us?"

"That is a trifle more difficult to explain, let alone understand." Andrée sighed sadly and shook her head. "Some people wrongly blame the Jews for various problems in their country. And it has led to an unfortunate idea of hating them. But it is not right that they do so. No one should hate another human being, and especially should not hurt them."

Renée nodded in thought, her lips now forming a slight smile. "That is what my mama says as well. That we should treat everyone kindly and forgive quickly."

Andrée returned her smile. "Your mama has the right idea about things. I hope you will remember that and believe it yourself."

"I want to," Renée confessed. "Can I, even though I'm not her daughter anymore?"

Stomach clenching to a painful degree, Andrée took the girl's hands. "You are and will always be your mother's daughter. Just because you are now Renée Braun does not mean you will forever need to be. I want you to remember your mother every day and keep her in your heart. And you must never give up hope that one day we will be able to bring you back to each other. All right?"

Renée sniffled once, then managed a small smile once more. "All right."

Andrée gave her an approving nod and turned her attention to both children as the train started moving. "What songs shall we sing while we wait for our stop, hmm? What are your favorites?"

The diversionary tactic worked, and soon both children were reciting their favorite songs and teaching them to Andrée, while Andrée taught songs to both of them in return. It was a delightful distraction for them all and allowed time to pass without any morose thoughts or reminiscences. Even Andrée needed the reprieve and was grateful for it.

What she did not expect was for the train to slow a full hour before it was scheduled to enter Crupet. And she certainly did not expect for the train to come to a full stop in the middle of the countryside.

Others had joined their car by now and were looking around with the same confusion Andrée was feeling. No one seemed to have any answers, and there was no sign of any railway employees coming through to give any.

The doors to their car opened then and men in plain clothes marched through, expressions determined.

One did not need to hear a single word to know they were Germans. The only question was from which tentacle of the Nazi creature did they hail? And would they be interested in Andrée or the children?

"Whatever they say," Andrée whispered to the children as she eyed the Germans, "do not reply. Whatever I say, do not reply. Give no answer whatsoever. Nod if you understand."

Both children nodded once, clamping their mouths shut.

The Germans walked slowly along the train car, asking only certain people for their papers. Young people, it seemed. But not children, she noted as one of the soldiers smiled at a young girl on her mother's lap. They did not bear the cruelty in countenance of the Gestapo, as far as she could tell, and their particular interest in the younger individuals on the train was unique.

What could they want with only the young adults?

The frantic beating of her heart settled slightly as she recalled the group known as the Werbestelle. The group "recruited" teenagers and young adults into what was actually compulsory labor. They enjoyed using the ploy that such work would save the families of Jewish teens, though she knew of at least three situations where a teenager who had agreed to go of their own volition was never heard from nor seen again, and then the families were arrested and deported.

So perhaps not the Gestapo, but no less nefarious.

Still, if it meant the children would be safe in this moment, she would allow the Werbestelle to be whoever else they were without any cursing.

She could always curse them in private later.

Andrée forced a smile onto her face as one of the Germans approached, his attention wholly on her rather than the children.

She would take that.

"Papers, mademoiselle," he ordered, though there wasn't harshness in his tone.

"Of course," Andrée replied. She reached into the inner pocket of her coat and retrieved her papers, handing them over at once.

He looked them over. "And what is your occupation?"

She cocked her head slightly, as her occupation was written on the identity card he held. "Teacher."

"And the children?"

Andrée had to bite back the urge to clear her throat impatiently. "These children are sick, and I am taking them to a nursing home in the countryside."

He glanced at them very briefly, then nodded and handed Andrée's papers back to her. "*Danke*, mademoiselle." He moved on, and soon, so did the rest of his company.

Andrée let herself exhale very slowly but would not say anything more to the children or anyone else until the train was moving again. She had heard too many stories of trains being stopped and passengers hauled off only to be placed on other trains headed for more dangerous places.

Once the entire train was searched and individuals of interest to the Werbestelle were identified, the rest of them could get on with their journey and lives.

She could only hope that there were no individuals of interest to them on this train. She could not bear the thought of young Jewish men and women, or teenagers, being sent to compulsory labor camps. Were those any different from the camps where people were being burned? She could not imagine so, and that made what she *could* imagine so much worse.

It could not have been many minutes more, though it felt like hours, before the train started moving again.

They were safe. For now.

Andrée looked at the children, forcing a smile she did not feel. "Well, that was a bit of excitement, wasn't it? Now, look out of the window there. Tell me what you can see in the countryside that we cannot see in the city."

CHAPTER 12

You must ensure through your behavior that Jewry never again has even the slightest influence on our people. Know the real enemy!

—NAZI FLYER, NOVEMBER 1941

"Her parents are gone."

Ida sank down onto a chair in shock, dropping the ration cards she had brought for the family. "What? I was only in their neighborhood yesterday, and no one said a thing about a raid."

Mrs. Brat shook her head slowly, hiccupping back a sob as she pulled a lace handkerchief out of her apron pocket and dabbed at her eyes. "Well, it happened. My Henrick was there when it did."

"Is he safe?" Ida asked with some alarm, thinking of the strapping fourteen-year-old and his good, kind heart.

"He got away, yes," Mrs. Brat told her, wiping her nose. "But it was . . . oh, it was horrible."

Ida closed her eyes in horror, feeling both hot and cold, fatigued and alert. Her rapidly spinning mind seemed now to be scraped and scorched by some obstruction in its mechanism wheel.

All she seemed to hear these days were the sad stories. The tragedies. Already this week, she'd had to move a girl who had already moved once because the wife of the household felt her husband was paying the girl too much attention.

Whether that was true or not, it was grounds for moving her, and the poor girl—Christine—was in her third location since being removed from her home. She would have further difficulty adjusting now and might never trust another soul.

Then there were the letters.

Incessant letters from those families who had not yet gone into hiding themselves and had not been arrested but wanted constant updates on their children. Constant reassurances of their children's health and safety. Constant connection to the children they had given over to the CDJ, a choice some of them seemed to be regretting now.

She did not fault any mother for longing for her child. But the risks parents were mounting upon them all by such communication was causing a strain Ida did not care for a jot.

How did one balance such emotions?

Shaking herself, more mentally than physically, Ida returned her focus to Mrs. Brat and the story she was about to tell.

"Anna's parents are known to us," Mrs. Brat began, her voice not quite steady. "This you were aware of from the beginning. Her father was an associate of my husband. At any rate, because of our past relationship, we have been keeping communication with Anna's parents. I know it is not the usual way of doing things with your organization, but it truly was better for us this way."

Ida waved off the tone of apology and defensiveness in the woman's words. "No matter. I trust you."

Mrs. Brat gave her a small smile before continuing. "Henrick went to the Storks' home with some food and also to retrieve a letter they'd written to Anna. It was our customary arrangement each week. Henrick was in their house, having just delivered the food, when the Gestapo arrived. He managed to flee on his bike and hid on the corner of the street, watching as the Storks were arrested and taken away. He returned home and told us what had happened, and asked me, 'What should I do, Mama? I didn't get Anna's letter.' He was so upset, not only that her parents had been taken, but that Anna would not have a new letter from them."

She paused, swallowing with some difficulty, her jaw quivering. "I had to tell Anna. It was . . . so horrible. She just sat there, tears falling, and she said, 'Papa said they wouldn't arrest him. He was in the German army in the Great War. He said he would show them a picture of him in uniform, and he would be safe. Why did they not come with me to your house?' And I had to hold the little one in my lap while her heart broke." Mrs. Brat broke off, pressing her handkerchief to her mouth.

A weight slowly pressed its full measure against the pit of Ida's stomach and, somehow, also against her lungs. To have such an experience in one's young life, and to be left wondering if her parents would ever return. And then for Henrick to see the arrest of people he knew. To have heard of roundups would be one thing, but witnessing one . . .

Mrs. Brat would be carrying the dark heaviness of both children's experiences for some time.

"Henrick is determined to find a way to get into Malines and find them," Mrs. Brat confessed weakly. "I've told him it is useless and dangerous, but he is determined that Anna shall have more from her parents." She shook her head. "What if they have already been moved from Malines, Mademoiselle Jeanne? What if . . . ?"

"There is no use in asking such questions, Madame Brat," Ida told her in as gentle a voice as she could manage with her own emotions. "Believe me, I have been asking them since the very beginning of this, and as of yet, I have no answers."

Mrs. Brat lowered her eyes, sniffling softly. "We will be well enough here, Mademoiselle Jeanne. We do not need ration cards; we have plenty to take care of Anna. Please, save those for others who are more in need."

"It is meant to help offset your costs," Ida tried to explain. "We do not want to put you out financially when you are sacrificing so much physically."

"It is no sacrifice." Mrs. Brat met her gaze squarely, the tears in her eyes doing nothing to lessen her determination. "We will take care of Anna as though she were our own, especially now that her parents have been arrested. And should the worst happen, she will always have a home with us. I appreciate your offer to help us financially, but I do not need to be paid in order to ensure that Anna is provided for."

Sensing this was not a fight to take on, Ida nodded and allowed herself to smile, the pressure against her stomach and lungs easing away in the face of such goodness and generosity. This was what she needed to be reminded of in the face of the evil and sadness all around her.

Ironically, this goodness was taking place *because* of the evil and sadness around her.

Perhaps it was only in the extremity of times that the weight of pure goodness could truly be appreciated.

The rest of the visit was rather efficient, given that Anna trusted her fostering family implicitly and was well cared for. She was a trifle more reserved than usual, but that was only understandable, given recent events. Ida made a mental note to ask about the Storks when she was able to get word to Maurice or Esta in Malines.

Her friends had managed to avoid deportation to a camp, thanks to the intervention of various influential people as well as the usefulness of Maurice and Esta to those who ran the camps, but only time would tell if they could continue to be so fortunate.

She could not offer such courtesies to the families of every child she hid, but this one was different.

Could she allow differences to creep into her work?

Could she make allowances for certain situations?

She'd never asked herself these questions before. Was she compromising her work by doing so now?

Ida took her leave of Mrs. Brat and Anna, her feet almost acting from their own memory as she made her way to the Little Sisters of the Poor convent. At least this time, she would not be visiting a convent alone, and at least it was her favorite convent of the bunch.

Brigitte, as the main contact for all of their Catholic associates, would be coming with her this time, and the two of them would be determining if the convent was prepared to take on children again. There were several requirements that would need to be met before it was safe to do so, including inquiring about any recent visits from the Gestapo, given what had happened the last time. But a meeting with Sister Marie-Aurélie meant that the Mother Superior, at least, felt that it was safe for the CDJ to begin their work there again.

It would be a relief to place children there once more. There were always students coming and going from boarding schools these days, and the convent had been able to keep their non-Jewish students as active as ever in the days since the staged attack. With all of that busyness, the addition of a few extra students was quite likely to go unnoticed.

But Jacques was a keen informer for the Gestapo, and far more observant than people gave him credit for. The convent could easily be under watch by some of his informants and assets, and the nuns could have no idea it was even taking place. It would all depend on how convincing he had found the situation, and if he considered Sister Marie-Aurélie trustworthy.

He was not a Catholic, so nuns did not hold much sway with him. They were on no pedestal, held no influence, and were under no rosy or hallowed glow in his mind. They were simply women in a religious order, and a religion in which he held no interest, to boot.

There was nothing preventing him from treating them as he would anyone else.

Brigitte was waiting for Ida just outside the convent, her posture as perfect as ever, making her seem taller than her small frame permitted. She was an impressive woman, and often accompanied children out of the boundaries of Brussels in addition to establishing connections with her fellow Catholics in their own resistance efforts. She was a determined individual, all matters of gender aside, and would have made an astonishing soldier, had such a position been available to a young woman.

Ida was delighted to have her on their side. She dreaded to think what Brigitte would have been capable of doing for the enemy, should her persuasions have tended that way.

"Good morning, Jeanne," Brigitte greeted with a smile, as she seemed to always be capable of bearing.

"Surely it is now afternoon, yes?" Ida looked up at the sun before looking at her colleague again. "Or is my morning only seemingly interminable but actually progressing at pace?"

Brigitte chuckled. "I believe there is time yet in the morning, but I will grant you the lengthy perception of your morning, given my own experience with welfare visits." She tilted her head toward the church. "Shall we?"

"Please," Ida agreed. "I am in need of the Mother Superior's good humor."

"She will be delighted to hear it." Brigitte turned to start the walk, waiting for Ida to join her side so they might walk together. "Bad morning?"

Ida shook her head. "Only emotional."

"Aren't they all?" Brigitte sighed, shaking her head. "Some days, we work and work and work, and somehow still feel useless in the face of it all."

"And then other days, it feels as though we've saved the world," Ida continued, shrugging her shoulders. "I'm not sure we'll truly feel the scope of victory or defeat until all of this is over. We've just got to keep going, haven't we?"

Brigitte looped her arm through Ida's as they entered the church. "We certainly have, and we certainly will."

Ida glanced at her friend as they passed the basin of holy water. "Don't you need to touch that?"

"If I were alone, I would," she replied without concern. "But as you won't, and I don't want to call attention to that, I will not. I think God will understand."

"That's how we feel about the mezuzah," Ida murmured.

"The what?"

Ida smiled at her friend's confusion. "The piece of Torah every Jewish home has in their doorway. We touch it upon entering or exiting the house. But we've all taken them down for the time being. It would be a simple way for us to be spotted. It feels unnatural entering one of our homes without it, even for me. I've been non-practicing for ages, and yet . . ."

"The traditions stick with you, don't they?" Brigitte hummed a sound that was a combination laugh and expression of thought. "I'm not sure Catholics and Jews are all that different, in that regard."

"Don't say that too loudly," Ida laughed. "Someone might curse you."

Brigitte grinned at her. "Not in this convent. Perhaps others, but not here."

That was true, in Ida's experience. The atmosphere and culture of this convent was truly one of warmth and acceptance from every person she had ever encountered, and that sort of attitude most certainly came from the top.

The Mother Superior had clearly cultivated the spirit of this convent, and it was a credit to her.

Not that she would accept such credit, but there it was.

They walked through the catacombs to Sister Marie-Aurélie's office and found her waiting for them at the door. She waved as though someone might scold her for doing so if it was too exuberant, but she could not contain the joy in her features nor in the action. It reminded Ida of some of the little girls they had hidden recently, their hand waves down at the level of their hips, but not lacking in exuberance.

Perhaps that was what was so charming about Sister Marie-Aurélie. She was, in truth, a child at heart.

"I could not believe my good fortune when I learned I would be seeing both of you today!" the Mother Superior gushed when they reached her. "What a treat!"

"Not many people use those words to describe visits from me, Sister," Ida assured her with a laugh.

Sister Marie-Aurélie raised a brow at her. "Then they don't know you like I do. Come in." She waved for them to follow her and entered her office, shutting the door behind them before moving around the desk and sitting in her chair.

"How have things been since the attempted raid, Sister?" Ida asked when they were settled, turning immediately to business. "Any more trouble with the Gestapo?"

"Not a bit," came the firm reply. "I anticipated having repeated checks, since they had been told we were housing Jewish girls that first time, but no one has come by, not even that miserable Fat Jacques. Now, perhaps it is only because we have not had Jewish students here, and whoever betrayed us the first time knows that, but we will not know until we try again."

Brigitte made a disapproving sound, her brow creasing. "And you think it is worth trying again? I would love to have children here again, Sister, but not acting as bait."

Sister Marie-Aurélie hesitated a moment, then seemed to slouch without losing an ounce of her posture. "I may have already tested something of the sort."

Ida felt herself actually slouch against the back of her chair. "You what? But we haven't placed any children here since last time—how did you . . . ?" She looked at Brigitte in desperation, but her friend looked just as confused.

"This was a private placement," the Mother Superior explained. "The neighbor of a member of our congregation. Our congregant approached the priest to ask what intervention might be possible, and the priest came to me. We housed the family for a few weeks, and when it was clear that no one was betraying us, we began to relax our restrictions on them. One fine day, they wanted to go out for a walk. I suggested that our garden might be the best option, as it is rather large but still enclosed and safe."

A curling feeling of dread began to claw at Ida's insides, and her fingers clutched the arms of her chair as though she could hold off the impending revelation.

"They chose to leave the convent for their walk," Sister Marie-Aurélie said on a heavy sigh. "We never saw them again."

Though she had anticipated it, Ida gasped at the result. Her eyes darted to Brigitte, who had closed her eyes in horror, her throat moving on a swallow.

"Maybe they wanted to buy something for the girls," the Mother Superior went on sadly. "Who can know the reason? They were such precious little girls. One might have thought they were twins, but they were over a year apart. Just the two girls and their parents. A loving, wonderful family. We haven't heard anything about them, and we don't dare inquire."

"But no one has been by the convent making inquiries since they've disappeared?" Brigitte asked, her voice pained.

The sister shook her head firmly from side to side. "Not even once. I would not have asked for this meeting if I had any lingering concerns." Her mouth quirked in a faint smile. "I have none. I firmly believe that if our sweet family had remained within our walls, they would still be here. And I believe we are once again a safe place for children, if you can trust us with them."

"Trusting *you* was never the issue," Ida said through suddenly dry and stiffened lips. "Nor your fellow sisters. But we do not know where the betrayal came from, and with times as they are . . ."

"A smaller number of children, then," the Mother Superior begged. "Please. We are desperate to be of use to our Jewish brothers and sisters. We have no worldly goods to offer for their aid, and our prayers have not ceased, but while God can work mighty miracles according to His will, we who have mortal hands must use them to do all the good we can."

Ida and Brigitte exchanged looks, their concerns clearly shared, but the offer so poignant, so pleading, and from so generous a soul . . .

"I will look at the requests coming in," Ida relented, biting the inside of her lip and shaking her head, "and see which ones might be suitable. Then I will have Brigitte examine the ones I am considering. If we both agree, we will come to you about placement."

"Thank you," Sister Marie-Aurélie said on a rush of air. "Thank you, my friends. It is God's work that you do here. I only wish to play a role."

Brigitte laughed very softly. "You have already played a role of great significance, Sister. No one could argue otherwise. Even Fat Jacques would agree, though he has nothing to arrest you for. One could even argue that you have done more than enough."

The nun shook her head. "No, I counter that argument heartily. There is no 'more than enough' when in the service of our fellow man. I have taken vows of poverty, chastity, and obedience, but nowhere in those vows does it say that I will also live by a vow of self-interest."

"There is a noted difference between self-interest and self-preservation," Ida protested.

"Not to me," the sister shot back with surprising vehemence. "I will not put my fellow sisters in harm's way, but they made no objections to our ruse for the Gestapo, and that was quite the uncomfortable experience. I have no doubt they will all agree with me on this."

It appeared to Ida that argument here was fruitless.

Perhaps argument anywhere was fruitless anymore.

Ida allowed herself to smile at this devoted nun. "What ages would you prefer, Sister? So that the children will blend in well with your existing students."

The conversation that followed was animated, but short, and then Ida and Brigitte were on their way out, parting at the gate and moving on to the next requirement of the day for themselves. Ida was not certain what Brigitte was working on for the present, but she had another family to visit.

Just one little girl, she had been told, though the age was not clear. One child was always easy to pick up and then settle somewhere. But Ida was feeling a little tenderhearted at the moment, what with the revelations of the day.

She would find the best situation she possibly could for this girl, no matter what it took.

"Jeanne! Jeanne, help!"

Ida turned quickly at the cry of distress, taking in the form of Claire coming toward her at a fast clip. "Catherine? What is it?"

Tears streamed down Claire's face, and she carried something in her arms. "I don't think she's breathing, Jeanne! Help!"

Ida looked more closely at what Claire carried and gasped. She held a blue-faced infant within the blankets. "Where did she come from?" she cried, taking the baby from Claire's arms and rubbing her back rapidly.

"I was in Malines just now," Claire told her amid gasping tears. "Maurice found a way for me to go into the camp officially as a social worker. I was seeing to some children when I was taken to see someone else. A woman had just had a baby, and she was afraid the Nazis would kill it. She had seen it happen to others. She begged me to take her baby out and get her to safety. She's only a few days old, Jeanne, and I cannot—"

Ida pressed her mouth over the infant's nose and mouth and gently breathed twice, then rubbed the baby's chest while Claire rubbed the back.

"I hid her in my sleeve," Claire cried, hiccupping slightly. "There was no other way to do it. No bags were allowed. And there were soldiers everywhere on my way out. I was only able to take her out just now, and she's so blue. Jeanne, please—"

"I am not God, Catherine," Ida told her quickly. "Give the child a moment."

Then, miraculously, the infant whimpered and gave a soft cry, followed by a much louder gasp and wail.

"Oh, thank God," Claire sobbed, unbuttoning her sweater and wrapping it around the baby. "Yes, that's it, child. Cry and scream and breathe and live. Oh, Jeanne . . ." Claire buried her face in her hands, her entire frame trembling.

Emotions welling within her as the tiny child wailed beautifully in discomfort, Ida put a hand on her friend's shoulder. "You saved her life, Catherine. You have fulfilled your promise to her mother. Do you know the child's name?"

Claire nodded from behind her hands. "Miriam Grinveld."

"Marie Geybels it is." Ida cradled the baby, bouncing her softly and blinking away her own tears. "Perhaps Marie-Claire Geybels."

Claire lowered her hands, smiling through her tears. "Really?"

"Why not?" Ida asked, handing the baby to her. "I don't think her mother would object to a tribute to the angel who delivered her child from certain death."

Claire tucked the baby close, beaming down on her as though she herself had given birth. "I know we are not supposed to have favorites in this work, Jeanne. But this little one is going to have my very special attention for the entire war. She will live on if I have to rescue her again and again."

"Very good, Catherine." Ida rubbed her arm and sniffled softly. "Let's get her back to the office and find some proper clothing and blankets. And we will find the safest place we can for her."

CHAPTER 13

The Jew must be destroyed wherever we meet him! In so doing we commit no crime against life, but rather serve life's laws of battle, which always oppose that which is an enemy to healthy life. Our battle serves to maintain life.

—NAZI PROPAGANDA DISCUSSION GUIDE, SEPTEMBER/OCTOBER 1944

"Six years old is a very good age, don't you think?"

"I don't know, Mademoiselle Claude. I cannot do very much at six. Maybe when I am seven, I can do more."

Andrée barely held back laughter at the creative thoughts and explanations of her present charge, Sarah—now Simone—who was completely unaffected by her departure from her parents for the moment. She had a very matter-of-fact attitude about the entire situation and had not shed a single tear, despite seeing her mother's visible ones.

Perhaps she did not fully comprehend the circumstances that were requiring her to leave her home. Perhaps she had been relatively shielded from the hardship and abuses taking place all around her. Perhaps her innocence had protected her from the fear that had been so prevalent in her community.

Perhaps she simply had the sort of nature that allowed her to endure life with a smile.

Whatever it was, Andrée was delighted to be escorting her, and faintly wished they were going a bit further than just the outskirts of the city so she might enjoy more time with her.

They approached the train station hand in hand, and Andrée squeezed Simone's hand, shaking it playfully. "Now remember, your name is not Sarah; your name is now Simone. You are Simone."

Simone nodded fervently, her young brow furrowing up as though she was forcing herself to commit the name to memory.

Whether the child thought they were playing some game of pretend or not was unclear, but Andrée knew she had no idea what was at stake. Simone would be the one to slip and say both of her names at the same time when asked by another child for her name. Simone might not remember that she was Jewish, but she would reveal details of her life that would identify her as a Jew to anyone who knew what to listen for.

But Simone would also adapt to her new life quickly. She would forget her life as Sarah, for the most part, and would embrace the situation around her. The reality around her.

Was she old enough to keep the memories of her mother stored in her mind and heart? Would she be able to recognize the woman who had birthed her and raised her to this point when they were reunited? Would Sarah be a name that remained familiar to her, even if she could not presently claim it?

Andrée had wondered a great deal about the children they would reunite with their families at the end of this awful war. How would those reunions play out? Would there be fear? Would there be relief? The parents would never forget their children, but children forgot so easily. The toddlers and little children they had hidden would almost certainly forget. Would the scars forming on their mothers' hearts from this separation be opened anew when their children failed to embrace them? And what of these children hidden in homes of other faiths? Not all situations would allow the children to continue the practice of their faith, such as it was, or permit them to be excluded from how the new family practiced their own religion. What if some of the older children truly turned to a new faith? The bonds in the Jewish faith and tradition were strong; how would families and communities react to such a change?

There were so many complicating factors in the prospect of reunion that Andrée was already overwhelmed by them. They were not even anticipating an end to the war as yet, and she was already dreading what lay at the end of it.

How could she let herself get to such a place? Of course, the families would want to be reunited. Of course, the children would eventually remember their families. Of course, they would remember the time before they were hidden, if they were old enough.

All would be well. Not necessarily right away, but eventually.

She boarded the train with Simone, finding a pair of seats opposite a well-dressed, pleasant-looking, middle-aged couple. Andrée helped to settle Simone, then sat beside her, ruffling her hair gently as the girl smiled at her.

After a few minutes, the train pulled away from the station, and Simone began looking out the window with interest at the passing scenery.

"It's so pretty," Simone said as they passed through older parts of the city. "I didn't know it was pretty."

"Brussels is a lovely part of the world," Andrée told her with a smile. "And in a few minutes, you'll see something even more pretty. Green fields and wide-open countryside."

Simone turned to look at her, eyes bright. "Really? With sheep?"

Andrée laughed and patted her knee. "Yes, dear. With sheep."

"Oh," the lady across from them gushed, "what a lovely little girl you are! What is your name?"

Simone smiled, then frowned and looked up at Andrée. "What do I tell her: my real name or my new one?"

Andrée felt as though her heart came to a screeching halt in her chest, her entire body going cold. She could not gauge the reaction of the woman across from her, nor that of her husband, as her eyes were on Simone, and she dared not look at the couple now. She kept her expression as blank as she knew how, though she could not have said if she had initially reacted in a visible manner.

"You are such a playful girl, Simone," Andrée told her with a light laugh, stroking her cheek. "Tell the nice lady your name."

As she had hoped, Simone understood the cue, and turned to the woman. "My name is Simone DuPont."

The fact that she had not said Sarah David was a miracle, and Andrée was certain her heart would not resume its usual beating pattern for quite some time.

"It is a beautiful name, Simone," the woman told her, sounding perfectly comfortable with the initial response.

Andrée looked at her, forcing her expression into one of apology for effect.

The woman winked. "My little girl was the same way. From the age of five until seven, she would not respond to Jeanne. We had to call her Madeline, Angelique, or Sophie, and it did not particularly matter which one we used."

Andrée laughed at the image, content to let the well-meaning woman believe what she liked about Simone and her imagination. So long as no questions were asked regarding her real name or new name, it would suffice.

Thankfully, the couple departed the train at the next station, waving farewell to Simone and Andrée as they disembarked.

"I'm so sorry, Mademoiselle Claude," Simone whispered when they were alone. "I forgot who I am supposed to be."

That was a painful thing to hear.

Andrée gathered the girl into her arms, hugging her tightly. "Oh, it's all right, sweet girl. I know I have asked a difficult thing of you today. Just try to remember from now on that you are Simone, all right?"

She felt her nod against her shoulder and pulled back with a smile. "Would it help if you thought of Simone as a princess? And you are now Princess Simone?"

Simone's eyes lit up, and she nodded eagerly. "I have always wanted to be a princess!"

Andrée nodded in approval. "Excellent. But you are a secret princess. No one must know you are *Princess* Simone. Just Simone. Only you and I know that you are a princess."

Now that a game had been set, Simone grinned, swinging her legs a little where she sat. "Yes! It will be our secret. I love this game, Mademoiselle Claude!" She turned to look out of the window again, no doubt watching for sheep once more.

Smile fading, Andrée put a hand to her brow, closing her eyes briefly. How did one explain to a child that this was not a game, but a matter of life and death? And yet, a fearful child is no child at all, so she could not be told, if innocence was to be maintained.

What game were they playing in this life? How soon would Simone realize that this game had no end to it? Would she ever come to understand just how close they could have been to utter disaster because she did not know the dangers?

What was worse, Simone's mother was pregnant and due to deliver any day now. They had contacts in the maternity ward that would help them to hide the Jewish newborns, and Andrée had explained to Simone's mother that they would come to collect the baby as soon as the doctors told them the time was right.

With renewed tears, Simone's mother had stared at Andrée in agony. "How can you be so cruel?" she had whispered, the words ripping through Andrée's very soul.

Yet she knew that the woman had not necessarily meant them toward Andrée. Yes, Andrée would be the one taking the baby away from her, but this woman knew full well it was for her safety as well as that of her children. She knew that this was necessary, and she had agreed to it.

She was asking the world how it could be so cruel. She was asking the Nazis how they could be so cruel. She might even have been asking her God how he could be so cruel.

Fate. The universe. Nature. Existence.

How any of them could be so cruel?

Not Andrée.

Still, it had hurt, and Andrée had no answers to give her but to squeeze her hand and promise to place the children together.

She hadn't told Simone, but her fostering family would know. When the child was delivered to their home, they would tell Simone of the relationship and of the child's name.

Its new name. Not its Jewish name.

The sight of rolling hills and sheep entertained Simone perfectly until their stop, and she had hugged Andrée fiercely when she had delivered her to the fostering home. Andrée promised to visit her and reminded her of their game.

Simone had winked, which made Andrée laugh heartily; and then Andrée was off, back to the train station and Brussels.

If Andrée had retained her childhood faith, she would have prayed for Simone just then. Prayed for her to love her fostering family. To be not only well treated, but well cared for. To become part of the family she was staying with rather than an accessory to them.

As it was, Andrée took only a moment to silently cast her wishes for those things out into the world.

If anyone was listening, they would know what to do with them.

She took a few moments on the train to Brussels to doze, knowing she would need the rest before fetching her next child. A one-year-old being delivered to her by his older brother. It was a complicated situation for the CDJ this time. The mother had asked them not to come to her house to take the baby. She could not bear it. So, she had asked that her son take the child away, as though for an outing, and then she would not have to suffer such final farewells.

Andrée had asked Ida for some kind of reasoning for this behavior, but Ida had failed to give her any. There was no understanding the heart of a mother who must part with her children, and they simply needed to do as she asked, if at all possible.

Andrée did not like the idea of a boy of ten having to act as an operative in their organization in this way, but they had little choice if they wanted to save these siblings.

They would pick up the ten-year-old in a few days, though if there were specific details associated with that assignment, Andrée had not been told.

She could only hope this ten-year-old boy would not always have to be the adult he was being forced to at this moment. He deserved to be a boy of ten, and nothing more.

The train arrived in Brussels sooner than Andrée had anticipated, no doubt due to her dozing off, but as soon as she disembarked, she was on the alert again. The meeting place to pick up the baby had been set for just outside of a café, which, thankfully, was only a few blocks from the train station.

Her eyes swept from side to side along the street as she walked, looking for any sign of Fat Jacques or Gestapo intervention. She always wondered if Fat Jacques would remember her face if he saw her again after their meeting in the café. Would he be watching for her in Brussels as she walked about, seemingly minding her business? Would he think anything more of her role in what had taken place at the café? Did he believe her to truly be only a social worker?

She was not a Jew, of course, so he would not be looking to round her up, but if she were suspected of helping Jews, she could be in danger indeed. But, according to Andrée's experience, Ida had been right: her Aryan appearance was her greatest asset. None of the Germans viewed her as a problem or as suspicious.

Imagine how any of them would feel if they knew the truth.

A clicking sound brought her attention to her right, and she saw a street photographer, his camera pointed in her direction. She frowned slightly, which prompted a wave from him, as though to reassure her.

Street photographers were a common enough sight, but what was one doing snapping a picture of her as she walked?

Andrée glanced behind her, out of curiosity, and nearly stumbled as she walked.

A German officer was walking some paces behind, his attention on shop windows. The photographer was at such an angle that he would have caught them both in his frame. Was he intentionally taking pictures of her? Did he know who she was? Did the German soldier behind her?

No one was shouting at her to stop, no one was rushing her in the street, and she had not reached her meeting place yet, so she had to keep going. Had to stick to the plan.

But her heart was now in her throat, beating furiously and drying her mouth, throat, and lungs with each and every pulse. Was she being compromised? Had she already been compromised? Was there some greater action taking place against suspect members of the CDJ?

Should she abort this mission now?

She kept on walking, hands tingling by her sides as she walked, knees unstable. She'd have to report this, but if nothing happened, and if no one followed her . . .

She turned a block, though her destination was directly ahead of her, and neither the photographer nor the soldier followed her. She walked hastily down the block and turned the corner, examining the street behind her as she did so. No one following. No eyes on her. No concern for her direction. She continued on her path, moving farther ahead than she needed to so she could better examine any presence aware of her on this route.

No one taking pictures here, no soldiers in uniform, no man in plain clothes interested in what she was doing, and, best of all, no sign of that odorous lump, Fat Jacques.

She might not be safe enough to do many things, but she felt safe enough to fetch the baby from his brother.

She rounded the block to circle back to her original destination, and saw, to her relief, a boy who looked to be ten holding a squirming, chubby toddler. No adult in sight of them.

And no signs of suspicious creatures hanging about any of them.

Which meant Andrée now became the suspicious figure, as the boy had never met her. She could only hope he had been given some sort of description of her, or, at the very least, been told what she would say.

As though waiting for a bus or tram, Andrée moved to stand beside the boy, attention forward. "What a pretty baby," she praised, glancing over and smiling at the young one.

"Thank you," the brother replied. "He is one year of age."

The poor boy was almost shaking with fear, his tone stilted and his words careful. "You seem to take excellent care of him."

He looked up at her, swallowing. "I try to. We all try to. He's only a baby, after all."

"That he is." Andrée smiled in what she hoped was a reassuring manner. "Does he trust others easily? Or is he inclined to remain with his family?"

"It depends on the stranger." The boy looked at his brother for a long moment, then leaned him toward Andrée. "You can try and see."

The lad was clever, she would give him that. Mature for his youth and well aware of the dangers around them. He knew precisely what they were doing here and why.

He deserved to be a boy, Andrée thought again as she bounced his brother on her hip, making the baby giggle. He deserved to be at school with other boys, getting into mischief and scrapes, and learning by experience more than by warning.

She would take him to Father André, if he had room. He took excellent care of his students and charges and encouraged an atmosphere of learning as well as fun. Perhaps there, this boy could regain what was left of his childhood.

If there was any remaining in him.

"He seems to like you very much," the boy murmured, examining his brother with almost pained eyes. "That's good, isn't it?"

Andrée smiled at him. "Very. Do you think you can tell your mother that when you return home?"

He nodded. "She won't get out of bed anymore, but she will be pleased to hear that." He looked up at her. "You will come to get me soon, won't you?"

"I will," she assured him. "You must try to prepare your mother for that. Pack your own things if you must. I know this is impossible for her, but it is for the very best."

"Papa said as much. Once we're gone, they can hide. That is the plan." He squared his shoulders and seemed to age five years before her very eyes. "I will remind her that this is the plan, and we will all be reunited when we can."

Andrée rubbed his arm, hoping against hope that he could keep that conviction within his heart, and that somehow, his parents would take it into theirs as well. "Precisely. Now, catch this next tram and return home. Your mother will be anxious. I'll be by to collect you in a few days."

"You promise?" he asked in a very young voice, avoiding looking at her.

Ah, so there was a child still within him, despite his learned bravado and responsibility.

Bless him for that.

"I promise," Andrée said with all the firmness of her spirit.

His head immediately lifted, and he looked at the approaching tram. "Good day, then, Mademoiselle Claude."

Andrée smiled, patting the back of his young brother, still safely tucked in her arms and none the wiser. "Good day."

She watched as he boarded the tram and as it pulled away before moving from her position and carrying the delightful little boy in her arms toward his fostering home.

She really liked the family he was being placed with. They had children aged three and four, and a new baby themselves. They had Jewish neighbors that had endured hardship and had hidden the adults from both homes until an escape was possible. They had never been questioned by the Gestapo as to their neighbors or their disappearances, and they often had visits from family from the countryside at various points throughout the year.

It was the perfect place to house a Jewish child who would stay for an indeterminate time.

A nephew from the country, they would claim. His mother has fallen ill and is unable to tend to him the way he needs, so he is staying with them until she is well once more. So, he would become young Henri Breyne, and he would know a loving, playful time with them. One could hardly ask for a better situation.

They were delighted to receive him when she arrived, cooing and gushing over his plump cheeks and bright blue eyes, his dark curls, and his attempts at walking, which were minimally successful. He was eager to please and was laughing uproariously at the antics of his new brother and sister.

How long until he realized that his mother was not here?

Andrée shook the dismal thought away and took her leave, knowing he was well settled here, which was all she could wish.

The fallout from the hidden children situation would not be known until all was said and done, and the reunions that were possible had taken place. Until then, she could not afford to dwell on those thoughts. It might lead her to question what she was doing, and that she could not allow.

At her first opportunity, Andrée found a phone and called her handlers at the committee.

"Hello?" came a voice she did not know well but still recognized.

"This is Claude Fournier," she said in a low voice. "And I may or may not have been set up today."

There was a brief rustling sound, then the murmur of other voices. "What happened?"

"I was walking toward a pickup," Andrée told him, looking around to ensure she was not overheard. "And a street photographer took my picture. There was a German officer walking directly behind me. Neither followed me as I altered my route, and there was no sight of them at the meeting spot. Nor did anyone follow me to make delivery."

She waited while faint sounds of discussion took place, unable to keep from biting her lip or shaking her leg as she waited for insight and instruction. There was so much still to be done, so much more that she was determined to do. She could not be compromised. She could not be taken off these assignments.

She would refuse. Change her appearance. Change her name and get new papers. Anything.

"Claude," returned the voice from the other end of the line, "we feel that your best option is to find the street photographer and get the negative of the photo. If we have that in our possession, we think you will be out of any danger. Can you do this?"

"Yes," Andrée said at once, not taking the time to consider how she might accomplish the task. "Yes, I will do that."

"Very good," the voice replied. "Contact us when you are successful."

The line disconnected, and Andrée hung up the phone, exhaling heavily.

Find the photographer, in a city of photographers, and somehow get him to give up his negatives. There would be more pictures than just the one of her on there, and he might have captured the photo of his entire career in those depths. Would he really be willing to give them up for her?

She took a moment to replay the few moments with the photographer in her head, trying to remember his likeness. He had waved at her, so she had seen not only the form of him from behind the camera, but had a general idea of his appearance and features. If he was focused on capturing a specific area of Brussels, he might still be near where he was a few hours ago. There was still plenty of light to the day, so perhaps he had not returned to his residence to begin processing his photos.

Andrée began retracing her steps, making no attempts to hide her blatant looking around at each individual who potentially resembled the photographer. She asked about him to nearly everyone she passed when she reached the area where the picture was taken, and a few were able to give her some general directions to find the man. Thank goodness, he was still snapping pictures of people and places in the area, so others recognized him.

She wandered up and down the streets where he had been recently spotted, and was delighted to find him at last, focused on a fountain in the center of a square.

"Pardon me, monsieur," Andrée said without any preamble as she strode up to him. "Do you remember taking a picture of me this morning?"

He turned to look up at her and got to his feet quickly. "Yes, mademoiselle. I do."

She smiled as kindly as she could while being filled with nerves and impatience. "Might I have the negatives of that? I don't wish anyone to know that I was about, and it would be embarrassing for me to have that picture published."

He blinked at her, then smiled with surprising warmth. "Of course, mademoiselle." He reached into his bag and pulled out a canister. He opened the lid to show her the roll of film within. "So you know I do not trick you." He smiled again and handed it to her. "For you, mademoiselle. And may you enjoy the other pictures you find on there."

Andrée looked at the canister in disbelief, then back at the photographer. There was no possibility this could be so easy, and yet he seemed in earnest.

How could he be so amenable and put up no resistance? "Just like that?" she asked, knowing he would see her doubt.

He nodded. "How can I resist the request of a beautiful woman?" His smile grew rather pointedly then.

Aha! That was a special kind of motivation, but certainly not one she had intended.

Whatever worked, she supposed.

"Thank you, monsieur," she replied as she tucked the cannister into the pocket of her coat. "Most generous of you."

Without any further conversation that he might take as encouragement or invitation, she turned on her heel and got herself out of the square as quickly as she could, taking care to alter her route as though she were on assignment. He was not quite the Gestapo or Fat Jacques, but her evasive actions were still required.

There was no time for flirtatious interest at this moment.

After reaching the sixth block away from the photographer, with no sign of him or anyone else following, Andrée allowed herself to sigh with relief. She started in the direction of her flat and stopped at the nearest phone to dial in.

It rang twice, then picked up. "Hello?"

"It's Claude," Andrée said, smiling her first true smile in some time. "I have the negatives."

CHAPTER 14

The Jew is the parasite of humanity. He can be a parasite for an individual person, a social parasite for whole peoples, and the world parasite of humanity.

—PAMPHLET FOR THE NAZI PARTY'S INTERNAL EDUCATION PROGRAM, 1943

Ida pinched the bridge of her nose, groaning to herself. "Are you serious?"

"Entirely. I met with her this morning, and Madame von Volden wants her to convert. So, she's asked to be placed elsewhere."

"I don't blame her." Ida shook her head and leaned her elbows on her desk, moving her hands to grip the back of her neck. "Poor Regina. She was so happy to be there. It was close enough to Charles that they were able to meet up on occasion. They've no one else, you know. The parents were taken, the oldest brother is somewhere in the war, a sister is in the camps, a brother went to a work camp to try to help."

Andrée tsked softly. "It must be serious for her to ask for removal with all of that."

"Asking a Jewish girl to convert and expecting her to do so *is* serious," Ida grumbled, squeezing her neck tightly. "She shouldn't have to be anything different while being hidden, aside from her name. It defeats the entire purpose of hiding them. If all of the Jews converted, there wouldn't be much of a problem."

"I don't know," Andrée murmured with a hiss. "I think the Nazis would consider that a false conversion and forbid it. Or exert worse pressure."

"Probably." Ida lowered her hands to her lap and sat back roughly against her chair. "If there is worse. But if anyone can find a way, the Nazis would." She pursed her lips, trying to think of a situation that would best suit Regina. But whatever she thought up would take her further from Charles.

Charles was with Madame Martine, and Ida wasn't particularly comfortable with that arrangement either. She had three children with her, all told, and there had been reports that German soldiers regularly called at her residence as well. The children were well, according to welfare visits, but Ida had the same feeling of discomfort whenever she thought of that arrangement.

"We'll find some place," Ida grumbled, sitting forward and beginning to toy with a pen. "Maybe the cartographer and his family would like to have her."

"I can check on that for you," Andrée offered, making a note in her diary. "We already know they are willing to take in Jewish children, so a visit wouldn't involve too many questions or too much time."

Ida looked at her operative with a raised brow, smiling a little. "Do you have something else in mind for me to do?"

Andrée returned her smile, looking almost shy. "You said you wanted to visit Yvonne. Why not do it today?"

"She is so busy," Ida protested, shaking her head and rearranging the papers before her just to make herself seem more occupied. "She's been working tirelessly since Ghert was arrested. She won't want to take some time to talk, not with all she has going on."

"You knew Yvonne before you came into the CDJ, right?" Andrée cocked her head, causing her smile to go crooked. "You are her friend."

Ida nodded, avoiding direct eye contact. "I am her friend, and I have been for years."

"Don't you think your friend, whose husband has been arrested and whose son now lives apart from her, could use a friend, even if she is exceptionally busy?"

The gentle prodding might well have been a jab in the side with a sharp stick by a determined seven-year-old, as it had a similar effect.

Ida squirmed in her seat and looked at Andrée with pursed lips. "I suppose."

Andrée laughed and pushed out of her chair, taking her diary over to one of the other desks. "You suppose. Well, why don't you 'suppose' while walking over to the main office and asking? I can manage here for a bit. Catherine and Solange are out on assignment. Can you rearrange whatever else is on your schedule to allow for a bit of friendship?"

"Fine, yes, I'll go," Ida groaned. "There is nothing crucial on my calendar until this afternoon. Perhaps I can convince Yvonne to go to lunch, or at least take a walk."

"Perhaps you can," Andrée allowed. "I think it would do you both good."

Ida looked at her friend, her roommate, and, in many ways, her confidante. "You think so?"

Andrée smiled over her shoulder, nodding. "I know so, Jeanne. I can hear you sometimes crying in the night. I think you need a walk with a friend. If Yvonne turns you down, against your better efforts, then I'll go for a walk with you."

It was the kindest offer Ida had received in a long time, and, for a moment, she wondered if she might actually cry now instead of later.

Or perhaps tears would be present both now and later. Or throughout. Perhaps she would always be close to tears until this war was over.

Or perhaps she would lose the ability to cry.

Her throat tightened with emotion, and she tried to swallow in spite of it. "Thank you, Claude. And the next time you hear me cry, you can say something. I know you cry as well."

"We all cry in private," Andrée replied without much emotion. "We'd never get through this if we cried in public as well."

Taking the finality in her tone as a cue to end the conversation, Ida pushed back from her desk and rose, walking toward the door and taking her coat off the peg. She slipped her arms in as she exited, and, per usual, started off in the opposite direction of the main office.

It was becoming habit now, taking long and roundabout ways of getting places. Particularly the places she regularly frequented. It was the best way to ensure that she wasn't followed, or, if she was, that the pursuer would lose interest or become confused as to where she was going. She hadn't felt followed as yet, and had no proof that she had been, but she could not trust that it would never happen. Or that she would never feel it.

She had dreamed of being discovered and arrested by Fat Jacques more often than she cared to admit, even to herself.

She did her best to breathe in and out slowly in the chilly air, though the day was fair, and the blue sky lightened her spirits simply by existing. Days upon days had felt like a dreary overcast, regardless of their actual state, and she had gone about them without noticing any of the weather's details. But today, she saw the blue sky.

And that was soul-lifting.

Ida even found herself smiling as she turned the final corner of her route, taking her onto Rue de la Brasserie, the offices straight ahead. Despite everything she and her family had been through, Yvonne had continued to work for the CDJ after Ghert had been arrested. She refused to go into hiding or to leave the city.

She was no longer living at the family home, but as Ghert had held no information about the CDJ offices in his briefcase, there hadn't been danger in the office becoming compromised. And Yvonne had argued with every single person who had attempted to convince her otherwise. She was as committed to this work as ever, and with the Heibers and her husband imprisoned, they would need all the help they could get.

No one could argue her point there, and her presence was inspirational to everyone else working. Any personal complaints or situations felt pitiful compared to Yvonne's reality, though she wouldn't have wanted anyone to feel that way. She would have said that they ought to think of the Heibers both being in Malines and what they must be enduring, knowing they were both there and unable to help those outside of the walls.

Ida had privately wondered if the Heibers might have had more comfort *because* they were together, but that was not exactly something she could suggest to Yvonne.

She entered the office and made her way toward the back, nodding at those she recognized and smiling at those she knew, but not taking the time to talk to anyone. There was only one person she was interested in speaking with, and if she allowed herself to become distracted by others, or even the work they were doing, she would not follow through.

She was already anticipating refusal of her offer, if not teasing for suggesting the idea.

But it couldn't hurt to try.

Yvonne was poring over paperwork at her desk, as occupied with her work as ever, and completely unaware of anyone's approach.

She'd never been driven to that extreme as long as Ida had known her. Something was driving Yvonne beyond her usual nature, and there was no need to guess what that was.

Ida cleared her throat as she reached Yvonne's desk, pausing there to smile in anticipation.

Yvonne looked up, an almost wild light in her eyes. She blinked, and the wildness disappeared, replaced by her usual warmth. "Ida! What a pleasant surprise! I didn't know you were reporting in today."

"I'm not," Ida told her friend simply. "I've come to ask if you'd like to go to lunch or for a walk."

That was clearly not what she had expected Ida to say, nor, according to her bewildered, almost startled expression, had she ever thought of the idea herself.

"Why?" Yvonne asked, her voice tight and stiff.

Ida eyed her friend with the sort of directness Yvonne had always appreciated from her. "Because we need it."

Why she had decided to include herself in the statement, Ida wasn't sure. Andrée had told her that she needed the interaction with her friend, but Ida hadn't let herself go to such a place in her mind. But now, facing this woman, knowing she would perfectly comprehend what Ida was struggling with, and that Ida might be able to help Yvonne bear the weight of her own burdens, she could not say that this visit was only for Yvonne.

Ida needed this, too.

How had Andrée seen that, and Ida had not?

Something wordless passed between the friends now, something that was deeper than expressions or edifices. It was as though Ida could feel Yvonne peeling back the layers of defense she had put up for everyone else and could peer into her very heart.

She'd always had that ability, but Ida had forgotten what it felt like.

Yvonne slowly began to nod, her lips not quite forming a smile. "Yes, I think we do. I am not hungry, but a walk would do me good." She got up and gestured for Ida to lead the way back out, taking her coat from the stand nearby and tossing it on without doing up any buttons.

Out in the bright day, Yvonne paused on the step, closing her eyes and tilting her face back in the sun, exhaling slowly.

Ida linked her arm with her friend's, content to wait for her to take this moment.

"Sometimes I forget that the sun is warm," Yvonne murmured. "More and more these days. The sun is always just what makes the day a day. But I forget that it's also warm."

"I understand." Ida rubbed Yvonne's arm gently. "The world is hard and exhausting. More for you, I think."

Yvonne returned her head and face to center and stepped down, starting to walk the block. "Just different for me. We all knew the risks going in. Ghert knew them. Maurice and Esta knew them. Odile knew them. And those of us on the outside still know them all too well."

Ida glanced at her, not surprised by the deflection, but not believing that Yvonne's suffering was the same as the rest, no matter what she said. "But?" she eventually prodded.

Yvonne did smile now, though there was no joy in it. "But I miss my husband," she confessed, her voice hitching. "I haven't heard anything since his arrest. I don't know where he is, if he is well, if he is even alive. I know nothing, and knowing nothing is worse than any outcome."

"Is it?"

She nodded. "I don't know if I should hope or not. I don't know what to dread. I don't know what to think or what to pray for. I am stuck in place, unable to move in any direction because I do not know in what direction my path now lies. It is paralyzing, Ida."

Ida pulled her friend closer, wishing that proximity would allow for a transference of emotion so she might bear some of her sorrows for her. "I'm so sorry," she whispered.

"A week ago, one of our contacts said that arrangements could be made to allow me to go and see Ghert in complete safety," Yvonne told her, lowering her voice.

"What?" Ida cried. "How? Where?"

"In the prison at St. Gilles," Yvonne said in a near whisper. "It had been suggested to him by someone, an Augustinian father, who we now suspect is a German agent. Our contact was unaware of the father's loyalties and thought it would be worth trying."

Something in the center of Ida's chest began to burn, the sensation becoming awkward and uncomfortable. It was too easy, too convenient an opportunity, and why would such a person offer such an opportunity so long after Ghert's arrest?

Unless he hadn't been transferred to Malines and truly had been kept in the St. Gilles prison all this time.

"Did you go?" Ida asked, unsure if she wanted to know the answer.

Yvonne sniffed once. "We have our own contacts in St. Gilles. Ghert was not there. If he is not there, he is either in Malines or a camp, if he lives. The Nazis would not bring him back to Brussels if they valued him as a prisoner. It would be an invitation for us to try to break him free."

Ida frowned. "So . . ."

"It was a trap," Yvonne said simply. "The father would have betrayed me to the Germans. No doubt, they suggested the idea to him. Perhaps I should take it as a sign that Ghert is alive and the Germans feel that, had they succeeded in their trap, it might have convinced him to give up information. Either way, our contact was most displeased to hear of the trap and apologized for wanting to risk my safety."

"He couldn't have known, surely," Ida protested as they crossed the street, a car slowing as it neared them, then speeding up once it passed them safely.

Still, it had made her limbs freeze.

"No," Yvonne confirmed. "He could not have known. All the same, he felt it best to move Paul again after that."

Ida nodded at the wisdom of the suggestion, then ventured to ask, "How is Paul?"

Yvonne sighed. "Too old for his age, too young to understand, too confused by all of the changes. I don't see him often."

"Why not?" Ida pressed before she could stop herself. "Isn't he safe?"

"Of course, he's safe," Yvonne snapped defensively. She took a breath, exhaled, then gave Ida a small smile. "I'm sorry. I don't mean to bark. I just . . ." She looked away, sighing.

"You don't have to tell me," Ida said quickly. "It's really none of my business."

Yvonne shook her head. "I need to talk. I didn't know it, but I do." She swallowed once. "It's hard. Being with him and being away from him. When I'm with him, he just wants me to stay. He wants to see me at all times. He cries so when I leave. He told his landlord that he is going to marry me so I'll always be with him."

Ida clucked her tongue sympathetically. "Oh, bless him."

"And he asks about Ghert," Yvonne went on, as though she hadn't heard her. "He says, 'Is Papa in Liège?' or 'Papa is working late?' or 'Does Papa know where I am?' and I never know what to say."

"Why would he think Liège?" Ida asked as Yvonne turned them around the next block. "Did Ghert go there often?"

Her friend was silent for a moment as they walked, her expression more distant than stoic. "We said he went away to Liège when he was arrested. It was easier than trying to explain. He has already had to adjust to living apart from us, to living in different places, to going by a different name . . ."

He was a hidden child, Ida realized. She blinked twice as the thought percolated in her mind, seeming to ignite various parts of her brain when it reached them. He was living the very life their Jewish children were enduring. He was, of course, a Jewish child himself, but his parents were not hiding. They were working with resistance groups. Practically running this particular resistance group. Ghert had been arrested in the course of working in the resistance group.

And Yvonne was showing no sign of letting up in her work.

"Ida? Ida."

Ida shook herself and looked at her friend. "What?"

Yvonne's eyes were wide and curious. "Where were you just then?"

"With our hidden children." Ida smiled at her. "And thinking how your Paul is just like them."

Yvonne looked away, sniffling once. "I've had that thought myself. I am terrified that if I don't visit him on occasion, he will completely forget who I am. I now understand how these mothers beg us to let them see or communicate with their children. Being forced to be parted from them is agony, even if we know it is for their good and our own. It is a piece of our heart living outside of us, and we're unable to touch it or hold it or even claim it as our own."

She had never heard Yvonne speak with such passion, let alone with such pain, and it made Ida ache to her core that there was nothing she could do to alleviate it. Nothing she could do to make it better. No promises she could make of a brighter tomorrow.

All she could do was continue to walk beside her friend, remind her that she was not alone, and continue to listen.

It wasn't enough. It wasn't nearly enough.

But it was all she had.

"And so, I work," Yvonne told her suddenly, her voice stronger. "I work with rage. I drown myself in our work so that I feel less broken, less helpless, and less afraid."

"Does it work?" Ida asked.

Yvonne's brow creased just a little. "Sometimes."

She said nothing after that, just continued to walk beside Ida and keep her chin up. That Yvonne was even upright was a feat, in Ida's eyes, but she was striding with confidence, or perhaps willpower, and moving forward.

It was nothing if not inspirational.

"Should we make our way back?" Ida suggested as gently as she could.

Yvonne surprised her by shaking her head. "No, I'd like to keep walking with you a while. Tell me about your work. How are our girls? How are the houses? Any issues I need to be aware of?"

"We're not having a business discussion on this walk," Ida protested, laughing at the rapidity of questions from her friend.

Yvonne sighed, more playfully than genuinely. "So be generic. I want to hear how *you* are doing, and I know you're doing a lot of work! This walk—much like this friendship—is not all about me. So, tell me what you need to, and let's both leave this walk feeling better."

There was no arguing with that, and Ida had to laugh as her friend swiftly and rather neatly took control of the conversation. But she would let her. If Yvonne wanted to help relieve Ida's burden, just as Ida wanted to relieve hers, it was only right that she be allowed to try.

"The girls are incredible," Ida began, the constant tension in her chest beginning to ease. "Truly, I don't know how we got so lucky with having them in our ranks."

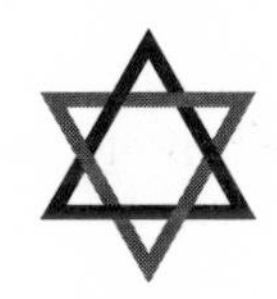

CHAPTER 15

Here is the Jew, as all can see,
Biggest ruffian in our country;
He thinks himself the greatest beau
And yet is the ugliest, you know!

—ELVIRA BAUER, GERMAN ART STUDENT AND CHILDREN'S BOOK AUTHOR, 1936

"Mademoiselle Claude, why may I not say that my name is Esther?"

Andrée smiled kindly at the girl beside her on the train, though she was close to exasperation. Not with her necessarily, but with the taking of five children at once to a convent near Ghent in winter. It was her own fault; she had said she could do it, but she hadn't thought through the specifics of the task when she'd said so.

A child in her lap, one at her side, and three across from them looking at her with wide eyes were quite the bunch to manage, though none of them were loud or rambunctious. They were quiet, well-behaved, and bore little resemblance to each other, so no one would believe she was travelling with a family.

If they were asked no questions, it would be no issue.

If there were questions, however . . .

"Mademoiselle Claude?"

Andrée returned her attention to the moment. "I'm so sorry, dear. Ask me again."

Remarkably unperturbed, she did so. "Why may I not say that my name is Esther?"

What could Andrée possibly say to such a deceptively simple question? It was one Andrée asked herself every time she picked up a child and gave them their new name.

She met the girl's eyes as directly as she could, given their position and height difference. "Esther is a marvelous and beautiful name, but where you are going, it is better that you should be called Jeanine."

That seemed to satisfy Esther—now Jeanine—and she looked out of the train window once more.

Andrée bounced the little boy in her lap, more to amuse herself than him. What else could she say? She had searched and searched, amidst all of the pickups and deliveries she'd helped children through, and she still had not found an answer that satisfied her.

How did one explain to a child that, right now, in this place, it was dangerous to be Esther, Rachel, Jacob, or David? How did you tell a child that she was being hunted? Or that he was being forced to wander away from his family at his tender age? How did anyone explain that to survive, you had to hide, and sometimes multiple times? And not only hide your person, but your name, your religion, your language, your heritage.

How did anyone tell these children that they had to be completely silent about their address, their family—their entire identity?

It was cruel. It was the only way to save them, but it was cruel.

And it was better than the barbarity that was the alternative.

Andrée hugged the little boy—now named Max—a little more tightly to her. He allowed it without complaint, unaware of just how precious he was to her in this moment. Sources of comfort were hard to come by, and when tears were her greeting upon procuring the children, and tears were what she felt when she left them, all she had were these moments with them.

Where she could appreciate that they were children. Where she could try to lighten the mood for them. Where she could entertain and play with them. Where she could build trust and help them approach the unknown with optimism.

If she could do nothing else during her custody of them, at least she could give them something bright in their ever-darkening world.

"Mademoiselle Claude," the little girl—now Clara—across from her suddenly said, smiling shyly. "Your eyes are the color of winter sky; did you know that?"

Andrée smiled back at her, oddly touched. "And yours are the color of warm chocolate. My very favorite."

The girl giggled and looked at her companions in delight. "And Delphine's are green like leaves on the trees at my *bubbe's* house."

Delphine shushed her at once, loudly, and looked at Andrée in horror. Clara covered her mouth with both hands, losing all signs of mirth that had been there.

It took a moment for Andrée to realize that Clara had said something in Yiddish, as she didn't speak a word of it. On some occasions, she might have been perturbed by the slip. But today, somehow, she maintained her serenity as well as her smile. "It's all right."

"I'm so sorry, Mademoiselle Claude," Clara whispered.

Andrée reached over and put a hand on her knee. "It's fine, Clara. Tell me more about that tree."

Clara gave her an uncertain look, but at Andrée's nod of encouragement, she went on. "It's very tall. One side of the leaves is green, and the other side is white. Sometimes the leaves look more gray than green. And it's a perfect tree to climb."

She continued to rattle away about the tree and its facets, entertaining the other children who had apparently only known life in the city. Andrée half listened as she looked around the train.

No one was looking in their direction. No one seemed even remotely interested in them. It was the best situation Andrée, or any of her cohorts for that matter, could hope for when escorting children to their fostering homes.

And yet . . .

There was something that Andrée did not like. Something about the situation that she was not comfortable with. Something that set her on edge and made her more alert than she had been just moments before.

She let her eyes slowly cast over each person in the train car. Many of the men wore fedoras, and many of the women had their heads down, but suddenly she didn't care about faces. She wanted to see the posture and tension in frames. Reactions to sounds. Points of focus, whether by eye or by some other method. Couples who were not actually couples. Anything that would stand out or strike her as unusual.

Anything that did not sit right. Anything that she might recognize as a tactic members of the CDJ might use when traveling together. She knew that there were members of the public who reported to Fat Jacques and the Gestapo. Could they be on this train? Her mind was awhirl with the dangers she and her associates faced every day.

She had witnessed friends being compromised, families being given up to the authorities. Contacts who had failed to show up for appointments with her comrades due to arrest. Families stating their willingness to host Jewish children and then suddenly entertaining Nazi soldiers in their homes. Those very same soldiers playing with children they had vowed to see crushed, thinking they were simply orphans of no consequence. Parents learning there were Jewish children hidden amongst the students at their children's schools and creating a scandal for the nuns . . .

And then there was the increasing tension she felt from all of the "almost" moments that had occurred of late. Those could frighten one to the core. Increasing requests for papers when on assignment. Being sometimes in possession of sensitive information but somehow managing to get away. Smuggling children out moments before a raid, confusing and enraging the authorities. Constantly being forced to face the real dangers and risks of opposing the Nazi regime.

Andrée looked through the train car with narrowed, keen eyes, even as the content little boy on her lap relaxed more fully into her.

Would any of these people here truly wish to round up little children and see them destroyed?

One should never be fooled by appearances; that much she had learned. Even an outwardly cruel person like Fat Jacques could be something more than an obvious villain. Most would never have guessed that he ought to have been one of the hunted. One of the arrested.

One of the imprisoned.

As though conjured from her very thoughts, a man raised his face as Andrée's eyes fell on him. The sight of the round, reddened cheeks, beady eyes, and thick moustache made her stomach drop, seemingly from her body down to the tracks beneath the train. He scowled, screwed up his mouth, twitched his moustache, then raised a newssheet in front of the majority of his face.

How could he be here? *How* could he be on this train? In this very car at this moment?

She had too many children with her to manage a full escape from this. She had false papers for them, of course, and for herself. Those ought to pass inspection. But if he recognized her from the café all those months ago, he might have more suspicions about what she was doing with these children, heading out of Brussels, and what business a social worker and teacher had with being an escort, and . . .

The paper shifted again, and she caught sight of his face once more.

Impossibly, somehow, it wasn't Fat Jacques at all.

She blinked once, then again, positive that she would soon see him once more in the features of this man, but he was not there.

The face was round and red, the hair was dark, the eyes were small, and the moustache was full, but the arrangement of features was all wrong. Had the similarities between the men been enough to convince her at first glance that it was the man she feared? Was she truly under so much strain that she was beginning to hallucinate the enemy within her presence? Or was she simply terrified?

Of course, she was terrified. They all were, every one of them. But they would not stop because of that fear. They could not.

Was she forgetting that?

She took in a slow breath, then released it as silently as possible, reminding herself of their safety, their security, and the provisions in place to protect them all on these assignments. No one knew she had the children on the train today, or where she was taking them. They would not be discovered here, and, most importantly, Fat Jacques was not on this train.

He was not here.

Andrée swallowed and placed the back of one hand to her cheek, wishing the hand was cooler so as to provide her some consolation in the moment. But at least she was not perspiring to an obvious degree, if her cheek was any indication. Children were remarkably observant, and if the group of them with her thought she was distressed . . .

"Who can see sheep out of the windows there?" she asked, unsure if she was interrupting any ongoing conversation. "Can you count them? There's so many!"

The girls immediately seemed to plaster themselves to the train windows to look at the sheep, counting in discord with each other and getting confused by the speed of the train and the numbers previously counted. Soon they were all giggling too much to count anything at all, and something about the sound did more to comfort Andrée than any breathing techniques or alteration of thoughts could have.

The children were what mattered here. They were the whole focus of their operation. Saving their lives, attempting to allow their parents to save themselves, trying to secure some sort of future for them that did not involve shame, abuse, or imprisonment.

Trying to give them any sort of childhood in a world that would have wiped them out entirely.

It was a humbling task, given the scale. And they were not perfect. They had not saved every Jewish child in Belgium, and they could not. They had no illusions of never losing a single Jewish child again.

All they wanted to do was save the ones they could.

As many as they could.

That was why she was facing fears and dangers to her own life. That was why she would combat her panicked thoughts and suspicions to keep going.

The children deserved a chance to survive.

The train came to a slow and steady stop at the next station, which was not theirs, and Andrée asked the girls to find the most interesting thing they could see from their windows while at this station. The girls observed everything from a red coat to a hat with flowers, and they took great pleasure in shouting out their discoveries with glee. Even Max strained for the window to see, but the only thing that captured his attention was a small, fluffy dog in the arms of a well-dressed woman.

New passengers came into their car, and Andrée paid little attention to them other than allowing her eyes the natural inclination to look at something new.

For the second time in a single train journey, her stomach dropped, this time taking her heart with it.

Four Nazi soldiers in full uniform loaded into the car. Laughing and chatting with each other, completely indifferent to their surroundings. Nearly all of the passengers in the car were uneasy now, tense in their seats and sitting up a little straighter. The only sounds were those of the girls still calling out things they saw, and their voices seemed too loud, too cheerful, too ill-suited for this entire situation.

But Andrée had no power to silence them. The sudden shift in volume and ambiance would be jarring, and she could not risk the Nazis noticing anything about them.

Max squealed when the dog he had been watching barked, and the Nazis looked over at him with smiles on their faces.

Smiles. Like any natural human might express when hearing the laughter of a child.

But they were not natural humans. They would have arrested her and these children if they knew who they were and what they were doing. They would have turned from smiling young men into the monsters they marched as. Proudly waving the flag that bore so much ill will and destruction to anyone who stood in its way.

Defiantly crushing the heads of men, women, and children that they considered lesser beings.

One of the soldiers looked at Andrée and smiled more broadly, nodding his head as though in some sort of compliment or praise for the brood she was managing.

She felt the corners of her mouth move to form the shape of a smile but could not be sure if she succeeded. Everything seemed frozen, without proper feeling, and she was slow to respond to any command she might have been given. She might have grimaced for all she could feel, and that wouldn't have done any of them any good.

But the soldiers took their seats and continued to talk among themselves, leaving the rest of their car to their own devices. Like any other passengers on a train might have done. Like Belgian soldiers might have done taking a train for leave. Like British soldiers might have done in a foreign land they were enjoying. Like the young men that they were in truth, and not like Nazi soldiers at all.

Could this really just be a coincidence? Could they simply be travelling to another destination and not interested in the passengers on this train at all? It seemed impossible, not to mention improbable, but the proof was before her. They were wholly focused on themselves and cared nothing for those around them.

It was a simple coincidence that she was on this train with them, taking Jewish children to a convent to hide them from Nazis.

She hadn't thought coincidences happened anymore. Not since the invasion. Not since she began working with the CDJ. Coincidences were traps. Plots. Dangerous. Deadly.

They were never innocent tricks of fate.

Yet here it was.

The train began to move again, and Andrée found herself checking the location of their bags, just in case a swift exit from the train was necessary. She did not fancy the idea of jumping from a moving train with five children, but she was certain she could turn that into a game if need be. Most things could be made entertaining with the right reasoning and enthusiasm.

How she would explain *that* in her report to the CDJ, she couldn't say. But extremes were sometimes needed.

She found herself unable to say a single word as the train moved to the next station, which was, fortunately, the one they needed. Until she and the children were off this train, walking freely, and arriving at the convent without any interference from Nazi soldiers, she would not breathe easy.

It seemed like an eternity before she felt the train slow again, and she released a quick, tight breath. "All right, children, gather your things please. Coats on."

The girls obeyed at once, and she helped Max with his coat. The train came to a full stop, and Andrée motioned that they should get up. The girls all took hands and started off the train in the direction she indicated. Andrée grabbed the bags and was startled to find one of the Nazi soldiers at her side, helping her with them.

"*Bitte, fraulein,*" he said with a smile, gesturing for her to exit.

It would have been rude to refuse, and a slight against his honor. She could not afford either.

"*Danke, Korporal,*" she murmured, eyeing the insignia on his uniform and hoping she'd guessed correctly.

At his nod, she turned and moved off the train with Max, feeling her heart pound in the soles of her feet as she moved.

Disembarking, she turned to reach for the bags, but the soldier whistled for the stationmaster, who came over like an obedient dog. "Take these for the *fraulein,*" he ordered, though he was not harsh about it. "Get her a cab. No fare."

"Of course, monsieur. Of course," came the blustering response as the stationmaster scrambled for the bags. "Right this way, madame."

Andrée forced herself to swallow her pride and revulsion, nodding at the soldier. "*Vielen dank.*"

"*Bitte schön, fraulein. Heil Hitler!*" He moved back inside the train before she had to respond, thankfully.

She might have spit upon the ground instead, and that would have had her shot.

"Madame?" the stationmaster prodded, nudging his head toward the way out.

Andrée exhaled slowly and turned to him with a true smile. "Yes, thank you, monsieur. And truly, I can pay for the fare."

He smiled, shaking his head. "With these precious little ones? I think not. It is my pleasure." He led them to the streets outside of the station and hailed a cab with more speed than she might have done. He helped her load the children into the cab, then banged on the roof of it to send it off.

Andrée shook her head at the ironic turn of events, and wondered even more now how she would explain the experience in her report. It was nice to take the cab to the convent, especially with the children and their small bags, but there was something about walking to the location hand in hand with the children that she would miss. Something innocent and playful, something actually resembling the childhood they were leaving behind.

Still, the sisters at this convent were particularly good, and she had no doubt the children would be loved and cared for.

Arriving at the convent, the cab driver got out quickly and took care of the bags for her, ringing the bell at the gate for the sisters. He tapped his hat and pinched Max's chubby cheek before leaving, no doubt returning to the station to collect a fare he might actually get paid for.

One of the nuns hurried to the gate, grinning when she saw Andrée and the children. "Oh! You must be Mademoiselle Fournier! And our beloved little children! Hello there!"

"Hello," the girls chimed in chorus, each of them seeming to use a different emotion to greet her.

She opened the gates and waved them in enthusiastically. "I'm Sister Marie-Joan. We have been waiting for you all day and are so happy to have you. Now, what are your names?"

The girls looked at Andrée, then at the sister.

"Delphine."

"Clara."

"Jeanine."

"Sophie."

There was something tragic in the recitation of their new names, something final and resigned that made Andrée want to cry. Made her want to take them all in her arms and tell them to forget everything she had said and become their true selves again.

But she knew better. And she kept silent.

"Darling!" the sister exclaimed. "You are such lovely, bright girls. Now, who would like some cake?"

The girls brightened in an instant, and Sister Marie-Joan laughed heartily. "I thought so. Sister Catherine there will take you to get some while Mademoiselle Claude and I talk."

Sophie looked at her with some suspicion. "What about Max?"

The nun crouched to her level, smiling. "He will have cake, too. I promise. I will take him myself."

That seemed to satisfy Sophie, and she happily skipped along with the other girls toward a beckoning Sister Catherine.

Sister Marie-Joan looked at Andrée with a more serious expression. "How was it?"

"Not without its stresses," Andrée admitted, hefting Max more securely onto her hip. "But ultimately uneventful. Jeanine didn't understand why her name had to be changed, but I think we've settled that for now."

"I'll keep an eye on her," Sister Marie-Joan murmured. "Poor lamb. And what about this fellow?"

Andrée gave Max an adoring smile. "He is as pleasant as they come. He doesn't say much, but he sees everything."

Sister Marie-Joan beamed at him before holding her arms out.

Max shied away, clinging to Andrée and eyeing the sister with suspicion.

"Oh, come now, my love," Sister Marie-Joan cooed gently. "Don't you want to go with the girls?"

He shook his head firmly, burying his head into Andrée's shoulder.

The tiny embrace was enough to crack marble into a thousand pieces, and Andrée felt her eyes burning. "It's all right, Max," she managed, prying him off her and handing him to the sister. "You heard Sister Marie-Joan. You can have cake."

He looked at Andrée with wide eyes, his lower lip trembling, his arm reaching for her.

Andrée took that hand and kissed it. "You will be so happy here, Max. So much love and joy." Her voice quivered, and she focused on the bags at their feet.

"I take it all that I need is in their bags?" the sister asked, now just as gentle in tone with Andrée as she had been with the children.

"Yes," Andrée said with a quick nod. "Ration cards, papers, clothing. All there."

"Excellent, thank you."

She put a hand to Andrée's arm, and Andrée looked at her almost against her will.

Sister Marie-Joan smiled, her own eyes swimming. "We will honor their family heritage, my dear. No one will try to convert them. They will be safe and loved."

Andrée nodded again, beyond words. She managed to mouth the words "thank you" but not much else.

The sister squeezed her arm. "God bless you for what you do, Mademoiselle Fournier. Surely a place of honor awaits in heaven for you."

"I don't believe in that," Andrée rasped against the rising lump in her throat.

"But I do," Sister Marie-Joan told her. "And if I have my way, you will have the honor nevertheless." She stepped back and rubbed Max's back. "Would you like us to hail you a cab?"

Andrée shook her head firmly, sniffing. "No, I would rather walk."

Sister Marie-Joan nodded, a light of understanding in her eyes. "Very well, then. Until next time, my dear. Say goodbye to Mademoiselle Claude, Max."

Tears fell down the young, chubby cheeks as his little hand waved at shoulder level.

Andrée tried to smile but failed. "Goodbye, my love." She dared not touch him, his arm or his cheek or his tears, for fear that she would not be able to leave. Instead, she turned and walked straight out of the gate and down the road toward the station.

And she did not look back.

A dozen steps later, her tears overwhelmed her, and she began to sob freely, her chest heaving with the force and depth of her cries. She covered her mouth to keep from being audible enough to disturb any around her, but there was no restraining the tears themselves. They fell from her eyes like waterfalls on swollen streams, tumbling over the obstacles of her cheeks, her nose, her lips, her chin, flowing and falling until they splashed onto her arms, her chest, and the ground beneath her feet.

She had adored Max like he was her own child and had done so with remarkable speed. He might have been carried within her and born from her very body for the tender feelings she had for him above all others. Yet it wasn't Max himself, as precious and perfect as he was.

He symbolized all of the innocents that were being so relentlessly hunted, and she was feeling the agony of the injustice, the upheaval, the desperation, and the shattered hearts of mothers and fathers everywhere who were losing their children for the sake of safety. So they might live.

And even then, there was no promise that they would not be discovered, in spite of all the protections in place.

It could all be for nothing.

And so, she cried. And cried. And cried.

Shamelessly and openly, she wept.

All the while making her way back to Brussels to do this again and again, as many times as it took until they were done.

If they ever were done.

CHAPTER 16

The Jewish people is the people of the Devil. It is a people of criminals and murderers. The Jewish people must be exterminated from the face of the earth.

—ARTICLE IN THE NAZI TABLOID, *DER STÜRMER*, JULY 1933

"What do you mean the girls are not here?"

Ida could not believe what she was hearing, and she stared at the woman in front of her as though a head had sprouted from each of the woman's ears.

"Just as I said, Mademoiselle Jeanne," the woman said with as much apology in her tone as possible. "The girls are not here any longer."

Ida pressed her tongue to the top of her mouth and to a few of her molars as she debated screaming at the woman, strangling her, or releasing a string of Yiddish curses that would mean nothing to her, but would cause Ida's ancestors to wake from the dead to scold her.

"Well," Ida said slowly, trying for patience in spite of herself, "if I didn't order their transference, and none of my superiors did, which I am certain of because I received no reports of such, then how, exactly, did two of the children I myself placed here suddenly disappear from the premises?"

The woman's eyes widened at Ida's tone. "The parents came to see them and took them away."

That was not the answer Ida had been expecting. "I beg your pardon?"

"The parents came," the woman said again.

"Yes, I heard that," Ida snapped. "What I want to know is how exactly the parents knew the girls were at this orphanage."

Color began to drain from the woman's face, and it made Ida more satisfied than she ought to have been. "The girls . . . wanted to send letters . . . so we allowed . . ."

Ida turned from the desk and rubbed one hand over her face, exhaling loudly. "Why did the parents take the girls back?"

"Well, because of the state they were in, of course."

The *what*?

Ida slowly lowered her hand and turned back to face the woman, almost shaking now. "The state they were in, madame? What state?"

What was it about panic that made people rustle through papers as though they were just remembering that they were in possession of some requested information?

This woman did so, frantically. Considering she was in charge of the orphanage, she ought to have ready access to all of the requisite information without much effort. Yet much effort was being exerted, and Ida noted such.

"They had been diagnosed with scabies, I see," she told Ida, completely businesslike apart from the faint sheen of perspiration that was forming. "And they were infected."

"The scabies?" Ida asked, more out of irony than anything else, keeping her tone clipped.

"Yes, mademoiselle." There was a faint throat clearing before she continued, "And possibly infested with lice. You know how they are."

Ida raised a brow. "Lice? Or children?"

"Jew children." She shook her head. "None of the other children have lice."

"Lice can't tell a Jewish head from a Christian one," Ida told her, her jaw tensing against her rolling fury. "And it would seem that your treatment of the children might have contributed to the state of them, if not caused it. Show me where you had them sleeping. Now."

The woman's eyes went round. "It's been cleaned and filled with new children, mademoiselle."

"And was it cleaned before the Jewish girls were sleeping there?" Ida shook her head, huffing in disgust. "You claim to be a facility of charity, you claimed you wanted to do your Christian duty, and yet you hold the same opinions as the Nazi barbarians we are hiding the children from."

"I beg your pardon," the headmistress snapped. "We would never hunt down children."

"No, you would just let them develop scabies, lice, and probably anemia, because negligence is so much better than death." Ida scoffed and turned. "Consider your charity invalid and your work with our organization terminated. Good day."

She did not stay to listen to whatever rebuttal might have been forthcoming.

It was always possible that children, regardless of race or religion, could become infected with lice or scabies or any other childhood affliction, particularly in places like orphanages and schools, which was why Ida and the rest had set up an inspection process. But there were so many places and increasingly fewer CDJ members to make those visits as frequently as needed. And those two little girls had paid the price for it.

But they were with their parents again, for better or worse, so that must have been some comfort to them.

How they were going to remain safe from the Nazis as an entire family unit was another issue entirely.

Ida would have to reach out to them or have Yvonne or one of the others do so, to see what help they could offer.

If they still wanted their help.

It was entirely possible that they'd blame the CDJ for the state their daughters had been in.

Ida would have a hard time not blaming herself, so she could understand that.

But now she had to focus on her next task for the day.

Ironically, it involved showing a hidden child to a relative.

The case had been brought to the head of the CDJ not long ago from a distraught grandmother whose entire family had been sent to the camps apart from herself and one grandson. The grandson had been under the CDJ's protection, attending a summer camp in the country, and would be sent on to a new location for the duration of the war, if not longer.

All that this grandmother wanted was to see her grandson and know that he lived.

No one was unmoved by the request, so as she was leaving Brussels on a separate train, they would have the grandson snuck between two trains to show her that he was well and whole. Then he would be placed on his train with one of the escorts and taken to his place of safety.

It was a risky undertaking, there was no question, but they could not forget what was at the heart of this entire enterprise.

Family.

If they could not help to maintain those ties when all was lost, what were they doing? The CDJ would retain the information to allow the family to get in contact when the war was over, but until then, there would be no additional information or access given. The boy would be as safe as any other child hidden by the CDJ.

His grandmother would know that he, alone, of all her grandchildren, still lived.

According to her letter, that would be enough for her to continue living.

It was an unremarkable return journey to Brussels, but Ida felt the agitation from the encounter at the orphanage twisting her stomach and pricking her heart as though it had been encased in thorns. She could not move but for scratches upon the surface, could not breathe but for the tender flesh being torn. It wasn't often that she dwelled on the situations in which the children they hid were living, or on how their conditions affected them, but she could not get the little girls out of her mind.

They had suffered in a place where they ought to have been safe.

Where they had been promised they would be safe. How confused they must have been! How sad and longing for their home and family! The only comfort they would have had would be each other, knowing they were not wholly alone but had their sister beside them.

She could see those sisters in her mind's eye. Could see them standing hand in hand, scabies, lice, and all, with silent tears rolling down their still infant-like cheeks. And, in her mind, their haunted expressions accused Ida as though she sat in a dock of some courtroom.

How could she bear this? How could she bear to place one more child without taking on stricter measures to ensure health and safety? Or to ensure that those who housed them did not view them poorly?

Would it be enough to work harder in any of those areas? Did they even have time to consider all of those things with the demand they were working under? It didn't seem possible, and yet it had to be. When help was offered, if from a trusted source, it had to be accepted. If they felt strongly enough to offer aid in these times, they must have been better than the alternative.

And yet.

And yet.

There would always be a *yet* somewhere. Nothing was perfect. Nothing could be, until the world was perfect.

If the world ever could be.

Disembarking from her train, Ida followed the crowd of other passengers off the platform before looping back around the porter's office toward the trainyard. She counted freight cars as she crossed over the corresponding tracks. After the fifth one, she turned and followed the tracks to the second of the connected boxcars.

Claire stood there with the boy, his small suitcase beside them, his shoulders squared, his flat cap in place. He was as neat and tidy as could possibly be hoped for when presenting a child to his grandmother, and the appearance of his legs and kneecaps told Ida that he would not be a child much longer. He was gangly, and would no doubt soon grow taller than not only Claire but all of them. He was already at Claire's shoulders, and his eyes held all too much understanding.

An adult already in so many ways.

Ida had to think quickly to remember his name. "Are you ready to see your grandmother, Francois?"

He nodded, but his set features could not hide the bob of his throat as he swallowed.

This was not just for the grandmother, Ida realized. Francois needed to see her as well. He didn't know anything specific about the rest of his family, which was extensive, as far as the letter had indicated. Parents, siblings, cousins, aunts, uncles. He might suspect what had happened, given they were allowing him to see his grandmother, but he wouldn't know for certain.

He needed to know that he was not alone in the world either.

If only they could have sent him with his grandmother! But with the borders being controlled as much as they were, with the risks involved in so many aspects, they had to remain separate. If they both survived the war, God willing, they could be reunited and move forward together.

Claire looked at her watch. "It should be ready at any moment. As soon as they blow the whistle, we'll move."

Ida nodded and put her hands on Francois's shoulders. "I know you will both want longer than we can give you. But for your grandmother's safety, and your own, we will only have a few moments. You must treasure this. You must replay it over and over in your mind until it is impossible to forget. Engrave it upon your heart. Do you understand?"

Francois dashed away a quick tear from one eye, sniffling before nodding. "I mustn't show my *bubbe* my tears. She'll never leave if she sees me cry."

Ida bit the inside of her lip hard as her own eyes began to burn. "You are the bravest boy I have ever met, Francois. And when her train is gone, if you want to cry, Mademoiselle Catherine and I won't tell a single soul."

A conductor whistle blew then, and Claire took Francois' hand.

"Let's go." She tugged him around the boxcar, Ida hard on their heels as they raced across the series of tracks.

They moved around one train still boarding, then raced alongside it and scanned the windows of the train opposite.

Two-thirds of the way down the cars, an open window dropped further still, and an elderly woman appeared, her wrinkled hands gripping the window as though it were her lifeline. Her eyes were opened wider than her visage should have allowed, but tears flowed freely, her smile threatening to extend beyond the constraints of her face.

"My darling one," she cried out, following the CDJ's condition to refrain from names or Yiddish. "You've grown so tall!"

Francois waved at her, grinning madly. "I'm almost as tall as my uncle now, I think."

His grandmother chuckled and reached a hand out as far as she could. "Touch my fingers, my love, so I know you are real."

Claire and Ida moved to help lift him up to touch her fingers, delight rampant on both faces of the family.

"H-how was your camp?" his grandmother asked, her fingers running over his. "Was it enjoyable?"

"Yes, it went well," Francois replied, his words growing tighter. "And now I'm off again. I will . . . write to you when I can."

His grandmother nodded rapidly, her free hand wiping at her cheeks. "Please do, my love. You will be in my prayers every morning and every night."

Francois kissed his grandmother's fingers quickly. "And you in mine, Grandmother. I love you."

The train whistle sounded, and the gears of the wheels began to turn, moving the train slowly forward. "I love you as well, my sweet. I love you so much. I am proud of you."

Their fingers separated as the distance became too great.

"Don't forget me," his grandmother called out, waving at him.

"Never!" he called back, returning her wave.

Then she was gone, the train picking up speed and rounding the turn to take them out of the yard.

Francois continued to wave, then hiccupped as his tears refused to be restrained, his face crumpling like the little boy he deserved to have been. Claire immediately pulled him into an embrace, and he buried his face into her shoulder, his entire frame shaking as he cried.

"Come on," Ida whispered, allowing herself to cry as well. "Let's get back before we get you prepared for your train."

Claire moved with him, not letting her arms slacken even the slightest around him. Ida stepped closer and rubbed a hand across his shoulders, and the three of them made their ungainly way back around the train cars.

When they had the privacy they sought, Claire murmured something to Francois that Ida couldn't hear, but Francois nodded and released her, moving to sit on the step of a nearby freight car, putting his head into his hands.

Ida watched him for a moment, then leaned closer to Claire. "What did you say to him?"

"I asked if he wanted some time to himself," Claire said simply. "He and I will have a lot of time with each other before we reach Ghent. He deserves to grieve privately before he's stuck with me."

"You have such a way with them," Ida murmured, shaking her head. "Children, I mean. It's in your nature, almost like the color of your eyes."

Claire gave her a look. "And you have the capacity to care and to sacrifice like no one I've ever met. What is bothering you?"

Ida glanced in her direction but did not quite meet her gaze. "Why should something be bothering me?"

"The way you said that I have a way with children. It was more mournful than complimentary." Claire shrugged, folding her arms. "I inferred, that is all."

"You infer correctly." Ida sighed heavily, her shoulders sagging under the weight of her morning. "I'm so tired, Catherine. Not with what we are doing, but with everything. Two girls were removed from an orphanage by their parents, who had been given their address by other parties. They were in such a weakened physical state that the parents took them back."

Claire clucked her tongue sadly. "Poor darlings. We can't inspect more than we already are, and what's to stop places from showing us one thing and the children living another?"

"You see why I am tired, then. Esta had such a way of managing things, and I find myself asking over and over what she would do, and I just don't know anymore."

"That's because you're not Esta," Claire said simply. "You're Jeanne. And you can only run it the way Jeanne runs it. Stop trying to be Esta and just be Jeanne."

Ida smiled slightly. "Jeanne isn't my real name."

Claire laughed once. "And Catherine isn't mine, but here we are." She cocked her head playfully. "We're all doing the best we can with the situation we're in, the provisions we have, and the skills we possess. We can't extend beyond the possibilities at hand. But maybe we can create new possibilities."

That was a weighty thought, encouraging though it was, and Ida exhaled very slowly. "Do you want to take over this job?" she asked with all the innocent hope in the world.

"No, I do not," Claire said with a laugh. "Please don't make me." She checked her watch again, sighing. "Time to find our train and get aboard if we want to avoid running. Will you be all right?"

Ida nodded her assurance. "Of course. New requests and new opportunities are coming. I'll have a better update after my meeting in a few days. You'll be contacted."

"Always am." She nudged Ida slightly, smiling with a wink before moving over to Francois. "Sorry, darling. Afraid we must go. Can you be ready?"

"Yes, Mademoiselle Catherine." He wiped at his eyes, looked up at Claire, and took a hefty breath. "I am ready now."

He wasn't, but at least he did not look as though he had been crying overly much. He got up from his step and brushed off his knees.

Ida smiled at him. "Good luck, Francois."

He nodded. "Thank you, mademoiselle. You as well." He held out his hand to shake, just like a man would have done.

He had grown up completely and entirely before her very eyes.

There was something profoundly sad in that.

Ida shook his hand firmly. "You will do very well. And remember what I told you."

Again, Francois nodded, but said nothing more. He turned to Claire, picked up his suitcase, and followed her around the box car.

If a boy such as he could continue going, in spite of all the losses and grief, then so could Ida.

There were many more children she could help, and help them she would.

CHAPTER 17

As Adolf Hitler stood before the German people twenty years ago to proclaim National Socialism's program, he also made the fateful promise to free the world of its Jewish tormentors. It is wonderful to know that this great man and Führer is keeping this promise! It will be the greatest deed in human history.

—JULIUS STREICHER, *DER STÜRMER*, 1943

Andrée rang the bell again, frowning at the door before her.

This was the appointed time and the appointed place, and yet no one had come to the door when she'd rung the first time. She was to pick up two boys and take them to Father André. All had been arranged with the parents, and all was agreed to. But no one was answering.

Her heart skipped exactly two beats before she pounded hard at the bell.

Had they all been arrested since arranging the children's affairs? Was she ringing at a newly emptied house?

She glanced up and down the street, wondering if she should knock as well, or if enough was enough. But she couldn't give up. Not yet, not if there was any chance.

But was there a chance?

She raised a fist to the door, preparing to knock, when it opened and a young boy stood there, his eyes somber, his cheeks rosy.

Andrée blinked at him for a moment. "Hirsch?"

He nodded but said nothing else.

That was the seven-year-old, then. He and his four-year-old brother were her children today, but usually the children were not the ones to let her in.

"Did your mother mention that someone was coming to take you and your brother away for a bit?" she asked him, forcing her tone into the gentle, kind, almost singsong voice she used for children more often than not.

Again, Hirsch nodded.

Andrée smiled at the lack of further response. "My name is Claude, and I've come to fetch you. Can I come in?"

He stepped back and let her in, closing the door behind her. "Mama is in bed."

"Is she?" Andrée asked, trying not to sound concerned. "Did she pack your bags?"

Hirsch nodded and pointed at the small suitcases by the hall table.

Well, there was that, at least.

But Andrée wasn't about to take these boys without their mother saying goodbye and being certain the woman could face it. She could crawl back into bed after they were gone if that was her wish. Andrée wouldn't even blame her for that. But what was she telling her boys by refusing to get out?

"Could you show me to her room, please?" Andrée smiled at Hirsch. "And then, perhaps, make sure your brother is ready to go."

Hirsch started down the hall, and Andrée followed, ignoring the family photos on the walls, as she always did in the family homes. She didn't need reminders of the happy families that once were that she was now breaking up.

It would make her think too much of the ones that would never be whole or happy again.

Hirsch stopped outside of a bedroom, peering in hesitantly. Still, he said nothing.

Was he normally this silent, or was it a condition particular to today?

Andrée put a hand on his shoulder as she moved in front of him and into the bedroom. A woman only a few years older than herself lay in the bed, covers pulled up to her chin, staring up at the ceiling as though memorizing its detail. She did not appear to have heard the bell ringing, nor the steps of her child coming down the hall toward her room. She barely seemed to blink, let alone breathe, completely unaware of her surroundings.

The Gestapo couldn't have got that woman out of bed at this point, but somehow, Andrée had to.

She moved to the side of the bed and crouched down. "Madame Blum, I am Claude Fournier, and I'm from the CDJ. I've come to take your boys. Do you still consent to this?"

Mrs. Blum blinked once, though it was difficult to tell if that was a response to the question or an involuntary reaction.

"You do understand the purpose of our doing this, yes?" Andrée pressed, leaning closer. "Why it is necessary?"

Again, there came a blink, and Andrée counted that as an answer now.

Was that all the communication she was going to get from her?

Andrée glanced at the doorway, noting that both boys now stood there, jackets and caps on, looking as though they might be off to school rather than leaving home for months or years.

Their eyes were on their mother alone.

Sighing, Andrée returned her attention to Mrs. Blum. "Madame Blum, I cannot imagine the devastation you are feeling at the prospect of your sons leaving you. I cannot pretend to comprehend the depth of your despair. I don't know that I would want to leave my bed either. But I need you to leave your bed for just a few moments, Madame Blum. Not for me, and not even for yourself. I need you to leave this bed and stand on your own two feet for your two boys."

Mrs. Blum blinked, but did not move, her eyes fixed above her.

"Your boys," Andrée went on, lowering her voice to almost a whisper, "need to see you up and out of bed before they go. Their lingering memory of you, the one that will get them through this separation, needs to be one of strength. They need to believe that you will still be here for them when the war is over. You and I know the realities of this world and this war, but they do not."

Andrée flicked her eyes quickly toward the boys, then back to their mother, swallowing hard. "Give them hope, Madame Blum. Your sons deserve to leave filled with hope. Let that be your parting gift to them. Then give in to your despair, if you must, once they are gone. Can you do that for them?"

Mrs. Blum blinked once, then again. Then she pushed the covers down and sat up, swung her legs to the side of the bed, and pushed to her feet. She didn't meet Andrée's eyes as she straightened her skirt, ran a hand over her hair, or squared her shoulders. She didn't even acknowledge her as she turned and walked over to her boys, and, judging by the way their countenances brightened, smiled lovingly at them.

Andrée slowly rose from her position and hung back as Mrs. Blum dropped to her knees and hugged each boy tightly, murmuring words only for them. Then she hugged both of them together, the only sign of her distress that of the strained arching of her feet and her toes digging into the carpet beneath her. Clawing at the ground in protest, digging for purchase in the only surface available, practically screaming aloud for some sort of reprieve, some deliverance from the pain.

Andrée had no such deliverance for her. No one did.

Mrs. Blum took her youngest boy's face in her hands, kissed both cheeks, and told him something, then repeated the actions with Hirsch.

Only when she got to her feet did Andrée dare go forward and take both boys by the hands, leading them back down the hall toward the door. "Grab your suitcases, boys."

They did so, looking up at Andrée with open, trusting expressions.

She smiled at them. "Say goodbye to your mama, then."

The boys looked behind them. "Goodbye, Mama," they chimed.

"Goodbye, darlings," she replied, her voice strong and full of adoration.

Unable to help herself, Andrée looked back at her as well.

She had both hands at her heart, her eyes on her children, tears flowing freely down her face. Then, to Andrée's surprise, her eyes raised to Andrée herself. Her lips formed the words "thank you," but there was no sound to them.

Perhaps no strength left for volume.

Andrée nodded in acknowledgment, feeling her eyes burn. "Come on, then, boys! We've got an adventure ahead of us!" She opened the door and led the little one out while Hirsch followed.

Once outside, she took both boys in hand again, grinning down at them. "As of now, dear Hirsch, you are Henri Ledent. You must only answer to this name. Understand?"

The newly christened Henri nodded, unperturbed by the change.

"And your brother," Andrée went on, shaking the hand of the four-year-old playfully, "shall be Maurice. Can you be Maurice, hmm?"

Maurice nodded eagerly, apparently thinking this was a game.

It would all become clear soon enough, but a game would do for now.

"Right, then," Andrée chirped in a bright voice. "Off we go!"

She led them down the sidewalk, turning on this block and that, passing a Nazi barricade with smiles from the soldiers, and potentially passing a few Gestapo members, based on their determined expressions as they walked. They all nodded their greetings to Andrée and the boys, tapping their hats as they passed.

Not one person looked at them with suspicion or stopped them.

It made keeping the lighter moods of the boys that much easier. They even started skipping once they were on the other side of Brussels. Their fostering home was in Vilvoorde, so they would shortly catch a tram, but the boys had such energy that walking to Vilvoorde might have been a better exercise for them.

Andrée certainly would not complain about an extended opportunity to walk. Everything seemed to be happening so fast these days, there was barely any time to comprehend what they were doing, let alone allow it to affect them. Actually enjoying a fine day with happy children was almost never an occurrence, which, naturally, made it all the more appreciated.

And she desperately wanted to appreciate it.

She was due at the maternity ward in the morning to remove another newborn from his mother. Those were always the worst ones for her. These new mothers who were almost literally having their children snatched from their arms just as they had entered the world and their lives. Whose glorious moments of joy in recent days would now be lost to bleak ones. Who would not even have the chance to know their infants before they were children, in most cases.

Who would almost certainly be reunited with children who had no love for nor knowledge of them.

The doctors helping them at the maternity ward looked after the distressed mothers once Andrée or her associates were gone, allowed the new mothers to stay longer than a typical birth, but what comfort and care could they possibly give that would be meaningful? That would even touch these mothers' pain, let alone provide relief of it.

She never had to see those mothers when she took the babies away. The doctors were very careful that she and the others go directly to the nursery and that the farewells between mother and baby take place before the CDJ's arrival. Physically prying an infant from the bosom of their mother would have been too cruel, and an already distressing experience did not need to become torturous.

It never got easier to take a baby away. One had to continually focus their thoughts on the safety of the child and the location to which they were heading, and that was all. They could not think of the keening family already wailing for their baby. They could not acknowledge that they were taking this new life away from the life it was born into. They also could not pretend this was some formal adoption that all parties wanted. That this was some matter of business and nothing more.

Yet their actions required that kind of mental distance. That same detachment. That same determination to see the task done. That same efficiency without particular consideration for the emotions involved.

Surely, they must be viewed with the same coldness by the family.

How can you be so cruel?

The words of Simone's mother still haunted Andrée, echoed in her mind every time she stepped through the doors of the maternity ward. It did not matter that she had not been forced to face the woman as she took her newborn son away. That she never had to face the mothers of any of the babies.

She heard their voices say the exact same thing again and again and again.

But she also heard the screams of the mothers with babies in those camps. Imagined screams and imagined cries, as she had never faced that horror, but the reports were beyond comprehension. She heard the wailing of infants being suddenly silenced. She heard the tearful attempts to soothe distressed infants by terrified mothers walking toward their death.

If saving anyone from such a fate was cruel, then Andrée must be cruel.

They all must.

For a living child in an unknown place was surely better than a dead child in a known place.

And that was something to which she must cling, if she was to survive any of this.

"Mademoiselle Claude?"

Andrée felt the innocent pressure against her fingers and looked down, shaking herself from the darkness of her thoughts. "Yes, Henri?"

His brow was furrowed as he looked up at her. "Are we going to ride that trolley?" He jabbed his finger toward one approaching, something about which Andrée had been completely and entirely unaware in her stupor.

She could not afford such distractions while on a mission.

It could be the death of them all.

"Yes, Henri," she replied brightly. "Well spotted. Now, Maurice, do you still have your suitcase?"

Maurice held it up obediently, his round eyes bright as he watched the approaching vehicle.

"Excellent, then we're ready to climb aboard!" She infused as much energy and enthusiasm into her voice as possible, knowing these two children in particular would pick up on any shift of emotions. She lifted them both onto the trolley with playful sounds, though neither had strictly needed her to, and managed to turn finding the perfect seats into a game for them.

By the time they reached Vilvoorde, both boys were laughing and smiling, behaving just as little boys their ages ought to. If they had lingering feelings about their departure from their home and their mother, they gave no sign of it for the moment. Andrée knew better than to suspect that she had solved all of their problems with her energy and attempts, her coaxing of their smiles and laughter, but it could not hurt the situation to bring some light in.

Perhaps that was her gift to the children she escorted and hid. Something to keep childhood within them for a little while in a time and in a world that was rapidly stripping them of that very thing.

The family waiting for them in Vilvoorde was delighted to have them arrive, welcoming them with open arms, with smiles and hugs, freshly baked bread, and a bedroom especially prepared for the two of them with a view of the nearby pond. It was a happy, bright, cheerful place with eager fostering siblings and an atmosphere of harmony and love.

This was exactly the sort of place that children should be allowed to grow up in.

This might have been the sort of place they had lived in before the Nazis had invaded.

Would Maurice remember his mother's tears when all this was over? Or would the woman with the blue apron and the cross necklace be the only mother he knew?

Andrée left the house with a smile, but that smile faded as she returned to Brussels, alone on the trolley and devoid of energy. As much as she appreciated the work they did here, as necessary as it was, as incapable as she was of stopping, there was no denying that it was the most exhausting work she had ever done. There was something soul draining about experiencing these separations again and again, something scarring, in a way, that she had never experienced.

What had she thought it would be like when she had taken this on? The idea of hiding Jewish children from the Gestapo had been a thrilling one, there was no denying that. She would have done far more reckless things to work against them, though perhaps not anything truly destructive, as some resistance groups were. She would have supported those groups, there was no question, but she drew the line at death for the sake of it.

Had she imagined then, when the idea had been presented to her, that she would be tearing families apart? With their consent, and with their being willing to endure such a sacrifice for the sake of the children, but even so. Had she dreamed that she would carry a weight on her heart that grew with every passing day? That she would lose sleep because of the nature of her dreams? That she would begin to view nearly everyone with suspicion? That she would not speak with her own family for over a year?

All of it was draining. All of it was exhausting. All of it tore at her heart and ate at her soul. All of it consumed her thoughts and seeped into her body.

All of it changed her.

If that change would be for good or not, only time would tell. Only the end of the war would tell. Only what was left of the world would tell.

But oh, was she fatigued by it all.

That was not to say that she was not also determined, invigorated, dedicated, and prepared for whatever eventuality might come her way. She was also those things. She would not rest while tyrants attempted to crush others beneath their perfectly shiny boots. She would not let innocent children be marched to death. She would not stand idly by while there was breath in her lungs and blood in her veins.

It was just the unending rigamarole of it all. The grinding of the painful, arduous gears of their secret work. The same processes playing out over and over again, the same tears of the mothers, the same hunting by the Gestapo, the same threats to the life they knew and the rights of the Jews to even exist.

Andrée walked to her flat without even thinking about the process, just trusting her feet to take her there, as they had done so many times before. She let her mind move and spread to whichever avenues it wished, hoping that somehow it would think of nothing and go nowhere.

What a relief it would be to have nothing to think of for a while.

She pushed open the door to the building and mounted the stairs toward her flat, one step after the other, each foot feeling like it was weighted down by cement bricks. She rounded the landing, and trudged up to the next floor, faintly wondering if her legs had the ability to get her all the way to her flat. They'd never failed her before, but this time, this day, she might not make it. She might collapse. She might just rest for a while.

Just until her strength returned.

But her feet and her legs did what they were designed to do, and she did find herself at the top of the stairs, turning left, and reaching her flat. Her fingers reached automatically for her keys, sitting, as they always did, in the inner pocket of her black raincoat. They inserted the keys into the lock, turned it, and pressed the door open, her feet taking over again as she walked in.

All of this without thinking through the processes. All just habit. All just a pattern.

She closed the door, locked it, and moved to the sofa in the living room, sitting down for a moment, then lying down and curling her legs up onto the cushions.

That was all she could do, and this was as far as she could go.

"Claude?" Ida called from the bedrooms. "Is that you?"

Andrée didn't answer, closing her eyes and hoping for rest.

Footsteps approached and stopped near her. "Claude?"

Breathing in and breathing out, slowly and beginning to shake in timbre, Andrée curled more fully into herself on the couch, faintly wishing for more strength, and also for a dreamless sleep to allow herself true rest.

Rest. When no rest could be found.

A blanket was suddenly placed over her, her shoes removed. And then a body sat near her head, lifting it to rest it on her leg. Fingers began to brush through her hair slowly and comfortingly.

Tears began to form in Andrée's closed eyes, and she let them leak out, knowing Ida wouldn't care, and let herself rest into the feeling of someone beside her, and fingers combing through her hair.

CHAPTER 18

He who fights the Jews battles the Devil.

—LINE FROM A NAZI CHILDREN'S BOOK, 1938

May 31, 1944

The entire time Ida was walking toward Beau Séjour, the café where she'd arranged to meet Madame Dumont, she thought about the raid at the castle in the Ardennes at the beginning of the year. The Nazis had been searching for weapons, but the castle had held no weapons. Instead, they had found a colony of Jews in hiding there. Men, women, and children.

All of them had been sent to the camp in Malines.

And, as far as Ida knew, all of them had then been deported to Auschwitz.

Why that was in her mind as she headed to her weekly meeting, she couldn't say. But it certainly had her on edge, and she did not like being on edge. It made everything suspicious and anything risky. Even meeting Madame Dumont, which was absolutely ridiculous.

Madame Dumont's husband worked for the AJB, along with Maurice Heiber, and he had done so from the beginning of Ida's involvement with the CDJ. As he could not risk compromise, his wife acted as the go-between, bringing them more requests for help and the requisite information regarding those who needed help. Sometimes, Madame Dumont brought Ida newly identified locations where the CDJ could find families needing help, but most of the time she delivered other requests from families—for trips, clothes, stamps, or news of children already placed. It was crucial to act immediately on the requests that came through the AJB, as the Gestapo could access all of the AJB's information at any time.

Sometimes, the CDJ would get to families found through the AJB just in time to get them out, but it was enough.

Ida had stopped trying to anticipate what information Madame Dumont would have for her. It was never the same from one week to the next, and their meetings took nearly two hours most of the time just to cover all of the information she wanted to share.

On edge or not, Ida was full of energy, and she wanted this meeting to be over quickly. She wanted to see the task done and move on with the business of her day, like all meetings and all days. Especially when she was carrying sensitive information, as she was now. Papers detailing the information for a dozen placements, among other things, and there was something about being in possession of such compromising information that she did not like.

Ghert Jospa had been arrested and taken away because of the information he carried with him while going about his work in their organization. Who knew what he was enduring, wherever he was, because of the information he'd been caught with? False papers were nothing compared to the paperwork they actually used in their day-to-day work, and she had no desire to compromise the families requesting their help. If she was captured with this information, those families would be as well.

And that was the problem.

She had to protect those families and those children at all costs.

Ida entered the café and moved to the stairs up to the terrace, jogging up quickly and then heading for the table where Madame Dumont sat waiting. "Good morning," Ida greeted as she took a chair. "Thank you for agreeing to the change of location."

"Not a problem, Jeanne," Madame Dumont replied with a smile. "It's a beautiful day, so why should we not sit and enjoy it?"

Ida grinned quickly, setting her bag on the ground next to her chair. "Exactly. We spend so much time in and out of places, sitting at desks and such, that we never really pay attention to the day itself."

"I tell my colleagues that we need some daylight every single day," Madame Dumont told her, tapping the table with a finger. "Whether the sun is out or not. That doesn't mean we get it, but we should." She shrugged, still smiling. "And we can certainly hope that the children do get some."

Nodding, Ida leaned her arms on the table. "I couldn't agree more. I have a dozen existing placement requests with me. How many more do you have for me?"

Madame Dumont folded her hands neatly together. "Seven. And three requests for stamps."

"Not as many as I was expecting." Ida made a face of surprise, raising a brow. "Bit of a relief, I won't lie. There's an awful lot going on right now."

"There is, indeed." Madame Dumont sighed with a heaviness Ida hadn't heard from her before. "The AJB is growing more and more useless by the day. We're puppets for the Nazis now, you know. I wouldn't stay in if it weren't for the protections it affords me, which allow me to continue to help you and the other groups."

Ida smiled sadly. "And believe me, we appreciate that you do so. It makes all the difference in the world."

"Then let us get started on today's work."

The two of them began to discuss the matters at hand in more detail, exchanging information they had relevant to the other, making suggestions about certain possibilities, and keeping the conversation relatively coded for the sake of their surroundings. Though the café wasn't crowded, it was habit now to not be explicit in any public conversation. Practically second nature, at this point, and details were always kept to only the most necessary ones.

Ida glanced toward the stairs as the sound of heavy footfall met her ears, and felt a coldness travel down her spine.

Fat Jacques was reaching the top stair with an SS officer beside him. Their eyes were on Madame Dumont, and they were headed in this direction.

"You there," Fat Jacques barked, pointing at Madame Dumont. "Are you a Jewess?"

To Madame Dumont's credit, she barely reacted to the accusation. "I beg your pardon?"

They moved to their table, both men towering over Madame Dumont's form. "Are you a Jewess?" Fat Jacques demanded again. "Show your papers!"

"Certainly," Madame Dumont replied without fuss, reaching into her bag for her papers. "I should tell you that my husband is a member of the AJB. You will find that card in my papers."

"So, you *are* a Jew." Fat Jacques sneered in vile satisfaction. "I knew it. I could see it from the street. You look like a Jew."

Madame Dumont raised a brow. "So do you. Ironic, isn't it?"

The SS officer roared something or other in German and hauled Madame Dumont out of her chair, her papers still in hand.

Ida bit back the impulse to ask what they were going to do with Madame Dumont, knowing that if she got too involved, she would become a target. But she could hardly let her friend and contact be subjected to abuse.

"Here is my AJB card," Madame Dumont told Fat Jacques, and his cohort, by extension. She showed them both the card quite clearly, holding it next to her face so they could compare the picture with her person.

Being married to a member of the AJB, and having proof of it, meant Madame Dumont was safe from their usual examinations, unless they had proof of specific actions that worked against her organization.

Ida had no such protections.

"Be that as it may," Jacques said, sounding upset as he moved in front of Madame Dumont, "I demand to know what you are doing here today."

Attention presently diverted from her, Ida slowly reached into her bag and pulled the packet of requests from it, sliding the bunch onto the chair beside her. The chair was mostly obscured by the tablecloth, the seat almost entirely hidden by the table itself, as it was pushed in. Unless they overturned the table or checked each chair, they would not see it.

Ida brought her hands back to her lap, trying to settle them as they shook ever so slightly. She knew she could not run, knew she had to wait, and knew that if anyone would be taken away from this meeting in the end, it would likely be her. Madame Dumont had too much protection and not enough proof of acting outside of her duties with the AJB. Fat Jacques and the SS officer might not like the AJB, but they needed them; and arrangements to protect AJB members from the same abuses showered upon other Jews in the area had been settled almost from the moment of the invasion. There would be a great deal to answer to if they upset that particular apple cart.

Ida, on the other hand, was nothing and no one.

And she had to wait.

Jacques and the officer came back to the table with Madame Dumont, whom they allowed to sit in her chair once more.

Jacques, however, now looked at Ida. "Who are you?" he demanded. "What are you doing in the company of a Jewess? Are you a Jew yourself?"

Ida showed them her papers, smiling tightly and waiting for their answer to her identity.

"Jeanne Hendrickx," Jacques read out. "Social worker. That does not explain why you are meeting with a Jewess."

"In my capacity as a social worker," Ida said as calmly as she could, "I sometimes take care of Jewish children. As, some years ago, I did with Spanish children during their war."

Jacques scoffed loudly. "It is not possible to compare the two groups."

Ida frowned at the statement. "No? War affects children."

"We are not asking about Belgian children," the SS officer told her, a malevolent gleam entering his eyes. "Only Jewish ones."

The fact that he was distinguishing between the two groups when she had not done so spoke of the true mentality here, the true hatred for Jews, no matter what the age.

Which meant her rationale would not be viewed as correct. Or allowed.

"Come with us," Jacques ordered suddenly. "Now."

Ida glanced up at him in interest. "Monsieur?"

He smirked at her. "The card is false, mademoiselle, as I am certain you are aware. Come with us. Now."

There was no refusing him, no denying anything, no point in attempting an escape.

She picked up her bag and flashed a quick smile at Madame Dumont, whose eyes were wide, but who said nothing. What could she have said that would have helped the situation for either of them? The only thing Madame Dumont could do would be to let the CDJ know that Ida had been captured so the appropriate measures could be taken.

What happened now was almost entirely out of Ida's hands.

Jacques and the SS officer followed her out, keeping close to her, and, when they exited the café, Jacques took her arm tightly, leading her to a nearby car. She was shoved in, and Jacques sat beside her, slamming the door shut.

"Are you a Jew?" he asked her again, this time emphasizing each word with precision.

Ida exhaled shortly but said nothing in response.

Jacques took her bag and began looking through it. After just a moment, he pulled out a letter and began reading it.

The sight of the letter made Ida cringe inwardly. It was a safe enough letter to read, her name was protected, but her address—her real address—was in there.

They would know where to search. She had to delay that as much as possible, if she could.

Which would mean giving him something.

"I am a Jew," Ida admitted, trying not to sound reluctant.

Jacques looked at her, his eyes narrowing. "You don't wear a star. We can have you arrested for that."

"I am in a mixed marriage," Ida replied. "You can look into that. I am not required to wear one in such a circumstance."

"That is no excuse," he argued, remarkably calm at the moment. "You are a Jew; you wear the star."

Though it could come back to haunt her, Ida heard herself reply, "You don't."

He looked at her then. Slowly, severely, and with more coldness than she could ever imagine. He might have killed her right then, had she not possibly been in possession of useful information for him and the Gestapo.

"You say you work with children," Jacques said suddenly, his voice harsher than before. "How many?"

"Recently, I've taken care of at least a dozen Jewish children." She looked out of the window, trying to keep her chest from tightening further with the stress of the moment.

"Who?" he demanded.

The car went over a dip in the road, jostling them all, and Ida closed her eyes, praying silently that she had done the right thing.

"Who?" Jacques asked again. "You will give us their names and their addresses."

"No," she told him softly. "I will not."

Someone in the car coughed, and she thought it was likely the SS officer driving, but she suspected Jacques was not refused often. Which made the satisfaction all the more delightful, in spite of her shaking hands and tightening chest.

"You will," Jacques said darkly. "And any children you give up will be sent to the orphanage in Wezembeek. They will be well looked after. Nothing will happen to them, I promise."

Ida snorted a soft laugh, shaking her head. Did he truly think she was going to believe him? She knew far too much and was not the least bit gullible.

"If you don't speak," Jacques went on, "it will be Breendonk."

"How will you send them to Breendonk if I don't give them to you?" Ida asked him, finding this whole situation ridiculous now.

"You, Madame Hendrickx. You will go to Breendonk."

Ida jerked and looked at him in shock. Every Jew or Jew sympathizer in Belgium was sent to Malines for holding, and then either kept there, or sent on to the death camps, usually Auschwitz. Breendonk was the third option, and it was nearly as bad as the death camps. Once a proud Belgian fortress near Malines, it was now an internment camp filled with torture and torment, where any remaining will and spirit was inevitably crushed. Jewish inmates were segregated from other prisoners the Nazis sent there, and kept in far worse conditions. Death was common at Breendonk, though not its express purpose.

To suggest that she would go to Breendonk was taking her crime to an extreme level, though she had not presently been accused of anything.

Other than being Jewish.

Which she was.

"Now you understand me, I think," Jacques said with a crooked smile that slanted his mustache awkwardly. "And just how serious I am."

Oh, yes, she understood. She understood very well. But he needed to understand how serious she was as well.

She pointedly turned and looked out of the window again, grinding her teeth and saying nothing.

Jacques said nothing further as the car moved through the streets of Belgium, turning eventually onto Avenue Louise and to the Sicherheitsdienst, or SD, headquarters, the intelligence agency of the SS. The car came to a stop and Jacques got out, letting the SS officer give the orders now. Two uniformed officers pulled Ida from the car and led her inside, but, oddly enough, not to any particular office or interrogation room.

They led her down a stairwell where the temperature seemed to decrease with every step. A narrow hallway led to a closed door, but it was soon opened by one of the guards escorting her, and she was shoved into the darkened room, stumbling and falling to her knees on the cold, gritty ground. The door slammed shut behind her, sounding like the clanging of a dungeon door.

There was an old lantern in a corner, barely flickering, but it kept the room from complete darkness. Ida pressed up from the ground, rubbing her hands to rid them of whatever was covering the ground. It didn't feel like sand, but it had the same sort of coarseness that irritated her skin. She glanced around, trying to get her bearings, and froze.

Four women sat on planks nearby, watching her. The room was not much wider than the four of them, so their appearance was somewhat intimidating from the perspective of the floor.

"Hello," Ida said slowly, unsure who they were or what was happening here.

"What have you done to come in here?" the second woman on her left asked.

Ida glanced at her, recognizing her on a second look. She had placed her son, a boy of twelve, but the woman had been too distraught to actually talk to Ida about it. All of the communication had been done with the father.

She would not give the woman any reminders now, not here in a false dungeon captured by their enemies. "I was in a café with a Jew. Then they found out I was one, too."

The woman hummed very softly. "What a crime." She looked to both sides of her and pointed at the woman on the far right. "Amelie has two children: one in hospital and one in hiding. She tried to escape from the Gestapo and injured her leg."

She patted the knee of the woman sitting to her right. "Jenny is Viennese and sings opera when she gets too depressed about her widowhood. She was arrested for sitting on a bench and being Jewish."

Now she touched the arm of the woman at her left. "And Maria had a baby two weeks ago in a maternal home. She thought she was safe, but the Gestapo raided. The baby was saved by one of the social workers there, but she was brought here when she ought to have been resting and nursing her child, but there is no help for her here." She rubbed Maria's back soothingly as Maria folded her arms tightly over her chest, wincing with a hiss.

"I'm Julia," she said at last. "And I have lost everything." She shrugged and sat back against the wall. "Don't mind the coal dust. It doesn't matter now anyway."

Ida looked at her hands, rubbing her fingers together and feeling the fine particles between the skin.

Coal. They had been put in a coal cellar.

Lovely.

Ida sat against the nearest wall, leaning her head back against the cold and probably filthy stone. Whatever was going to happen to her, she just hoped her documents had been safe where she'd hidden them.

She could not bear the thought of families and children being compromised because she had been caught. And they didn't even know who she was or what she had been doing yet, they only knew she was a Jew. Perhaps they'd never know that she was Ida Sterno, given her paperwork had her married name of Hendrickx and her false first name of Jeanne. All of her paperwork in Brussels was under that name. No one knew who she really was.

So long as that remained true, her work should be safe.

How long she sat there in the cellar with those women, Ida wasn't sure. Time wasn't measured there. There were no windows to cast shadows that could indicate anything, and there was not light enough to have a hope of reading her wristwatch.

Suddenly the door was thrown open, and the SS guard who had been with Jacques when Ida was taken stepped in. He took her arm and hauled her out of the cellar, muttering rapidly in German. Ida knew some German, but not enough to keep up with his rambling.

"Time for interrogation?" Ida asked, pretending it might as well be a party she was now invited to.

The SS officer did not respond, nor did the younger one on her other side. But everything was clear enough when they reached the top of the stairs and took her outside once more. A car was waiting, and Fat Jacques stood outside of it.

"And now, Mademoiselle Hendrickx," Jacques said almost with glee, "we are going to see your flat."

"It's Madame Hendrickx," Ida grumbled, wrenching her arm from the hold of the Nazis.

Jacques gave her a look. "You'll forgive me if I don't quite believe your marital status, mademoiselle. Or your having a mixed marriage. You've already given me one false identity today. Why should I trust any of the paperwork regarding you?"

He had a point there, she would not deny it, but she wasn't going to tell him so, or give him the satisfaction of discovering any information whatsoever.

Ida sat in the back of the car once more, surprised when both soldiers got in as well as Jacques. "So many escorts," she mentioned almost absently, smiling at Jacques.

He startled her by smiling back. "Oh, there are others, but they are already at your flat. We wanted to get started going through your things as soon as possible. It will be so much easier for you if you tell us where to look."

Ida bit the inside of her cheek, praying quickly that Andrée was not at home. That she would not come home during this. That she would be spared all of this. Once they truly looked into Ida's records, they would find out who her roommate was, and if they discovered the falsifications there, it could bring down their entire operation.

"Well," Ida said with a dismissive sniff, "what are you looking for?"

"Documents regarding hidden children, Mademoiselle Hendrickx. What else?"

CHAPTER 19

Every Jewish slander and every Jewish lie is a scar of honour on the body of our warriors. The man they have most reviled stands closest to us and the man they hate worst is our best friend.

—ADOLF HITLER, *MEIN KAMPF*

There was something to be said for a good day's work done.

Andrée hadn't felt so satisfied with the course of a day in so long that she had forgotten what it felt like. Her burden hadn't been entirely removed from her shoulders, but it was easier to breathe today than it had been of late. She would be able to sleep without excessive thoughts or tears tonight and would be able to face the morrow with fresh energy.

She sighed contentedly as she rounded the landing, starting up the final stairs toward her flat. A smile spread its way across her face, and she imagined Ida slicing them both some bread to have with tea as they relaxed before retiring. She had missed dinner, which was not unusual, but Ida always seemed to have fresh bread for them even if Andrée had missed the meal.

She glanced up at their door and froze on the stairs.

A Nazi seal was across the door. That meant they had been inside, and it was forbidden for anyone but them to enter. It was illegal to break a Nazi seal. And they would know if . . .

Andrée swallowed hard, one hand going to her throat. She forced her feet to keep mounting the steps, unsure what she would find or what could have happened. Were they compromised? Had the Nazis found their documents? Ida had been hiding a few notebooks in their house since Esta had been taken, so if the Gestapo had searched the flat, it was entirely possible that they had found them.

Not that they would know how to read the notebooks, considering the sheer number of them and what was documented in each. But they would certainly know it was something, and it would put a great many people in danger.

The seal crossed the doorjamb, of course, so Andrée could not enter without breaking it. They would know she had been inside. And it might clue them into something they had missed.

If the flat was sealed now, then Ida could not be home.

Andrée stumbled back a step, staring at the seal in horror.

Ida.

Where was she? Had she been captured? Was she safe?

She had to know, had to find out, had to inform someone, if nothing else. Before anything else happened, before she looked into any other risks, she had to make certain that Ida was safe.

Andrée turned and flew down the stairs, not bothering to take care with her steps or their volume. If the building was being watched, if the Gestapo were lying in wait for her, they would know exactly where she was, but she didn't care. She would risk it to get out of the building and find some answers.

She didn't know where the CDJ headquarters were. Never had known. She knew only of the office she worked out of with Ida and the others in the children's department in Rue du Trône. But she did know how to call in, and that would be enough for now.

Once out of the building, no one stopping her or even appearing, she raced for the nearest phone in the street. She did not dare hope that the place was not being watched, but as she had not been arrested yet, perhaps there was a little time.

But it could only be a little.

She put coins in, and dialed the number, her arms and legs quivering as though she were out in the middle of winter. She could barely keep still, her heart pounding in a thunderous way, her pulse seeming to echo in various parts of her body in random intervals. She wanted to run to some safe place, scream until her lungs collapsed, then curl into a ball in some corner and wait to be found by someone with the ability to console her.

"Hello?" answered a voice from the office.

"This is Claude," Andrée said quickly, her voice trembling somehow more than her frame. "My flat has a Nazi seal on it. I don't know where Jeanne is or what has happened."

She heard rustling from the other end of the line, and a few other voices, though none of them were speaking to her directly.

"What do I do?" she asked before anyone could say more. "What's happened? Do we know?"

"Jeanne was arrested during a meeting today," came the would-be calm voice. "We had a report from her contact. They must have searched the flat."

Andrée hissed and looked around, half expecting to see Fat Jacques poking his head out from one of the nearby bushes and waiting for her. "You know what Jeanne has there, right? We have to know if it's safe. If any of us are safe."

"Where are you now, Claude?" demanded the voice. "Are you safe?"

"For now," she answered, still scanning her surroundings. "I'm on Rue de Belle-Vue, a block and a half from the flat. No watch seems to be in place."

"Stay there. Is there shelter?"

Andrée turned to look behind her. "Yes, there's a building of flats with a porch alcove I can wait in."

"Do that. We're sending Raoul to your location. You need to get into the flat. He'll assist. Take anything you need from the flat along with the documents, then go to your office. We'll rehouse you and get you new identity papers as soon as we can. You'll be running the department now, Claude. Do you understand?"

"Yes." Andrée swallowed hard, nodding in spite of being alone. The nodding was not for the voice on the end of the line.

It was for herself.

She was now in charge of the children's department of the CDJ. Esta was gone, Ida was gone, but she was still here. She and Paule and Claire, but she had been the one living with Ida and knew the details well. She was the one who had to get into the flat and retrieve the notebooks, if any were still there. If any of the books had fallen into the hands of the Gestapo, it would disrupt what they were working toward. Any information in the hands of the Gestapo was damaging, even if they would not understand it, nor comprehend what else was out there. They would not have all five books, as there were some still stashed in their office, but there were enough notebooks in the flat to compromise a significant portion of the operation.

And destroy countless lives.

This would all be on Andrée's shoulders now. She would have to take on the stresses that she had seen Ida carry, and the weight of all the hidden children in their records. And all of the new requests that needed to be fulfilled. And all of the future requests that would come in.

There was no point in asking herself if she could do it. If she was up for the challenge. If she even wanted to take on all of this. None of that mattered. She *would* do it. She *would* meet the challenge. And she *would* do the very best that she possibly could to ensure that Esta and Ida had not been arrested in vain.

What she wanted had become immaterial ages ago, because ultimately, what she wanted was to see these Jewish children safe.

She'd go to the ends of the earth if required to do so.

She hung up the phone and shoved her shaking hands into her coat pockets, moving to the porch alcove she had mentioned only moments ago. It was not quite a hiding spot, but it would keep her out of plain view of the street, and if it started to rain, which was always a risk this time of year, she would be protected from that.

It was a small consideration now, rain. A mild inconvenience, but it wouldn't change anything. Wouldn't change her mood. Wouldn't impact her night in any significant way. Wouldn't be a soothing song to help her sleep.

Wouldn't be anything at all, really.

Maybe it should rain. It might complete the morose picture the evening presented. It should rain on depressing occasions just for the sake of having the weather match her emotions.

She had no idea how long it would take Raoul to get to her location. She didn't even know who Raoul was. Not that it mattered. Anyone from the CDJ would have been a stranger to her apart from those who had worked with her. If the main office felt that Raoul was the best person to help her get into her flat and remove what was most important, she would trust them.

How they were going to keep the Nazis from seeking her out, she wasn't sure. Her name was on the lease documents for the flat. It was a false name, of course, but if they knew Ida, they could easily know Andrée.

Andrée leaned against the wall of the building, looking up into the lantern-shaped light above her, letting her mind move to Ida.

What was she enduring now? Had they sent her straight to Malines? Was she being held somewhere in town? Interrogated? Harmed? Did they know who she really was?

Was she afraid?

Ida had been such a help to her in the time that they'd been working together. Such a mentor and a dear friend. None of this work Andrée had done or would do would have been possible without Ida's devotion and determination. Her commitment to the vision of the CDJ. Her certainty of their mission. Her complete sacrifice of her own safety and security to the greater good of these Jewish children.

She was truly the heart and the backbone of their operations.

How Andrée would manage without her, she could not imagine. How any of them could do this without her remained to be seen. But it was what they had to do, and she would have to have the patience to wait until they had answers regarding Ida's condition.

They had the ability to get certain information into Malines, if need be, and some information could come out of it. The Heibers had been kept in Malines, for whatever reason, rather than sent on to Breendonk or a worse camp. Perhaps it was Maurice's connection to the AJB that had kept them there. Perhaps it had been intervention from influential individuals. There were a great many possibilities, none of which Andrée was privy to.

What had happened to Ghert Jospa, however, was a mystery.

He was certainly not in Malines, but more than that was not known.

They would be able to find some information about Ida when some time had passed. How much would depend on what was done and when.

And then they might know if there was any intervention to be made.

"Claude?"

Andrée turned her head to her left, seeing a tall man in a dark coat and flap cap, his jaw covered in scruff. "Raoul?"

He nodded once.

Andrée did as well, wondering if the motion shook as much as her body seemed to. Fear gripped her, licking at every joint and limb with the sting of a fire and the foreboding of being tied to a stake.

Was she about to learn of the utter destruction of all of this? Or might there be a glimmer of hope for them all?

Or, worse still, might there be Nazis within the flat, waiting for her arrival?

She forced the sense of doom down with a swallow, then pushed off the wall and indicated the way toward her flat with a nod of her head. "This way."

They started the block and a half walk, saying nothing. Andrée knew what her task was, and she figured Raoul did as well, and likely to more detail. What was there to discuss?

To her surprise, Raoul did not move toward the door of the building when she did. Instead, he tilted his head away from it, and Andrée followed, more curious than fearful.

He led her around the corner of the building and pointed up at the windows, silently asking which was hers.

Was he completely daft? How could they possibly climb their way up to the second story windows of her flat? Even if she would be capable of such a thing, she was not dressed for anything so extreme. Plus her legs had not stopped shaking since she had noticed the Nazi seal.

But needs must, she supposed, and she walked toward the far corner, pointing up to the two windows closest to it.

Raoul nodded and looked around the small side street for a moment before moving to the rain barrel at the corner and waving Andrée over.

"Stand here," he told her in a low voice. "I'll help you hoist up along the drainpipe to that flower box there." He pointed to the ledge of the flower box that hung from Ida's window, though no flowers had grown there yet. "You should be able to edge your way close enough to reach the railing of the second window and secure yourself there."

Andrée nodded as she looked up at her path, every swallow and breath within her burning in her throat and chest in anticipation.

"Are the windows locked?"

She blinked, trying to think back to that morning. "I don't know," she admitted. "I may have latched them."

"Not a problem," Raoul told her easily. "I can take care of that. We'll get to the railing and take things from there."

Before she had too much time to think, Andrée moved to the rain barrel and took Raoul's hand to get up on it. She gripped the drainpipe and looked up its length, feeling a firm resolution seep between the cracks of her abject fear.

She would get into that flat and retrieve the notebooks. There was no other alternative. She would not give the Nazis more time to examine the space and discover their location, if they had not done so already. She had risked her life for this operation, and this was simply another avenue she must risk it on.

"Ready?" Raoul asked from his position on the ground.

Andrée did not even bother nodding. She raised her right foot to the tiny bracket and used it to steady herself as she reached higher on the pipe. She pulled herself up as high as she could, clenching her legs around the cold metal of the pipe. She reached up again and heaved with all her might, feeling as though she were only moving a few inches at a time and yet a mile.

Raoul was soon under her, pressing her legs further up and giving her a steadier base of support. He tapped her feet and brought one to his shoulders, holding it tight. Once both of her feet were secure on his frame, she could reach higher still and repeat the almost agonizing motions of dragging herself up the pipe's length.

Yet the flower box was nearly within range now. She could see it clearly, and a few more times pulling herself along would have her there.

Just a few more times.

Again and again, she reached along the pipe, arms shaking with the effort of holding her own weight as she tried to move and maintain her hold on it. Her thighs shook with the pressure of keeping her secure, and her fingers throbbed with the tension she was forcing into them. The smoothness of the metal did not help, and she slipped a time or two, but never more than a fraction or two, mercifully.

Then suddenly, the top of the flower box was within reach, and Andrée raised her hands as high as she could on the pipe, groaning as she pulled herself up just a bit further. She stretched her leg out until her shoe was firmly on the flower box, then reached her hand out for the top of the window.

All she had to do was lean forward. Lean and trust that she was stable enough to keep from falling.

Holding her breath, she gave over to the motion and somehow gasped at the same time as her other foot found purchase on the flower box, her free hand gripping the cool stone above the window for her very life. A surge of elation rushed through her, but she could not revel in it. Not yet.

Easing her way along the flower box, Andrée kept her eyes on the railing of the next window. That was her way in. There was not space enough here to do so, but the area might as well have been a full terrace in comparison to this one.

The railing was an easy reach from her position, and she gripped it hard as she swung her body over, sliding her feet between the balusters and onto the small platform. She climbed over the top of the railing quickly and checked the window while Raoul followed her path along the pipe and window box, doing so with more speed and ease than Andrée had managed, naturally.

"I think it's latched," Andrée murmured when he reached her. "Sorry."

He waved that off and pulled out a switchblade from his pocket. He flipped the blade open and reached for the separation of the two windows. He slid the blade along the tiny gap, then quickly twisted his wrist. Andrée heard the telltale click of the window latch sliding back.

Together, they pried open the windows and climbed into the flat.

As she had feared, the place had been overturned from top to bottom. Her bedroom was in complete disarray, and, further into the flat, things only got worse.

Drawers in the kitchen were open, books had been yanked off the shelf, the cushions had been tossed from the couch, and she could see from her position that the other bedroom had been gone over with just as much enthusiasm. There was an odd sense of violation in seeing her home like this, something like offense and vulnerability at the same time, and a hint of humiliation to top off the emotional cacophony.

A general sense of rawness, really.

For a moment, all she could do was stare at the mess.

Raoul came up behind her, whistling low. "What do you think?"

Right. They had a task to do. She could not afford to be emotional about this.

Andrée immediately looked at the rug in front of the couch. It lay perfectly intact, perfectly in line, and perfectly undisturbed. She moved forward and crouched, flipping the rug back and exposing the floorboards beneath. Pressing a corner of one of the boards, she pried up the now raised opposite edge, pulling the board off entirely.

Three notebooks sat in the newly exposed space, just as Ida had placed them.

A rush of air burst out of Andrée's lungs. Tears filled her eyes, and she managed to smile in spite of them. "All good. Safe and secure." She pulled them out and replaced the board before rising and tucking the books under her arm.

Raoul also wore a smile. "Perfect. Did you need to pick up anything for yourself?"

"Probably." She returned to her bedroom, pulling a carpetbag from her bureau and putting the notebooks safely within. Other items were scattered all over the room, and suddenly she didn't care much about what she took with her. Sighing, she began picking up just a few things from the floor, tossing them into her bag haphazardly.

She clasped her bag and left, turning to Ida's room more for observation than anything else. It had also been tossed, no rhyme or reason to any of it, and the bureau sat open.

Andrée smiled very slightly at the sight of it, knowing one thing for certain now. "Raoul? They must have brought her here. A bag is gone that she did not take this morning."

"Really?" The note of encouragement in his tone bolstered Andrée as well. "Then she would have seen . . ."

"Exactly," Andrée answered as he trailed off. "She knows they don't have the books." She turned from the room and grinned at Raoul. "There's that, at least, right?"

He nodded, returning her smile. "Absolutely." He nodded at the bag in her hand. "Ready?"

"Ready." She glanced around the flat without emotion, exhaling with a new sense of satisfaction. "Absolutely ready."

They returned to her window, climbed out, and closed the windows behind them. With annoyingly lithe movements, Raoul swung his legs over the top of the railing and lowered himself until he was only gripping the platform of the window. Then he suddenly dropped.

Andrée rushed to the edge, looking down in horror.

He stood perfectly well, looking up at her and brushing his hands off. "Toss down the bags."

Andrée did so. She hoped he wouldn't expect her to be so haphazard on the way down. It looked a lot further down than it had looked up.

Once the bags were down, Raoul peered back up at her. "Swing over and lower yourself down gently. I'll move this crate over to stand on so I can reach you faster. Just a short drop, but I'll have you."

There was no question in his voice, no offer of another way, so Andrée swallowed the fire in her throat and hooked one leg over the top of the railing, then the other. She turned to face the building and allowed herself a very small breath before crouching down and gripping the balusters with quivering, clenching fingers. She forced her feet out from under her, arms trembling as she carefully lowered herself down.

Her legs swung a little as she tried to find Raoul's grip but felt nothing there. Exhaling in short gasps, she forced her right hand to move to the platform, then the left, and lowered herself further.

"Nearly there," Raoul called up.

Andrée closed her eyes and let herself hang fully from the ledge.

Hands clamped around her ankles hard. "Right, don't crumple. Let me pull you." Raoul guided her feet to his shoulders, then raised his hands to her knees.

Her fingers ached as her body stretched, her muscles screaming at her with the anxiety of letting go.

"Lock your knees, lock your core," Raoul instructed, "and let go."

Andrée bit her lip and did so, going as stiff as she dared, and was startled to find his hold on her perfectly secure.

"Right, then," Raoul told her in a much calmer voice. "Crouch down and climb off me, then we can get out of here."

It took a few moments of rather monkeylike antics that reminded her of some of their dear children, but then she was down on the ground, and so was he.

That was that, then.

"I'll escort you to Rue du Trône, if that's all right with you," Raoul said almost absently as they walked out of the side street and back onto the main road. "I don't anticipate any problems, but we must be certain after what happened with Jeanne."

"I wasn't aware you knew where the office was," Andrée replied, giving him a quick look.

He shrugged. "I didn't before tonight. We know what we need to know when we need to know it."

"I suppose that's true." She twisted her mouth in thought. "Do you know what happened with Jeanne today?"

"Some. She was meeting with a contact from the AJB. They questioned the other woman first. Apparently Fat Jacques thought she looked Jewish, so he asked the questions. She presented her AJB card, which spared her arrest, but he didn't trust Jeanne's papers."

"Jacques himself arrested her?" Andrée shook her head, sputtering in disbelief. "What are the odds? That man is a vulture."

Raoul snorted softly. "He is, indeed. Much to answer for. Anyway, Jeanne had the presence of mind to pull her documents from her bag and hide them at the table. Her contact found them after the arrest and took them to safety. It's been retrieved, so I suppose it's your information to use now, isn't it?"

That was a humbling thought. Ida's work was now Andrée's work. Her contacts were now Andrée's contacts. Her meetings were now Andrée's meetings.

There would be much to do, and not much time to adjust to the change.

Andrée continued walking toward the office on Rue du Trône, now doing so silently. There was too much to consider, too much work to do. As far as they knew, Ida was alive. If they allowed her to pack a bag from her flat, they were either maniacal or not planning to kill her immediately. If they thought she had valuable information, which seemed to be the idea, given the state of the flat, they would probably keep her alive as long as possible for the information she possessed.

If she was that valuable a capture for them, then interrogation would be her fate.

Ida was in her forties, and her health was good. But what sort of tolerance would she have for the pain they could inflict upon her?

How would she do if they sent her to a camp?

People are being burnt.

Andrée shook her head, desperate to clear the words she'd first heard nearly a year ago. She refused to contemplate the possibility of Ida being sent to a camp like that. Refused to allow the worst-case scenario to become the truth in her mind. Refused to give into the abject despair so easily accessible in these times and circumstances.

Ida was one of the strongest women that Andrée knew. If anyone could endure the troubles that would be inflicted upon them, it was Ida. If anyone was determined enough to withstand trials, it was Ida. If anyone could give the Nazis as good as they got, it was Ida.

And Andrée was not going to let Ida down.

She was going to live up to the expectations that Esta and Ida had set for the children's sector of the CDJ. She was going to continue the work they started and make certain there was no lapse in the quality of their care and their efforts. She was going to do everything she could to get as many children out of danger as possible.

She was going to do this.

How, she wasn't sure. But the how did not matter as much at this point as did the conviction to do so. The details did not matter. The complications did not matter. The pressures, the stresses, the dangers, the burdens—none of it mattered.

The children mattered. The families mattered. The operatives mattered.

The work mattered.

And Andrée was going to get it done.

CHAPTER 20

We must always keep in mind what the Jew wants today, and what he plans to do with us. If we do not oppose the Jews with the entire energy of our people, we are lost. But if we can use the full force of our soul that has been released by the National Socialist revolution, we need not fear the future. The devilish hatred of the Jews plunged the world into war, poverty, and misery. Our holy hate will bring us victory and save all of mankind.

—ERNST HIEMER, *DER STÜRMER*, 1943

Ida sighed wearily as she was dragged from the coal cellar by soldiers again. She'd been in there for at least two days now, but possibly more. She'd been questioned once upon her return from her flat, but they'd gotten bored with her lack of responses and sent her back to the cellar.

Jenny and Amelie had gone now, taken out by soldiers and not returned. Julia didn't speak anymore, and Maria just wept for her pain and for her baby. Ida didn't bother talking at all, finding no relief or purpose in it. Until it was decided what would be done with her, she just viewed the time in the cellar as an opportunity to declutter her mind and take whatever rest she could.

Not that life was comfortable in a dark and cramped coal cellar, but they'd let her bring her bag of belongings in with her, so she had a makeshift pillow. She had slept in more uncomfortable places recently, like benches in well-lit train stations, in the course of her work. Having almost complete darkness for sleep was a relief.

Now, of course, she was probably due for more questioning.

Maybe now they would decide what to do with her and get her settled in one place or another. She would love to be able to adjust to a new way of life rather than being kept in this state of irregular and intermittent existence.

She was taken up the stairs again, her feet working perfectly well, though she was being pulled along as though she was unconscious. Then, to her surprise, she was taken up another flight of stairs, the hallway and rooms much brighter and filled with more light than the ground floor had been.

They turned roughly two doors down, the room wide and comfortable, containing large bay windows and an ornate desk to one side. No one else was within at the moment, but Ida was made to sit in a chair in the center of the room before the soldiers who stood behind her.

Then they waited.

How long wasn't clear; Ida could not have even said what day it was. But she looked at her hands, wincing at the filthy state of them. She began to pick at the dirt and grit beneath her fingernails while she waited, treating the experience almost like an interview for a job she didn't really want.

Would Fat Jacques be present for this particular interview? Or would it be the Gestapo alone? Would they bring in the SS or leave it to the plain clothes? Or would she just sit here and enjoy some light for a change?

That would have been an interesting form of torture. Bringing captives out into the sunlight for short intervals. Showing them what clean spaciousness was available. Allowing them to sit without risk of splinters or soiling of coal dust. And then returning them to complete, damp blackness.

How it would motivate anyone to do anything would likely depend on the mental state of the prisoners, but Ida was fine for now.

Steps in the hallway met her ears, and she continued to pick at her nails pointedly.

Two people entered, and Ida did not bother to look up as they did so.

Without any sort of preamble or introductions, one of them stepped forward and began barking at her in German.

The second person spoke soon after. "Who was the lady with you at the café?"

Ida picked at her nails, focusing on a particularly stubborn piece of coal.

More German.

"Why were you with her?" the translator asked, though it seemed to take him a long time to translate.

She flicked her eyes at him, and his eyes were fixed on her; he was not considering the German beside him at all. Was he trying to help her or was he simply slow at translation?

The German huffed. "Who is her husband?" the translator eventually asked.

Ida raised her brows and resumed picking at her nails.

"Just give us the names of the hidden children," came the slow translation. "The true names. And addresses. If you do this, no harm will come to you. You will not have to leave Brussels."

It was almost word for word what Jacques had said to her the night she was arrested, and it had not worked for him either, much to his irritation.

Ida let her eyes move to the German asking the questions, and just smiled.

He smiled back. "I want to help you," he said, according to the translator. "I think it is wrong not to think of yourself in times like this. I can help you; I am one of the kind ones. If you will just give me the information, you won't have to suffer anymore."

It took an almost agonizingly long time for the translator to relay all of that, and Ida was growing more and more convinced of the intention of such a slow speed. She looked at him again, wondering if he had children himself. If he had sympathy for the children she had been helping and the cause she had been engaged in.

Was he Belgian? Was he sympathetic to Jews? Did he simply draw the line at children? Whatever it was, she was certain that he was trying to help, unlike the officer with his obviously false claims.

Yet this questioning was fairly innocent, all things considered. Was it an attempt at indicating worse things to come?

"Tell me something," the German apparently said, losing the pretend kindness. "Anything."

Ida shrugged a shoulder. "I have taken care of Jewish children pursued by the Gestapo. What could be more natural, since I am a social worker? I have hidden perhaps fourteen of them. And I am in touch with some priests and the like who get me the money necessary for their upkeep."

It took a long time for the translator to relay this to the officer, and Ida found herself smiling at that. It might have seemed like a good chunk of information she had passed on then, but she knew it was nothing they did not already know once they considered it.

She was a social worker. She was hiding children. People in religious orders were helping.

All details they knew and had known.

And that was all she would confess to.

"We would like to know the names and addresses of the priests," the German stated, via interpreter, folding his arms.

"I am sure you would," Ida replied, folding her own arms to match him.

When she said nothing else, the German glared at her and said something else.

Ida looked at the translator for understanding.

"He demands the answers," the interpreter said simply, his tone implying it was fairly obvious.

Ida gave a helpless gesture, then folded her arms once more.

"We will beat you for the answers if you do not give them to us."

We? Who did he think was going to join him in that? Beating a woman, really?

"We will bind you. Restrict your food and drink. Forbid you sleep."

Considering there had been zero intimidation tried by this man as of yet, his threats weren't exactly striking the proper tone he might have wished. It felt more like a comedy than anything else, and had she thought it would help her case, Ida would have actually laughed.

Instead, she only gave him a tight smile.

He growled, irritation clear in any language, and stormed out of the room, the interpreter remaining behind.

Was that it? Ida scoffed to herself and sank back against her chair.

The interpreter cleared his throat, and she looked up at him.

His expression was full of warning.

A new officer came into the room then, and his expression was full of disgust at her.

Her smile faded ever so slightly.

He roared at her in furious German, the delay of the interpreter doing nothing to lessen the feelings involved. "Who is helping to hide the Jewish children?"

Ida swallowed but said nothing.

"Which religious frauds are assisting you?"

She looked down at her fingers and began picking at the nails once more, though her fingers shook a little more this time.

The officer came closer and shouted at her ear. "We will hunt down anyone you care about and send them to Breendonk. To the torture camps."

Considering her brothers had left the country and her husband hadn't seen her in years, there weren't many people in that category at risk.

"Tell us what we want to know!" Flecks of spit hit Ida's cheek while she listened to the translation.

She shook her head, only pretending to pick her nails now. She was shaking too much to do more. There was something about the fury directed her way that had that effect on her. Sent her quivering from head to toe and making her head swim. She wasn't necessarily afraid, but she would never claim to be unmoved by the rage.

It wouldn't make her give them the information they wanted, but it would make her look weaker.

More vulnerable.

Breakable.

The officer yelled at her a bit more, then left the room unsatisfied.

Ida closed her eyes as he left, taking a moment to breathe to herself.

But only a moment.

A third interrogator entered and started by shaking her chair violently. "You will tell me what I want to know," he hissed in her ear, his voice resembling a snake. "Everything I want to know. In detail."

Ida tightened her jaw, grinding her teeth together.

She would not give them anything. Not one single thing.

"The priests," he said in a dark voice. "The nuns. The convents. All of it. Every religious institution you know. Names and addresses." He backhanded Ida suddenly, the sting of his hand on her cheek more like fire than she expected. She could feel the scratches his nails had left in their wake, crackling like lightning on her newly sensitive skin. It felt like a branding, in a way, and there was no escaping the humiliation of the experience.

Or the indignation.

She imagined herself digging her heels into gravel out in the world, anywhere away from this room, resisting in a more physical sense than was possible now.

Anything to solidify the resolve in her mind.

"Do you know how easy it would be to break you, little Jew?" he rasped behind her, picking the chair up with her in it and dropping it back to the floor, literally rattling her. "And how fun?"

Ida inhaled deeply and exhaled the same.

"Dirty, little Jew." He spat, the blob of moisture hitting her shoulder.

He said more things, but the interpreter said nothing.

Ida opened her eyes and looked at him, her eyes questioning.

"That," the interpreter said simply, "was a great deal of foulness."

There was something almost funny about his matter-of-fact explanation for his silence. About his unwillingness to translate what was said.

And the Nazi tormenting her wouldn't even know.

It was a beautiful thing.

The Nazi shoved her head forward hard, making something twinge in her neck and her head feel as though she had gone through some wall. But then he stormed out of the room, slamming the door behind him.

The guards behind her chair had not moved from the positions they had taken upon their arrival.

Perhaps they were used to this sort of thing.

What a terrible thing to become accustomed to.

A new man entered the room then, and he stopped right in front of Ida. "Get up," was all he said, according to the interpreter.

Cautiously, Ida did so, her knees shaking immediately upon standing.

There was no time to find her balance before the man shoved her toward the corner of the room. She stumbled on her way, and was pushed just as hard again, until she crashed into the walls. He grabbed her shoulder and whirled her around, holding her tight into the corner, immediately beside one of the bay windows. He could have pushed her through the glass and onto the ground below if he'd moved her a few centimeters to her left. It might not be a catastrophic fall, but it would have done enough damage.

"I don't think you understand how trivial your resistance is," this new man said, according to the poor interpreter, who was still trying to keep things slow for her. "How futile."

There was nothing futile about resisting the Nazis, no matter what they wanted anyone to believe. And considering what she was hiding, and what was at stake, there was nothing trivial about it either.

"You tell me what we want to know," he ordered, shoving her hard into the corner again. "Every name and every address. Or I will send you to Breendonk, have you locked in a cell, and have food and water completely withheld until you have written them all down."

Something new and impulsive lit into Ida as he continued to push and shove her against the walls, and she shook her head from side to side, even as her head was rammed against those walls by his force.

He said something very harsh, snarling in a feral manner, and reached into his jacket, withdrawing a gun. He cocked it quickly and pressed it to Ida's chest.

Hard.

Then he laughed. Chuckled like he'd thought of something particularly humorous.

Ida swallowed, though it did not do anything to relieve the dryness in her mouth and throat. The perfectly circular rim of the gun barrel against her chest was all she could feel otherwise, pressed against her in such a way that she could not move in any direction without increasing that pain.

He leaned in, slowly and methodically, continuing to chuckle. The sound was echoing in her ears and reverberating down her limbs, wrapping around her spine, and invading her thoughts.

"Stubborn little Jew," he whispered, his breath cascading over her face. "Tell us."

Ida tried to swallow. Once, twice, and even a third time.

But she could not do it.

Her interrogator suddenly burst out laughing, loudly and with some genuine delight, somehow. He pulled the gun from her chest, still laughing.

Something in Ida broke, some band of tension that had taken hold of her body, and she began to laugh as well. A nervous, panicked, half-hysterical laugh that had her gasping painfully.

He ordered something as he turned away from her and left the room. The interpreter hurried his translation for her. "You're to be taken back down to your cell," he said in a rush as he took his leave as well.

Ida could manage a faint nod for him, but nothing more as one of the SS soldiers took her by the arm and hauled her from the room. This time, she was dragged, her legs completely without strength, though they hadn't been touched by anyone during the course of the questioning. She was, quite simply, exhausted by the experience. Fairly well and whole, apart from the stinging in her cheek from the blow.

But drained in all other respects.

Half-carrying her, muttering to himself, the SS soldier brought her down both flights of stairs and deposited her back in the coal cellar. He dropped her onto the ground and pushed her legs out of the way of the door with his foot before closing the door and securing the latch.

Ida lay there on the floor for a long while, just breathing. Her legs began to shake, trembling and quivering with the aftershocks of her experience. Her lungs matched them, still allowing for inhalation and exhalation, but seeming to shiver as they did so. Her throat was now painfully dry, the desire to quench her thirst bordering on agony, but there was nothing to drink in their cellar.

That was part of the pattern there.

She pulled herself back to her usual corner where her bag still sat and laid her head upon it. Her mind contemplated the contents for a quick moment, and she recalled her mealtime treasures of watercress and cottage cheese.

It was not water, but it might do the trick.

Pushing herself up, Ida opened the bag and pulled them out, nibbling on the watercress as though it had come from the heavens itself.

"All right there, Watercress?" Maria asked softly.

Ida smiled in the darkness at the nickname her cellmate had given her and nodded, though no one would see. "For now, Maria. I'm all right for now."

CHAPTER 21

That is the Jew! He is the drone of humanity. He is the exploiter of the labor of others. He is an enormous danger for all the nations. If one overlooks this danger, whole peoples can be destroyed. History is rich in examples that prove to us that the Jew has ruined millions of people.

—LINES FROM A NAZI CHILDREN'S BOOK, 1940

It was the biggest assignment Andrée had worked out yet. Six children to be placed, and preferably together. But she'd done it. She had a place for them and a willing family to claim them as cousins.

The single father would be thrilled and relieved.

Andrée would not pretend that they could do this all the time, or even frequently, for families. There were just not enough places for multiple children at one time, and the risk of travelling with more than three children at once was great. And getting worse by the day, it seemed.

But the pain in this father's eyes as he had pleaded for help for his children had been too much to bear. This man, who had done everything in his power to raise his children alone in this horrendous time, now needed help. And the only thing he had specifically asked was that his children be kept together, if at all possible.

They had already lost their mother. He couldn't bear to have them lose each other when they would already lose him to hiding.

And she had done it.

Not alone, of course. There had been a great number of resources for her to call upon to find the perfect place for these children, and each person she had contacted had worked with the same passion and drive she had been filled with. They had all come together to find a solution that would work for this family.

She had not been this excited to relay information in ages.

It had been only a few days since she had taken over the children's sector, and she still felt as though she were treading water in a rough sea, but she finally had the sense that she was at least treading that water in the right direction.

Surely that was all she could do at this point.

She passed a pair of Nazi soldiers on the walk and smiled rather cheerily at them, if for no other reason than because she was on her way to thwart yet another one of their plans to destroy a family. They returned her smile with nods and smiles of their own, continuing on their way.

Someday she wouldn't have to smile at Nazis anymore. Those were the days she worked and yearned for.

She turned at the next block and walked five houses down, advancing to the porch and ringing the bell, feeling the odd desire to dance a little while she waited. She resisted, of course. She couldn't approach something like this being that lighthearted, no matter how relieving the solution was.

The door opened and the oldest child stood there, looking rather worried and drawn, the shadow of tears in her eyes.

Andrée sobered at once, all desire to dance having vanished. "What's happened?"

The girl stepped back and let Andrée in without a word, just a small sniffle.

"Where's your father?" Andrée demanded, afraid he had been taken away from these children.

"Here, Mademoiselle Fournier," the low, resigned voice answered from within the house.

She followed the voice and found the man in the kitchen, sitting at the table, looking more dejected now than he had when he first asked for the CDJ's help.

Andrée breathed a little more easily at seeing him there, but the relief was minimal. "What's happened, monsieur?"

He rubbed at his brow and slid a piece of paper across the table to her.

Andrée picked it up and read quickly. It was an order to report to the authorities. She had seen these orders time and again in her work, usually when she picked up the children and took them away. Or strewn across the street in the aftermath of a razzia.

But now . . .

"When did this come?" Andrée all but growled.

"Not ten minutes ago."

Her mind flashed to the two soldiers she had smiled at on her way here, and she suddenly wished she had tripped them instead.

She shook her head, pressing her tongue to her teeth hard. "No," she snapped. "No." She tore the notice in half, then in half again, and then one more time. She slammed the pieces on the table and looked at the man. "Pack a bag. For yourself and for each of the children. We're changing the plan. You are all coming with me. Now."

He stared at her as though she had lost her wits. "What are you talking about, Mademoiselle Fournier? We cannot possibly—"

"We can," Andrée overrode. "And we will. I came to tell you that I had a placement for your children all together, and now I am telling you that you are going as well. We will come up with some story, put you in a neighboring house, have you work as a gardener for the nearest convent, I do not care. But neither you nor any of your children will be reporting anywhere that the Nazis order."

He blinked, then rose from the table. "Children! Up to the rooms! We are packing!"

The next several minutes were a flurry of activity. Andrée helped the children pack a bag each, aside from the youngest two, who would share a bag, and got them changed into travel clothes as well. The father got his bag packed and explained the plan to the older children while they packed, and the entry filled quickly with the six bags.

"Food," Andrée instructed the oldest girl. "Anything that we can travel with. Nothing excessive, just enough to get us where we're going."

She nodded and dashed into the kitchen.

The little ones were putting on coats now, each of them bearing stars.

Andrée shook her head. "Not those coats, darlings. Do you have any without stars?"

They stared at her in confusion, so young that they likely did not recall ever being without their stars.

"Never mind," Andrée murmured, yanking on the stars of each and tearing them from the coats. It would leave the coats looking a little frayed, but no more than any other well-worn coat in Belgium.

It would have to do.

Moments later, they were all assembled, and Andrée looked at them. "We are going to travel as a family," she explained in a straightforward tone. "I will pretend to be the mother of the family. We are going on holiday to the country. Just smile and act as though we have planned this whole thing. We will see to the details later. Understand?"

Everyone nodded, even the youngest two, who clearly did not understand anything.

Andrée opened the door and gestured for them to go out. She picked up the youngest as well as the bag for the little ones, then put her arm through that of the father's. The second oldest child, a boy, closed the door to the family home, and returned to his bag at once.

Not one of them looked at the house after that.

"Let's go," the father announced cheerily, his voice almost convincing.

As a pack, they walked together toward the train station. The older siblings held the hands of the younger ones, apart from the one Andrée carried in her arms. If anyone thought the sight of them together was strange, they made no comments as they passed the group. No one appeared to think anything of it, which was exactly what Andrée had wanted.

What she had expected.

She could feel the stiffness and apprehension of the man whose arm she held, but he held his head high and continued to walk with them. He was the one to start the games with the children as they walked, encouraging them to find things beginning with a certain letter he called out. It had most of the children laughing as they walked, and seemed to do the trick of reminding them all that they were still a family and that they were in this together.

None of them knew Andrée all that well, but they trusted her enough to go with her without much thought. She felt the weight of that trust and would not see it misplaced. She would house this family with her own if she had to. In her parents' home, if she must.

Luckily, she did not think that would be necessary.

A truck approached on the street, and the children clumped together, some of them whimpering.

"It's all right," Andrée told them, continuing to smile. "They're not for us."

She didn't dare suggest what, or whom, the truck was for, given the realities of life at present, but she was confident it was not for them.

She had to be.

Sure enough, the truck rumbled on by without even slowing for their procession. Everyone seemed to breathe a sigh of relief at that, and Andrée began to whistle a jaunty tune.

One of the girls caught on and began to sing along, or at least hum when she didn't know the words, but it did seem to lift the spirits of the others while they continued to the station.

When they arrived, Andrée purchased the tickets for the entire group, being excessively sweet and gracious to every worker, every guest, every person. She wanted their faux family to be viewed with fondness from the very first moments.

Adorable, happy children with a mother and father, all heading out to the country on a holiday.

That was what they needed to see.

She loaded the family onto the train, got everyone situated, and settled the youngest child on her lap, encouraging her to sleep, if she could. The father took the next youngest and did the same, and only when the train moved did they speak.

"Thank you for this, Mademoiselle Fournier," he murmured, his voice thick. "I know this is not what you had planned on, or when, and likely not what you are supposed to do."

"What I am supposed to do," Andrée replied softly, "is see children and families to safety. Which is exactly what I am doing now."

He chuckled, stroking his child's hair gently. "People don't say no to you very often, do they, Mademoiselle Fournier?"

Andrée managed a smile herself. "Not often, no. And I don't usually give them the chance to."

"Well, we will be eternally grateful for that. Thank you, again." He nodded fervently, and turned to the child on his right, speaking softly.

Andrée looked at the children across from them, all seeming to stare at nothing, just moving with the motion of the train.

Would they find themselves smiling over something genuine soon? Over something that was not forced? Over something spontaneously joyful or fun?

That was what this was all about. Putting the smiles back on the faces of children.

She needed to see the children smile again.

It wasn't a particularly long train ride they had to take, and the family that had agreed to take in the children were perfectly understanding and willing to help the children's father when they learned what had happened. They assured Andrée that they had the room and the means to house him as well, and that they would be more than happy to host them all for as long as needed, even without aid.

Andrée protested, of course, and promised they would receive all the aid possible for the CDJ to give.

They deserved nothing less.

Once back on the train, Andrée focused on her breathing, which was actually quite difficult to keep steady. The stresses of the day and their sudden appearance had taken a toll on her that she had not allowed herself to experience until now. It was not like her to tear up an official notice in irritation, but it had felt like the right thing to do.

It *was* the right thing to do.

Getting the entire family out had been the only solution.

How she would explain that to Yvonne and the others, however . . .

She shook her head as she got off the train back in Brussels. Yvonne would understand. She would comprehend exactly why Andrée had done it, and probably support her fully in it.

Or else simply not make her write up a specific report on it.

After all, the children were exactly where she had planned to place them all along.

The fact that their father was also with them was beside the point.

Andrée shoved her hands into the pockets of her coat and forced herself to let her shoulders droop as though she were relaxed. Perhaps if she made a concentrated effort to *appear* relaxed, she might actually relax. It would start with not being so tense, even if she had to remind herself not to be so tense.

But everything was tense these days, not just her bearing.

She was waiting to hear back on the success of smuggling a child out of the Malines camp, courtesy of Maurice Heiber, who had become an unofficial camp leader during his time there. The interventions of Queen Elisabeth herself had prevented the deportation of the Heibers, and having them in Malines had done a great deal of good.

As much as having them in any camp at all did anyone any good.

This child had been caught up in a raid before they could get him to his fostering home, and Andrée felt responsible for his being in there. He was only two, the poor thing, and a camp was no place for a child to be. Especially without parents. Though there would be some good and worthy people there to make sure he suffered as little as possible, it could not replace the safety and security of being free.

It would be difficult to smuggle adults out of the camp, given the careful stock that was taken of those interred there, but children were less tracked and recorded. And a child of two could be easily misplaced when no one was paying attention to him.

Or so she hoped.

She entered the office at Rue du Trône with a groan, a little fatigued by the unexpected excursion, but not displeased with its outcome. She had families to visit still but needed to update the notebooks before anything else.

To her surprise, Paule was at a desk, working at some notes herself.

"Solange," Andrée greeted, smiling. "I expected you to be out."

"And I will be shortly," Paule told her as she dotted the end of her present record. "But we had a sudden change today."

"Another one?" Andrée rubbed at her brow. "I just finished with a sudden change. A complicated one."

"Well, this one was not so complicated." Paule turned in her chair, grinning at her. "Maurice got the boy out."

Andrée gaped for a moment, then matched her friend's grin. "Did he? Oh, thank heavens! Where did you put him? How did it go? What location did you secure for him? Is he well? Was he hurt?"

Paule chuckled at the rapid succession of questions. "Slow down, dear Claude. You'll wear yourself out before lunch. Maurice claimed the child was ill and had him taken to the *Hôpital St. Pierre* for diphtheria. I reported to the camp as the social worker to take him there."

"Hospital?" Andrée shook her head in disbelief. "How are we going to get him out of a hospital? What is Maurice thinking?"

"Maurice is thinking," Paule said with some severity, "that the child will die. Not in actuality, of course, but he will be made to die according to records. Then we will take him to a house."

Andrée sank onto a chair, exhaling in a huff. "You see? This is why

Maurice and Esta ought to be out here instead of in there! That is a stroke of genius!"

"It is a desperate move only made possible because he *is* in that camp." Paule rose from her chair and patted Andrée on the head like a child. "You have your own genius, Claude. Don't envy others theirs." She moved to the coat rack and plucked hers down. "635 is going to 32. I know they said last time they were full, but not all of their students returned this term, so they have room now."

"Fine," Andrée said with a wave of her hand. "Be safe."

Paule waved back and exited the office, leaving Andrée alone in the workspace.

She had so much to do. She had so much to check and examine and see to, but she wanted nothing more than to breathe and remember how to smile in moments of private solitude. To smile because of something unrelated to the success of her work.

She thought back to the sweet little singing that accompanied her whistling earlier in the day, and, though it had taken place in the course of her work, it seemed more genuine than a great many things lately.

And that sweet little singing made her smile.

CHAPTER 22

But education alone cannot solve the Jewish question. A people that recognizes the Jews must also have the strength to deal pitilessly with the world enemy. Just as the danger of poisonous snakes is eliminated only when one has completely eradicated poisonous snakes, the Jewish question will only be solved when Jewry is destroyed. Humanity must know that in the case of the Jewish question there can only be a hard "either/or." If we do not kill the Jewish poisonous serpent, it will kill us!

—LINES FROM A NAZI CHILDREN'S BOOK, 1940

"*Aufstehen! Jetzt! Du gehst! Jetzt! Schneller!*"

Ida held up her hands as she got to her feet, waving at Maria and Julia to do the same. "All right," she tried to soothe, hoping not to be prodded again by the rifle in the soldier's hand. "We don't speak German. No speak Deutsch."

"*Schnell!*" he barked, gesturing for them to come out.

Ida grabbed her bag, along with Maria's arm, and moved toward the cellar door. Maria had grown feverish lately and was weakening quickly. If they were going to Malines, perhaps Maria could be treated by a doctor.

If they were going somewhere else . . .

The three women were prodded up the stairs from their coal cellar and into the courtyard of the building. The sky was still dark, and Ida could not see the horizon to tell if dawn was approaching yet, but it was certainly early. There were other people waiting in the courtyard, perhaps twenty or so, and they spanned ages. Some old and some young, mostly women but a few men as well, and none of them looked particularly well.

Ida supposed she probably did not look well either. She hadn't been interrogated again, which had been a blessing, but there had been more mockery of them lately when they had asked soldiers for things. Even for something as simple as the chance to relieve themselves.

"Oh, I haven't the time," one had said in perfect French.

"I can't find the key," another had said at one time.

All a joke for them, and a stark inconvenience for the three women.

Would things be better or worse where they were going next?

A truck rumbled into the courtyard, and the canvas was pulled back by one of the soldiers in the courtyard. "In!" he ordered. "To *Mechelen*!"

Mechelen. The Dutch name for Malines.

A destination. And an acceptable one, given the alternative.

The group trudged to the truck and started the process of entering. There were no support points for them to grab onto, so the smaller women and older people struggled to get in. There was no help from the soldiers, naturally, so they had to help themselves. Ida did what she could to assist, though the lack of proper food lately had weakened her more than she would have liked.

Still, they were soon all aboard, and as they were trying to settle themselves, the truck took off. The abruptness threw them all together, some on top of each other, squeals and grunts and groans filling the space as they tried to right themselves. There was nothing within the truck for them to hold onto, so they held onto each other.

Ida looked around the truck bed as they jostled along the cobblestone roads of Brussels. There weren't even any benches in this truck. No suitable place for anyone to sit.

It was not designed to be sat in, she realized. This was not a truck designed for transporting people. It was for transporting items.

Things.

Not people.

Another bump in the road threw them together, and a young girl's shoulder slammed into Ida's arm.

"*Pardon. Het spijt mij,*" the girl murmured.

Ida smiled at the sound of Dutch. She did not speak it well, but so many in Belgium did. "*Ja, zeker,*" Ida replied.

The young woman smiled a little and pulled out a sheet of paper and a pencil from her coat, beginning to sketch.

Ida stared at the paper, an idea striking her. "Have you more?" she asked. "Erm . . . *Meer? Schrijven?*"

The girl glanced at her, her smile spreading, no doubt due to Ida's poor accent. "Yes," she answered. "Here." She handed over her paper and pencil, as well as an envelope from within her cloak.

Where she had procured these things could not possibly be comprehended at the moment. Ida had writing utensils and such in her belongings, but not on her person. This girl, for whatever reason, had been slightly more clever than she, and Ida was so grateful for it. She began to write quickly, hoping her words were legible enough. She wrote her false name and where she was headed, a few details about her state, then listed the social work office on Rue du Trône as the delivery address on the envelope.

It would have to do.

She handed the pencil back to her new friend and shoved the letter through the cracks in the truck bed. It fell through to the ground beneath and, with it, Ida's hopes of any sort of rescue.

If rescue was possible.

Brussels soon disappeared from view through the back of the truck, and then so did Vilvoorde. Lovely views and places that Ida had known so well in recent months and years as she'd helped children to safety.

Now she was being taken out of these places, and sent into danger rather than safety. Forced to endure the very things she had been trying to save children from.

Perhaps there would be children in the camp she could tend to or comfort or help. Families that might benefit from her experience in social work. Or life. Or her work for the CDJ.

Anything. It would take her mind off her own suffering if she could do that.

She winced as the truck thundered over new roads, the change in quality meaning only one thing.

They had arrived in Malines.

Ida closed her eyes, forcing herself to swallow. For two years, the Dossin Barracks at Malines had been something feared by all who had been persecuted in Brussels. Being sent to Malines, for most, meant eventual deportation to Auschwitz. And while reports were never explicitly clear about what happened in Auschwitz, it was well known that no one came out of that place.

And now Ida was going to be in those barracks. This entire truck would be.

For however long the Nazis saw fit.

The truck turned into the barracks courtyard and came to a stop. Again, Nazi soldiers yelled at them and waved rifles. Some of the truck's occupants screamed as they were forced out, directed roughly to stand in a line nearby. Their luggage was taken from them and tossed aside, no care or concern for the owners or contents displayed.

A tall, severe man stood at the head of the line, hands behind his back, a horse crop in his grasp. He said little, from what Ida could see, but the line proceeded toward him steadily. People split off in one direction or the other after seeing him, and when Ida reached him, it became clear why.

"Jew?" he grunted, giving her the same disapproving look he gave them all.

Ida nodded once.

He jerked his head to her right, and she followed the line of others heading toward the barracks themselves.

They filed into a room one after the other, and a stern-faced woman handed each a cardboard box with numbers on it.

"One forty-four," she told Ida without feeling. "Transport twenty-six."

A number. No longer a name, but a number.

There was an odd sort of irony in this. She had been turning children into numbers for years now, not that any child knew what their number was. The number was a code for their safety, but each child *was* a number. And had a new name to keep them safe. A new identity to keep them alive.

She had been given a number instead of a name. To strip her of life.

The line continued into another room of the barracks, this one oddly chilling.

A man in a VNV uniform walked around the person in front of her, examining him and yelling out things in Dutch. A VNV working with the Nazis! Ida had known they were doing this, of course. The VNV—the *Vlaamsch Nationaal Verbond*, or Flemish nationalist party—had made a deal with the Nazis on their invasion of Belgium. But she had yet to see one acting as jailer for the Nazis.

He had an exceptionally long countenance, this man, his face naturally sullen by the dimensions. When he spoke, his mouth bore large teeth, and his jaw worked in a strange manner. Yet there was nothing abnormal in his manner or his bearing, other than the sheer ruthlessness he exuded. He could not have come to this rank of his with any deficiencies noted by recruiters, superiors, and fellow officers.

He reminded her of something, but she had no idea what. Someone, perhaps, though she was certain she had never seen anyone look like him.

What was it that made him of such interest to her mind at present?

He pushed the man ahead of her along and waved for her to come in. He walked around her slowly, and she could feel his eyes raking her in a strange manner. Not predatory or with any interest, but somehow just as thorough and just as unsettling.

He yelled out again in Dutch, though the words weren't as familiar to her as her conversations in the truck had been. Then she was shoved ahead.

Ida walked on, all of them following the line like cows headed for slaughter, not knowing what lay at the end, only knowing this was the path.

Dogs barked somewhere in the vicinity, and there was nothing playful in the sound. It was as though they, too, hated the sight of the Jews.

A series of somber-faced, poorly dressed figures came next, and they stepped forward as Ida reached them.

"Your brooch," one said flatly, holding out a hand. "And the watch."

Ida's mouth fell open and she thought to protest, but one of them shook their head very slightly.

She looked ahead to the others and saw one handing over jewels, another his keys, and yet another some money.

Their identities were not enough; now they had to be stripped of anything valuable they possessed.

With some agitation, Ida pulled off her watch and gave it over, followed by her brooch. The ring from her hand was taken off, the one she had been given upon turning fifteen. Her bag was taken, and the purse removed from it.

Then all four thousand francs she had brought, which Fat Jacques himself had suggested she would need when he had allowed her to pack a bag in her flat, was removed and the seemingly empty purse placed in the box around Ida's neck.

The VNV officer walked up the line of them now, making adjustments he thought were necessary. Cutting off buttons, tearing epaulets from jackets, slicing into bags. There was nothing in it but destruction, though; from what she could tell, they weren't looking for anything hidden.

He reached Ida and took her bag, slashing it randomly and focusing on ruining the lining. Stamps, papers, her compact, a pencil—all of it fell free to the ground. Then he put it in her box, the purse now flat, as though it had never been an item. Her pockets were thoroughly searched, but she had nothing remaining in them.

She stared at the man directly, daring him to look her in the eye.

He never did.

A horse, Ida decided then. That was what he reminded her of.

An ill-tempered, cantankerous, poorly bred horse.

He sniffed at her and moved on.

They all stood there for what had to be an hour, and then, finally, they were free and escorted from the room.

A series of screens greeted them in the next room, a poorly dressed attendant standing beside each. They were lined up at the screens according to gender of the attendant, and Ida moved forward when indicated and stepped behind the screen in front of her.

The attendant moved to her and reached for the collar of her blouse.

"What?" Ida protested, leaning away and grasping tightly at the filthy linen of her blouse.

"Your clothes, mademoiselle," the attendant told her. "It is required."

Ida blinked, unable to believe what she was hearing. "I am to be divested of my clothes?"

"Inspected, mademoiselle." She gestured for her to get on with it, so to speak.

Face flaming, Ida began undoing her own buttons, glaring at this woman, who had no control over what went on here or her assignment, if her state of expression and dress were any indication. She was probably a prisoner here herself and was forced to subject her fellow man to this humiliation.

Which was worse? Enduring the humiliation or participating unwillingly in doling it out?

The attendant stooped and worked at Ida's laces, removing her shoes when she could.

Fully stripped of her clothing, Ida stood behind her screen, wishing there was some place, any place, to hide. But no, she stood here naked while the Horse looked through the soles of her shoes, cut her corsets, ripped open her hems. She could see all of this. She could see him doing the same to all of the clothing, all of the shoes.

What did he think they were going to smuggle into the camp in the soles of their shoes or sewn into their hems? It was utterly ridiculous and entirely unnecessary.

The only reasoning could be, of course, to further their humiliation.

The dirty, ruined clothing was then returned, and Ida did her best to reassemble herself with some dignity, though it was clear there was no dignity to be had in this place.

Her small group of now completely disheartened prisoners traipsed back out into the courtyard, waiting for the rest of those transported with them to suffer the same fate. Their luggage was taken from the pile it had been tossed in and walked to a particular corner of the courtyard.

There it was opened, and all of the contents examined. Items of value were removed and set aside. Everything else remained.

Very little seemed to be remaining.

The man with the horse crop, who had been at the first line Ida had stood in, now played with dogs in the courtyard, chatting with another officer as he did so, laughing and clearly enjoying the fine weather of the day, in spite of the dozens of workers circling the yard to go about their tasks.

Other soldiers seemed to just circle the courtyard like caged dogs, no rhyme or reason to their being there, and something soulless in their demeanor.

Was that what this camp turned a person into?

"Number 144!" a voice called out.

Ida jerked belatedly, realizing she was that number, and she looked around for the source of the voice.

An officer stood at a doorway in the rear of the courtyard, staring at her with impatience and waving her over.

Heart racing, Ida walked over, tattered and dirty, stripped of pride and property, and utterly dreading what else could await her on this day.

She was led, with a few others, up two flights of stairs and then down a hall. She counted the doors, and when they reached the eleventh, their officer stopped and gestured for them to go in.

The room was disgusting.

A double row of bunkbeds was arranged, rags and clothes hanging from the head of the mattresses. There were cardboard boxes of all sizes scattered throughout the room, open and untouched, no doubt containing whatever sad possessions the inhabitants were allowed to keep. There was a stench to the room, too, but not one that could easily be placed.

Men, women, and children were in the room, some lying in their beds, clearly unwell, and others clustered together in groups. But they all stared at the newcomers, the same hollow, hopeless eyes in each and every face.

And this was where she was to stay. Among crowded strangers and mixed genders?

What fresh hell was this?

Ida shook like a dried leaf as she moved to a vacant bed, gingerly sitting down and praying that she would not burst into tears or howl like some sort of trapped animal. Yet those were her inclinations. She was no longer Ida Sterno, Jeanne Hendrickx, or any other human creature.

She was number 144. A Jew.

Nothing more.

And, apparently, nothing was less than that.

The door closed, making Ida flinch, and she sensed someone approaching her. She moved back in anticipation, but a kind-faced man from within the room crouched before her.

"Hello," he said gently, his French careful, but not great. "I am Dago, the head of the room. I promise you that things are not as bad as they seem. You get used to it. I am here to help, and, if you like, you can go wash and change into something new."

Ida looked at him as though he had appeared from some magical forest she had never heard of. "Wash? I haven't washed in days; I haven't been allowed."

He smiled sadly. "Yes. But here, it *is* allowed. Come, I will show you where."

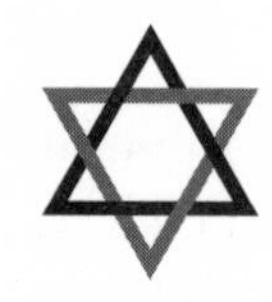

CHAPTER 23

Tapeworms and the Jew are parasites of the worst kind. If we want to free ourselves of them, if we want to be healthy and strong again, there is only one cure: their extermination.

—LINES FROM A NAZI CHILDREN'S BOOK, 1940

"Ugh, still no word on how I can get into the Dossin Barracks to see Jeanne."

Claire turned in her chair, raising her brows. "Did you think there would be? It is a camp run by the Nazis, Claude. It is not easy to sneak in, let alone get back out."

Andrée looked at her doubting friend with a hint of a scowl. "They do allow visitors, Catherine. You went yourself."

"Not easily," Claire shot back. "We have connections in the camp, and they are working on it. You need to let them work within their means."

"I know, I know." Andrée sighed and shook her head. "I just want to see her and make sure she is all right. Let her know that we have kept going. Anything, really."

Claire made a sympathetic sound. "Of course. We all miss her terribly. But not everything can happen at the pace we are used to here. Just relax. Have some water. Take a breath."

Andrée laughed softly. "Water is for external use. Wine is for internal use."

That made Claire laugh out loud. "Where did you hear that?"

"Probably my father, who can say?" Andrée grinned at her friend and fellow operative. "But I cannot take a moment to relax now. I need to go pick up the little Weinberg girl."

"Rivka?" Claire turned more serious at once. "Have the neighbors agreed to take her? I know they took Chaim, but I hadn't heard about Rivka or Simeon."

Andrée closed the notebook she was writing in and handed it to Claire to be replaced. "Simeon went to another neighbor across the street. They have a son of a similar age, so it will work out well to be cousins, or some such. No one seems willing for Rivka, so I am going to pick her up."

"At the house?"

"No, the café just three blocks south. I'm told it is used often as a hiding place for Jews when the raids are in the area. They are used to the situation, so it should be simple enough." She shrugged and fetched her coat from the rack in the corner.

Claire put her hands on her hips, brow creased. "Nothing about this is simple anymore. Be careful, Claude."

Andrée smiled a little. "Always." She gave her friend a quick salute and left the building at an easy pace, trying to focus more on the little girl she was going to retrieve than on her friend trapped in the camp at Malines.

It had been weeks now since Ida had been arrested, and they had received word a few days afterward that she was being transported to Malines. It was both good news and bad news for their band. Malines was close and had connections, but it was still a horrible place, by all accounts, and there was no knowing what she would endure while she was there.

But it was not Breendonk, and it was not Auschwitz.

They had to hold onto that. So long as Ida remained at Malines, there was every reason to hope.

Prisoners could not receive letters from within the camp, but notes were passed, and Andrée had tried her best to get such notes to Ida, though she had no idea if they got through. Nothing had come back out for her. Or for anyone, as far as she could tell.

Had Ida found the Heibers? Had she found anyone that she knew from life outside the camp? Was life at the camp such that there was socialization? Or were they somehow confined?

She knew that most of the people that went to Malines were only going *through* Malines, so to speak. Held there until they could be taken on. The ones that stayed were probably of use somehow to the camp commandant or organizers, or, like the Heibers, had too many requests from the right people to move them anywhere.

Were those same powers working to keep Ida there as well?

This was information that Andrée was not privy to, but she would have loved to know.

She scoffed to herself as she continued toward the café. Hadn't she just been telling herself to focus on Rivka instead of Ida?

It was a difficult shift, given her near-constant concern for her friend and mentor, but she had to put that concern aside for now. Contain it in a chest that could be opened and explored at a better time. Not to be ignored, just to be rescheduled.

She had grown used to this sort of rearrangement of her thoughts as she had been working in the CDJ. She could not become distracted by outside thoughts and concerns when she was picking up a child or escorting one to safety or doing a welfare check. She could not think of friends when facing the Gestapo. Could not think of her mother while avoiding Fat Jacques.

There had to be structure to keep her wits about her and her attention sharp.

And she needed to engage that structure now.

Andrée was sorry for little Rivka. Her parents had desperately wanted to have their children go to neighbors where possible. They felt it would allow them to be more comfortable than going elsewhere and might improve the chances of the children doing well in the new situation. Chaim was very young, so that had been easy. As Andrée had told

Claire, Simeon's friend had persevered with getting him to stay in his family.

But Rivka . . .

From what Andrée had heard, Rivka was the sweetest of little girls. Not demanding or loud, never asking for excesses, obedient and docile. She loved dolls, Andrée recalled learning, and had given each of them a name. Would she have a doll with her today, or one in her suitcase? How had she chosen which doll would come with her? Or had she brought more than one?

If she had packed her own bag, she might have packed *only* dolls. That would provide some amusement for all of them.

And some interesting complications for Andrée where temporal needs were concerned.

Perhaps she could give Rivka a new name that had belonged to one of her dolls. That might be something she would like and might give her something from home to cling to in her heart.

Andrée tied the belt of her black coat as she walked, more out of habit than anything else, and turned the corner, heading directly for the café now. It was a clear favorite establishment of the community, if the number of people coming and going these past months was any indication. Quieter now, but she had passed it many times over the months, and it had always been busy. When she had discovered that the local Jews hid there when they could, she had liked the place even more.

Any place that made the lives of those around them better was one of which she would approve.

The proprietor had agreed for the café to be a pickup location when needed, and today, she needed it to be.

She pushed open the door and waved at the woman behind the counter, who smiled in greeting.

"Coffee, mademoiselle?" she asked.

Andrée nodded gratefully. "That would be wonderful, thank you. And a pastry, please. Whichever you think best."

Understanding dawned in her eyes and she gave Andrée a quick wink. "Of course, mademoiselle." She set about to work and Andrée looked around the café.

A little girl with dark hair sat in a booth in the corner, ribbons tied at the ends of her braids in neat little bows. She was somber and quiet in demeanor but clutched a cloth doll against her and pretended to brush her hair.

Andrée approached her with a smile. "Rivka?"

Wide eyes, a mixture of brown and green, looked at her, answering without a word.

"My name is Mademoiselle Claude," Andrée told her gently. "I'm here to take you somewhere. Did your parents tell you I would?"

She nodded. "They said you would change my name. What is it?"

Andrée crouched down, keeping her smile as easy and natural as possible. "What would you think of Rose?"

Rivka suddenly beamed, the change like that of the dawn itself. "I love that name. My other doll at home, the one with the green dress, is named Rose."

Well, that was easy enough.

Andrée took the girl's hand and held it in both of hers. "Then from now on, you are Rose. Do not answer to your other name anymore, all right? Only Rose."

Rose nodded, returning to her previous seriousness. "And my last name?"

"Wauters," Andrée recited. "Can you remember that?"

"Yes, mademoiselle." She focused on her doll once more. "Can this dolly still be Madeline?"

Andrée laughed very softly. "Yes, darling, she can. Now, where is your suitcase?"

Rose pointed to the counter. "Behind there."

"I'll go get it, hmm?" Andrée patted her head and moved toward the counter, noting the cup of coffee and the pastry waiting just nearby.

Perfect.

The door to the café suddenly burst open, a number of men entering. "Gestapo!" the first one shouted. "We will search the premises!"

Several café customers jumped to their feet in fear and began moving back toward the counter, herding away from the guns now pointing around the room.

Andrée ducked behind a few people, double backed to the table, and took Rose by the hand, tugging her quickly out of the booth, and pushing her toward the counter. The café employee took her from Andrée as soon as they were back there, then grabbed the suitcase and ushered Rose toward the kitchen.

The proprietor came out of the kitchen, all of the action at his feet hidden by the counter. "What is the meaning of this?"

One of the Gestapo came to him, sneering. "We have been told that you are hiding Jews here."

"I?" the proprietor asked, his eyes wide. "Where?"

"That is for us to discover," the Nazi replied with a grin. "Come out from behind there. Now."

A few customers started inching toward the doors, but guns were swiftly swung in their direction. "*Nein!*"

"Everyone will stay here," the first man shouted in clear French, "until you have been questioned and released. Meanwhile, a few of my men will start the search." He nudged his head toward the kitchen, and four of his men went around the corner and into the kitchen.

Andrée closed her eyes, praying to any God that existed in any faith that Rose had been hidden better than the Gestapo could look.

How had they just happened to come in here at the same time she was picking up a child? Of all the cafés in Brussels, they had to choose this one at this exact moment? Had someone told them that a child would be hidden in this location today? Was their arrival based simply on rumors of the Jewish community regarding this café, and all of this was just poor luck on her part?

But it couldn't be a coincidence. She knew it.

They had to know something. They could not just be here on a whim.

Rose needed to be safe. If she was safe, Andrée could cope with the Gestapo here. Could be questioned. Could be arrested, if it came to it.

But if the Gestapo found Rose in all of this . . .

Andrée would never forgive herself.

The employee came out of the kitchen, pushed by the Gestapo and prodded by their rifles. Other kitchen staff came as well, each looking as nervous and apprehensive as any other. But nowhere was a child in the mix.

Andrée tried to catch the eye of the employee, and once the Gestapo men focused somewhere else, the woman looked at her. Looked upward without moving her head. Looked back at Andrée.

And winked.

At that wink, Andrée felt something in her chest give way. Something that released several emotions, none of which were easily defined.

"You!" one of the men shouted, coming to Andrée and grabbing her arm.

Fear like Andrée had not known since returning to her old flat rushed to the surface in a wave. "Yes?"

His look was severe, his eyes narrowing. "What are you doing here?"

"I just . . ." Andrée stammered, struggling for words.

She never struggled for words. Ever.

She managed a swallow. "I just came in to make a phone call." She gave a helpless gesture, averting her eyes.

Out of the window, she saw, to her horror, a public phone in plain sight across the square.

She had just said she'd come in to make a call, and less than a hundred yards away was a public phone, which she would have used if she'd truly had to make a call.

She had just signed her own death certificate.

Why hadn't she been paying more attention to her surroundings? Why had she allowed her thoughts to be so scattered? If she had trusted in others to save Rose, she might have concocted a better story for herself. With a better story, she could continue to work and save children. But her carelessness was going to get her arrested and probably land her face to face with Fat Jacques again.

Would he remember her from their previous encounter? Or did he ruin enough lives to render him confused by the volume?

A soft grunt came from the man in front of her, bringing Andrée's attention back to the present, and to him.

"Do you know anyone here?" he asked without much interest.

Andrée shook her head quickly. "No one."

"Papers."

"Of course." She fumbled within her jacket for her new papers and handed them over, her fingers trembling.

If the man noticed, he made no sign of it. He looked at her papers, looked at her, looked at the papers . . .

Andrée had never been so grateful for the efficacy of the CDJ and their paperwork in her entire life.

"You may leave," he said as he shoved the papers back at her. "Go straight home."

"Thank you," Andrée said in a rush, moving before she had refolded her papers. She pushed open the door of the café and began walking, somehow managing to get her papers folded and shoved back into their usual pocket.

Then her lungs seemed to catch up with her mind about what had happened, and they began to shake.

Not tremble, not quiver, but shake. Her entire chest shook. Then her torso. Her arms. Her legs. She just shook, enough that she would swear the hair upon her head shook as well. Her breath came and went in rampant pants, acting in the pattern of normal breathing, but barely resembling the actions at all.

Breathe, she reminded herself. *Breathe.*

Except she was breathing.

She was walking.

She was . . .

Gasping painfully and looking over her shoulder, expecting Fat Jacques himself to be there, walking easily behind her. Yet no one appeared.

She realized then that she wasn't a far enough distance from the café to be turning around and looking. If she acted at all suspicious, the soldiers inside the café would surely notice her and rush out to arrest her. She was incredibly easy prey.

Which made her worry. Had she made it easy for the Gestapo to find her? Had they been watching her for some time? Had someone betrayed her? How else could they have known she was there?

Maybe the Gestapo knew about the children's sector already. Obviously, they knew it existed, but maybe they knew more than they'd let on. First Esta, then Ida, and now her. Maybe they had known about all of them.

Maybe Ida had given them her name during torture. Did they torture people in the Dossin Barracks at Malines? But Ida wouldn't have known about today's operation or information in Andrée's new papers.

What mistake had Andrée made to bring the Gestapo to the café? Had they followed her from the Rue du Trône office? Was Claire in their grips now? What about Paule? Had the Gestapo gotten ahold of the notebooks?

Breathing was suddenly difficult. Everything was tightening across her chest, her ribs refused to expand for breath, her face was turning warm, and her pulse was racing. Her arms began to feel heavy, like a force greater than gravity was pulling on them. Her legs tingled behind her knees, her feet struggled to find balance, her ears . . .

Her ears could suddenly hear only very loud, very rushed, very deep breathing, and even that was fuzzy.

Andrée felt her throat clench, choking her and preventing even a single swallow. She looked around her, all around, searching for this force that was turning her into the very embodiment of chaos. But more than that, she sought escape.

Any escape.

Any help.

Any hope.

A small side street was just ahead, and she moved toward it, almost stumbling now, her vision not quite clear. Her fingers gripped at the brick of the buildings, her nails catching on the rough surface almost painfully.

She collapsed into the side street, the world tilting in nearly every direction. She pulled her feet up, curling into a ball to keep from dangling them visibly.

And then she found tears.

How had they formed? She remembered no burning in her eyes, no welling of moisture, no trickling of those peculiar beads of salt and heartache along her face. But here they were, rivers of her very own, cascading freely down the features of her face, containing every gasp and pant of her frantic lungs in their depths.

She bit into the fabric of her coat to stifle any sounds of her crying but could not seem to stop the crying itself. It just came, wave after wave, mingling with the poor excuse for breathing in a way that made her head swim.

Yet the tears also made her deepen those breaths. Made her lungs work differently. Made her so tired that natural patterns began to resume without force. Not all at once, not easily, but with a gradual progression that covered her like a tattered blanket.

No one had rushed on her here. Did they wait for her around the corner? Were they waiting for her at her new flat? At the office? Were they even now looking for Claire and Paule? Or Yvonne? Her contacts?

Where had the errors been? And how, if Rose had managed to escape this raid, were they going to get her out safely?

It all could have ended for Andrée right there in that café. Perhaps not for the entire children's sector of the CDJ, given there were still others to work, but it would have been the shortest term any leader had held.

It still could be.

Her heart seemed to stop entirely at that point. Then energy roared to life through her once-tired limbs, and her panicked breathing suddenly became focused and controlled.

She could not stay here. She could not stay anywhere until she was sure that she had not been . . . that they had not been . . .

But they had to have been, hadn't they? If such a simple assignment could be compromised, how could the entire operation not be?

Andrée forced herself to sit up, her head swimming ever so slightly as she did so. She waited for balance to return to her mind, for her ears to stop ringing, for anything to feel like her own again.

Then she got up, left the side street, and walked.

She walked for twelve blocks, then turned left and walked for fourteen blocks. She turned right and continued for three blocks. She turned right again to double back on herself for seven more blocks.

She took side alleys that became dead ends. She walked to the Palais de Justice, then down to Gare du Nord. She walked along St. Alphonse, and she walked up and down Rue Royale. She walked down to her old flat on Rue de Belle-Vue.

She kept moving, kept going, avoiding the office and her home, but avoiding nowhere else. She even walked by the SD offices on Avenue Louise.

No one cared that she walked by. No one tried to stop her. No one raced out to get her. If anyone had followed her, they would have been utterly lost by what she was doing.

She was a little lost by it herself.

Darkness had fallen hours ago. Her feet ached, burning in places where she knew there would be sores later, and her legs cried out for mercy.

But until she was sure that she would not compromise herself or anyone else, she could not stop. Could not rest. Could not go home.

Somewhere in Uccle, she stopped at a phone to call the office, mostly so they would know she was safe, as she would have missed some appointments. They were apprised of the situation and assured her that someone else would go get Rose and make sure she got to her designated location safely.

Andrée hung up the phone, looked up at the rising full moon, and continued to walk, wondering when she would know that she was safe.

If she would know.

CHAPTER 24

The Jew . . . is nothing but a dangerous parasite from which we Germans had to free ourselves were we not to perish slowly but surely as a people.

—NEWSLETTER FOR NAZI YOUTH LEADERS IN FRANCONIA, FEBRUARY 1944

The black bread and hot water were even more disgusting than usual today.

Her stomach had gotten used to the indignity of the meal, so it rumbled in hungry satisfaction despite the protesting of her tongue.

Ida forced herself to continue chewing, knowing better than to not finish. The last time she had done that, food had been withheld for three days, and she had been hit in the face several times. Just until her eyes had swollen enough to make seeing difficult.

Then she had received more punishment when she was slow to respond to orders or required motions, her limited eyesight apparently no excuse.

There were never any excuses.

She forced the final portion of her bread into her mouth and took a swig of the nearly painfully hot water. It burned, but it softened the bread enough to make chewing easier.

Small mercies.

The whistle sounded, and everyone stood from the tables, moving to deposit their poor excuses for plates into the pile. Those assigned to dish duty would take care of the plates, but that wasn't Ida's assignment.

She did her best to leave a clean plate for them, but others demonstrated no such consideration. It wasn't that they wanted to make life harder for their fellow prisoners; they just no longer cared about anything at all.

That was easy to do in here.

Ida had done it quite a few times herself but had worked hard to not make it a permanent state of mind or being. She had no desire to give up on life itself, no matter how bleak the present appeared. She had little hope for great changes in the future, but she could do nothing if she was dead.

Alive, she might at least be of use.

Besides, she had connected with Maurice and Esta again in the barracks, and having them close made her feel less alone.

Esta had been put to work as one of the secretaries in the camp, usually working with newly arrived transports. She had, at least three times, if not more, changed the addresses of known resistance workers when they'd been brought into camp and made to turn in their keys so the Gestapo would not be able to search their true homes. It was a small thing, considering what else was submitted to and suffered, but it seemed to make a difference to those she helped.

Maurice worked in the kitchen for children. But he had made enough connections throughout the camp and held enough respect there to be allowed certain freedoms that led to unique opportunities for helping his fellow prisoners. Last week, he'd somehow accrued a number of missing belongings and returned them to their rightful owners. Nothing that would be missed from the stash of goods the prison guards had collected, of course. But small items like a good razor and other basic necessities that were a godsend in this place.

Ida had heard rumors that he'd even been able to help a few people escape transport to one of the other camps, but he refused to comment on that.

She wouldn't doubt his abilities there.

"Time to wash!" one of the VNV officers shouted in his native tongue.

Ida had learned that particular phrase rather quickly. She had hated this part of the process early on, and nothing about it had improved, but she had grown so accustomed to the horrors that the words no longer triggered any sort of reaction.

The women filed into the washroom and stripped themselves to the waist to wash. As per usual, not one of them had gotten halfway through before a pair of VNV officers entered to "ensure the rules were being kept," or some such other lie. The officers always muttered to each other in Dutch during this, and any woman who stopped the process of washing would be struck across her bare skin.

It was not worth the objection.

Even now, Ida barely blinked at the disruption.

She finished her washing and rearranged her clothing, then helped the much older woman next to her to right herself. She nodded at the gratitude in the woman's eyes, both of them knowing not to speak.

Speaking during washing was also a problem.

They filed back out of the washroom, and Ida caught sight of Horse Head, her least favorite, and the camp's most vicious, VNV officer. He saw her as well, and, like always, he grabbed her hair and yanked with all his might as she passed. When he had first done this, she had fallen out of the line and stumbled, her scalp aching. Now . . .

Well, now she stumbled, her scalp tingled, and a chunk of her hair wound up in his hand.

He laughed and made a show of dropping the hair bit by bit to the floor.

Ida and those with her proceeded to the courtyard, following the usual pattern of each day. They would engage in activities created by the guards while the SS searched the rooms for any contraband, items of value, glimpses of life or pleasure. And while any who were unwell and in bed in the rooms received beatings with leather straps or blackjacks to the soles of their feet.

It wasn't enough to torment the prisoners with such actions in the middle of the night, as was the guards' favorite pastime. The middle of the day was also viewed as a perfectly good time to abuse those already unwell.

There were no humans in this place. There were only the real animals and those they viewed as animals.

"Run!" one of the guards ordered as the prisoners entered the courtyard. "Go! Now!"

They all did so, following along the perimeter of the courtyard. Most of the prisoners limped at least a little, due to recent lashes upon their feet. But some, like Ida, who had recently taken a turn in the torture bunker just outside of the barracks, and had gaping and still-healing sores on their feet and bruises in various places along their legs, exhibited an even more complicated gait.

A pair of guards cocked their rifles loudly and began chasing the pack of them. "Faster!" they shouted, laughing together. "Faster, or we'll shoot!"

An older woman sobbed as she tried to move faster, and Ida's heart went out to her. Only the week before, the woman's husband had been shot for not going as fast as the guards liked during this very activity. There were no jokes in this camp. No idle threats. No humanity.

There was only danger and the moments when that danger escalated.

"Jump!" came the next order.

Like a herd of blind sheep, the prisoners began jumping. Ida's left leg still throbbed from yesterday's blow with a rifle butt, so jumping was more difficult than usual. Even more so when she landed, but at least she could put more weight on her right leg most of the time.

"Lower!"

She bit the inside of her lip against the searing pain in her leg as she was forced to stoop further for her jumping.

"Left leg only! Jump!"

Tears burned at the corners of her eyes as she jumped on her injured leg, bending as deeply as required and feeling every muscle scream in agony as she did so. Her knee shook more with every landing, and her balance, already poor, was best described as flailing. But there was no thought of refusing, or of using her right leg for rest, or collapsing to the ground.

It was too soon to take the beating that would result from failure to comply. She had only just regained proper hearing in her right ear and ceased having intense headaches in the daylight. Returning to that misery would be too brutal.

The feeble prisoners continued to jump on their left legs alone, the guard now laughing and speaking with his associate about something rather entertaining, it seemed. The guards paid no attention to their prisoners, nor did they seem to care what they were doing. But orders had been given and must be followed on pain of death.

"Close your eyes," one of the guards suddenly shouted. "And skip!"

Ida almost groaned at the command. Blind skipping, as it was called, was one of the more humiliating "exercises" prisoners were forced to do, and the guards' laughter always rang out whenever people fell, collided with each other, or hit one of the barracks walls. More than one inmate had received nasty wounds that needed tending due to blind skipping, and the number of those injured in the exercise had only increased as time went on.

It was cruel, these routines labeled as "healthy exercise" for prisoners. There was nothing healthy about them. The exercises were entirely designed to dishearten those involved, to strip them of any remaining pride or dignity, to remind them of how weak and vulnerable they really were to those who ruled them, and to emphasize the fruitlessness of resistance or refusal.

After a dozen or so people were too injured to continue, the order came to stop, and the inmates gradually formed a ragged line, waiting for their next order.

"To the truck!"

Ida groaned, knowing what was to come.

They all raced to the nearby truck as fast as they could, almost frantic, as rocks were thrown in their way. All existing pain was ignored for this. It had to be.

"What are you doing?" a guard bellowed. "Get back here and line up!"

Ida and the rest raced back to their previous position, forming as perfect a line as they could manage. Those who had not reached the truck had to turn in place and race back with them, barely making it before the next direction.

"West wall!"

They dashed to the wall, setting their noses against its cold stone.

"Line!"

Back to face the guard they went, eyes forward like soldiers.

"Truck!"

With scattered scampering, they returned to the truck yet again.

"Touch it!" he screamed, as some of the stragglers were already turning back for his next instruction. "Touch it now or you'll all be taken down to the shed!"

Ida shook her head as they came closer to the truck. She knew the guard was going to shout again before they really could touch it.

He always did.

"Back here, you lazy Jewish dogs! Now!"

They returned to him, lining up, every one of them panting hard from the exertions. Some of them shook, some of them leaned into others, but most of them were able to stand firm.

For appearances, anyway.

The soldier walked along the line of them as though inspecting his troops, and he stopped directly in front of Ida, staring into her face. She kept her eyes forward, careful not to look at his face or his eyes. Just straight ahead as though there was nothing and no one there.

"Eyes down, Jewish vermin," he sneered. "We'll have that pride knocked out of you yet."

Ida cast her eyes down, saying nothing.

A sudden glob of moisture hit her right cheek, and she did her best not to react. Spittle was a common weapon, and, while degrading, it was not worth reacting to. There were no indignities here, only realities. The prisoners were forced to exhibit silent endurance and mute obedience, allowing themselves to be dragged here and there by the commands of others, incapable of independent thought or action.

They were lemmings, she thought to herself. Following one another, even if it led them right over a cliff, at which the Nazis would undoubtedly laugh hysterically as the prisoners tumbled to their deaths.

"To your work," the officer ordered, suddenly sounding bored with the entire game. "Quickly now, or you'll get thrashed."

Ida allowed herself a sigh of relief as she turned from the courtyard and headed to the laundry. She wasn't permitted all that much freedom by having an indoor position, but there was some privacy and space to think. She had only one task: to unravel the sweaters that came in so the wool could be repurposed. She had never been told where the sweaters came from, and she had never asked.

She never would.

Entering the empty room, she sank onto her usual stool and covered her face with both hands. There were no tears to shed, not anymore. There had been a month of silent tears before they had all dried up. Before she realized that tears stung the wounds on her face. Before she understood that tears encouraged the guards.

Before tears no longer provided relief.

Now she just breathed and reminded herself who she was. What she was. *That* she was.

Sometimes, just the reminders were enough.

Inhale . . . exhale . . . inhale . . . exhale . . .

Ida smiled ever so slightly on the last exhale. Her ribs did not ache as much today. That was a relief. Her first week in the camp, she had endured a horrible beating, mostly from the boots of the SS and VNV, and the bruising still had yet to fade completely. The pain had been excruciating. Every breath, every movement, every attempt to sleep had sent sharper and sharper bolts of pain ricocheting through her frame.

And heaven forbid she ever had to sneeze or cough.

But today, the pain was dull.

It would be a good day.

She picked up the sweater from the top of the pile at her table and began to unpick its threads, fingers no longer tender from the work, rapidly flying across the lines of wool once carefully woven together to form the article. Once the weather turned cooler, she would have to try to set a few items aside, if possible. There were some very frail figures here, and a few children who were looking rather waiflike. They would need all the help they could get to keep warm when the chill came.

If she began setting a few pieces aside now, would she have saved enough to make any kind of difference? And where would she store the sweaters for safety?

Maurice might have an idea. She'd ask the next time she saw him.

"Jeanne, I've got someone to help you for the day," his voice suddenly sounded from nearby.

Ida turned with a quick grin. "I was just thinking about . . ."

Her voice trailed off when she saw who stood beside him in the doorway.

Andrée.

She was dressed very poorly, rather perfectly blending in to the mix of inmates in the camp, her fair hair covered with a rag. She was smiling in a way that told Ida she had not been arrested to enter this place.

She had come on purpose.

"This is Mary," Maurice told her clearly, his eyes widening. "We want to see how she does here in the laundry. You'll only have an hour. I'll be back then." He squeezed Andrée's arm, winked at Ida, then left.

Ida could only stare at Andrée in shock, words entirely beyond her capacity.

Andrée, on the other hand, began to cry. "Oh, Jeanne!" She rushed over and hugged her tightly, so full of warmth and goodness that Ida was tempted to shy away from her influence.

But instinct, dormant though it had been, soon returned, and Ida shoved up to her feet and embraced her friend more fully. "Claude! Oh, Claude, how are you here? *Why* are you here?"

"Seeing you, of course!" Andrée said with a laugh, rubbing her back. "Do you think I would have myself sneaked into the Dossin Barracks for my own amusement?"

Ida pulled back, somehow smiling amidst her disbelief. "But the risks! Claude, you shouldn't have!"

Andrée scoffed and waved a hand. "Of course, I should. Maurice and I have been working on this for weeks. And Frank has been a most excellent help."

"Frank?" Ida repeated, racking her brain. "You can't mean Frank, the Jewish head of the camp?"

"The very same!" Andrée chirped. "Having a half-Jew, half-German at the head of things is mighty useful. The Nazis don't hate him more than they do the inmates, so they trust him more, never suspecting that he identifies more with the inmates than with his countrymen." She grinned and patted Ida's shoulders. "Never fear, we are safe for an hour."

Andrée's smile faded as she felt Ida's shoulders again, her clear eyes raking over her frame quickly. "Oh, Jeanne . . . you are so frail. So small. And these bruises . . ." She touched Ida's cheek very gently, but Ida still winced at the contact.

"It's nothing," Ida assured her, taking her hand and sitting. "Honestly, this is a great improvement."

Andrée swallowed and sat on a nearby stool, scooting closer. "I wasn't sure you'd still be here. Maurice told me it's hard to keep anyone from being deported."

"I was supposed to leave on the twenty-sixth transport," Ida murmured, shivering at the memory. "We were all assigned a number and a transport when we arrived. But somehow, when the day of transportation came, I was spared. I watched everyone else load up. Every person that I was supposed to be with. A tuberculosis patient, a blind man, a woman paralyzed in both legs, a woman six months pregnant, a four-month-old baby. No one is spared here. They screamed as they left. Fear and worry and fatigue and despair . . . I'll never get that out of my head. And—" She looked down at her hands, the filthy nails and calloused fingers seeming to bleed anew in her mind. "And I was ashamed."

Andrée gasped. "Ashamed? Why?"

"Because I was staying, and they were not. We are not free here, but we are alive at least. I don't know if any of them still are. And it is hard to live with knowing you should be dead with them, if they are."

"Oh, Jeanne . . ." Andrée took her hands, holding them in both of hers, effectively cupping the image of blood pooling in Ida's mind. "You mustn't allow yourself such guilt. Don't you think you were spared for a purpose? If I've heard rightly, Queen Elisabeth herself intervened for you. And not her alone, but others, too. We've all worked so very hard to keep you here, if we cannot get you out."

Ida shook her head. "But why am I more deserving of saving than they? Who do they have to intervene for them? No one."

"Maurice tries," Andrée reminded her, the gentleness of her tone like a weak slap to Ida's soul.

"I know he does." Ida nodded, swallowing hard. "I know. And I know there is a difference made in saving even one life, but it all feels so helpless in here."

Andrée glanced behind her, faint sounds of the Germans in the courtyard making her frown. "And I trust the blasted Nazis don't help with those feelings. The SS, indeed. One might as well call them Slayers of Souls."

"When I was in Gestapo headquarters," Ida murmured, the faint memory seeming like years ago rather than scant weeks, "they would have Romanian and Hungarian SS members guard us at night. I don't know if they were conscripted, but they were kind to us. One of them was a man in his forties, and when the Germans had turned their backs for the night, he opened our cell doors and allowed us water and light. He kept us company, telling us about his family and showing us pictures of his wife and children. He did not hate us, but he was in the SS."

"I've never heard of such a thing." Andrée stared, wide-eyed with shock. "And he wasn't in trouble for it?"

Ida smiled very faintly. "Who was to know? It was the night watch. There was another one, practically a boy. He had a fiancée, and he showed us her picture. She was just lovely, smiling and bright. All he wanted to do was return home to marry her and to live freely. He was not afraid to tell us all this, or to treat us as humans. He did not want this war. This position. He was not filled with hatred toward anyone."

"He deserves that life," Andrée said with a sigh. "We all do."

"He may very well get it. The rest of us, however . . ." Ida shrugged, then began coughing, the sound racking and choking, thunderous in the small, enclosed room.

Andrée rubbed her back. "That sounds painful. Are you well, Jeanne?"

Ida nodded, gripping at her now throbbing sides. "Yes, for this place. My lung was injured after some treatment I received at the hands of our wardens out there. It's never been quite the same, but truly, I have no fever or illness."

"Treatment? You mean torture."

The word sounded worse coming from the mouth of someone who had no idea what was endured here. And, as if her friend were a child, Ida felt the need to shield her from the true horrors.

"Beatings are part of daily life," Ida hedged, looking away. "My friend was beat about the face and forced to stand facing a corner for two hours for not saluting one of the SS guards."

Andrée growled darkly. "And where is your friend now?"

"Deported. I could not tell you where." Ida forced a smile, praying it looked better than it felt. "But it is so good to see you, my dear!"

Andrée did not smile back. "Because you can see me or because I am here?"

Ida felt a weary sigh well up within her. Andrée had always seen more than she was supposed to. Why she thought this would be an exception . . .

"I see how sunken your eyes are, Jeanne," she went on. "I see the cuts and the scars. I see the swelling and the discoloration, and I can feel the very bones of your hands. They are killing you in here, only more slowly than elsewhere."

"We are already dead to them." Ida could not help the flatness of her tone and did not bother trying to soften the truth with a smile. "You cannot kill what is already dead."

Ida sighed, looking back down at her hands. "I met a girl here not long ago; she was only fifteen. But she was not afraid. She told me that she does not feel alone. She recalls passages of the Torah that she had been taught and had read. She recites them to herself. And she said she has no questions because of that. She has faith, and that faith strengthens her, even in this." She shook her head. "She was transported to a camp."

"I have never had faith in anything like that," Andrée admitted, her tone raw. "I've seen too much to allow me to have faith."

"I wish I had her faith," Ida whispered. "I would love to feel that I am not alone."

Andrée suddenly leaned forward, seizing Ida's hands tightly. "Hold on, Jeanne. There are rumors from reliable sources that the Nazis are going to leave soon. Don't let them kill you. We need you when this is over. The work has continued since you've been here, and will keep going, but I need you to come back out. To help me put these families back together. Hold on and find a way to hope."

Somehow, by some miracle, Ida's eyes began to well with the first tears she'd shed in weeks. "I will always hope in you, my friend, even if I cannot find it anywhere else. We can have faith in each other, and in the work we do."

"Yes," Andrée urged. "Faith in the ability of good people with the right motivations to create change in the world. That is what we can do and what we will continue doing."

Ida nodded, one of the tears falling, stinging a cut somewhere on her face. "Tell me what you are doing, Claude. I want to hear everything."

CHAPTER 25

We will strike our external enemy just as we put an end to our internal foe. The end of this war will mean the destruction of the Jews.

—ADOLF HITLER

The Germans were preparing to leave.

The news was spread all over the city, but no one dared believe it could be true. Whispers were everywhere—in the cafés and the schools, on street corners and in shops. All the Belgians needed was to actually see the trucks leave. Then they would know.

Or they could simply open their eyes and stare.

The Nazis on the streets were more agitated, more prone to hurling abuses at any Jews they saw, and the raids were increasing with a fury that Andrée had never seen. It was as though the Germans could not believe for themselves that they were going to have to leave, that they might not win this war. They had to continue desperately clinging to the power they abused until it was stripped from their fingers.

If they knew they were leaving, they were keen on leaving as much destruction as possible in their wake.

"Claude! Claude!"

Yvonne Jospa burst into the office on Rue du Trône, breathless and panting, her cheeks red and her hair wild.

Andrée shot to her feet and rounded her desk at once. "Yvonne, what is it? What's happened? Are the Nazis pulling out?"

Yvonne shook her head and waved a folded paper at her. "Word from Frank at the barracks in Malines. He has been ordered to have all of the homes of AJB members emptied, and all evacuated. To be taken out of Belgium entirely and moved into their other occupied territories."

"Are you serious?" Andrée leaned hard against her desk, her feet unsteady. "Where will they evacuate first, and when?"

"Wezembeek and Brussels," Yvonne panted. "By tomorrow."

Andrée put a hand to her brow. "That's probably a hundred homes. What is the plan?"

"We are already mobilizing everyone we have to help get everyone out of the homes with their necessities," Yvonne said, her breath finally starting to stabilize. "But there are so many children, and they cannot . . ."

"Of course. Of course." Andrée thought quickly, clicking her tongue as she ran through possibilities. "There's a convent in Auderghem. The Sacred Heart. It's large and they've offered help several times. Can we spare teams to install and prepare bedding and furniture supplies there? I can get my escorts to take the children from houses in small groups. It's far enough away to not be obvious, but close enough to not be difficult."

Yvonne was already nodding. "Yes. Absolutely. I'll send telegrams to contacts from the other networks; I am sure they can spare people to be escorts tonight."

"I'll get Solange, Catherine, and Brigitte," Andrée offered, grabbing her coat as they both moved for the door. "We don't have any time to spare. We can't move anyone until nightfall, but the preparations must be ready for when we do."

"Exactly. I'll meet you at Gare du Midi in an hour with the addresses. Would you liaise with the Mother Superior at the convent before we send our first groups? I'll telegram with the urgent need so the preparations can start, but . . ."

Andrée was already moving away from Yvonne to find her operatives. "Yes, I will." She waved quickly and hurried off, trying to recall where the others would be that day. If she remembered correctly, no one was being sent particularly far today, which served their purposes well.

A full-scale evacuation of the AJB families, of those Jews who had worked for the very organization created to conspire against them by assisting the Nazis in registering and tracking other Jews in Belgium. It was true that the AJB was the means by which the CDJ sometimes obtained information in advance of the Gestapo and was able to intervene and rescue children before a raid. But in reality, the AJB was nothing more than a puppet group that claimed to be assisting Jews while actually enabling their rapid destruction.

Now members of the AJB were to be treated just like all the other Jews of Belgium had been—and by the very oppressors they had unwittingly helped.

Or perhaps helped only to try to spare their families.

They were Jews, after all, even if they had once been useful to the Nazi cause.

There was a phrase Andrée's father used to repeat when she was a child that sprang to mind, and it swam about her head as she walked.

Cursed be the man that trusteth in men.

Where her father had taken the maxim from, she couldn't recall. He had only ever said that it was "in the Bible," but as her father was not a regular student of scripture, she could not necessarily believe the Bible to be the source. But she could believe the meaning of the words.

Trusting in the safety promised by the Nazis was a fool's errand. Was never going to come to fruition. Was only ever going to delay the inevitable.

The CDJ had beaten the Gestapo in their attempts to capture families time and again where requests for help had been made. They had done the impossible and stolen children away under the Germans' very noses at times. Their contacts had even assisted children who were known by the Gestapo to be hidden in very specific locations, as had been the case at Sister Marie-Aurélie's convent.

Could they accomplish the same task again, but on a much grander scale, all in one night?

It was one thing to say that they would do it or die trying, but the latter might be more probable than the former, in this case.

Andrée shook her head and moved a touch more quickly to track down her team. They needed to move, and move fast.

Hours later, Andrée was at the Sacred Heart convent in Auderghem, watching the rearrangement of furniture and placement of beds with satisfaction. "I cannot begin to thank you enough for allowing this, Sister."

Sister Antonia rubbed Andrée's arm. "Of course! We mustn't allow these families to be caught up in one final sweep of Hitler's arm in Belgium."

"Final?" Andrée looked at her in surprise. "Do you know something I don't?"

The sister smiled a little. "I have a sister in Douai, mademoiselle. They've just been liberated, and she says the Allies' next objective is Brussels. The end is on its way."

Andrée grinned without shame at that. "Sister, if that is true, I just might praise the Lord."

"Don't exaggerate so," the Mother Superior chuckled. "I'll praise Him for us both."

"You won't try to convert me, Sister?" Andrée asked, nudging her.

The nun shrugged. "I leave conversion in the Lord's hands and His power and leave choices to people's own hearts. I serve God and I serve my fellow man. If you wish to seek the Lord, I'll help you do so. If you do God's work with your own hands, and do not wish to see it as such, who am I to try to convince you?"

Andrée made a soft sound of impressed consideration. "You are a very interesting sister, Sister."

That made Sister Antonia laugh out loud. "Well, we can't all be cross biddies with the might of the Almighty in our rulers, can we? Go, I'll see this organized. Get those families out. We'll be ready for them. Try not to be afraid."

"When you are doing something that you feel is absolutely necessary," Andrée told the kind nun, "fear is in the background."

Sister Antonia smiled gently. "In my world, child, we call that letting your faith be stronger than your fear."

Andrée thought about her father's maxim. Trusting in man may bring about a curse, but there was no mention of *women* in the saying, and she was more than ready to place her trust in the woman who stood before her.

They all had to.

The sun was beginning to set as she exited the convent, and she nodded in satisfaction at the growing darkness. They could likely start moving families now, and might have to, given the limited number of hours in the night. But if Sister Antonia was right and the Allies were practically at their gates, there was no way the Nazis were going to look particularly hard for these people after they were gone.

Another point in their favor tonight.

Andrée walked as quickly as she could back to the office in Brussels, her fingers rubbing together in anticipation. Claire and Brigitte were overseeing the escorting of families in Wezembeek, while she and Paule were doing Brussels. They had managed to recruit some assistance from the other resistance organizations, as Yvonne had hoped, so there would be plenty of hands to see this done. The children would come with them, the parents would go with Yvonne and others who could find suitable places for them. No one wanted to split up in this sort of confusion, but these families, of all the families that had been helped, had the best chance of reuniting soon.

Of not losing a single family member.

Of still being a family.

Paule was waiting for her on the corner of Rue de la Brasserie, as arranged, and said nothing as Andrée reached her. She only stepped to her side and walked with her, the same energy and alertness palpable in her frame.

They had memorized the addresses, as usual, and hidden the proof in their shoes. In many respects, this was no different than any other assignment they had accomplished in the last few years.

It was simply on the largest scale imaginable.

With a faint clasp of hands, the two of them parted on the next street, heading for separate homes assigned to them.

Andrée walked directly to the first one without deviation in route, her eyes scanning the streets for any trucks and seeing none. All the trucks seemed to have vanished these days.

Yet more signs of the end being nigh.

She knocked on the door firmly and almost jumped with the rapidity of response. Worried parents and two small children crowded the doorway, looking at her with trepidation.

She smiled down at the little ones. "It's a lovely night for a walk. Shall we?"

The two of them came with her, holding tight to her coat as she moved to the next house, and the next, collecting a total of five children, and proceeding with them all to the convent. There was no joking or singing this time, no games as they walked. There was no attempt to lighten spirits, other than whispering for the children to hold hands and pretend they were ducks.

They could draw no attention to themselves tonight.

Until the Allies were *actually* in Brussels, none of them were safe.

Andrée led her little troop of ducklings quietly along the streets, feeling rather proud of them, though there had been no time for introductions or instructions. They moved quickly without dramatics or whining and looked after each other on the way. One of the little girls stumbled and lost a shoe, and before it could even be noted, two others had helped her retrieve and replace it.

Somehow, these children had formed a bond with each other in mere minutes. They had no thought for self above others. They were a group, and they would stick together.

They were the first of the children to arrive at the convent, and Sister Antonia could not have been more gracious in her welcome. They were ushered in, handed off to the most cheerful, pleasant looking nuns Andrée had ever seen, and the scent of freshly baked bread seemed to waft through the entire place.

What child would not want to spend the night in such a warm place?

There was hardly time to consider the perfection in it, however. She had been to only three houses thus far, and there were dozens more to go.

Throughout the entire night, she walked back and forth from the convent to the houses, ferrying children in groups of five or six at a time. She occasionally saw Paule or one of the borrowed operatives with their own little flocks, but more often than not, she was entirely alone in her efforts. Her assigned efforts, that is. They each had specific responsibilities this night, and failure in even one of them would result in trouble somewhere.

Apart from her own frequent delivering of children, the only sign she had that the night was succeeding was the number of beds she was seeing filled. They were gradually filling up more and more as she brought her little groups in, and some of the nuns had even taken to reading stories to clusters of the children, who, for whatever reason, were not sleeping. Andrée recalled the times when she, as a teacher in a boarding school, had been able to read to children late at night herself. When her job had been so simple and yet so fulfilling.

She had never loved anything more than that.

When comfortable in such a scene, children would lean upon her, cuddle up to her side, or lay their heads on her lap. Take her hand or lean their teddy bears against her as they strained to see the pages. She became a sort of mother to them in those moments, and the fulfillment of such a role was an honor and a delight.

Could she have imagined, in those nights she spent reading to the children, that she would spend years with different children in a far different capacity? Hiding them from a great evil at hand and ignoring the blemish that was the star they were forced to wear? Those stars that signaled a lesser creature, a target of hatred, a mark of shame. That forced each wearer to stand out, not with the light a star ought to provide, but with victimization and with permission to be mistreated.

To become nothing.

She had once read that a star that could be seen in the sky was a star already dead in its existence.

The yellow fabric stars worn on the coats of Jewish children these past few years had also signaled death, in one way or another. They signaled the end of a life and a way of living. The end of childhood and innocence. The end of respect and humanity.

The end of goodness.

But soon, all that could be done away with. The stars of evil would vanish, and humanity might begin to be restored. Life could resume for all, and respect could return to the world.

Children could be children once more.

It might take a generation, but she would see it done, if she had her way.

She would see children as children again, and she would see them smile for joy.

Andrée walked back to Brussels from the convent again, one more group of homes on her list. She barely felt the fatigue of the night, though she was certain she would once she stopped moving. It was something she had learned in all the time she had been working in this capacity. Continuous movement was the thing to keep her from exhaustion and fatigue. To keep her from despair and collapse. To keep her heart and her head in line with each other.

Action. Always, always action.

Her feet had gained enough strength and callouses on them to take the load. Her legs had grown accustomed to the strain. Her head knew full well how to operate in such circumstances. Her heart still beat with steadiness and determination. Her arms could still carry any child that needed her to. Her fear, never fully gone, had learned to stay somewhere in the background.

This was who she was now. Her entire identity and her sole purpose for existing. And even when this war was over, whenever it was over, there would be more work to do. Setting to right what they had been forced to disrupt. Reuniting what had been torn apart. Returning life where there had been a kind of death.

And after that . . .

Well, who knew what lay ahead after that? The world was not a perfect place, wars or not. There would always be injustice somewhere and a need to do good. Surely something would come to her as an opportunity, just as this had.

What hope did she have for any sort of quiet life after this?

Why would she even want one?

She laughed to herself as she reached the house she needed and knocked on the door. A quiet life. What would that even look like?

Four children came out to the porch with her, their eyes full of trust and light, in spite of the darkness, shining with complete confidence in her to get them to safety, and a willingness to do exactly as she asked. The parents assured her they had already been contacted by the adult operatives and would be right behind them, so to speak.

They moved to one house across the street and picked up a toddler and an infant, both of whom were rather sleepy.

"I can take one of them, mademoiselle," the oldest of the four others offered, holding out her hands with confidence.

Andrée smiled at the dear one, wanting to cry at the noble spirit she saw before her. "Take the baby, then. I trust you'll be able to get him back to sleep better than I can."

She smiled and tucked the baby against her, making sure the blanket was secure and the infant fully covered.

Andrée took the toddler, shushing her and resting her against her shoulder, rocking slightly. "Will you be all right?" she asked the parents. "Dawn is not long from now."

They nodded, their worry evident. "We are leaving now. Thank you, mademoiselle. Thank you so much."

"Of course," Andrée told them, not certain she had ever meant words more. "Of course." She nudged her head at the children. "Take hold of a hand or my coat, darlings. We've got to go for a very quiet walk now."

They all nodded and began to walk, the journey a touch awkward with recurrent tugs at the back of her coat, but the little fingers were a sign to her that each precious one was still with her. She would take those tugs every single time over a vacancy of feeling. There were little whispers among themselves, but, as the other groups had, no one even tried to treat this occasion like a typical stroll with siblings or friends. There was a solemnity to the occasion, and yet . . .

Andrée felt, this time, at least, that she might as well be bearing a torch as they ascended some great mountain. Each of them stronger than they knew, especially the children. The higher they climbed, the closer hope became. The torch grew brighter. The path became easier.

It was still a mountain, by all means, but the progress became less and less of a burden. Because they could see how far they had come, because they knew that hope awaited them, because they were not alone but walking together. They were moving forward in spite of their fear. While feeling that fear. While fighting that fear.

It was a humbling, powerful vision in her mind. The tender toddler who was now sleeping against her, her moist breath dancing at Andrée's neck in precious intervals, could very well have been her own child at this moment. Her own future that she carried into the distance. Her own life that moved forward toward hope.

She was forever changed by this night, by all of the nights she had spent with these sweet children that had needed her. What a privilege it was to *do* something in this world rather than just *wish* to.

What would become of these children she had hidden? What would they do with their lives? How would the world improve because they were in it? Would any of them remember her?

That was a less important question, but she wondered it all the same.

She would remember them. Each and every one. They had left a mark on her heart and an impression in her soul. They were part of her, pieces of the heavens she had treasured up within herself.

She had lived an entire lifetime in the last few years. She was only twenty-two, and her twenty-third birthday was days away. But she felt at least fifty in so many ways. Aged without aging. Mature without maturity. Grown without growing.

Perhaps the children she had hidden were all also older than they appeared now. Perhaps they always would be.

She reached the convent once more just as the sky in the east began to pale, and Sister Antonia grinned at her in welcome.

"All here?" Andrée asked as she ushered the children in, keeping the delightful toddler for herself.

"One more group from Wezembeek, and then yes." Sister Antonia heaved a sigh, shaking her head. "You've done it, mademoiselle."

Andrée shook her head. "Not until the last child arrives. And then not until Yvonne says the other attempts were successful. And then"—she managed a smile—"not until we can hear the frustrated cries of the Gestapo when they find all the empty homes."

Sister Antonia laughed and took hold of two children's hands. "Well, let's go get settled into beds, and we'll see if we can't hear all of those things."

They had barely gotten the children settled, including Andrée's little toddler, when Brigitte arrived with the last of the children. Her face was strewn with tears as they arrived, her smile brighter than the sun at noon.

"We've done it," she whispered to Andrée, coming directly to her for an embrace. "I've just seen Yvonne. We've done it, Claude."

Andrée released a surprised breath and hugged her colleague close, her own tears not far behind. Relief had never tasted so sweet, had never felt so victorious. The impossible had been accomplished, and yet again the Gestapo had been thwarted.

It hardly seemed possible, but the end, it seemed, was finally here.

Andrée and her fellow operatives all waited at the convent for several hours, until the sun was well risen, before they dared leave. They would check back in on the children in a few days, but knew they were in excellent hands with the sisters.

Wandering back into Brussels, a neighbor to one of the homes they had visited in the night informed them: the Gestapo had come at dawn and found nothing in the homes, had left emptyhanded but for some trinkets.

He grinned as he shared this and waved as they left.

No words were shared between the four operatives as they walked back. The night had been too profound, their success too great.

As though to capture their feelings to perfection, church bells began to ring, seemingly from every corner of Brussels, if not from Belgium herself. Showering the streets with music and celebration, though the cause was not immediately clear.

"Is it a holiday?" Claire asked as she laughed, pretending to cover her ears.

"Not that I'm aware of," Paule answered, grinning and squinting up at the skies. "It's not even the right time of day for bells."

Brigitte looked at them with wide eyes. "You don't think . . ."

They all sobered, staring at each other. Was it possible? Were the Germans gone? Could Brussels be its own once again?

Andrée looked up the road, toward their offices on Rue du Trône, not far from where they stood. A lone figure was walking down the street in their direction, limping slightly, but standing tall.

The bells continued to ring, and those in their homes began to pour into the streets, cheering and crying and embracing one another.

Andrée felt something catch in her chest as she watched that figure approach them, the bearing and appearance as familiar to her as that of her own mother. She bolted from the others, racing forward with a surge of energy that only those bells could have given her.

Ida grinned broadly at her approach and opened her arms just in time to catch Andrée's embrace, though it nearly knocked her over.

"You're alive!" Andrée cried, laughing and crying all at once as she hugged her dear friend. "You're free!"

"Yes," Ida choked out, pulling back and looking at Andrée with clear bright eyes. "I am free. We all are."

Andrée shook her head in disbelief. "It is so good to see you, Ida."

Ida grinned at the use of her true name. "And you as well, Andrée." The others reached them, and hugs were shared all around.

When the novelty had waned and they stood together in the square among the ringing bells and celebrations of the town, Andrée looked around her, exhaling with deep, exhausted breaths, but in pure satisfaction. "Well, ladies, I supposed now the real work begins."

Andrée Geulen and Ida Sterno pose together at the end of the war.

AFTERWORD

This is the lesson: never give in, never give in, never, never, never, never—in nothing, great or small, large or petty—never give in except to convictions of honour and good sense. Never yield to force; never yield to the apparently overwhelming might of the enemy.

—WINSTON CHURCHILL, HARROW SCHOOL, 29 OCTOBER 1941

Throughout the time that the CDJ began hiding children in Belgium, it is estimated that nearly three thousand children were successfully hidden. Their work continued after the war, reuniting as many families as possible. They were particularly successful, thanks to the ingenious methods set up by Esta Heiber in her series of notebooks detailing which child was living where and under which assumed name.

In some instances where parents had perished, children stayed with their host families, went to existing family members, or were sent to Israel through the Youth Aliyah program, which specifically sought to locate child survivors in displaced persons camps.

Many attempts were made by resistance members to capture Fat Jacques, whose real name was Icek Glogowski, but none were successful. He was sentenced to death *in absentia* in 1947 but was never found to fulfill his sentence.

In the case of both Nicole and Rivka/Rose, other CDJ operatives were sent to pick them up after the Gestapo had left, and they were taken to safe locations for the remainder of the war.

Odile Ovart and her husband Remy died in the concentration

camps. Their daughter, Dédée, went on to start a foundation in their name that specializes in finding homes for needy children. They were named to the Righteous Among the Nations by Yad Vashem for their work.

Ida Sterno, 1944, taken shortly after her liberation from Malines.

Ghert Jospa, Maurice Heiber, and Esta Heiber all survived their imprisonment.

Ida Sterno never fully recovered from her time in the Dossin Barracks in Malines. She continued to work as a social worker in aiding Jewish survivors until her death in 1964 at the age of sixty-two.

Andrée Geulen continued her work after the war by becoming actively involved with the Aid for Israelite Victims of the War. She married

Andrée Geulen walking in the street in Brussels, 1944, on her way to pick up a Jewish child. German officers walk behind her.

a Jewish man, Charles Herscovici, whose family perished in the camps, in 1948. They had two daughters.

In 1989, Andrée was recognized as Righteous Among the Nations by Yad Vashem. She continued to meet with some of her "hidden children" for the rest of her life, and she never forgot a single name. She died in 2022 at the age of one hundred.

ACKNOWLEDGMENTS

Thanks to my father, Pat Connolly, for alerting me to this story when it crossed his path.

Thanks to the Kazerne Dossin for their extraordinary museum and the countless hours of research that have been put into it.

Thanks to Dr. Anne Griffin, Dorien Styven, and Nicolas Burniat for helping me get this project started and headed in the right direction.

Thanks to Nicola and the rest of the team at the Wiener Holocaust Library for providing me with access to crucial documentation surrounding the hidden children of Belgium, the CDJ, and Andrée and Ida themselves.

Honored thanks to Yad Vashem for their incredible records, which provided so much insight and detail about the Righteous Among the Nations as well as the revered lost during the Holocaust.

Thanks to Professor Shaul Harel, author of *A Child without a Shadow*, for his friendship and guidance, for his stories, and for sharing his life and his work with so many.

Thanks to Heather Moore and Jen Johnson for keeping me from the darkness when this story threatened to overwhelm me.

Thanks to the incredible team at Shadow Mountain, as always. Lisa, Chris, and Heidi, you are a venerated Cerberus in this work that I ever strive to please. It is an honor to consider you my friends as well as my mentors.

AUTHOR'S NOTE

"Every hidden child has a story."

—PROFESSOR SHAUL HAREL

The journey that was the process and evolution of *Hidden Yellow Stars* is one that was heaven-sent, and there is no question in my mind about that. It all started when my father was reading the news online and found an article about the death of Andrée Geulen, a Belgian woman who had just turned one hundred and had hidden Jewish children from the Gestapo during World War II. Knowing I am always looking for good stories in history, he sent the article to me to read.

I read it, and I loved it. So, I began looking into her story even more, learning about the life she had led and the people she had worked with. I learned about Ida Sterno, how she had been captured in the end and forced to endure all manner of torment in the barracks in Mechelen. I learned how deeply Andrée loved the children she worked with and how she remembered them for the rest of their lives.

And the rest is history.

To say that the research for this project was difficult is an understatement. To learn of the specific suffering of these children and their families, the fear that they lived with constantly, and the losses many of them faced was harrowing. There were many tears shed on my part as I struggled to comprehend how such horrors could have happened in the first place, and my gratitude for and appreciation of brave figures like Ida and Andrée soared. I *had* to tell the story of these children and of those who saved them, and I had to do them justice.

One of the most extraordinary opportunities I had throughout this project was to visit the Dossin Barracks, now the Kazerne Dossin, in Mechelen, described in this book by its French name, Malines. There is a remembrance museum there as well as the original barracks, where a memorial has been created, and what I learned and felt in that hallowed space will stay with me for life. The very walls seem to echo with the cries of those who passed through there, as well as those who stayed. I could watch Ida's procession from room to room upon her arrival in my mind as I walked that space myself, feeling the humiliating and harrowing experience in a new and profound way.

During my research and writing process, I was fortunate enough to make contact with one of the surviving hidden children, Professor Shaul Harel, who provided me with extraordinary details beyond what his own account in *A Child without a Shadow* says, and who remained friends with Andrée Geulen for the rest of her life. He became a symbol of hope for me as I worked through this project, illustrating the goal that Ida and Andrée, as well as the others in the CDJ, had for their work.

The barracks at Malines (Mechelen) today.

What was still more extraordinary in my research is that, thanks to the work of the incredible souls at Yad Vashem, I was able to identify extended members of my own family that had suffered death in the camps at the hands of the Nazis. We had always suspected that there were some distant relations who had died in the Holocaust but had never found names or details to prove it, due to the loss of records in the region throughout the years of destruction and persecution.

I found the details for the aunt and uncle of my great-grandfather, their children, and, in some cases, their young grandchildren. For a family as loving and inclusive as mine, the identification of so many that had been lost not only from this world, but from our own knowledge and awareness was humbling. I hope to honor them with this book and to tell the story of their people—of my own heritage through that family line.

When Professor Harel learned of this discovery of mine, and my partial Jewish heritage, he told me, "So you're in this book, too." Those powerful words have stayed with me ever since. Though my family was not part of the Jewish community in Belgium, though I myself am not Jewish, Professor Harel sees this story as part of my own. He, who lived through this, believes this is the story of me and my people as well. What an honor and tribute that is!

The names of the children rescued by the CDJ throughout their work are kept private, both in record and in this book. Any names given and used are fictional, but their stories come from real accounts. The same applies to the families that gave them up, the families that housed them, and the majority of the nuns mentioned. Sister Marie-Aurélie, however, is a real figure in the story.

All accounts of the treatment of children in their fostering homes, for good or for ill, come from real records, either from the children themselves or from those who worked with them.

The story of the baby being saved from the camp at Malines was spoken of by Andrée Geulen often, although the gender of the baby and the social worker who rescued them is now unknown. The baby did indeed go on to live through the war.

The ingenious system of coded notebooks set up by Esta Heiber and maintained by Ida Sterno and Andrée Geulen was set up as follows:

- Notebook 1: The child's real name and their assigned number.
- Notebook 2: The child's number and the new false name with their date of birth.
- Notebook 3: Numerically ordered name code with the true parent address.
- Notebook 4: The locations hiding children, each location having an assigned code.
- Notebook 5: The code name of the child next to the location code number.

The account of Ida Sterno's treatment after her arrest comes from her own accounts. The names of those she was in a cell with, apart from Jenny, have been created here, as their true identities are unknown.

The VNV soldier known in this book as Horse Head was indeed a real individual whose real name is not recorded. He made an appearance in reports from three separate individuals who had been interned at the Dossin Barracks in Mechelen. In their reports, he was known by the German version of that name: *Pferdekopf.*

NOTES

Quotations at the beginning of each chapter that come from various forms of German propaganda were, by and large, translated by Randall L. Bytwerk, a historian at Calvin University who maintains a Nazi Propaganda database hosted at https://research.calvin.edu/german-propaganda-archive/ww2era.htm#racial.

Chapter 1: Language used to reference the badges that Jews were made to wear in Nazi Germany beginning in 1939 and in German-occupied territories beginning in 1941 and 1942 (see https://www.holocaustcenter.org/visit/library-archive/holocaust-badges/).

Chapter 2: Adolf Hitler, *Program of the German Workers' Party,* read to two thousand Germans in Munich on February 24, 1920. Artifact available at United States Holocaust Memorial Museum, courtesy of Patrick Gleason.

Chapter 3: "Das Ende der jüdischen Wanderung" ("The end of Jewish migration"), *Nationalsozialistische Monatshefte* (*The National Socialist Monthly*), May 1933, 229–31.

Chapter 4: Text appearing on a propaganda slide, United States Holocaust Memorial Museum, photograph number 49821, courtesy of Marion Davy.

Chapter 5: "Die Lösung der Judenfrage" ("Solving the Jewish question"), *Nationalsozialistische Monatshefte* (*The National Socialist Monthly*), May 1933, 195–97.

Chapter 6: "Wann ist die jüdische Gefahr beseitigt?" ("When will the Jewish danger be over?"), *Der Stürmer,* no. 19, 1942.

Chapter 7: This headline appeared on the front page of a special edition of the anti-Semetic tabloid *Der Stürmer*, published by editor Julius Streicher (see Randall L. Bytwerk, *Julius Streicher: Nazi Editor of the Notorious*

Anti-Semitic Newspaper Der Stürmer [New York: Cooper Square Press, 2001], 89, 208–10).

Chapter 8: "Der Kampf gegen den Teufel: Alljuda offenbart seinen Vernichtungsplan" ("The battle with the devil: Pan-Jewry reveals its destructive plan"), *Der Stürmer,* no. 37, 1941, 1–2.

Chapter 9: "Bolschewismus und Synogoge" ("Bolshevism and synagogue"), *Der Stürmer,* no. 36, 1941.

Chapter 10: "Der heilige Haß" ("The holy hate"), *Der Stürmer,* no. 18, 1943.

Chapter 11: *Die jüdische Weltpest* [*The Jewish World Plague*] (Munich: Zentralverlag der NSDAP, 1939), 8.

Chapter 12: From a four-page flyer explaining and justifying the mandatory wearing of the yellow star, "Wenn Du dieses Zeichen siehst . . . Jude" ("When you see this symbol . . . Jew"), November 1941, 4.

Chapter 13: This quote comes from a 1944 issue of the *Sprechabenddienst,* a publication that Nazi party members used to guide discussions at an evening meeting—called a *Sprechabend*—where party members discussed the Nazi approach to various ideas and events. See "Parole 21: Den Juden kennen heißt den Sinn des Krieges verstehen!" ("To know the Jews is to understand the meaning of war!") *Sprechabenddienst,* Sept./Oct. 1944.

Chapter 14: G. G. Otto, *Der Jude als Weltparasit* [*The Jew as world parasite*] (Munich: Eher Verlag, 1943), 4.

Chapter 15: A verse from the anti-Semitic children's book *Trau keinem Fuchs auf grüner Heid und keinem Jud bei seinem Eid* [*Trust no fox in the green meadow and no Jew on his oath*] (Nuremberg: Stürmer Verlag, 1936), 5.

Chapter 16: "Die Geheimpläne gegen Deutschland enthüllt" ("Secret plans against Germany revealed"), *Der Stürmer,* no. 27, 1933.

Chapter 17: "Der Weg zur Tat" ("The way to action"), *Der Stürmer,* no. 5, 1943.

Chapter 18: Ernst Hiemer, *Der Giftpilz* [*The Toadstool*] (Nuremberg, Stürmerverlag, 1938).

Chapter 19: Hitler, Adolph. *Mein Kampf.* Pg 319. https://archive.org/details/meinkampf0000hitl_s5q9/page/318/mode/2up?q=slander.

Chapter 20: "Der heilige Haß" ("The holy hate"), *Der Stürmer,* no. 18, 1943.

Chapter 21: Ernst Hiemer, *Der Pudelmopsdackelpinscher* [*The Poodle-Pug-Dachshund-Pinscher*] (Nuremberg: Der Stürmer-Buchverlag, 1940). Each chapter in this children's book compares Jews to a specific animal. This particular quote comes from the chapter comparing Jews to drones—stingless male bees.

Chapter 22: Ernst Hiemer, *Der Pudelmopsdackelpinscher* [*The Poodle-Pug-Dachshund-Pinscher*] (Nuremberg: Der Stürmer-Buchverlag, 1940). Each chapter in this children's book compares Jews to a specific animal. This particular quote comes from the chapter comparing Jews to poisonous serpents.

Chapter 23: Ernst Hiemer, *Der Pudelmopsdackelpinscher* [*The Poodle-Pug-Dachshund-Pinscher*] (Nuremberg: Der Stürmer-Buchverlag, 1940). Each chapter in this children's book compares Jews to a specific animal. This particular quote comes from the chapter comparing Jews to tapeworms.

Chapter 24: *Führerinnendienst des Bundes Deutscher Mädel in der Hitler-Jugend*, Gebiet Mainfranken 39, February 1944.

Chapter 25: This line from Adolf Hitler was quoted in a newsletter distributed to leaders of the Hitler Youth in the Franconia region of Germany (see *Führerinnendienst des Bundes Deutscher Mädel in der Hitler-Jugend*, Gebiet Mainfranken 39, February 1944).

Afterword: Winston Churchill, "Never Give In." October 29, 1941. https://winstonchurchill.org/resources/speeches/1941-1945-war-leader/never-give-in/.

Author's Note: Author's personal conversation with Professor Shaul Harel.

BIBLIOGRAPHY

Abramowicz, Myriam, and Esther Hoffenberg. *Comme si c'était hier.* (*As if it were yesterday.*) 1980. National Center for Jewish Film. Documentary film.

Altman, Bracha. "Eyewitness Account by Bracha Altman of Her Experiences as a Young Jewish Girl in Belgium during the German Occupation." October 28, 1955. Reference number 1656/3/9/374. Courtesy of The Wiener Library.

"Andree Geulen-Herscovici." Yad Vashem website. https://www.yadvashem.org/righteous/stories/geulen-herscovici.html.

"Andrée Geulen: Elle a changé leur vie." ("Andrée Geulen: She changed their lives.") Commune d'Ixelles website. https://www.ixelles.be/site/877-Andree-Geulen?.

Balteau, Bernard. *Children without a Shadow (Les enfants sans ombre): A Story of the Resilience of the Spirit.* 2009. Derives—Jean-Pierre and Luc Dardenne. DVD.

Berger, Joseph. "Andrée Geulen, Savior of Jewish Children in Wartime, Dies at 100." June 7, 2022. *New York Times* online. https://www.nytimes.com/2022/06/07/world/europe/andree-geulen-dead.html.

Block, Gay, and Malka Drucker. *Rescuers: Portraits of Moral Courage in the Holocaust.* Santa Fe, NM: Radius Books, 2020.

Bytwerk, Randall L. "Nazi Propaganda: 1933–1945." German Propaganda Archive at Calvin University website. https://research.calvin.edu/german-propaganda-archive/ww2era.htm#racial.

Corthals, Michéle. "Geulen-Herscovici Andrée." Belgium WWII website.

https://www.belgiumwwii.be/belgique-en-guerre/personnalites/geulen-herscovici-andree.html.

Decoster, Gérald. "Andrée Geulen, dite 'Mademoiselle Andrée' et le sauvetage des enfants juifs." ("Andrée Geulen, known as 'Mademoiselle Andrée' and the rescue of Jewish children.") RTBF website. https://www.rtbf.be/article/andree-geulen-dite-mademoiselle-andree-et-le-sauvetage-des-enfants-juifs-10899277.

Dumont, Frédéric. *Un Simple Maillon.* (*A Simple Link*). 2003. Les Films de la Memoire. Documentary film. https://vimeo.com/ondemand/unsimplemaillonfr/535891385.

Fajerstein-Heiber, Esta. "The Rescue of the Children in Belgium. The Conditions in the Camp of Malines." 1957. Reference number 1656/3/9/266. Courtesy of The Wiener Library.

Frye, Chapa. "Anonymous report on Chapa Frye (Madame Vve. Engelszer) a resistance fighter in Belgium." February 1956. Reference number 1656/3/7/258. Courtesy of The Wiener Library.

George, Bernard, Ambre Rouvière, and Olivier Wieviorka. *Les Combattants de L'ombre: 1939–1945 Des Résistants européens contre le nazisme.* (*Shadow Fighters: 1939–1945 European Resistance Fighters against Nazism.*) Albin Michel, 2011.

Geulen-Herscovici, Andrée. Oral history interview. August 4, 1988. The Jeff and Toby Herr Oral History Archive. United States Holocaust Memorial Museum. RG-50.012.0033. https://collections.ushmm.org/search/catalog/irn506516.

———. "The Rescue of Jewish Children in Belgium." 1957. Reference number 1656/3/7/1046. The Wiener Library. Eyewitness account. Digitized copy at https://www.testifyingtothetruth.co.uk/viewer/fulltext/105666/en/.

Groisman, Hava. "Eyewitness Account by Hava Groisman [Mrs. Yvonne Jospa's] of the rescue of children initiated by the 'Comite Defense de Juifs' (C.D.J.) in Belgium." February 1956. Reference number 1656/3/7/253. Courtesy of The Wiener Library.

Harel, Shaul, Dalia Harel, and Ela Moscovitch-Weiss. *A Child without a Shadow: A Memoir of a Holocaust Survivor and a World Famous Doctor.* eBookPro Publishing, 2021.

Heiber, Maurice. "The Jewish Children in Belgium." 1956. Reference number 1656/3/9/274. Courtesy of The Wiener Library.

Heinsman, Reinier. *From the Children's Home to the Gas Chamber: And How Some Avoided Their Fate*. Independently Published, 2021.

"Help for the Jews: A Ray of Hope." November 17, 2009. Website for the Jewish Museum of Deportation and Resistance, now Kazerne Dossin. https://web.archive.org/web/20091117193206/http://www.cicb.be/en/help.htm#CDJENG.

"In memoriam Andrée Geulen," January 1, 2022. Kazerne Dossin: Memorial, Museum and Research Centre on Holocaust and Human Rights. https://kazernedossin.eu/en/nieuws-item/in-memoriam-andree-geulen/.

Jospa, Ghert. "The Belgian Resistance and the camps of Breendonck and Buchenwald." April 1956. Reference number 1656/3/7/272. Courtesy of The Wiener Library.

Kam, Laura. "The sad truth about Jewish informants during the Holocaust." *The Jerusalem Post* online. January 22, 2022. https://www.jpost.com/diaspora/antisemitism/article-694232.

Kronberg, Ethea. "Eyewitness account by Ethea Kronberg of the measures taken by the Nazis against the Jews in Belgium." February 1956. Reference number 1656/3/9/242. Courtesy of The Wiener Library.

"La poulette orange." ("The Orange Chick.") Songs & Rhymes from Belgium. Mama Lisa's World website. https://www.mamalisa.com/?t=es&p=2868.

Meinen, Insa. "Face à la traque. Comment les Juifs furent arrêtés en Belgique (1942–1944)." ("Facing the hunt. How Jews were arrested in Belgium [1942–1944].") *Les Cahiers de la Mémoire Contemporaine* no. 6 (January 1, 2005): 161–203. https://doi.org/10.4000/cmc.978.

Moskovics, Jim, et al. "Andrée Geulen, l'institutrice bruxelloise qui a sauvé des milliers d'enfants juifs pendant la guerre, fête ses 100 ans." ("Andrée Geulen, the Brussels teacher who saved thousands of Jewish children during the war, turns 100.") September 6, 2021. BX1 Médias de Bruxelles. https://bx1.be/categories/news/andree-geulen-linstitutrice-bruxelloise-qui-a-sauve-des-milliers-denfants-juifs-pendant-la-guerre-fete-ses-100-ans/.

Paldiel, Mordecai. *Saving One's Own: Jewish Rescuers during the Holocaust.* Lincoln: University of Nebraska Press, 2017.

Perelman, Chaim. "From Malines to Auschwitz." September 1943. Reference number 1656/3/8/891. The Wiener Library. Eyewitness account. Digitized copy at https://www.testifyingtothetruth.co.uk/viewer/full text/105998/en/.

Rozenzayn, Chaja Rywka. "Erlebnisse in Belgien und Auschwitz." ("German Experiences in Belgium and Auschwitz.") 1940–1945. Reference number 1656/3/9/425. The Wiener Library. Eyewitness account. Digitized copy at https://www.testifyingtothetruth.co.uk/viewer/fulltext/106393/en/.

Steinberg, Maxime. *Dossier Bruxelles-Auschwitz: la police SS et l'extermination des Juifs de Belgique.* (*The Brussels-Auschwitz dossier: the SS police and the extermination of the Jews of Belgium.*) Brussels: Van den Bossche, 1980.

———. *Extermination, sauvetage et résistance des Juifs de Belgique: Hommage des Juifs de Belgique à leurs héros et sauveteurs, 1940–1945.* (*Extermination, rescue and resistance of the Jews of Belgium: Tribute of the Jews of Belgium to their heroes and saviors, 1940–1945.*) Comité d'hommage des Juifs de Belgique à leurs héros et sauveteurs, 1979.

———. *La Persécution des Juifs en Belgique (1940–1945).* (*The Persecution of the Jews in Belgium [1940–1945].*) Brussels: Editions Complexe, 2004. Digitized copy available at https://books.google.com/books?id=AbK_Qs ZLMV0C&printsec=frontcover#v=onepage&q&f=false.

Sterno, Ida. "Augenzeugenbericht Ida Sterno II. Teil (Folge)." 1957. Reference number 1656/3/8/1093. Courtesy of The Wiener Library.

———. "Eyewitness account by Ida Sterno of her experiences of hiding Jewish children in Belgium." 1957. Reference number 1656/3/7/588. Courtesy of The Wiener Library.

———. Testimony on the work as operational head of the Childrens Section of the Comité de Défense des Juifs du Front de l'Indépendance. European Holocaust Research Infrastructure. Reference number kd_00220. Archival information at https://portal.ehri-project.eu/units /be-002157-kd_00220.

Tenenbaum, Marcel. *Of Men, Monsters and Mazel: Surviving the "Final Solution" in Belgium.* Bloomington, IN: Xlibris Corporation, 2016.

Van Praag, Roger. "Organisation and Administration of the Belgian Resistance." December 1956. Reference number 1656/3/7/1112, 1113. Courtesy of The Wiener Library.

Vromen, Suzanne. *Hidden Children of the Holocaust: Belgian Nuns and Their Daring Rescue of Young Jews from the Nazis*. New York: Oxford University Press, 2010.

Wachsmann, Oskar. "Eyewitness account by Dr. Oskar Wachsmann of the conditions for Jews in occupied Belgium." September 6, 1955. Reference number 1656/3/9/410. Courtesy of The Wiener Library.

Zmigrod, Irene. "A Social Worker's Report on her Experiences in Belgium during the Time of the Nazi-Occupation." February 1956. Reference number 1656/3/9/262. Courtesy of The Wiener Library.

DISCUSSION QUESTIONS

1. What struggles and problems did Andrée Geulen and Ida Sterno face in this book?
2. How do Ida and Andrée change, grow, or evolve throughout the course of the story? What events trigger these changes?
3. How would you react if you were in the situation that Andrée and Ida were in?
4. Do you think you would have been able to give your children to the CDJ to hide from the Gestapo? Why or why not?
5. Each chapter begins with Nazi propaganda about the Jews. How did these quotes affect the tone of the story for you?
6. The character known as Fat Jacques was never captured to face his sentence after the war. How does this impact his character arc for you?
7. How did reading of Ida's experiences in the camp at Malines impact you?
8. Imagine being one of the hidden children in Belgium. What do you think you would have struggled with most? What might have gotten you through the experience?
9. What surprised you most about the book?
10. How does the book's title, *Hidden Yellow Stars*, work in relation to the book's contents?